The Sorrell

Book One

Ezra's Song

Written by Ellis B

Titles in The Sorrello Sea series

Book One: Ezra's Song
Book Two: Rhapsody's Secret
Book Three: Tianna's return

This book is dedicated to my son Simon, and my daughter, Fleur.

Part One
The Stowaway

Part One: The Stowaway

Introduction

Why Roden Jarrus ever took to piracy was a bit of a mystery. His methods weren't exactly conventional and opinion of him was divided. It took the unexpected arrival of a girl to begin a sequence of events that would ultimately link him to the past he'd rather forget, the present which confounded him and a future that he could never have anticipated.

The Sorrello Sea had long been the favoured route for cargo ships. Its balmy, warm water was kinder to vessels than the unpredictable Cantico Ocean, where winds and storms challenged all ships, fueling the mariner's superstitions of fearful monsters and demons lurking below the water, angry and ready to devour them. The Sorrello Sea, in contrast to Cantico, rarely altered from its temperate state. The cargo handlers navigated its' waters smoothly.

The group of four Islands, with the good fortune to be lapped by the Sorrello, were peaceful places, bathed in the heat and warm winds of the tropics. The only threat to the cargo ships, making their regular passage between the larger land masses of Alamande and Tarantella, were the pirates, who claimed the Sorrello Sea and the nearby straits of Auretanea, as their own, and viewed any cargo carriers that strayed from the ocean as legitimate targets.

Passing through the straits was, therefore a risk for the cargo men, but preferable to being swallowed whole by the Cantico Ocean during bad weather. The ships took their chances on the Sorrello Sea and if they were intercepted by pirates, their crews paid a heavy price.

But there came one group of pirates, more unusual than the rest, led by a man with vengeance in his heart. He was driven, not by greed, but by the determination to right a great wrong. To that end, he and his crew came to dominate the Sorrello Sea, looting the cargo vessels and striking fear into his victims as they crossed with their cargo… unless they agreed to play the game…his way.

Chapter One- Pirate Attack

It was late in the afternoon as the pirate galleon stalked her victim, a cargo carrier of moderate size, cutting across the Sorrello Sea, seeking to avoid the wind on the wider ocean. With daring and skill, the pirates brought themselves alongside, ready to cut down any opposition, making any maneuver to escape impossible for the navigators of the smaller vessel.

The agility of those pirates, who were predominately young and fearless, was unsurpassed. Using ropes and grappling hooks, they launched themselves across the thin gulf of water that separated their vessels and descended among many terrified crews. Their cutlasses drawn, they were always ready to cut down any opposition. The ritual was precise and perfected to maximize their terrifying effect and loot the vessels swiftly with little objection.

The first man to drop onto their deck stood out from all the rest. His height and stature were impressive. He was powerfully built with a smooth, shining head and had the challenging features of his tribal ancestry. He looked around with a dark and menacing intent. Seizing the nearest man, he twisted his arm painfully up his back, then placed his sword under the man's chin, pulling his head back with the flat of the cold, deadly blade. The cargo man closed his eyes, convinced he had taken his last breath, and uttered a silent prayer.

"Who is in charge here?" demanded the half-naked warrior with a snarl, "Speak! Or I'll open your throat!"

The horrified man stuttered a name and with a trembling arm, extended a finger to point further along the deck. The other pirates, swinging themselves aboard, arrived in noisy, high spirits, shouting and whooping to maximise the terror and disturbance. Young and irrepressible, they held the unfortunate crew at knifepoint, alternately mocking and threatening their hapless victims. To them, it was fine sport as they waited for their own pirate Captain to take over. The warrior released his first captive by throwing him hard to the deck, stripping the man of his only weapon, a small knife. He kicked the fellow over with the toe of his heavy, black boots, then he strutted around impatiently, his fists arrogantly placed against his hips, awaiting orders.

The pirate Captain arrived, to stand alongside his formidable second in command, thus blocking the cargo foreman's vision of his own men, to intimidate him further. The Captain was as tall and strong as the warrior but his voice was less formidable, and he took his time before he spoke, walking about the deck and examining the cargo, as though he already owned it.

"If you co-operate with us and give me what I ask for, no man need die," he said slowly, without looking particularly at any one. His voice was controlled. He saw no need to raise it. In speech and manner he had an almost leisurely air of self-assurance, born of earlier successes. This was almost too easy. There was only one question he wanted answered. "Give me the name of the merchant you work for." The cargo foreman looked from one to the other of the pirates but had no desire to oppose them. His mouth had gone dry.

"Merrick, Sir! This cargo all belongs to Merrick, Sir." The frightened man, eyeing the Captain anxiously, tried to gauge if his answer had been sufficient. The smooth skulled warrior cast threatening eyes slowly around the ship, ensuring nobody moved.

The Captain's deep blue eyes, that normally held a glint of good humour, darkened at the name which was anathema to him. "Merrick," he mouthed with loathing, and spat. "Then these containers are ours!" he declared to his men.

Another grim faced pirate advanced, much older than the other two and possessed of a rough voice like stony gravel. He gestured to some half dozen men to help him. They were selective in what they chose to take, forcing the cargo bearers at knife point, to prize open any unmarked crates, before beginning to remove the valuable cargo onto the galleon. From somewhere further along the deck came the only protest.

"You can't be doing that!" blurted out one young foolhardy cargo handler. His inexperience of the sea lending courage to a face not yet showing the desperate fear of the others. "Tis more than our job's worth to arrive in Tarantella without the cargo," he argued.

The pirate warrior, whose sour expression alone was enough to curdle a man's blood, rounded on the one who had the temerity to challenge them. Still grasping the knife so recently purloined from his first victim, the warrior let it fly from his hand. It whistled past the man's chest, narrowly missing his heart, thudding into the wood as it grazed the flesh of the man's shoulder, pinning him painfully to the crate he was vainly trying to protect. The pirate walked towards him, seized him by the throat and drawing back his fist, punched the man hard. As he slumped forward, the warrior released the knife from the man's blood soaked sleeve and drew back his powerful arm to draw the blade across his neck.

"That's enough!" said the pirate captain sharply. The warrior looked around, suddenly stilled by the command. The Captain shook his head and approached. Sometimes he wondered if he'd made a wrong decision in accepting this savage into his crew. The warrior, a fearsome creature, relaxed his arm and placed the knife back in his own belt.

"We have not come here to kill," the Captain said with authority, as the warrior stepped over the man, nonchalantly. His slow, dark eyes turned towards the Captain. There was a momentary threat of defiance in his manner, but he capitulated. "Let's be away from here," the Captain shouted to his men. They had got all they had come for and prepared to depart.

The traumatised cargo handlers watched as their assailants began to leave. Miraculously, it seemed to them, no-one lay dead, although more than one of their number were blooded and bruised. Their foreman remained where he stood, much shaken, but also puzzled that the pirate Captain seemed less murderous than he'd first supposed him to be. The agile leader of the buccaneers prepared to swing confidently away to his galleon. Before he went, he tossed something small and hard which hit the deck in front of the bemused man. "That is for your trouble gentlemen. Until the next time we meet, and mark me well, there will be a next time!" he shouted across to them. He turned away laughing, and with his own good humour restored, descended upon his own magnificent galleon.

The foreman of the cargo carrier waited until he felt it was safe enough to move without being fired upon, then he picked up the purse from the deck. As his crew rushed to bind the wounds of the injured men, he tipped the contents into his hands. He turned the heavy coins over in his fingers, before looking across at the galleon, now drawing away in the water "It's gold," he declared with astonishment "Well, I'll be damned! The pirate has left us a purse of gold!"

On their galleon, The Zenna Marius, the pirates made merry. With raucous laughter, shouts and curses, they celebrated another easy victory, watched by their Captain, an inspiring figure with laughing eyes that shone in a good natured face, his thick, black hair barely concealing the gold loop that hung from his ear, identifying him as one of their own. Close beside him stood his counterpart, the smooth headed warrior of exotic appearance and indeterminate ancestry.

His expression darkened otherwise handsome features, with especially large, penetrative eyes that flashed dangerously. A brooding, menacing undercurrent suggested he might never be far away from violence. The mysterious looks were matched by an equally mysterious name, Te Manu Manmou, often shortened to Manu. He acted as second in command to his new leader, Captain Roden Jarrus. They were both proud adventurers with the potential to forge a long partnership, but were still wary of each other and were not always of like mind. Jarrus took advantage of the simmering heat that Te Manu generated on their raids. It was also useful that he quelled any opposition within Roden's newly assembled crew, with the efficiency of a lightning bolt, but it came at a price. From the Captain's point of view, it was like harnessing a tiger. "How many times do I have to stop you from killing the poor bastards?" Jarrus reprimanded the warrior mildly.

"The man opposed you, Captain. He had no respect," answered Te Manu coldly. He was not used to criticism and fought down the resistance that threatened to erupt at any moment.

"The man bore no weapons. He opposed me with words and for that you were prepared to cut him down," persisted Jarrus.

"They must learn respect and do as we say," replied the warrior.

"They will learn to co- operate and that is not the same thing at all. From now on, Manu, there will be no more killing unless it is on my orders. Is that understood?"

The man breathed heavily, his brooding face like stone. It was never certain that he would obey. A dangerous tension existed between them that lasted several seconds until the warrior seemed to make a decision and forced himself to accept the command.

"Aye, Captain," he acknowledged grudgingly, refusing to meet his eye.

"Good man." replied Jarrus, concealing his own relief at what could have become another dangerous standoff between them. "Now, let's check this cargo and see how rich a haul it's been."

In these early days of Jarrus's piracy, some of the merchandise carriers made the fatal mistake of defending their cargo against being looted. The buccaneers were equal to anything and among their number were a few impulsive men who would not hesitate to kill any opposition if they deemed it justified. Gideon was one of those. Larger than his counterparts, he had the might of an old bear, and had more than once tightened those massive hands around a man's neck and squeezed until his victim, purple and gurgling, became a lifeless corpse. Gideon had once boasted the strength of those massive hands, but knew that the Captain had little interest in his stories and would rather use milder means to get what he desired.

The warrior, Te Manu, with dagger or sword, showed no remorse at cutting down men ruthlessly. His face, always dark with intent, was formidable to everyone. The pirates did not expect to be challenged, and showed no concern at spilling blood. The Captain, less murderous than some of his men, and sometimes despairing of their aggression, always gave the cargo crews a chance to co-operate. Irrespective of the mayhem they inflicted in order to obtain their looted goods, he threw a purse of gold at the feet of those he had robbed. You would have thought his men might have mutinied, but for the fact that they saw in their Captain a just leader who rewarded them generously and treated them fairly. In fact, Captain Jarrus showed little interest in keeping much bounty for himself. He had the ability to get what he wanted. The chase and the looting was sport enough for him. Of the spoils, he was strangely contemptuous, so under his leadership, his men fared well and were content with their share of any plunder.

Over time, rumours of this strange pirate crew spread far. The cargo men had mixed feelings about what went on. Some of the encounters on their ships could almost be called civil. A sort of illicit trade upon the sea became established. A strange coexistence developed, where the cargo men watched out for the galleon, almost sailing into it on their numerous crossings, and were disappointed if Captain Jarrus and his crew did not intercept them.

Via some of these same cargo men, the rudiments of distribution began around the coastline of the three closest Islands of the Sorrello Sea, namely, Auretanea, Petriah and Scalos. Using hidden coves and inlets, the pirates rowed ashore, bringing goods secretly to land, that were resold cheaply to the Islanders, turning contraband into coins, and everyone benefited as a result of the curious trade. The only ones who were angered were the grasping merchant owners whose cargo was spirited away. It never happened predictably enough to prove; and try as they might, they were outwitted in a time when many pirate vessels roamed the seas. Captain Roden Jarrus received inexplicable, tacit support from one or two dignitaries in high places, who used a quiet authority to frustrate the merchants' attempts to get him arrested, whenever he appeared on land. Why he should ever escape justice, remained a mystery.

There was plentiful talk in the taverns, the kitchens, yards, and workplaces. Many folk were for the pirates, as there were those firmly against them, but the consensus of opinion was that they had provided the townspeople with supplies they would otherwise never have seen. In time, there was only the distant memory of any life being lost that could be laid at the pirate's door. In fact, when unopposed they did not cheat the cargo bearers, and traded the contraband fairly.

"As I sees it," began old Mikhael, who had established a regular rendezvous with them, under the cliffs in Auretanea, "They don't give me no trouble, and I don't raise any. Some of 'em are rough 'uns, I'll grant you that, but you has to speak as you finds a man, and I'll warrant that Captain's a good 'un, despite rumours otherwise. No! I'm for 'em I am."

Several men surrounding Mikhael nodded at his words, and Artemus was one who lent voice to them all. "We wouldn't be buyin' half of what's needed goin' down no regular path. Prices are always too high for folk. I says those merchants are rich men who could give summat back if they chose, and seein' as they don't give it willingly, well, we has the pirates to take it for us. 'tis fair and square seen like that."

The gulf between the supporters of the pirates and those of the rich merchant owners became ever wider. A rumbling under current of anger and frustration was steadily growing and threatened the peace. Tension was in the air and rumbled on, slowly building as the years passed, although daily life continued much as it always had. The seasons changed and the barometer was set fair for so long it seemed like the needle was stuck, but life, even in that slow paced world like the barometer, could not stay the same forever...

So, now we must leave the past behind and travel forward in time to one particular day, more than a decade later. A day that began much as any other. The pirates anchored their ship off the Island of Auretanea, and rowed with their goods to a secret meeting place as they had numerous times before, but on this occasion, a strange wind of fate was blowing in their direction and, as a result, nothing would ever be the same again.

Chapter Two - The Bay at Auretanea

A young swarthy man sat lazily reclining beneath the mast of the galleon. His knees were raised, and with his toes pressed against the base of the wooden shaft, he comfortably held his guitar. His complexion was attractively dusky against hair that was black and wavy, uncut and curled at the nape of his neck. He was unshaven. His eyes were brown with sweeping lashes and his profile was still youthful enough to be quite beautiful. His shirt was open in the heat, his face bent towards the instrument he played. He acknowledged no listeners, but raised his head and softly began to sing. His voice, as captivating as his looks, drew anyone who was close enough to stop and listen.

There were some men left on board the galleon. It was not easy to guess how many might be listening. Some had gone on the long boats with heavy crates of cargo to draw up on to the beach. Several of the ship's crew waved in recognition towards the three or four Islanders who appeared along the shoreline to meet them in this secret place, as they had many times before. Across distant cries of welcome, the man with the guitar continued playing on the deck of the galleon, while some of the crew watched and waited patiently for the exchange of goods and money to be made. The musician's name was Ezra. He did not seem to care if anyone paid attention to his words, even though he enjoyed making up verses in his spare moments; yet perhaps someone should have listened, for there was something prophetic about today's rendition:

'Roll away white waves, and crash upon the shore.

Must I risk the hangman's noose to trade with you once more?
Pay me with a maiden to take away to sea,
And bid her come with riches to change my destiny.'

"Another song Ezra? What's that you're singing about now?" called the Captain, as he strode towards him.

"Nothing new Captain, I just put some more words together," he replied lazily with his soft accent, as he squinted up at Captain Jarrus in the strong sunlight, and smiled.

"Well if it's girls you're singing about, they'll be plenty enough once we hit the brothel in Petriah," promised the Captain as he stared across the bay to focus on the men who were trading beneath the cover of the cliffs. His easy smile evaporated and his brow furrowed as he watched them talking on the beach and he became more tense, as the minutes grew longer while he surveyed the scene. The men in the distance showed no sign of moving. "Why are they taking so long? Every minute carries the risk they'll be caught. We ought to be away by now"

The warrior, taciturn and sombre, appeared beside his friend. He seemed puzzled at this outburst. "Relax, Roden. They all carry pistols," he said.

The Captain, impatient to be away, was only partly mollified. "The last thing I want is trouble here in Auretanea," he said. "It's one thing to take a pistol to a man at sea but quite another to aim at him on his own land. We could soon be proved to be murderers if something goes wrong and one of our crew gets trigger happy down there." Te Manu's mouth narrowed slightly.

"Life is cheap," he replied carelessly. "We are already wanted for dealing contraband. The penalty is the same. They can only hang us once."

"Even so, I want us away from here." said Jarrus.

The Captain drummed his fingers on the ship's rail. Ezra laid aside his guitar. It was unusual to see the Captain agitated. Roden glanced at him. "Oh well," he sighed, punching the rails, attempting to play down his concern. "After today we will soon be in Petriah. At least we are tolerated there by Governor Cavendish and Ezra can have the real thing instead of singing about it." He smiled, the usual good humour returning to his face. Ezra grinned and picked up the guitar to strum a few more chords before the men returned.

Above the sparkling sea, white birds circled, calling to each other. Wild and free they sailed upon warm air currents, coasting and floating with wings outstretched. They swooped, then soared into the sky, gliding effortlessly around the sandy bay, above the waiting pirate galleon. Far below them, beneath the grass topped cliffs, waves rolled gently inwards, breaking rhythmically upon the shore. Further out to sea, a blistering sun had turned the deeper water to an inky hue and upon this dazzling water sat the sailing ship. The glinting sun reflected upon the metal fitments, turning each one gold in the bright light of mid-day. It bleached white the huge canvas sails as they billowed in a warm breeze; the magnificent galleon lay upon the blue water.

The birds above the Island of Auretanea had a panoramic view. They saw the ship as though it were turning in a complete circle beneath them as they flew a full three hundred and sixty degrees around and above it. The land spread out like a patchwork quilt beneath them. A sprinkling of villages, flat grassed plains, a town with a small castle, the battlements of whitened stone, standing upon the highest point, looked out over the Sorrello sea.

A single bird descended towards the ship that rested upon the water. It flapped its wings and folded them upon the horizontal bar of the top mast, shaking several feathers into place, before it settled down. The scene was idyllic and peaceful and for a few quiet minutes nothing seemed to be moving; at least not upon the sea but, on land... Someone was watching them.

High above the cliff top pounded the dull, regular thud of a black stallion, carrying a young girl across the land. She rode hard, the loose sleeves of her garment blowing backwards as she raced across the plains and beneath the cover of trees, emerging into brilliant light, then disappearing into dappled sunshine. There was an urgency connected with her speed. It was as if she was leaving something behind in a great hurry or was it that she was riding towards something that may not wait? She was frantically racing against time, to arrive, who knew where?

The girl began to ride the ebony horse towards higher ground, slowing all the time until she reached a place commanding a good view of the bay looking out towards the Sorrello Sea. The horse's hooves slowed to a trot and gradually became still. The black stallion shook his mane and lowered his head to chew the long grass. The girl sat astride him, but leaned forward to stroke and pat the animal's hot, black neck.

Sitting upright once more, and shielding her eyes from the bright sunlight, she gazed all around. She sat there for some time wondering which direction to take, whilst absently stroking the velvet coat of her beloved stallion who, almost three years earlier, on her fourteenth birthday, she had named, Whisper. As she dropped her eyes from the horizon to the bay, her attention focused on a ship, a large cargo ship, and the seed of an idea began to germinate in her mind.

She dismounted and stepped nearer to the cliff edge. Running her hands through her long, dark hair, the girl pulled it back behind her ears with slender fingers to hold it off her face while she peered down. Boats were pulling in to the cove beneath and indistinct voices drifted upwards towards the circling birds overhead. They must be the voices of cargo carriers unloading goods, she decided.

Then, she began to talk aloud to herself, the way she had always done, whilst playing with her dolls. It was a habit she had never entirely left behind. She would not do it if there was any chance of being overheard, of course that would be madness. She was conscious that it was a childish thing. The girl liked to think her horse could understand and thereby often excused herself from the foolishness of talking to empty air.

"Goodness Whisper! What a drop! If I were to fall down here it might be days or weeks before anyone would find me." She straightened her back and ran both hands through her heavy hair, combing it back from her pretty face with her fingers. "But certainly, it would be kinder to be found at the bottom of the cliff with my neck broken than to be fated by the ordeal that awaits me if I stay," she added dramatically.

The girl stepped back and studied the cliff more carefully, walking along as if trying to discover a route that would lead her downwards without plummeting her to a crushing death on the rocks below. After a while, she seemed satisfied and wandered back towards her horse who was grazing contentedly, occasionally flicking his ear at a fly, but otherwise preoccupied and certainly unconcerned by human affairs. The girl lay her hand upon his nose. "You must go home without me," she told him earnestly. "You do understand, don't you? I cannot go back, not right now. It is vital that I go to get help, even though as yet, I'm not sure how." She frowned and her forehead creased. "I hate to say goodbye to you, but this must be done. Now *go* Whisper, *go!"* And so saying, the young girl pushed the horse's hind quarters and slapped his glistening rump, saying firmly, *"Home,* Whisper! *Home!"*

The horse stopped chewing for a few moments and turned his handsome head to look at his mistress, as though expecting her to remount. "Oh dear!" sighed the girl with some concern as to what she should try next. Then, summoning what was her most authoritive voice, she told him in what were unmistakably commanding tones, *"Home,* Whisper! GO! GO! GO!" and shooed him. This time, the young black horse with large brown eyes recognised the signal and tossing his mane, trotted off under the trees, homeward. The little girl inside, surfaced long enough to say aloud, "Well. This is it. I really am alone now."

Taking courage in her hands she began her faltering downward climb. At intervals, she found it possible to weave a zigzag route across wide hillocks of chalky cliff ledges, fringed by tussocks of grass and the odd trees that grew at impossible angles, being tentatively rooted. These stopping places afforded her a safe resting place, from where she could study the ship afar and listen for the voices on the beach below. As she descended, she made exclamations of frustration, catching her clothing, stubbing her toe, and scratching her ankles against brambles.

The dress proved a liability to her and caught on everything it touched. She wound the pale fabric around, as if wringing out washing and found that by knotting the garment between her knees, she could at least free her legs and gain more freedom of movement. She was neither demure nor ladylike moving in this fashion, but her progress was faster and before long, the girl could see how to reach the sheltered bay at the bottom of the cliff.

A sandy beach stretched into the distance along the shore line. It had taken her a fair time to reach sea level but had proved infinitely less risky than taking a steeper path. With relief, her sore feet pressed into warm, soft sand. She had lost one shoe half way down and kicked off the other, having abandoned hope of retrieving the first. She glanced up at the route she had taken and then finding shelter in the occasional recesses at the foot of the cliff, made her way to where she hoped the long boats might be tied. The girl was slim, agile and light footed and in no time at all, she saw them.

Peering around a small rock, she located the source of the voices heard from above and watched a group of men deep in conversation some distance away. Crates and barrels were piled upon the beach with some already stacked upon the handcarts. It was easy to pick out who were most likely to be the cargo men, even at this distance. They were at the peak of age, health and good looks that nature bestows upon the young. Some were naked from the waist up and others wore open shirts but their skin all had the same tanned hue as befits men who toil all day under the sun. They were barefooted, with knee britches.

They seemed to be in deeper conversation than one might have expected over the exchange of goods, but it was to her advantage. Immersed in talking, they showed scant regard for the longboats and did not once look back at them, whilst the narrow vessels bobbed, quite abandoned at the edge of the water.

"Something bad is happening hereabouts," confided the aged Islander who went by the name of Artemus, to his listeners. "I don't know how much longer we will be at liberty to go about our work, either up at the castle kitchens, or down here with you. They came ashore and took up places in all our taverns, ale drinking, cheeking the landlords, not paying their way; They was asking too much about the castle, and wanting to know about the guard there. I've avoided 'em all so far, but more keeps arriving and the more of 'em that comes, the more they act like they've got a right to be here."

"We're not comfortable an' that's a fact." added his friend, Mikhael. Several other Islanders nodded at this. Artemus went on. "There's a rumour flyin' about that this is just the beginning of a long held plan by Baron Lussac, to leave his land of Scalos and disrupt ours here in Auretanea." Gypsy swung the sacking over one shoulder from the cargo they had recently delivered, and looked pensive "What business can the Baron want with Auretanea?" he asked, quietly. "Has there been a quarrel between these Islands?"

Mikhael beckoned him closer. "He came here from Scalos, months ago it was. My old woman works up at the castle, same as me. She hears things. Servants talk, Gyp."

Artemus agreed. "That Baron Lussac is off his head. He was after courting the Princess of all people! Well, he didn't get what he come for, oh no! She give him short shrift. Got a real fiery temper, that one, despite her looking like an angel. Anyway, she refused him, outright. He demanded an apology or compensation or summat which he didn't get. Next thing, he's storming back to Scalos, right ruffled and making threats as he goes. Then, all sorts of things happen. The King's advisers turn up with a load of others from Petriah. Right agitated they are. There's rumours the Baron wanted a share in controlling the sea passage which is queer since Scalos is nowhere near our stretch of water. Trouble ain't gone away Gyp. Mark me, it's still brewin'. More Scalos soldiers pourin' in and none of 'em in power seems to know what to do about it."

The men talked a while longer

"Just you be sure to tell your Captain, they are slowly taking over this Island," said Artemus, "If we ain't here when you return, look lively about you 'cos you'll know it's too late for poor old Auretanea and for us, especially if them soldiers start patrolling our sea straits. They'll make us pay to send out our fishin' boats next. It's an invasion, it is. You wait and see if our days aren't numbered!"

Gypsy looked across the bay towards the galleon, peaceful upon the water. Could things really be as serious as old Mikhael and Artemus suggested? It seemed so tranquil. Mr. Baines would need to talk to the Captain about the ship's stores if there was going to be danger in coming back. They relied on getting fresh produce from the Island, as well as trading there.

Mr. Baines was an interesting fellow, a good ship's cook, who had taken the cabin boy Jonah, under his wing when the lad had been picked up destitute, two years earlier. Jonah and Mr. Baines got along well together from the start. They made a good team. Jonah came under Mr. Baines' protection if the men got a bit too rough or rowdy and Mr. Baines, being the provider of decent food, never had any trouble from even drunken men aboard the Zenna Marius. He was a quiet man himself, reticent, perhaps, except with youngsters. He was alright with them. Never given to an outburst or bad humour, that was Mr. Baines, a contented sort of man.

"Come on," said Gyp, We best be taking the boats back. We've been here too long already."

"Hey up Jonah, lad," called Mr. Baines, and a boy came splashing along the shoreline towards them.

The girl had watched the men talking for some time. They seemed very involved with whatever they were discussing and she was too far away to see their faces or hear their conversation. She reached the last crevice in the cliff that would afford her cover before she had to take the risk and break away in order to run to the side of the boats. Timing it carefully, she calculated needing only a few seconds, certainly not more than a count of ten, when she would be totally exposed. She watched the movement of the men on the beach, studied the incline of the heads of those most likely to spot her, and watched their movements. Seeing they had not lifted their eyes, she decided to run like the wind and if nobody noticed, she would hurl herself onto the sand behind or between the longboats. Running on sand was harder than it looked, yet she reached her goal without obstacle and threw herself, panting, into the damp, golden mud.

Protected by the wooden vessels, she waited and listened, and then carefully, keeping as low as she could, she stretched one leg along the side of the boat, hooking her foot over the side. It was uncomfortable, but when no sound came, she carefully hooked her elbow over the same side and paused before raising her other arm. Biting her lip in determined effort, she could now just about look over the edge of the boat. No-one was approaching. She could see sackcloth and tarpaulin in the bottom of the second one.

With one almighty heave, she tipped herself onto the edge of the boat and into it, immediately burying herself beneath the tarpaulin cover. The boat moved against its neighbour, and caused ripples and movement the girl had not anticipated. She held her breath wondering how long it would be before the boats resettled. Nobody had been close enough to see or hear any disturbance. She dared to relax a little, and breathed out slowly. Her foot touched something round, flat and smooth beneath the sackcloth. It was a leather water flask.

She reached it with as little disturbance to the boat as possible. To her great relief it was more than half full. The girl unscrewed the cap and lay on one elbow drinking, drinking. The blessed relief of water ran down her chin and into the nape of her neck. She took care to leave some in the flask, and lay down as comfortably as she could make herself.

Sometime later, she heard voices and holding her breath, for fear of discovery, she felt the movement of three or four people climbing into the adjoining boat. She heard the voice of a young boy shout, "Do you want me to fold the tarpaulins before we cast off Mr. Baines?" The girl strained anxiously to hear the reply.

"No. Jonah lad. We'll make time later. We've spent long enough here already and must get back to the ship."

A youth, not long into his teens, took up the oars, and with Gyp and Mr. Baines, began to row steadily, towing the empty cargo vessel behind them. "What was you all talking about for so long?" Jonah wanted to know. Gypsy winked at Mr. Baines.

"There's soldiers from Scalos on the Island," answered Gyp. in his slow, quiet tone, narrowing his eyes and his lips devilishly at Jonah, "and they say as they're looking for a cabin boy last seen in these parts some two years ago- wanted dead or alive for thieving, they said." Seeing Jonah's blue eyes widen, Gypsy began to smile. Jonah, realising he was being teased, shook his head of white blonde hair and smiled broadly, before breaking into laughter.

"Now then! Now then you two!" admonished the voice of Mr. Baines, trying to restore some order. "'Tis true them Scalos soldiers have arrived in enough numbers to cause upset, but what they are come for is not cabin boys. An' certainly old Artemus and Mikhael would have told us more if they had knowed more. We'll tell Captain, cos as sure as I'm sitting here, I can tell both of thee there is no love lost between our Captain and the Baron of Scalos."

The girl was alert and listening although she could see nothing. So, it was Artemus and Mikhael who had collected the cargo. The girl knew them well, and the Captain of the cargo ship they were approaching did not like the Baron, and word was spreading about the soldiers from Scalos. This was indeed useful to hear.

At length, the boats came alongside the ship and the girl felt ropes and a hoist put in place to raise them. She gripped the seating slats above her and pressed her feet hard against the sides in an effort not to be tipped out. The girl held her breath inside the boat as it was winched, feeling it rise in the air, and into its resting position on board. Mr. Baines and Jonah climbed up the rope ladder that hung over the side of the ship. Gyp. went to take the purses of coins to the Captain. Jonah was about to climb into the cargo boat to retrieve his water flask and jerkin.

"Leave them tarpaulins," shouted Israel tersely, from further along the deck. "Go up to the crow's nest and look about you before we weigh anchor. Captain says we're to be away from here and me and Josh got back an hour since. You're all late. Captain ain't best pleased."

"Aye, Sir," shouted Jonah, happy to oblige, and once again the rowing boat was left undisturbed.

"When do we eat Mr. Baines?" shouted Israel, whose stomach was well aware of the lateness of the hour.

"Not more than long if I don't send the boy to attend the boats first," replied Mr. Baines. Jonah jumped down the last six feet of rigging. "All clear." he yelled to Israel, as he ran after Mr. Baines who was heading towards the galley at a brisk pace.

"Food first, Jonah! Always food first." shouted Mr. Baines, cheerfully.

Chapter Three - Pirate Company

The Captain sat with his men, tankard in hand. He was an astute man; a shrewd leader, able to think carefully and exercise good judgment. He had a well-disciplined crew under his command and was supported by his most trusted friend, a fearful warrior of some renown.

The Captain, in his wisdom, knew all his men. He would speak plainly before them. He would eat and drink among them. He expected their loyalty and got it. He was not afraid to discipline but he was just and fair minded. He earned the respect of all the men who sailed with him and few would wish to leave the crew of the graceful galleon, Zenna Marius. The Captain sat now, attentive to Mr. Baine's and Gypsy's faithful retelling of the conversation with the elderly Islanders who had traded with them on the beach.

Mr. Baines had something appealing about him; nudging his late forties and carrying slightly too much weight around his middle, he was speaking earnestly. His straight brown hair had a habit of flopping over one eye and the corners of his light brown eyes wrinkled into good humoured lines whenever he smiled, which was often.

Self-effacing, he was a quiet man in ship's company preferring to listen more than talk, unless the subject was food. The exception to his reticence was always young Jonah. They worked well together normally preparing all the food either in the galley or, when possible, out on deck, enjoying the air. Ship's cook was an essential role and Mr. Baines operated with complete independence from being sought for any task that did not involve food. Where Jonah might be spirited away on other errands, which it has to be said, he cheerfully undertook, Mr. Baines was left to get on and that may have accounted for his regular expression of contented wellbeing. Mr. Baines did not look quite as content as he spoke now.

"Thing is Captain, if old Mikhael speaks true, we could be risking our necks to trade again at Auretanea, until we know what's going on there. I picked up some supplies today right enough, but there's not as much as usual and if we can't load there with fresh stuff, the distance we sail will see us run short."

Captain Jarrus was an enlightened man, prepared to listen to any problem and he would not underestimate the importance of preserving the diet and good health of the men under his command. What Mr. Baines was saying was important. They were all aware that there were those inland who would like to see them arrested. It seemed in Auretanea, that risk may have significantly increased.

"I do not have an answer to this Mr. Baines," answered the Captain truthfully. "If the supplies you bought today are not sufficient, we will take more on at Petriah, until we can find others prepared to trade with us. Governor Cavendish can be trusted. I will seek him out while we are there and see what he knows of the unrest in Auretanea. We all need a few day's ashore." A fresh thought occurred to him.

"We must be careful in seeking a new source of fresh supplies, though. Even in Petriah we can never be sure who our enemies are or with what trickery they may try and outwit us. I have to say I have been edgy since we were in the bay today. Something misgives. I don't know what or why." He paused in the doorway and looked back. "You're sure no-one else was watching you on the beach? You noticed nothing unusual? "

"No Captain," they replied, shaking their heads.

"Very well," acknowledged Jarrus, but he hesitated, looking thoughtful just for a moment, before he moved away.

In the cabin, Te Manu listened respectfully to the Captain. "The men must speed up the exchange of goods and not get into overlong conversation on the Islands. They're becoming too casual." he was saying. Gideon stood nearby.

"All of the Islands or just Auretanea, Captain?"
Te Manu asked.

"All of them, at least until we know more of what is going on. We must be even more watchful. There is a restlessness in the air that we would be fools to ignore."

Te Manu pursed his lips, his brow set in a heavier line. He was picking up unusual caution in his friend.

"Then what shall I tell the men about their leave in Petriah?" he wanted to know. "They expect to spend several days inland relaxing among friends. Petriah has always welcomed us so long as we've kept to the places we know."

Captain Jarrus was not to be persuaded. "Not any more." he answered. "I feel an uneasiness this night. When the men are unloading they are not sufficiently watchful. They are not alert enough and must be quicker. I charge you with making that message understood. If there is trouble here, there might also be trouble in Petriah. The men must keep their wits about them."

"Very well Captain," answered Te Manu "Shall I speak to them now?" The Captain nodded, his thoughts occupied.

Te Manu left Roden without further comment but caught Gideon's eye as he walked out of the door and up the three steps to cross the deck. The Captain had introduced an element of misgiving. He was preoccupied. Something was definitely bugging him.

Gideon remained in the cabin. There wasn't much he didn't know, especially the risks of being on land for any length of time. That was why they sailed away and hid the ship for careening. It didn't do to risk the scaffold. He had spent a lifetime working on sailing ships. He could remember the days when men handled rows of cannons on the biggest vessels amid the smoke and fire of battle that he'd heard about as a boy and couldn't wait to experience. He'd run away to sea when much on Jonah's years and worked hard but learned much. Adventure stayed with him, and his love of the big ships never deserted him.

Only two small guns remained on Zenna Marius. She had been stripped out years ago, and Gideon with huge hands made like shovels, that had done their share of all heavy duties in times past, polished and maintained them still but, had found more useful work, becoming the ship's carpenter instead. He worked with love and pride and turned good wood to a thing of strength and beauty. His craftsmanship helped assuage the distant memories when those same hands had killed. There were still those who said that the mighty Gideon could snuff life out with a single blow from his fist, but it was no longer Gideon's boast. He had forgotten such things.

These days, he was just as fearless, but added to that was an unshakable, loyal, dependability. He loved the galleon as if she were a woman, regularly taking the helm and talking to the old ship as he guided her through winds and gauged the tides. He was a slow man and thought about the Captain's concern. He was older than the others and knew when to keep his counsel.

"Well, Gideon. You seem very quiet. You've heard me speak. What say you to all this?

"Aye, Cap'n," he replied slowly, in the gravelly voice that suited his bear like frame. "I hear thee." He shifted slightly on the bench but couldn't be hurried. "There's always good sense in everythin' you say, Sir," he said, eventually."

"And?" invited the Captain. Gideon shrugged. The cogs and wheels of his mind turned. He wasn't sure what to think. It was a funny business and no mistake.

"Maybe Te Manu, don't want to stir up the men til there's proof there's more in it, and right now who knows what's goin' on? All I knows Cap'n, is talkin' on the beach be the only way we pick up news from inland, be that good or bad. We needs to be doing that, Sir, Wouldn't do to miss anything important. Like today fer instance, with Arti and Mikhael. It might have taken time but that were important, what they told Gyp and Mr. Baines."

The Captain gave a wry smile to Gideon's words.

"You're right to say there's no proof we may be at greater risk than we ever were, but something is gnawing at me Gideon, and it's been upon me since we lowered our boats in Auretanea. I can't shake it off." They drained their tankards.

"Could it be that old Artemus and Mikhael's warning has done it to thee?" suggested Gideon.

"Could be," agreed Jarrus, frowning as he thought about Scalos. "but I felt it before then."

Had the young girl been close enough to watch or listen to the most senior men on board, she would have found much to interest her and she might have begun to question her earlier assumptions about them, especially whether they really were what they had first seemed. They were an odd mixture of nationalities and shared no common ancestry. They professed no measurable affinity to any place and seemed instinctively distrustful of anywhere except the open sea. They were risk takers. Then, there was their choice of dress. They either wore long boots, turned at the top with a deep cuff, or went bare foot. Their shirts were slashed to the navel or they were bare chested. They wore britches with wide buckled belts in which they carried an assortment of weapons; knives, daggers, pistols or cutlasses.

They carried gold about their persons in ear rings, amulets, chains and pendants. They were mostly unshaven and without exception, their hair was long and tied behind them or loose and curling at the collar. Each had rugged good looks, untamed by any sort of genteel living. Their naked skin was tanned by constant exposure to the sun and the wind, their muscles developed by hauling on ropes, climbing, loading and manning the rowing boats. All were capable of killing. None would be slow to draw a weapon.

If the girl had been able to see them, she would have noticed that a few carried scars with pride, a declaration of some past encounter. She would have blushed at their naked torsos, the well-developed chests made hard and healthy by the demanding, physical work on the galleon. She would probably have decided by now, that these men were no ordinary cargo handlers.

They were unmistakably... BUCCANEERS!

An hour passed... The ship was out on the Sorrello Sea, near the open ocean and the men's minds were set upon the destination of Petriah. It would take some time to reach. The galleon was big and slow and needed the deeper waters to navigate successfully where the winds were in the right direction.

Petriah was a favourite stopping place after weeks or occasionally months, at sea. The taverns on the coast and the nearby brothel were hospitable to the buccaneers, and over time, Jarrus had established important contacts there. The Captain was affable and liked. The Governor, a brilliant diplomat named Fabian Cavendish, approved of Jarrus despite his unorthodox trade. Cavendish governed from Petriah but oversaw the smaller Kingdom of Auretanea.

He had the unenviable task of keeping a balance with the wealthy merchant ship owners who persistently tried to buy favour to gain office and influence government. Cavendish saw the misuse of power that such men already evinced over trade. They inflated prices to make themselves richer and only sought trade with the larger Islands beyond the Sorrello group of four, denying the smaller populations access to commodities because they did not want to burden themselves with their needs. It angered Cavendish that such men would happily sit in a position of comfort and power at Petriah without investing in the local

Islands. The rich merchants hated buccaneers like Jarrus, which only served to make Cavendish more tolerant of the Captain and his crew, especially when he heard that Jarrus traded at reasonable prices on numerous small Islands with tiny populations that would otherwise be denied merchandise.

It seemed odd that Governor Cavendish was not more measured in his attitude. There seemed to be an imbalance between his objections to the merchants whose trade was after all, within the law, and his affinity with the pirates, who operated outside it. Consequently, there was more than a ripple of discontent in Petriah with the merchants more determined to get themselves elected to positions of power by fair means or foul. Cavendish was powerful, but for how long was less certain and the pirate Captain Roden Jarrus knew it.

Raucous laughter and ribaldry abounded on the galleon as the crew anticipated their arrival in Petriah and talked about how they would spend their earnings there. Te Manu Manmou had decided to be circumspect about the Captain's misgivings. He had certainly delivered due warning that trade on land must be speeded up and that they needed to be more vigilant since soldiers from Scalos were infiltrating Auretanea, but he stopped short of suggesting that Petriah might also be off limits and for tonight would say no more to the men.

Roden Jarrus swung idly in the hammock, rocking with one foot on the wooden floor. He enjoyed the men's bawdiness and joking about the delights of the women awaiting them in Petriah, deciding not to depress their lewd spirits with his own uneasiness. Te Manu, however, watched them with the eyes of a man charged with the responsibility of controlling this body of vigorous, testosterone driven men, whose thoughts were turning to carnal pursuits now that they were about to be released from weeks of heavy, manual labour.

Te Manu also rested in a hammock but sat with both feet firmly upon the floor. He was always a striking figure, even in repose. It was in his bearing; the way he carried himself, warrior like in appearance, muscular in physique and with a brooding disposition. There were similarities between him and the Captain, both were self-assured, handsome individuals of similar age but looking very different. A great deal of Te Manu's intimidation lay in his penetrating stare; his way of fixing a man in his sight with a glowering look. He was fierce and could silence any man with a single word. His voice was deep, his accent, exotic and darkly masculine. With the exception of three men on board, he was rightly feared.

Roden and Gideon did not fear him and Rhapsody was amused to be Manu's closest friend, but Rhapsody was at the other end of the ship, happily engaged with his medicinal reserves of opiates and does not yet concern us.

Chapter Four – Stowaway

All this time the young girl had stayed inside the boat until everywhere about her seemed to fall quiet. She had taken advantage of the men's universal departure to eat, but the smell of cooked food reminded her that she had not eaten since early morning and another pressing need was making itself felt in her bladder. As planning goes she was utterly unprepared for being so far from home, having no fresh clothing or food or drink to sustain her. Driven by impulse, she was now paying the price for her impetuosity, being hungry and uncomfortable in a gown that was damp, torn and soiled. She purloined a small knife from the jerkin that had been left in the boat, and peered out from the tarpaulins. Seeing the deck deserted, she moved stealthily from the rowing boat and crept out of sight behind two packing cases. An open barrel stood perilously close to the exposed deck but, in the fading light, to approach it seemed a risk worth taking. She reached it without difficulty and helped herself to two moderately sized mangoes which, aided by the small knife, she devoured quickly from the hiding place behind the containers.

The girl settled herself as comfortably as she could, consoling herself that if she could purloin just one or two more fruits by daybreak, the ship would surely arrive at Petriah, where she could make her escape. She comforted herself with the thought that only one night need be spent in this cramped fashion. Crouching or kneeling was out of the question since whatever position she settled upon would have to be held for as long as possible and even slept in when the mariners returned after their supper. Sleeping in the rowing boat held no appeal since the base had been so wet that her gown was quite soaked and had it not been for several sheets of sacking that she had wound round herself, she would be quite chilled, despite the balmy air. She was seized by a sudden spasm of cramp in her left leg where she had been sitting awkwardly. Her immediate remedy of drawing up her toes sharply to relieve the pain was easier said than done in the confined aperture between the wicker case and the side of the cabin wall, where she hid. She ached now and was weary too, but with little chance of sleep, determined herself to stay awake and be vigilant.

She peered out from the security of her hiding place. The lightweight container, although large, had a very convenient wickerwork lid and a sizeable gap between the box and its hinges gave her an excellent view of the deck without being seen. Several voices, from somewhere in the middle of the ship, were approaching the deck, presumably men to take over the early evening watch. Gideon appeared and took a customary walk around before he would relieve Joshua at the helm. Then Gypsy appeared. The three talked amiably together, unaware that a pair of grey/green eyes was watching them intently.

During the next few minutes, the girl had her first opportunity to look at them closely. To her naive eyes, they did not appear quite the way she had imagined them. Their mismatched clothing, their untamed hair, the very swarthiness of their appearance seemed more akin to a wildness of nature, as if they lived all their lives at sea and not in some pleasant little dwelling on land somewhere, with wives and children waiting for their return from the merchant ships. Her eye fell upon the weapons in their belts and remembering all she had been told about such costume, the girl suddenly gasped. With sickening certainty, she knew she had made the most terrible mistake, and following that sharp intake of breath, her eyebrows lifted and her beautiful eyes became round in alarm. These were not cargo men. This was no ordinary cargo ship. The men she had so carefully concealed herself among must be... HAD to be... and she whispered the appalling word to herself..."PIRATES."

With her pulse racing, the girl searched her mind for anything that might help her find a more reassuring explanation of the world into which she had unwittingly placed herself. Nothing in her head served to ease her fearful mind. Everything she had ever heard about piracy, flooded her thoughts. She had heard they were murderous, bloodthirsty and dangerous. They were violent plunderers, merciless in their looting. The list went on in her fevered mind without one redeeming feature. The girl knew she had to get out of this terrible place but how? How?

And then... It happened.
She inadvertently leaned upon the packing cases for support, so great had been the shock, and instead of standing firm, one slipped; not by much, just a little, but enough to draw the attention of one of the three men, who turning round sharply, now homed in on the containers. Fresh in Gypsy's mind was the warning that Te Manu had so recently served them all about being more vigilant. Given that all of them had a predisposition towards suspecting anyone and anything, Gypsy was quickly flanked by Joshua and Gideon.

Gypsy raised one finger silently towards his lips, moving stealthily towards his prey, intent on making the other two advance without a sound. He slowly closed his right hand over the hilt of his cutlass and began to withdraw the smooth blade. Gideon and Josh nodded to each other, as they too, unsheathed their swords. Gypsy waited. His usually amiable, dark eyes and quiet smile was replaced by grim concentration. His long, brown curls swept his face in the light wind. He did not move. They stood a few feet apart ready to strike. Gypsy nodded towards Joshua who, with a raised voice called out.

"Alright! We know you're there. We have drawn our weapons. Come out with your hands on your head, man. Show yourself!"

Nothing happened. The girl behind the packing cases had frozen in terror. This could not be happening. Joshua exchanged a look with Gypsy. Had he not been absolutely clear in what he had demanded? Had he not sounded fierce enough when he spoke? Gideon realised such hesitation could be their undoing. The infiltrator might not be alone on the galleon. He did not wait before sounding the alarm that would be taken up as it was wrung all over the ship.

"STOWAWAY! STOWAWAY! STOWAWAY!" he roared. There followed a great commotion.

To the girl cowering nearby it seemed as though a hundred feet came running from all over the deck and were converging on the place where she had desperately curled up trying to make herself invisible in the recess. Voices that had shouted from afar came perilously near. She would not open her eyes and covered her ears in a futile attempt to block out the nightmare that was only just beginning.

On hearing Gideon's shouts of 'stowaway', the Captain let fly with a raging stream of expletives. *"What did I tell you!"* he yelled as he and Te Manu raced up the steps and on to the deck.

The tension in the air all around them was palpable. The blood was up. They were poised to kill and would be merciless to infiltrators. Roden Jarrus strode towards the scene. With a masterful voice, he shouted, "Come out or die." And so saying, he kicked the container viciously with his boot, venting all his anger and disquiet of the last few hours upon it, when he alone had sensed something was amiss. The wicker crates were sent sprawling and with a pistol in his hand, he reached down and dragged the recumbent figure from it's refuge and flung the body on to the deck. There came a scream as it was thrown, a primeval scream of abject terror that announced to every man present that the stowaway was no rough necked man but almost certainly just a youth with a voice not yet broken:

Yet whatever they thought, did not prepare them for the villain lying upon the deck at the Captain's feet, for when he reached down with the point of a pistol aimed at the hideaway, he was met by the upturned face of the loveliest girl he had ever seen.

The effect upon the girl of so many men with cutlasses raised and a pistol inches away was paralyzing, but equally, the vision of the girl upon each man was just as mind stopping. The Captain, nearest to her, was completely taken aback, like every other person present. Their blood lust was replaced by total surprise.

"Land sakes," the Captain uttered, and then added, quite unnecessarily, "It's a girl!"

She was the closest thing to perfection, a jaw dropping beauty with jet black hair against a creamy white complexion. Her eyes were enormous, but most arresting was their colour of extraordinary grey as she peered up from the floor. Te Manu instantly ordered a complete search of the ship and directed the majority of the men to cover all areas of the galleon. With swords or daggers in hand they hastened away and Te Manu went with them, shouting instructions for who was to go to the decks, the bow, the stern, the cabins, the quarter deck and so on. The few remaining men did not take their eyes off the girl as, one by one, their companions returned to the Captain, having found nothing.

She looked petrified with fear and in her face was innocence and youth. She was neither a child, nor yet a woman, and hovering in that half way place disturbed the men standing over her until Jarrus told them to lower their swords, but he did not give orders to put them away. With the initial search of the vessel revealing no other stowaways, the Captain now concentrated on the dilemma facing him.

"Stand-up," he commanded, in tones that he hoped were authoritative without terrifying her further. Slowly, with a movement graceful and liquid, the girl raised herself to her feet. A silent wave of awe rippled through the crew as she appeared, exposed before them. Her gown of palest blue was muddied and where it had become soaked, clung to her body in wet patches like a fine layer of paint, following the delectable contours of her breasts, the flatness of her belly and the sweep of her hips, all of which the garment rendered virtually transparent before their eyes. It was obvious she concealed nothing upon her

42

person. Her small feet were bare and when the Captain brought his gaze to her face once more, he saw the large round eyes of grey/green watching him with an expression of despair. Her prettily shaped mouth opened as she suddenly realized the inadequacy of her clothing and she tried to smooth the clinging folds of her gown, aware that the silk material was revealing all the curves of her figure.

She drew back behind the wicker case, the sackcloth still wound around her black hair, she waited tremulously for her fate. The girl was, perhaps, five feet four in height and had the softest, palest complexion that was, perhaps, the result of fear draining the blood from her cheeks. The length of her hair could not be seen but would probably fall way down her back. There was a fragility about her which was borne of unworldliness, yet she was a stowaway, and as such, had to be dealt with.

No man spoke, but Jonah the cabin boy, being too young to hold his tongue, decided she was a mermaid and broke the silence by proclaiming loudly,

"Cor, she's beautiful ain't she?" There wasn't a man standing who would have disagreed with Jonah, though no-one dared voice a word of it. Roden Jarrus knew that whichever way he played it, the fate of the girl lay entirely in his hands. A whole company of men would be wondering what he was going to do.

He could covet her himself. Not a man would dare question it or opine otherwise. He was the Captain. Then again, he could throw her to the crew for her punishment and let them amuse themselves despite her screams. He might just lock her up, imprisoning her on starvation rations for daring to come aboard and outwit all his attempts to make the ship secure, or he could simply arrange for her to disappear without trace, over the side. No questions would be asked and none answered. All of this flashed through his mind while he steadfastly watched her, but the one overriding and compelling instinct within him was to offer his protection. As their eyes met and her delicate gaze settled upon him in exquisite desperation, he knew that was exactly what he had to do.

Jonah's outburst had caused the girl to move her eyes in his direction. She identified him from recent memory as the boy from the rowing boat whose water flask and knife she had used. He was near enough her own age and she briefly wondered if he might have more sympathy for her plight. Transferring her attention to Jonah seemed to prompt Jarrus to say something quickly, just to recall her fascinating eyes to once more meet his own. Deliberately moderating the level of his voice, he asked "Who are you?" She looked resolutely towards the Captain, but, surrounded as she was by men with knives and swords, remained mute, rendered incapable of speech or coherent thought by the fear that gripped her.

"Ow do we know she understands us?" ventured Gideon, who, of all the crew, was most touched by the girl's tender age and delicacy. "Could be she's not from these Islands."

Israel stepped forward. "Ezra could ask her. He knows a language or two." There were quite a few nods at this. "Aye, ask Ezra" echoed several others while the girl shivered at this sudden surge of vocal assent.

"SILENCE!" thundered a deep voice that resonated around the ship.

The men instantly drew back as Te Manu strode across the deck. He approached the Captain and appraised the girl standing behind the packing case in front of them. He scowled at her, but said nothing. Ezra made his way forward.

"Ask her who she is in every tongue you know, Ezra," commanded the Captain.

"Aye Sir," said Ezra, obligingly," but if she speak to me fast and more than her name, I will not understand which language she talkin', Captain."

"Just do it," replied Jarrus. Ezra tried, in several languages, but the girl merely blinked at him whilst trying to commit to memory any names as she heard them. She was struck dumb by the formidable presence of the glowering warrior, whose severity numbed her completely.

Had Captain Jarrus but known it, the confusion caused by having such an audience staring at her was totally inhibiting and just too much for the girl to deal with. Her eyes did not leave the half-naked man with gold bands across his muscular upper arms. Her attention was riveted upon him. It was like watching an angry lion who might pounce upon her at any moment. The Captain was becoming more irritated by his crew than by the arrival of the stowaway.

"This is getting us no-where," he told Ezra.

More in exasperation than expectation of getting any response, he clapped his hands loudly in the girl's direction, to draw her from her hypnotic and petrified fixation upon the second in command, and asked distinctly, "What is your name?" The girl jumped visibly at the loud hand clap and instantly looked at the Captain. The shock simultaneously served to unlock her speech, for she took them all by surprise when in the gentlest voice of dulcet tone, she replied nervously

"My name is Tianna, Sir."

There was an audible rustling among the men assembled who exchanged her name with each other lest some at the back had failed to hear it.

"Tianna. She's called Tianna." they muttered only to be silenced by Te Manu's menacing roar in their direction for a second time.

"SILENCE!"

The girl jumped out of her skin. The Captain's eyebrows rose and an intuitive gleam crossed his face as he realized that she needed to be treated with some care in order to get her to say more. "Who brought you here?" he asked more quietly. Realizing she was not going to be instantly dispatched, the girl tried to co-operate. "I came alone, Sir," she replied for his hearing only. Almost at once, the warrior challenged her statement.

"SHE LIES, Captain," he announced, decisively. "She has not managed this without an accomplice. Others got her to this ship, or they boarded it with her." He turned the sourest face upon the girl as he spoke with venom, then, he turned upon the men with almost savage intent. "SEARCH AGAIN!" he shouted, "Do not return so swiftly this time. Uncover every place. Leave nothing untouched. Strike at every corner, however unlikely it is to conceal a man or boy. Now GO!"

The girl looked at this fearful being, tempestuous and forceful in manner and bitter in expression. He would kill her. She was certain of it.

It took several searches of the ship before Te Manu was satisfied that no other stowaways could be concealing themselves on board. He instructed men to remain on watch in the lower decks and patrol the cargo hold. His persistence was thorough, and did him credit, but yielded nothing. He walked back to the Captain. There were only a handful of men surrounding the girl, the rest having been re-deployed in searches or ordered on watch. The Captain continued to keep her standing.

"There is only one other possibility, Roden," said Te Manu, in an undertone, "and that is the least palatable."

The Captain ran his hand thoughtfully over his chin. He knew what was in his second officer's mind and voiced it. "You think one of our own crew has a motive of his own for bringing her on board? A deal has been struck to take her somewhere perhaps?" he suggested.

Te Manu nodded. The girl, calling herself Tianna, tried to protest that it wasn't true. "No. That did not happen. I came alone," she cried. It had been hours since she had parted from her homeland. No liquid had passed her lips since she had been in the long boat. She was overwhelmingly tired and too fatigued to think any more. Exhaustion made her almost cease to care what happened.

Te Manu Manmou regarded her with suspicion, choosing to view her as their enemy until it was pronounced beyond all doubt that she was not. He looked at her as though a dreadful feud was unavenged between them because she had the temerity to protest at their assumption. How dare she challenge his authority! Slowly, with great effect and deliberation, the warrior began to draw his own sword from its sheath because she had interrupted.

"Tell us who brought you here if you want to live." He spoke coldly, his words heavy with malice, the blade against her skin. The girl swallowed hard. She could scarcely stand for trembling. Her heart thudded in her chest. This is not what she had expected to happen. It had all gone horribly wrong. Her eyes wanted to close. The Captain interceded.

"That's enough, Manu!" he said quickly, stepping between them. Te Manu replaced his sword in deference to his Captain's command, but the girl was traumatized and lost all composure. She had the strangest swimming motion in her head as the images of the men standing close to her became hazy and obscure. To her disbelief and distress, a puddle began to appear around her feet as she could hold on no longer and in complete anguish, she cried out in shock and disgrace. Gathering the wet gown in one hand and fretfully cramming her other trembling hand to her mouth, she tried to step to one side. Things seemed to sway before her eyes. Almost inevitably, she overbalanced, slipped and fell, catching the side of her head hard against the metal hinged corner of the crate as she went down. The pain took effect as she cried out and blackness engulfed her, then, there was nothing. The girl lay quite motionless before them.

For a brief moment, they wondered if she was dead. Gideon, thoroughly alarmed, looked from one man to the other. Te Manu looked at the Captain, the grimness in his piercing dark eyes, had disappeared. Roden Jarrus raised his eyes to heaven. "That's how you get a girl to co-operate is it?" he asked with considerable irony in his voice. Te Manu looked suitably shocked himself, but remained typically defensive of his actions. "I never interrogated a woman before," he replied, staring down at the crumpled form on the deck, as though she were an animal, and seeing the puddle beneath her, added scornfully, "Do they always do that?"

"Only when threatened with having their throats slit," retorted the Captain, furious at his second in command. He tried to think fast but his mind would not cooperate. They both stared at the girl before he yelled, "Now what the hell are we going to do?" but without pausing for Te Manu to reply, added hastily, "And don't suggest throwing her overboard!

The remaining men watched the scene, turning their gaze from the girl to Te Manu, then to the Captain and back again to the crumpled girl lying motionless before them.

"Alright!" exploded Jarrus, determined to resume control. "We will learn no more tonight. I will decide at daybreak what is to become of her. She will be kept in the cabin under watch for now. All hands depart, save you, Gideon, and you, Manu. You stay here."

They watched the crew move away and the Captain issued an order to swab the deck clean.

"Carry her to the cabin, Gideon," ordered the Captain. "Put her on the bed." He turned to Te Manu, shaking his head at the girl lying on the deck. "I hold you responsible for this. You will watch her and sit up all night if need be. She is no use to us dead. I will have to go and talk to the crew before anyone can turn in. God what a night!"

Te Manu pursed his lips thinking that had the stowaway been a man, things would have turned out far better. He would have had the infiltrator dragged from unconsciousness to his feet, with a bucket of cold water in his face, then marched below deck at the point of a pistol for interrogation. If he survived the ordeal, which was unlikely, he would be thrown into a cage to await his fate. Satisfying though such thoughts were to Te Manu, he decided against voicing them.

Gideon stood over the prostrate girl, figuring what to do next. He bent down, turning his head at angles, considering the best approach to the task. "How exactly would you be wantin' me to do this, Captain?" he asked after an interminably long time. Jarrus stared at him blankly. It had been a simple enough command, for God's sake! He hesitated, not certain, himself.

"How the hell should I know?" he finally exclaimed. Gideon thought again. "Shall I sort of throw her over my shoulder, Captain?"

The Captain considered it. They all did, as they stared down at her, none of them sure what to do next. After some deliberation, the Captain made a decision.

"Look. Just do it. Just lift her up, but do it carefully. Not like she's a sack of rice. She's taken quite a knock."

Gideon reconsidered the problem from all angles before tentatively sliding one immense arm beneath the girl's slumped shoulders and the other behind her bent knees to raise her up and across his chest. Her head fell against his shoulder. Her long black hair, suddenly freed from the sacking, floated over his arms. Gideon was surprised at how light she felt.

"Why, the little creature don't weigh nothing at all," he told them, and proceeded to carry her with remarkable care down the three steps to the cabin where he used the weight of his broad shoulders against the door, to pass through. Gideon lowered her gently, across the wide bed. The Captain went to assemble his men and address them about the incident, leaving Te Manu and Gideon with the unconscious girl.

For some minutes, they sat watching her, Gideon sitting on the long bench, clutching his cap anxiously, afraid to make a sound less she should waken, and Te Manu leaning against the table, his arms folded, his feet crossed at the ankles, looking grim. The only indication of life emanating from the girl was the steady rise and fall of her chest, otherwise she was deeply asleep.

"How d'you reckon she did get on board then?" Gideon whispered aloud.

"She was planted," replied Te Manu, scathingly.

Gideon frowned. He had heard the girl protest before she had collapsed and was inclined to believe her. He studied her in his unique slow way. The delicate hands and fingers, the clear complexion, the silk of her clothing, all indicators that she was more of a lady than peasant and, unpainted, so probably very young and not one of the working girls who hung about the town courting men's favours.

"Well, all I know is, I never hurt a woman, an' don't intend startin' now wherever she's from an' if she is a plant, then I say the guilty man is the one who put her here and him's the one to be punished, not she!" Te Manu did not respond but knew full well that Gideon would be wholly disapproving of any attempt to do away with the girl. The big man turned towards the door to leave, then he hesitated, looking back at the warrior. "You're not gonna..." and he gestured towards the sleeping girl, as his concerned eyes hardened towards Te Manu.

"No," answered Te Manu, tersely. "I'm not." Gideon nodded, satisfied, and went out, leaving them alone.

Tianna would only retain the dimmest memory of the hours that followed. Heavy with exhaustion, she continued to sleep, probably aided by concussion from the blow she'd sustained when falling. The room was so dark and the mattress so thick and comforting, it was as if she was putting down roots from where her languid body sank into the bedding. Her eyelids did not flicker. From her shoulders all the way down to the small of her back, she seemed drawn into the softness. Her limbs were leaden and immobile. Her senses registered only silence and relief, enabling her to sleep on. Hours passed. At intervals, she imagined she was floating away, and as her body was raised, she tasted water, then sank back into sleep.

Outside, night had fallen. The moon was full and the sea, calm, gently moving the galleon like some gigantic cradle as she dreamed. A silver stream of light bathed the moving ship as it glided silently through the darkness towards tomorrow.....

Chapter Five - Cabin Girl

Daybreak came early.

In the cool dawn voices became audible as men woke up and the galleon came alive. The crew, refreshed by sleep, emerged from below deck.

Some threw water over themselves and began to crudely wash. Some ascended the rigging, attending to the constant demands of the complicated ropes, vital to adjusting the sails. There were daily routines to begin and things to set moving. The wheel was taken over from the men who had finished the last shift of the night watch. They were a healthy crew led by an enlightened Captain. The galleon brought them to friendly Islands often enough to take on clean water and fresh food, which was plentiful in the warm hemisphere where they sailed.

Roden Jarrus was a confident Captain of the Zenna Marius, and a contented man. He loved the sea and his command of the ship. Occasionally, he felt his sense of duty and responsibility towards the welfare of his crew, prevented him from becoming a true pirate, whatever that was. He had too much integrity to be a ruthless buccaneer, but his soundness of mind meant that he exercised good judgement and made right decisions, and as a result, he was liked and respected by all who served under him.

He had no taste for wanton violence but recognised that side of him was not something to boast about on a ship full of the most rugged individuals. It frequently fell to his friend, and second in command, Te Manu Manmou, the warrior of mixed descent and exotic looks, to meter out discipline and punishment. Te Manu could seem sullen and harsh yet he had learned a great deal from the Captain, and together, they ruled effectively. If the Captain was in danger of letting sentiment affect decisions, Te Manu would challenge him. If Te Manu became overzealous, the Captain did the same. Neither man hesitated to draw the sword or the pistol if threatened. Neither man would baulk at blood, but the Captain was slower to spill it. Men of all dispositions could feel respect for the leadership. It was a strong ship with a loyal crew and held to be the best.

The cabin was still quiet and dark inside, save for the square paned windows. Dawn light played on the eyelids of the slumbering girl. She moved her face away from the intrusive shaft of light, gradually becoming aware of the sounds outside. Before opening her sleepy eyes, her mind tried to make sense of the noises. In a state of half wakefulness, she dreamily believed herself to still be at home in her own bright bedchamber. She opened her eyes and blinked in the direction of the light. Peering at the windows, which were in the wrong place for her bedroom, she suddenly remembered she was on the ship. During those first waking moments, Tianna's mind raced.

Her first thought was 'Where am I?' but a quick survey of the cabin assured her that she was still on board and had not been taken off. The thoughts that tumbled together next were concerned with her last memories of the grim and taciturn pirate who wanted her life.

Tianna briefly questioned if she was dead, but dismissed it as absurd and followed it instead with the possibility that she might be injured from that fearful sword. However, the realisation that she was suffering neither obvious blood loss nor pain, diminished the need for more than the most cursory self-examination. Her arms and legs were as normal and everything between the two seemed unscathed. Her next thoughts hovered around her captivity.

Tianna wondered if she might be tied or bound in some way, but on kicking off the rough wool blankets, she proved there were no restrictions of any kind upon her. 'Then the door is certain to be locked,' she decided, and she considered this must be her prison, until she saw quite distinctly that there was a large iron key on the inside of the door. Her senses, by this time fully awake and sharp, informed her that she was in fact warm, breathing and lying on a mattress of considerable size and depth with a quantity of pillows and rugs around her. As the daylight grew brighter, she began to look around the cabin.

There was the door with a key and two dark wooden steps down to the floor. Across two thirds of the room was a table of considerable size, under which were two long benches fashioned from lengths of smooth wood. A rod supported curtains of some heavy, dark fabric with large metal rings that were pulled aside and this curtain screened the bed which recessed into a sort of bay. The mattress was wide, almost extending the width of the cabin and fitted like the cushion in a window seat, into a solid wooden box. It could easily have slept four people of moderate proportions.

In each wall were shelves and compartments where scrolls, maps, ink, compasses and various mathematical and nautical instruments sat among almanacs and books of various thicknesses. Small hand tools wrapped in rolls of coarse fabric nestled among the spy glasses, telescopes and pens that filled the smaller cubby holes. She sat up, scrutinizing the cabin with curiosity. There was an orderliness here suggestive of something more civilized than her limited understanding of piracy.

Tianna folded down the rough blankets, which although numerous and heavy were not dirty as she had imagined they might be. Everything had a density to it, the furniture and fabrics being thick and durable but not uncomfortably so, and nothing smelt musty as it might have done.

Only at this moment did Tianna realize first with bewilderment and then with shock, that she no longer wore the damp and grass stained gown. Where it was, she had no idea. She was wearing a long shirt that was clean and dry although several sizes too large. It was loosely fastened with a knot. It slowly dawned upon the girl that in order to be wearing the garment at all, someone must have removed her own clothing, for she certainly could not remember removing it herself, and what was stranger still, someone had attempted to redress her while she slept. Adopting the childish habit of talking to herself when alone, she said aloud,

"Do pirates lend stowaways clean shirts?" but didn't have time to consider an answer because at that moment her attention was drawn to an approaching footfall at the door, a solid sound of heavy boots and the click of the latch being depressed.

Sickness, borne of panic, erupted in her chest and engulfed the girl as the door opened and the silhouette of the Captain filled the aperture, blocking the streaming sunlight. In a flash, Tianna sprang from the bed, and hugging the shirt around her, stood with her back pressed against the furthest wall, like a cornered animal preparing to make a dash for freedom past its assailant. The Captain advanced no further into the room, but quietly closed the door behind him, conscious of the all-consuming terror that his appearance had invoked. "Hey, easy now, easy." he attempted to speak calmly with a deliberate quietness designed to soothe rather than provoke. Her wild eyes conveyed all the fear of last night. The Captain stepped slowly into the room and placed the pewter plate he had been carrying, on the table.

The girl tried to slide further into the recesses of the cabin. Her heart was thumping and her breathing was rapid. She was fighting down nerves of such magnitude that a mounting hysteria caused her to shake uncontrollably and a silent scream tried to escape her lips. The Captain tried not to move but held up his hands in a gesture of capitulation. "Whoa," he said in a tone that matched his amiable eyes. A genuine bewilderment played around his mouth. He had not expected her to react so violently. "I'm not going to hurt you, okay?"

She swallowed, but neither moved nor answered. He admired the way she looked in a man's shirt which he had recognized at once. "You must eat. By my reckoning, you've had nothing since afternoon yesterday." He spoke very quietly. She glanced at the plate but clutching the shirt defensively, did not come forward. The Captain decided on a different line of approach. "I'm going to leave you for a while. When you have eaten we are going to talk." He paused. "Okay?" His eyebrows lifted, waiting for a response. She nodded. His face relaxed. "Good," he said and went out, but removed the key, locking her inside, just in case she decided to bolt.

When she was certain he had gone, the girl moved. Her shoulders dropped and she emitted a long sigh of relief. This ordeal was taking its toll of her nerves for sure, but acute lack of food was also weakening her spirit. Tianna straddled the bench and stood over the plate of food. There was bread and cheese, nuts and fruit beside a tankard of liquid. Until the first mouthful she was unaware just how much she had needed food. She ate hungrily and drank the cider from the tankard. Although finding the taste strong, it was not too unpleasant and served to wash down the meal. The repast done, and fortified once more, the girl sat upon the bench and waited. To pass the time she studied everything within the room but neither reached out nor touched anything, upon the shelves or in the alcoves, not wanting to incur the wrath of these dangerous beings. Tianna remained where she was seated, watching and listening, alive to every sound beyond the door, and her eyes rested upon the dappled sunlight that played upon the table and lit the room in patches from the square paned windows. She had time in this solitude, to compose herself and think. Tianna was not timid by nature. She was intelligent and resourceful and told herself sternly that she could apply calm reason to this dreadful predicament in order to assess her chances. It occurred to her, that as she was not only still alive but clothed and fed, there could be no immediate intention of doing away with her.

However, with the door now locked from the outside, she may be of more use to the pirates as a hostage and for that very reason would be careful not to tell them everything they wanted to know. Perhaps she could get away with half-truths if she was clever. It wouldn't do to be deceitful and found out to be a liar. Their anger at being misled would surely seal her fate. This was not going to be easy but, the girl decided, the Island of Petriah could not be far off and she had heard them talk of going there only yesterday, while she was hidden in the rowing boat. Perhaps she could give them the slip when she wasn't guarded.

At length, footsteps descended to the door of the cabin. It was all Tianna could do to remain seated and not retreat to the wall again, but she had heard only one pair of feet. She tensed. As the key turned and the latch was depressed, it was the Captain alone who entered. During his absence, Roden Jarrus had made it plain to his crew that he would tolerate no disturbance whilst questioning the stowaway. He was still aggrieved by yesterday's fracas which had left the girl unconscious on deck and no doubt contributed to her current state of terror this morning.

He had also had a word with Mr. Baines and requested spare garments from Jonah that might be used to dress the girl, since no clothing had been found with her. Jonah obliged readily, as he did with every request, but had misgivings about the teasing he might endure from the pirates, if it became generally known. Mr. Baines was mindful of it. "I'll say nothing about it and no more will you," he told Jonah, "and if anyone asks we'll say as we don't know where no clothes come from, see?" But Jonah looked sceptical and unconvinced.

The Captain also knew he had to obtain answers to his questions or there would be rumblings of discontent among the men who were rightly suspicious about the girl's arrival on board. Being Captain to such men as these, carried risk as well as responsibility. If they trusted his decisions, he could pull anything off, but if they felt he betrayed them by setting a girl's interests above their own safety, then mutiny was an evil consequence for any pirate Captain. He re-entered the cabin knowing that he had to cover his own back and she knew that in order to survive, she had to do the same. He locked the door behind him as he entered. It unnerved her to be locked in with him. Rigid, she watched him as he placed himself directly opposite where she sat. Jarrus made a small comment of satisfaction that she had eaten the food. For the first time they observed each other carefully and despite mutual distrust and uncertainty, each approved of what they saw.

The girl beheld a man in his early thirties, but to one of Tianna's youth might be any age at all. He was dressed in high boots and tight fitting, buckskin britches. His cream shirt was finely made with wide sleeves and a generous collar, over which he wore a jerkin made of hide. His dress was dashing and well fitted, his poise, assured, and his appearance striking. His thick dark waves, neither cut nor cultivated, gave him a raw masculinity and his penetrative deep blue eyes held such attraction that it almost embarrassed the girl to look at him. Had they been introduced under any other circumstances, Tianna's heart would certainly have fluttered and she would have blushed at her reaction to him. As it was, she scarcely dared hope that the Captain might have a soul to match his kind voice or his looks. His eyes, fringed by black lashes, beneath strong brows, were warm eyes, set in a well-proportioned face with attractive features and suggestive of a humour that matched his seductive voice. He had a strong, angular jaw with a wide neck and broad shoulders. He was assertive when speaking and very much his own master, but he had a refined voice, an educated voice, and she guessed it was deliberately moderated because he was speaking to a woman. The manners and delivery of the Captain were at odds with the perception Tianna had of pirates, and in the quiet recesses of her mind, she questioned why a man of his breeding was thus engaged.

"Your name, if indeed it is your own name, is as lovely as your appearance," he opened the conversation gallantly, with a smile. He spoke as a gentleman, she thought. "I will call you Tianna, and introduce myself as Captain Jarrus. You will call me Captain or Sir when you answer me. Agreed?"

It seemed to Tianna that as the odds were against her, there was little to be gained by refusing. She nodded.

He seemed satisfied. "Try not to be so afraid. I only want to talk to you. You are on my galleon, the Zenna Marius, Have you heard of it?" She shook her head. He waited, studying her closely.

He frowned very slightly. If this were true, she had not been foretold of any plan to target his particular vessel. "How did you get on my ship?" he asked directly, his expression suddenly more intent.

The girl knew she could not be evasive with this man and brevity would not satisfy him. She did not want to make an enemy of the only one who seemed cultured enough to treat her justly. She decided to tell the truth as far as she safely dare. "My name really is Tianna," she said, looking into his eyes with an openness that engendered trust.

"I hid inside your cargo boat, beneath the sacking, I wanted to travel to Petriah and hoped this cargo ship might be going there after Auretanea."

The Captain listened. He had been right after all, about the landing party. Not one of them had spotted her on the beach. She had obviously come from that Island, and thought they were legitimate traders.

"Why couldn't you take a smaller vessel to get to Petriah?" he challenged her. The reply surprised him.

"I didn't want to be discovered trying to leave. There are soldiers from Scalos everywhere and they watch the beaches and stop the boats." Jarrus sat forward.

"Does anyone know you have come?" he asked. She shook her head. "No. I ran away with others to get word out to Petriah before our Island was cut off by the soldiers." This was even more perplexing.

"Where are your companions now?" he enquired.

"I don't know," she answered. "Some left on horses to reach boats anywhere they could find them."

"Who sent you?" Jarrus asked her again. She only repeated what she had said the night before. "I came alone."

The Captain considered the girl in front of him before asking any more questions. Like Gideon, he decided she was not a peasant girl, nor would she be an innkeeper's daughter and not in servitude of any kind that he could think of. It was hard to place her. He did not want to ask the wrong questions and find she had spun some fabricated web to deceive him. There was something wary in her answers that suggested they were playing some evenly matched game. He deduced that he would learn as much from what she did not say if he read the hesitations and expressions on her face correctly. She was, he considered, the loveliest looking girl he was ever likely to see, and made all the more so by her earnestness and seeming entirely unconscious of the effect she had on him. She seemed on a mission of great importance and looked straight at him, meeting his eye with her responses, but choosing not to say too much. There was no natural subservience in her manner, despite her fear of him, and he sensed a lively intelligence behind her eyes. Jarrus felt sure that under any other introduction, the girl would be confident. She was not challenging, but exuded a poise, and an assertiveness that made her regard him with equivalence. She made an immediate impression on him and aroused his interest. She was clever and presented a mystery that he fully intended to unravel. Intrigued, the Captain continued, and knew he would not be asking Te Manu to advise him.

"So you wanted to alert Petriah that something is happening in your homeland. A brave endeavour for a girl alone, so why were you out on such a mission? Did you have no brother or father to undertake the task?"

"No Sir. I left the castle with many others who work there. There is talk of it being seized."

"The castle? And you work there?" he surmised.

"Yes," she answered. "My mother has a position in the residential apartments." Everything she had told him began to slot into place and she fitted like the errant piece of a complicated jigsaw puzzle. She was in service after all, but in the privileged sector and must likely be of good character, and background.

"What is your last name and where is your father?" the Captain asked. Almost at once he perceived a change in her demeanour. She became defensive. His question triggered the girl's fears of being held hostage by the pirates. Thinking quickly, Tianna decided that she must make plain there would be no financial gain by keeping her a prisoner until some ransom could be secured for her release. She must give this buccaneer no reason to hold her. She must plead poverty. "I have no father, and therefore no name," she replied, and lowered her eyes as she said it.

Roden Jarrus interpreted this to mean the girl was almost certainly illegitimate and shamed at the confession, but it could equally mean she did not want to answer. He ran his hand across the back of his neck and raised his eyes to the ceiling of the cabin as he thought. It was trying and not a pleasant exercise to question her so closely. He considered the last off loading at Auretanea. The men on the beach had told his crew much the same of the marauding soldiers and their own fears of intimidation at the castle. They had to decide whether to leave or risk being held there. To justify their desertion in the face of invasion, they might well decide to try and get out and any number might volunteer in pursuit of finding help overseas, however reckless the journey. The picture painted by the girl was the same as he had been told, general fear, unrest and hasty decisions made by the growing intimidation from Scalos.

Tianna turned a look of expectation upon him, the grey/green eyes wide, the full lips slightly parted and her head, delicately inclined to one side, as if trying to read her fate, by guessing what was in the pirate's mind. There was still something of the butterfly about her. Jarrus recognized that fear would very quickly cause her to back away again unless he proceeded carefully. He changed tactics. "How did you expect to survive as a stowaway?" he asked, but the deep blue eyes held a twinkle and his voice was gentle. She dropped her defence and gave a small apologetic smile at the stupidity of her actions. "I considered eating your mangoes and hiding for a night or two until your ship reached Petriah," she answered guiltily. "I would have paid for them, but I brought no purse."

The Captain smiled at her optimism. "I don't think we need worry about that." he said. "The journey in the galleon will take a full week and only then if the wind is over the stern or the quarters to be favourable," he informed her. "We are much slower than the smaller vessels you know of. We cannot enter some ports where the water is too shallow. That is why we have to launch boats a good way out at Auretanea, but Petriah is good for us. It has deep water and a well-constructed dock."

Tianna was dismayed. To have encountered pirates was bad enough, but to dwell among them for seven days before seeing land held unimaginable horror. She could not contemplate surviving on a ship with such hardened men, who might do anything to her. "I...I thought it would only take a day," she faltered.

"So it would, well, less than two if you had travelled further to the east of the Island and taken a smaller ship, but we sail on a broader route that keeps us further out on the Sorrello Sea and near the ocean. It is safer for us. We are wanted men."

The girl listened to this news carefully, realizing for the first time that she should have ridden her horse, Whisper, over a far greater distance before dismounting. She fell silent.

"You cause me a problem," the Captain said, interjecting her thoughts, and frowning. "I could keep you in here for a day but I cannot keep you inside a cabin for however long we are at sea, and I don't yet know how much you heard on deck whilst my men were talking and unaware of you." She looked frightened. "I will propose something to you. You may gain passage by working on board as a member of my crew. How does that sound? The deal is this. I need answers to my questions. In return, you have safe passage until I release you, so long as you remain on board and do not go below deck, and are visible at all times."

Tianna shot him the first smile. It was a smile of relief at not facing certain death at the point of a cutlass, and of the excitement borne of pending liberation bound up with youthful optimism. At this moment she presumed the Captain would give her freedom at Petriah. The smile was a transformation. Her already beautiful face, lit with a smile, became radiant, lending her an almost irresistible attraction. It simultaneously captivated and unnerved him. The flash of that smile could be misinterpreted.

"I accept your terms, Sir," she replied, gratefully.

"Very well," he responded, "but you are to be careful on a vessel full of men. You are to give no word or gesture that could entice my men towards you. Do you understand? To use your bewitching eyes or that intoxicating smile to attract them will result in your being confined in solitary state until we reach land, so be careful. Do you understand?" She nodded.

"You will be given appropriate, better fitting garments and report to Mr. Baines on deck. He is ship's cook. You will get on well with him and work hard." As he stood up to leave, so did she.

"Yes, sir." she murmured.

"The correct response is 'Aye Captain,' he replied with some amusement.

"Yes, Sir. I mean, Aye Captain... Sir," she added as an afterthought, becoming rather confused. Roden

Jarrus looked at her and would have laughed but for the fact he must not relax his defences against one who was effectively his prisoner and a stowaway at that, who may or may not be lying. As she prepared to step over the bench, he noticed the extraordinary length of her glossy black hair for the first time as it cascaded across her shoulders and down her back. She could have almost sat on it. She looked up at him and they shared a questioning glance more meaningful than any recent conversation had conveyed. There was an affinity between them, an unconscious mutual recognition of refined manners and breeding. It was there but for a second, yet held them both. He hesitated, arrested by this unspoken unity, but was made uncomfortable by it. Finding the need to break the moment, he enquired quickly and somewhat awkwardly, "How is your head? You banged it when you fell." Embarrassment welled up inside the girl. She remembered wetting herself through fear and slipping but nothing else. "My head is a little tender, Sir," she confessed.

"Hmmm," he responded, "Show me." Tianna gingerly raised her hand towards her temple.

The Captain made the decision to stroke her hair away behind her ear, to see for himself. In that moment of physical touch, the girls' heart skipped a beat. She winced as his hand revealed a grazed area with heavy, purple discolouration at the side of her forehead. He frowned at the discovery, pained that she should have been injured. She lowered her eyes, the dark lashes sweeping her cheek. Tianna was discomforted by his attention. The Captain's jaw softened at her embarrassed submission. His unexpected kindness had confused her. "I have an ointment here in the cabin which you may use." he said, turning to the crowded but orderly cubby holes. He placed a small jar on the table. "Tianna," he spoke her name quietly. "Be careful to tell me only the truth." He drove the words home. "In return for your honesty, I will help you." Then wondering if his decision to place her on deck was akin to displaying a diamond among jewel thieves, he went through the door.

"Here! Take these," he shouted over his shoulder and threw a bundle of clothes in her direction. "Dress quickly, I shall return for you soon."

Chapter Six - Shipmates

The cabin door closed as he mounted the steps, but no key turned in the lock this time. Left alone in the cabin, Tianna turned her attention to the garments on the bench. She took the items and spread them on the table, before holding them up against herself. They were quite unlike anything she had in her previous wardrobe. There was a white shirt but cut smaller than the oversized garment she had difficulty keeping around her and it would almost certainly be a better fit, but the britches were something else! They were short in the leg and had a bib of sorts. She supposed the shirt must tuck inside the waistband.

Tianna did not want to delay in a state of undress in case the cabin door opened before she had finished fastening the clothes. She hurriedly abandoned the larger shirt and placed her arms into the smaller one, finding it to be well suited to her size. The girl sat on the edge of the bench to step into the britches and pulling them up, discovered them to be a snug fit around her bottom but slightly too generous around the waist. A belt of rope, fastened tight around her middle pulled the excess fabric in and the bib and braces served to tuck the shirt tails neatly inside.

She had no shoes and peered down at the unusual effect of being bare legged. Never before had Tianna dressed like a boy. The clothes had been cut for the less curvaceous shape of a young male, but the trouser legs, frayed through age, were rather becoming and sat tightly hugging her thighs, finishing, not embarrassingly short but more in the region of her knees. The bib covered where the shirt was inclined to gape. All in all it was practical and surprisingly comfortable, giving Tianna more freedom of movement than she had ever known before.

The Captain returned and called from the top of the steps, "Hurry up!" With no tie for her strong, black hair, she left it free from restraint and went up the wooden treads outside the cabin, stepping into dazzling sunshine. The freedom of light, air and warm sunshine on her bare skin was intoxicating after the restrictions she had known inside. It was as though her senses were heightened and exhilarated by the sounds and smell of the sea and the brightness all around the ship. She gazed in wonder at the masts rising up like gigantic trees from the deck that seemed to touch the sky and the rigging with its astonishing number of ropes that were held in perfect symmetry, taut and spaced as beautifully as a spider's web. She gasped at the enormity of the ship, her eyes following the flooring that ran endlessly in perfectly fitted smooth planks as far as her eyes could see.

Tianna had never contemplated that a ship could be so vast and so beautiful. It moved with a slow grace that she could feel and the sails were so enormous and powerful above her head, that she felt she was in the keeping of something living and breathing in its own right and merely being guided by the many men who were constantly calling to each other, working tirelessly to manoeuvre her through the winds and waves. Tianna was so excited by her first impression of the galleon that she almost forgot to be afraid of anything. She was awestruck by the enormity of the beautiful ship, and it showed in her face.

Her hair blew in the wind as she peered upwards, in the dazzling sun, to the flapping, billowing sails. She placed both hands behind her head to catch her hair from the constant breeze and drank in the new sights, the smells and sounds that enveloped her, watched by the crewmen nearby who now gazed upon the girl with a mixture of curiosity, suspicion, distrust and fascination, all at the same time.

Tianna gazed upon it all, and was enchanted by it. Suddenly she saw the Captain waiting for her with another man, Gideon, close behind. Her smile had been in response to the powerful sensation of being enthralled by such a ship, and was not meant to be seen by the two men. She hastily corrected herself and remembered she was among dangerous people. Her initial reaction to stepping upon the deck had not been missed. The girl's spontaneous delight was genuine enough. It pleased Gideon and others nearby, despite their reservations about her. They were proud of the Zenna Marius, and rightly so. The Captain was quietly relieved. There was a delightful optimism to the girl despite her circumstances, he reasoned.

But, as she began to move towards him, Roden stood stock still and ran his hand over his chin, thoughtfully, considering her attire, and, more especially, the sway of her hips each time she walked. It bothered him. She had been lovely before, but dressed like a boy only served to reveal her shapely limbs and soft contours, exposing her to much wider appreciation. He knew the risk he was taking in bringing her out on deck.

The Captain decided to walk ahead of her. She was stunning. Her complexion seemed shades darker than he had initially thought. Seeing her in the sunlight made him fleetingly wonder how she came to be such a breath taking combination of dusky skin and extraordinary, wide spaced, pale grey eyes.

"Follow me," he instructed. The girl obeyed, nervous but excited by the adventure opening up around her. The crewmen on deck all turned their heads but did not dare gaze for too long with their Captain present. They all had work to attend, but some gave raised eyebrows and knowing looks to each other after she had passed them, conveying obvious appreciation of the girl's physical appearance. They were men after all.

Some distance away, Jonah sat with a container of sweet potatoes. Tianna stared at him, relieved to recognise him as the open faced youth with bleached hair and eyebrows who she had seen yesterday. He had a ready inclination to smile broadly. The boy jumped to his feet at the approach of the Captain and responded enthusiastically in his replies of "Aye, Captain," to every sentence, but he momentarily glanced at the outfit worn by the girl and hoped it would not be attributed to him. The girl was brought before Mr. Baines who affirmed that she would be kept properly occupied alongside young Jonah, and learn much. The Captain left her in Mr. Baines charge.

Tianna felt instantly vulnerable as Captain Jarrus moved away, but she squatted beside Jonah in the hot sunshine and immediately offered her help. Jonah gave her a broad grin and handed her a small knife. She wasn't sure whether to accept it, having purloined one from the jerkin left in the longboat which she had left behind the packing cases, after being discovered there.

"Keep it," he said pleasantly, "You can fix it to your belt. It'll come in useful for lots of tasks."

Tianna thanked him and looked at Mr. Baines, whose face wore its regular, quiet smile of benign approval of things. She sensed that both he and Jonah were happy.

"Now you two young 'uns," he began kindly, adopting the style he always took with the cabin boy, "There's lots to do. There's potatoes to prepare and while they're cooking, the fruit needs a careful checking. We always has to be sure that no bad or bruised one is missed where it could affect all the others it touches, so you need keen eyes for the job and mine aren't as good as they used to be, so I'm relying on you two to get the job done, then we'll need plates ready for the stew. Got that?"

His good natured eyes creased at the corners as they both responded positively. Tianna noticed a quietness to Mr. Baines way of speaking that was his own natural reticence at putting himself forward. She sensed that however busy they might need to be, hurrying a task was not part of the plan. She also surmised there was a fondness between Mr. Baines and Jonah, and briefly wondered if they might be father and son. Tianna sat among the potatoes, determined to learn how to do the job properly, grateful for being placed with the affable Mr. Baines and Jonah, who was at least nearer her own age.

On the far side of the galleon, Te Manu Manmou had addressed the crew. With his severe and low voice, delivered with the brooding glower that was so typical of his perversity, he warned them all of the hellish consequences of any transgression involving the girl. The penalty for any man who touched her would be a flogging with the cat o' nine tails. They must not see her as fair game, but as being the possession of their

Captain who would decide the infiltrator's fate in his own time, before they reached Petriah. She was an enemy. The consequences of fraternizing with an enemy were dire. The men were quiet. It was obvious to one and all that Te Manu harboured the most resentment towards the girl who had dared to trespass.

Meanwhile, unaware of any negative reaction to her, Tianna found time passed swiftly. Jonah was not inquisitive about her, but very keen to talk. He wanted to impress her, and to that end became a mine of information about the pirates, who he admired for their notoriety. She learned that Jonah guessed he was fourteen years old and had no living family. She heard from him that some areas of the ship were off limits on account of his age and these would be off limits to her too, he supposed.

"I must never go where there is rum drinking at night," he told her confidentially, "on account of them sometimes getting dreadful drunk down below. Mr. Baines says it's because I'd hear such terrible words and see such wicked things a goin' on that it would be enough to make my hair curl and never straighten again, if I was to see it."

Tianna was fascinated. Her eyes widened and she gave a shiver at the thought of pirates being so alarming that they could have such an effect upon one's hair. Jonah warmed to his subject. He wanted to romanticize the pirates and horrify her too, to maximum effect, believing that she would relish it all as much as he did, no matter how exaggerated the telling might be.

"Course, one day I will be just like 'em." Jonah told her proudly, to impress his new friend. He filled her with trepidation about the strange and murky world below deck, where the sweated labour was hardest in the bowels of the ship and men who seemed scarcely human, remote and distant, would gather of a night around a great table with their tankards and fill the air with oaths, laughter and brawling presided over by the infamous Te Manu Manmou. Tianna's fertile imagination pictured the scene of drunken fighting and violent disagreements, where men crowded into the chaotic atmosphere at their peril.

The potatoes had been peeled, the fruit sorted, and Mr. Baines' timely intervention prevented further forays into the imagination. He showed Tianna the arrangements for the orderly stacking of clean pewter plates and the rows of tankards that had useful lids with hinges allowing a drink to be carried without spillage. The young girl was surprised at the quantity of plates needed to provide a meal for every man and she staggered under the weight of trying to lift too many from the shelves until Mr. Baines took half of them away.

"'Ere, 'ere you go easy lass. No more 'n a few at a time for you to try liftin'. Pewter is heavy stuff."

They set about ladling a hot stew into bowls with plenty of potatoes and began distribution. Some would go straight to the men on deck who would eat where they stood. Some would come to be served direct from the galley. Some would be taken to the dim world of the lower deck and placed ready upon the enormous table for the hungry men's repast, a job undertaken only by Mr. Baines himself, on account of its being off limits to Jonah.

Tianna was told who to serve and although it scared her very much to approach them, she went about leaving the plates of appetizing victuals for each man on deck and began to identify names with faces. Some men stared at her suspiciously, with hardened faces, resenting her existence for being among them. She withdrew rapidly as soon as she had set down their plates, feeling the glare of antagonism. Tianna dared not wait. A few nodded or grunted, failing to meet her eye, but she felt their critical gaze burning the back of her head as she hurried away. One or two even muttered their thanks, ominous though it sounded. One or two smiled as they grasped the plates from her into their own hands, but whether it was with a smile or a leer, she wasn't sure, and retreated even faster from them. Once, she lost her orientation back to the galley, and afraid to ask, stood petrified for a few moments, until approached by a fair haired man, who had been watching her appreciatively from the side of the ship.

Joshua came across slowly. His casual movement, as he made his way in her direction alarmed her more than if he'd hurried. He took his time and when directly in front of her, he looked her up and down and the man's mouth began to pull up at the sides in a suggestive smile. "I'm Josh," he said simply, with mischievous eyes. The girl swallowed and tried to smile but found to her consternation that she had begun to shake.

"You needn't be that afraid," he told her, "I'm only going to tell you the way to the galley."

"Oh!" she sighed. "Thank you."

"You're welcome," he smiled.

Tianna took a deep breath and tried to relax. He was not many inches above her own height and had a mass of dark blonde hair, thick and so tight like thatch, that it would have defied any combing. His eyes were bright blue and full of impertinence. There was a defiantly cheeky attitude in his manner that made the girl think he would make fun and trouble, given the opportunity. He winked at her and she blushed. It made him laugh, but he kept his word and pointed out the way she should turn to get back. She murmured a tremulous word of thanks, to which Josh bowed and said, "At your service ma'am."

She smiled shyly in his direction, and when he saw it, he gave a slow whistle and rolled his eyes as though bowled over by her. It made the girl take to her heels and hasten away, hearing his laughter behind her. She did not know what to make of Joshua, but hoped he was alright, even if meeting him had unnerved her.

Tianna returned to the safer company of Jonah and Mr. Baines who was informative about how long fresh food could be expected to last, the best means of storage for dry goods, the damage that could be done by weevils and the importance of keeping things clean and separate in order to avoid contamination.

He was a man ahead of his time, along with the far sighted Captain, who knew to skimp on wholesome food was a deadly economy. Tianna gave all the appearance of taking in the information, which was the only safe way forward, given that she was wary of them all and totally unable to relax her guard for a second. She was unsettled; conscious that many pairs of eyes followed her every move, yet they all turned away from her direction quickly, if she looked around.

If Mr. Baines was aware of this voyeurism from the other men, he didn't reveal it, demonstrating instead a near perfect show of normality as he talked to her about the use of oil and spice in food preservation. The girl grew tired, having been alert and guarded all day, whilst trying to overcome her tremendous fear of the pirates.

As the softer light of evening fell, she relaxed a little and found her intense weariness not altogether unpleasant. The tiredness was the result of work thoroughly undertaken during a whole day in the fresh air. She ate on deck, surprised at the delicious flavour of food, when truly hungry, the very same food she had helped prepare. It seemed tastier to her palette than anything she had eaten before. Such hunger and appetite were new to her. She ate with surprising enjoyment of her food, despite all her trepidation.

That evening, a leisurely atmosphere descended with the setting sun. Miles from home, Tianna sat on deck. She quietly listened to the pitch and fall of voices, catching random words of conversation as the sounds drifted on the warm wind. Words became interspersed with snatches of song or a note of music that reached her ear but were muffled by the wind and flapping sails of the majestic vessel that was home to them all.

Jonah named all the pirates who were within their range of vision, explaining the skills each possessed which were essential to manning the great ship. There was a ship's carpenter, a sail master, a cooper and many more. The cook she already knew a little and feared him least. Jonah told her small things about each one; things to impress or amuse that served to imprint each man as an individual in her mind. She wanted to enquire more about Joshua but was too much of a stranger to pry. She wanted to know if Jonah was ever afraid of the pirates but decided it was far too soon to ask such questions.

As dusk fell, the Captain emerged from a company of men further along the deck and bade her follow him. He was less friendly and rather off hand in manner towards her, made necessary by the watchful eyes of his crew. She jumped to her feet, immediately guarded and apprehensive again.

"Go to the cabin and sleep now before the men receive their rations," he instructed her, without preamble. She knew better than to delay. He seemed crisp and impatient. Had they all been kept waiting for her departure before being issued with rum? She hoped not. It would be another black mark against her to deepen their resentment. The girl knew she should not be there at all, and had only been tolerated today because of the Captain's orders. It was frightening to be so vulnerable, but their deeply held prejudice of stowaways was understandable. She had transgressed a law of piracy that could have ended her life and still might. Tianna said a hasty goodbye to Jonah and Mr. Baines and hurried to the cabin, hearing the key turn in the lock before the Captain walked away. He pocketed the key, thus ensuring no man could take advantage. To Tianna's understanding, it was an act of imprisonment and convinced her that she was indeed captive and would be held for sale or ransom just as soon as the pirates could work out her worth.

She lay in the dark, turning the events of the day over in her mind. Lots of things did not add up. She could not equate the barbaric reputation of pirates with the consideration she had been shown. It puzzled her that Mr. Baines and Jonah were such civil beings and obviously content to live on the galleon, Zenna...Zenna... Whatever it was called. The thought of the beautiful galleon warmed her. And the Captain,

What of him? He was a gentleman, pretending to be rougher than he really wanted to be, wasn't he?

She shook her head in weary confusion. Her mind drifted to the memory of Jonah curdling her brain with stories about the men she had seen; how Gideon could kill with a single blow, and the prowess of the warrior and Israel with their cutlasses who could slice a man in two. Then there was the twilight world below deck where angels feared to tread. The galleon was a paradox of vice and virtue. However, one thing was manifest and it had been announced with the turning of the key in the lock. Unless they intended to kill her, she was certainly a hostage. There could be no other reason for the Captain to confine her to this room. She must therefore, be careful not to reveal her real reason for going to Petriah, and with that thought in mind, Tianna fell asleep.

Chapter Seven - Divided We Fall

The Captain made his way to find Te Manu. He knew there would be criticism of his decision to treat the girl with kindness. Usually Jarrus and Manmou managed situations comfortably between them, but this was different. They seemed diametrically opposed on how to handle the stowaway and Roden was aware that anything threatening their safety, drew Te Manu's darkest side. He hoped the arrival of the girl would not cause a deep rift between him and his friend.

Te Manu was below deck when the Captain came to take his rum. The warrior's sultry mood fitted well with the sombre surroundings of the dark panelled middle deck, where most of the men would sleep. His eyes flashed the moment he caught sight of the Captain. "You take a big risk, Roden, bringing her to work on deck," he told the Captain, bluntly. "What do we know about her? Suppose she is lying and has another motive for coming aboard? Have you questioned her more since this morning?"
"I will ask her more tomorrow." Roden declared.

"She should not have freedom, either on deck or in Petriah," said Te Manu, darkly.

The Captain toyed with the handle of his tankard and sighed. "I can't keep her locked up for the whole voyage," he retorted.

"We need access to the cabin," complained Te Manu.

"The documents stored there relate to our contraband. Suppose she is looking for them?"
"Everything that should be under lock and key is safe. I saw to that," replied Jarrus. "I know how you feel

about her, but if she stays in sight of everyone on deck, there is safety in numbers for her and for us."

"I still don't like it. A female among the men will cause unrest. They are already under sentence of the cat if they so much as touch her, and what envies and jealousies can she rouse between them, Roden, if she has come to make mischief?"

The Captain considered the implications. "Do you suspect she may have links with Baron Lussac's men from Scalos?" he suggested, more to deflect the tension between them. Te Manu considered this.

"It's possible. But we have enemies too among the merchants. How do you know she is not from a merchant's family, one of the ship owners who we have regularly plundered? There are several I can think of who would have us hanged. Is she here to find the evidence to condemn us, and report what she found in Petriah?"

The Captain reflected on his friend's mistrust. "I can't see any merchant setting his daughter among pirates, can you? But I grant you that she could be in the pay of merchants," he conceded.

"Or in the pay of the Baron's men," added Te Manu. "If his plan is to dominate the straits of Auretanea, like has been told you, we are going to sail into a trap. The Baron despises pirates too, remember, and another thing, what happens if we are caught with a girl of breeding on board? If she turns out to be gentry, the charge will be kidnap. They won't have to find evidence of looting to hang us, just finding the girl will be enough to get us locked up."

Jarrus became thoughtful. Te Manu pressed his point.

"All I'm saying is, don't trust her just because she's young and female. Watch her hourly. Have Baines report every question that she asks. She came as a stowaway for Christ's sake! Remember that. We wouldn't give any privilege to any man who got on board that way."

Roden Jarrus drank from the tankard and held the vessel in front of him with a concerned look in his eye.

"I will question her closely." he conceded.

"Well, you bloody well better get some answers because there's men on this ship who are watching us and aren't going to take it well if they think you're putting her safety above theirs. It won't be long before one or two start asking where your loyalties lie. They are not going to sit back and watch you jeopardize their lives through sentiment. Putting her on deck will make some of them resent the liberty, and things could get ugly, really ugly. I already feel it festering."

There was a long silence.

"If her story is not convincing, we will have to set a trap to make her show her hand," said Jarrus, contemplating what could be done.

"You'll need to do it before we reach Petriah then, Captain," said Gideon, who had been listening in the doorway. "Because Manu speaks true about the men. There's a rumblin' sure enough. I've been listening to them and while most of 'em are ribbing Mr. Baines about the girl in good humour, there are some who don't want to see the joke." Gideon sensed the girl was in much danger from suspicious men among the crew and although he understood Manu's disquiet, he didn't want to see the girl snuffed out like a candle by any one of them.

Te Manu stopped chopping the tobacco with his knife, to look at Gideon. "Yes," echoed Te Manu. "and what does she think you're gonna do when we get to Petriah, just let her go?"

Roden Jarrus looked at them both. "I can't take that risk," he said decisively "If she was planted, then her very existence jeopardizes our lives." Gideon asked the inevitable question. "If we can't leave her in Petriah, Captain, What 'appens to her then?" Te Manu got up to leave. His voice was black with malice. In his eyes, she was a threat. "We make damn sure we know who she is before we land." He sounded venomous. "And if not, she has to disappear, the same way all of our enemies have gone before." From the depths of his dark mind, worked a dangerous and terrible brooding, contemplating the girl's fate, but as yet, the means were undefined, yet poison slowly festered within. He kicked aside the bench with ferocity and threw the knife he had been using into the table with such savagery that it thudded and stuck firm, standing upright, vibrating with the force. The Captain and Gideon watched him go.

Knowing Te Manu's penchant for violence, both realized that the girl's very survival rested on her answers tomorrow. They stared at the knife embedded in the wood with the violent energy of being thrust there. It affected them both.

Joshua had entered and been there long enough to catch the chilling words and to see Te Manu's departure. He saw the knife in the table and understood at once. "He can't mean that, can he?" he asked them. Gideon shrugged unhappily and growled incoherently. The situation was not good.

"You know what Manu is like." answered the Captain.

"Yes, but we don't kill women, Sir. Least, I don't want any part of that."

"I know Josh," acknowledged Roden, "I know."

The girl asleep in the cabin was causing untold ripples of disturbance that threatened to divide the crew. Te Manu's rigid attitude could stir up an even bigger revolt among them. Gideon looked grave. Jarrus's brow was furrowed. The likelihood of the girl being raped or murdered depended upon the Captain suppressing the antipathy and distrust already voiced with vehemence by a few. Tonight, Roden Jarrus wished Tianna had chosen any ship other than the Zenna Marius. The clouds were gathering.

The girl woke early. She had not slept well. Too many thoughts had passed through her troubled mind, making themselves felt in nightmarish dreams. She missed the small comforts of home which were in stark contrast to the very baseness of life on the galleon. The toilet and washing facilities were crude in the extreme compared to what she had known. There would be no relief until she could break free of the pirates. She resigned herself to another day of toil on deck but suddenly remembered being locked in.

Tianna sat up and was surprised to find a meal left on the table, the plate bathed in light streaming through the window. The noise outside suggested the hour was later than she had first thought. She ate quickly and crossed to the door to try the latch. To her surprise it opened. Tianna dressed in a hurry and made her way up on deck, hoping not to arouse the displeasure of Mr. Baines, by arriving late. She need not have worried. Amiable and busy, he simply handed her a scouring cloth and set her to clean the morning's dishes. She had been there not a full half hour when the Captain approached. "A word, Mr. Baines. You'll be good enough to excuse the girl for one hour."

"Aye, Captain," answered Mr. Baines, agreeably. Tianna got to her feet.

"Follow me," he said shortly. The girl obeyed as the Captain walked swiftly towards the cabin she had only recently left. She had to run to keep up, and followed him hastily down the steps. Jarrus had been reflecting on Te Manu's opposition to the girl's lenient treatment on board, and his strong objection to her freedom on deck. It had preoccupied him all night. It troubled him that Gideon was asking what they were to do with her on reaching Petriah. In truth, the Captain had no idea, but the discontent in Te Manu and others was likely to increase, and he, Roden, could lose control of his galleon if the crew began to argue about the fate of the stowaway or considered his handling of the situation to be inept. By the time he confronted the girl, the man had had little sleep and what there had been was disturbed by the recurring thought that his authority, as well as the girl's safety, were compromised. He was in a predicament that was becoming dangerous and so was she. The Captain indicated that she should sit next to the window. Tianna stepped over the bench and slid herself into the corner, while he took his place opposite. His manner had changed, and the girl was instantly alert.

"Remind me of your connection with Auretanea," he demanded, abruptly. Tianna's guard instantly went up.

"I was born there," she replied, carefully.

"And you are high born, are you not?" he guessed.

She was a little taken aback by the directness of his approach, but could scarcely disguise her class.

"Yes Sir." This was assuming the unpleasantness of an interrogation.

"You said your mother worked at the castle. Are both your parents in the direct service of the royal family, perhaps?" he suggested. Tianna hesitated. She had told him yesterday she had no father. Was he trying to trip her up? The Captain read her expression of surprise. She was thinking quickly, now more convinced than ever that the pirate's intention was to sell her or demand a ransom for her release. "My mother is a lady in waiting Sir," she informed him. "I have no father."

Fear did not totally dissolve her feistiness. Inside her head, a defiant voice added *'so you won't take ransom money that way, Captain!'* She did not like his curtness. Roden Jarrus was prematurely pleased with his progress. A lady in waiting with a daughter of this girl's age, would not risk being held in a castle overtaken by enemy soldiers from Scalos. That fitted. So far, so good. She had been telling the truth.

"How old are you?" he demanded. It was impertinent to ask a lady's age. The girl bridled.

"I am soon to be seventeen," she answered.

It was the Captain's turn to be surprised. His eyebrows rose and he stared at her, dumbfounded. He had taken for granted that she was at least three years older, not by her appearance, for in truth, Jarrus had only the vaguest notion of how sixteen might look any different from nineteen. He had simply assumed that to infiltrate his ship so capably, she had to be older.

"Are you telling me you are only sixteen?" he asked, totally disturbed by the revelation. The girl nodded and bit her lower lip, wondering if it was a worse transgression to be sixteen years old than it was to be a stowaway. The Captain was contemplating something vastly different. She was little more than a child! No wonder she had come aboard without a second thought and expected to arrive a day later in Petriah. She was young enough to believe she could achieve anything she set her mind to, and would take no account of the risk. The impulsivity of the girl! The recklessness! The stupidity! It plunged him into greater turbulence than before. Te Manu was suggesting they dispatch a girl who was little more grown than a child!

He drummed the table as if trying to resolve a great problem while the girl watched him blankly. Suddenly he got up and walked around the table so he was standing close behind her. He leaned forward, bending over her, altogether too close for her comfort. His breath fell hotly against her ear. "Who were you going to see in Petriah?" he demanded.

"No-one!"

"You had no-one to go and see?" he persisted.

"No!"

"No destination? No place to attend?"

"No!" she was becoming defensive and agitated. "I don't know anyone in Petriah," she protested passionately. She was uncomfortable with his rapid questions being fired from behind. The Captain changed course. "Have you heard of Baron Lussac?"

There was a sharp intake of breath, a definite reaction that the girl instantly tried to cover. She became tense and guarded. "I have heard of him," she allowed. "I know all my people are concerned for the freedom of the sea. We will be cut off in Auretanea if he has his way." This was common knowledge and told Jarrus nothing that he didn't already know. The girl's reaction had been extreme, at the mention of the Baron. It was as if she had been caught out, and had more personal knowledge of the man than she cared to admit. He resumed his place opposite the girl. He fixed her with a piercing stare to which the girl returned unflinching eyes. It had become a standoff, like some dreadful game where each of them, playing for high stakes, used intellect and calculation to outsmart the other. Neither of them trusted the opponent, for opponents they had become.

Jarrus was changing his opinion of the girl he had pledged to protect only twenty four hours ago. He began to consider Te Manu might be right and that she had been lying throughout. The name of Lussac had hit her like a rock. She knew him. Jarrus was certain of it. Tianna sensed danger creeping towards her, engulfing and isolating as lies are wont to do, to those least suited to telling them.

"I will ask you again, Tianna, who are you going to see in Petriah?"

She believed he was fishing for a contact from whom he could extract a ransom for her life.

"I told you. I don't know anyone in Petriah," she said again. The effort she brought to her denial was too much. She knew she had failed to convince him.

"Very well," he said quietly, with a delivery cold as ice. "Then you have no need to go there..."

"Oh! But I must!" she interjected, and stopped just as suddenly, turning her face away and averting his gaze in guilty admission.

"You will stay on this ship," he told her. Tianna was mortified, angered and became more distressed.

"You said you would help me" she accused him through a blur of tears, blinding her vision, which began to roll silently down her face.

"I asked you to be honest with me," he retorted angrily. "Instead I am sure that you are concealing the truth. If there is no-one waiting for you in Petriah, you have no need to leave my ship. You will stay until you tell me who you were going to see."

The girl could have opted to confess everything, but fear, distrust and stubbornness combined to make it impossible. She was certain the pirates had intended all along to keep her for gain, and would imprison her until they had a good price. She wept openly now at her fate. The Captain had no time for this. He realized the danger to them both, of supporting a stowaway who lied. "Get back to work until I decide what is to become of you," the Captain ordered, severely, holding open the door. She had little option but to pass through, crying bitterly. Tianna had lost the kindness of the pirate Captain.

Jarrus was angry and greatly troubled yet must appear to have the matter in hand or there would soon be a revolt among the men, the like of which had never happened. He was drained. He would now have to confess to his men that the girl was withholding the truth. There was no option but to think up a plan to get a confession from her. If he could not succeed in this, her future and his were in peril. Te Manu would be hard to convince that Jarrus could do it. Te Manu would extract the truth at knifepoint and death if this went wrong. The Captain of the Zenna Marius, sat at the table and stared into space.

From beneath black, glistening eyelashes, Tianna's sadness made her weep for lost freedom. It was cruel to emerge into such a beautiful morning where the sun shone too brightly and the cloudless blue sky spread too wide and far above her, promising a freedom of the spirit where her melancholy heart could not fly.

Out on deck, a warm wind greeted Tianna and slapped against her skin as if rebuking her gently for crying. She took a deep breath in an effort to recover her composure. She would not accept that all was lost. She had outwitted them to steal aboard and she would outwit them to get off, even if it meant diving over the side! The young girl may have been more afraid than resilient had she realized how her very survival was to become the subject of their discourse. The girl wiped her eyes with the back of her hands, trying not to show her disappointment, and braved the day.

She was fortunate to be assigned to Mr. Baines. He acted no differently, whether or not he sensed she'd been thoroughly upset by the interview with the Captain, although he had heard the obvious frustration in the Captain's voice when he emerged from the cabin to ensure responsibility for the girl was properly handed over. Mr. Baines carried on in his usual quiet and optimistic way, affording Tianna the time and space to feel better. He gave her small tasks and did not chivvy her to get them finished. Once or twice he noticed her with her head on one side, flicking hair away from her face, sniffing and wiping her eyes with smudged hands. Mr. Baines felt sorry for the lass even if she wasn't being honest with them. There was probably good reason, if she was in the grip and power of some powerful merchant. Her day passed without further incident, although she had a headache that persisted. She did not see the Captain again.

The girl did not feel like talking much and remained subdued with thoughts centred on escape. She knew that within two or three days they would see the outline of Petriah from the galleon. Then she would take her chance. For now, she would accept her situation passively, to avoid attracting undue attention, until the ship neared land, when she would attempt her escape by swimming ashore. Tianna reasoned she would only need to be out of sight for the shortest time. No suspicion would be aroused until Mr. Baines noticed her absence, and, bless the man, he was never worried about the time, nor seemed in any hurry.

She sought permission to retire early and Mr. Baines, although surprised that she wanted no food, agreed. Jonah was disappointed.

"I thought she liked us," he said.

"I think she still does," replied Mr. Baines.

"Is she ill then?" asked the boy.

The man sighed. He hadn't wanted to involve Jonah, but he'd hear something soon enough from the others. "Thing is, Jonah, Captain got angry with her. She's a stowaway, remember, and as such, he could punish her hard if he wanted, lock her up, just give her bread and water, that sort of thing, but he give her a chance to tell truth about where she were going and she won't say. Captain's certain she's lying and that puts him at odds with all of us for being too lenient." Jonah may have only been fourteen, but his background had been a hard one. He knew the value of telling lies to protect yourself.

"It ain't so bad to keep quiet Mr. Baines. Sometimes keeping your mouth shut saves you from a beating."

"Aye Lad, could be she's afraid to tell the truth," agreed the ship's cook.

Unbeknown to Tianna, the Captain had decided that a few more of his crew should become involved in trying to trap the girl into saying something. To that end, he assigned her to work with a few of his most trusted men and told them to engage her in conversation. There had been a distinct shift towards Jarrus's idea since they had discovered she was only sixteen. If Te Manu was still for dispatching the wench, it was tantamount to murdering a young 'un, and few would say they were up for that. Unlikely though it was to yield results, they went along with Jarrus, at least for the time being.

So it was that Tianna became a maid of all work, and what work! It had to be up on deck. The Captain would not risk her being below and falling into the clutches of Te Manu, or the labourers. She swept and she scrubbed. With Israel, she worked hard to cut and mend the sailcloth, wielding heavy shears through tough material or forcing eyelets into the resistant fabric for the longboats. With Gideon, she sanded and varnished where he had replaced weathered timbers. With Ezra she learned how to plait rope. None of it was easy work. The tools were made for men to use and she lacked any experience of physical labour. Each day she presented herself, concealing any resentment of the work or the men, and did her best. Of the Captain, she saw nothing.

At first the men remained wary of her and she of them, but their attitude became less hostile and they were making more effort to communicate. Tianna had a vague idea it was intentional. They began to talk to her, awkwardly at first, whilst showing her what to do, but starting other conversations, asking about names and places along the way that she might have known; except she did not know and therefore was not drawn by any of it. They soon discovered it was easier and made the day far more pleasant if they tried to be friendly, rather than scare her half to death but Tianna remained frightened of them all and they knew it. So they put aside their own suspicions of her, to encourage her to relax her guard. That was Captain's orders. It entertained them, rather than irritated them, when she tried new skills but got them wrong. It was something of a novelty to teach her and find she finally got it right. They began to laugh at her mistakes and, to the girl's credit, she never displayed bad humour and would fight down her own fear of them, occasionally flashing a breath-taking smile in their direction, or trying to suppress her own giggles when they laughed at her, and she forgot to be afraid. The men started to become accustomed to her and none found her any trouble. It seemed hard to believe she might be a threat.

Tianna decided she did not like Israel. She could not master the sailcloth, except for threading rope through its rings, but it wasn't so much the work as his reluctance to look her in the eye, and he had least to say, giving an impression of surliness.

Gideon, on the other hand, despite his gruffness remained favourable to the girl, and although she was initially afraid of him, Tianna began to find he was almost as agreeable as Mr. Baines. He was gentle with her, almost frightened she might break, so took care explaining how things had to be done in certain ways and he praised her to the stars for everything she did.

She smiled at him so often, that he melted inside and a fondness developed because he thought she was an angel and she thought he was a gentle giant. It wasn't easy being a sixteen year old girl, trying to navigate a sea of emotions that kept her in childhood one minute and propelled her towards womanhood, the next.

Ezra pressed buttons that awakened a sleeping sensuality in the girl that expressed itself in terrible shyness. Some ten years older than Tianna, he was a handsome Latino with eyes that winked at her provocatively. He was a romantic at heart and sang all day long as he worked. He spoke in his own tongue, saying sensual things to her that he would never have dared, had she understood, and he amused himself by getting her to repeat things back to him. She half guessed that what he got her to say was impertinent, and when she challenged him, he laughed and denied it was anything other than a few harmless words about the weather. Plaiting ropes was hard on the hands but they took their breaks and Ezra would produce his guitar and sing to her. She quickly lost her heart to him, in a girlish crush. She began to eat and sleep again and returned to work with Mr. Baines and Jonah each evening. Thus the days passed rapidly, with long hours spent in the company of one or other of the crew every day.

Tianna was discovering in those long days of sunshine, that although collectively, the pirates were indeed a fearsome body of men, as individuals, they were people with histories just like any other. She had started to glimpse their characters, and her fears grew less. With Jonah alongside, who told her more about them each evening, she found a natural affinity with the galleon and an embryonic liking for a handful of its crew. There had been scant sign of the Captain in these four days and of the warrior, she had seen nothing since that terrifying night when he had threatened her. His work probably kept him among the many dangerous men of shabbier appearance who toiled in the bowels of the ship in a world of sweated labour.

She suspected they were former slaves, presided over by that monstrous man whose orders were never challenged and who killed randomly, if he was out of temper, which she guessed was often. Thank goodness he occupied a twilight world where she never had to go. She shivered at the thought of him. The girl's imagination supplied chilling pictures of the two senior men on board, in the absence of any facts. Deeply ingrained upon her memory was the Captain's declaration that she had no business in Petriah. The girl's mind turned to thoughts of making her escape.

By the fifth day, the girl's behaviour had provided no fresh clues and time was running out. The Captain resolutely refused Te Manu the opportunity to go anywhere near the girl, let alone question her. He would not allow her to be pre-judged and was still intent on finding a way to unravel the mystery without recourse to Te Manu's kind of threats, intimidation or violence that might all too easily end in her demise.

Captain Jarrus decided to call a meeting. The night was warm, the atmosphere as relaxed as it could ever be under the circumstances, and the girl was uppermost in their conversation. Joshua arrived late. He took a seat next to Gideon.

"I just gave her some oil for her hands. Nasty blisters she's got. The kid's not meant for work like ours, and she's tried really hard."

"I don't think it's my work has hurt the lass," said Gideon, who considered her appearance perfection, and did not like any thought of her being marred.

The Captain wanted feedback on how the four days had gone. "Now, what say you, Mr. Baines? You've spent more time working with her than any of us. What do you think?" asked the Captain, determined to dredge up something useful from his scheme. Mr. Baines, quiet and good, assumed his usual cheerful manner. "I never once seen anything that would make me dislike her. Seems open to orders and willing to work. Started to laugh a bit with young Jonah too. Just a couple of kids sparking off each other whilst they work. She's not asked questions of anybody that I've heard and don't seem to have picked up on anything that's been said in her hearing, neither. I don't think the lass knows anything about cargo, contraband or anything like it." Gideon nodded. "That's my reckoning too, Captain. If she had been set up she would have been asking summit and poking around, wouldn't she?" Gypsy rested against the wall. He felt that he ought to make some sort of contribution. "Why don't we just ask her if she's been set up?" he suggested, because he did not like all the subterfuge.

"Cause she's 'ardly gonna say yes, is she, ye daft beggar," Gideon replied gruffly, turning round in his seat.

The Captain shook his own head in disbelief at the way this meeting was rapidly going downhill. He turned to Israel, with even less hope. "Well, what can you add to this?" he asked. Israel frowned. "She's bloody useless to my work," he answered, "Can't manage the needle and nearly stabbed herself twice."

"It's you what's hurt her hands then!" rounded Gideon, accusingly, and Joshua agreed with him.

"Oh for fucks sake!" stormed Te Manu, who had heard enough, and was irritated beyond measure. "Who cares about her bloody hands? She wasn't put there to help you get your blasted work done. You were meant to find out what's making her tick. She would have spoken up by now if I'd been left to deal with her," he raged. Jarrus was irritated by his second in command and showed it.

"Yes. I'm sure you would, if you'd had your way, but your trouble is, you never know when to stop, Manu, and you're so goddamn sure she's been planted on us, that it wouldn't matter what you did to get her out of the way."

They all began to talk at once. There were times when Roden Jarrus wished his voice was louder. It didn't always do to have a voice that was naturally softer toned than Manu. It gave an impression that he wasn't as determined. Come to think of it, it wasn't much help being considerate either. Look where this little episode had got him! The blasted girl had got under the skin of just about everyone and revealed absolutely nothing.

"Can't we just take her back to Auretanea and dump her where she came from?" asked Israel.

It was a solution.

"Or she just disappears," suggested Manu, darkly. They all stared at him. He looked at each of them in turn. "I could do it. Quick and clean, while she sleeps. Nobody can prove she was ever among us, and nobody finds out that she's gone to the bottom," he said, whilst picking his nails with a small, sharp knife.

"Except you've just told all of us - and I don't like it," growled Gideon, dangerously. He rose and took a step toward where the warrior was sitting.

Te Manu was chilling. "No knife then," he decided "No blood. Strangling's easier, but then, you know all about that Gideon, don't you?" Te Manu was being provocative. Gideon disliked being reminded of his past.

"She's a girl!" Gideon roared at him, rising to the bait with an ominous look in his eyes, ready for a fight. "A kid. You ain't never killed a woman or a kid and nor have I. I ain't for having any part of that."

Israel would never dare confront the warrior like Gideon, but he was equally opposed to his ideas. He sat staring at his hands, his face betraying little.

"I don't like it either," he said. "I don't want the death of the kid on my conscience. If there's a vote, you can count me out of supporting this one."

The ominous silence was almost palpable. Te Manu broke it. He sounded really angry with all of them.

"Nobody ever got one over on me, and I ain't going to the gallows because one girl made you all lose your senses. If I don't kill her, what are you gonna do with her? Tell me that." The question hung in the air.

"Ask Ezra," suggested Josh, attempting to break the tension. "I bet he could think of something to do with her. She likes him, and that guitar of his." Thank god for Joshua! The hell fire coursing through Te Manu's veins was offset at once, because the others laughed. They had all seen and heard Ezra on deck with the girl. A smile relaxed each hardened face. Jarrus had been thinking. "Something has to frighten her into telling us who she was going to see. An ultimatum of some kind. Her freedom balanced against something more precious than just telling us, and I think Josh has just given me an idea how to do it."

They all turned expectant eyes upon the Captain.

"Gyp, go and take over from Ezra. Tell him I want him down here, right now."

Chapter Eight - Revelation

Ezra had been briefed on the part he had to play. He had raised his eyes at the instruction to kiss the girl, having been warned only days before of the severe penalty for touching her, but agreed to act the part once the reason was explained. The set up was intended to discover the truth about her, if she was put under duress.

  On that fateful morning, Tianna's sixth day at sea, something was in the wind. The day began as any other, except a number of the crew knew something she did not. Ezra was surprisingly comfortable, his temperament being suited to flirtation. He was confident of giving a good performance, and orders were orders. He also had an inner belief that Te Manu would never actually harm the girl. If bets were taken, Ezra would say that Manu would consider it a shameful thing to do away with any woman. He had seen enough of the warrior to know that the brothel women did not fear him and seemed fascinated by him. It had sometimes intrigued Ezra that there seemed to be another side to Te Manu that he hid from them all. If Ezra was right, Tianna's life had never been in danger, despite all the evidence to the contrary. There was a lingering element of doubt though. Te Manu could become dangerously insular with his thoughts and here was provocation, in the form of a young girl who had recklessly stowed away, challenging all that had gone before and dividing the men in their loyalties. Such a thing had never happened and so no-one could really predict the outcome.

When Tianna emerged from the cabin, there was an atmosphere of expectancy, of something waiting to happen. She looked around once or twice as she made her way to find Ezra, and glimpsed several of the deckhands who were less familiar to her, but they had seemed to be watching her and as she turned, they looked away. It was an odd thing and hadn't happened since her first morning on deck. It made her slightly apprehensive although Ezra behaved much the same as before. The girl had the strange notion that the deckhands were watching Ezra too. She mentioned it to him.

"Take a no notice of them," he shrugged, carrying on as normal, although his manner was more casual than usual as they worked, and he began to sing to her. Suddenly, Ezra made a grab towards her, in full view of everybody. Tianna was taken by surprise, pulled completely off balance and falling towards him, he made to kiss her. She was shocked but had no time to react before there came instant noise and activity around them. The girl had been about to admonish him mildly for his forwardness, which to her had been made in foolish jest, when the atmosphere darkened and a voice, vitriolic and damning froze her where she stood.

"SEIZE THAT MAN!" shouted the angry and forbidding warrior who she feared most.

She stared in his direction to see the owner of the voice that had paralysed her. He stood a few yards away, the imposing, dreadful man they called Manmou, his taut and glistening muscles, giving him statuesque proportions His iron arm was extended, thrust towards Ezra with a rigid, accusing finger.

"TIE HIM TO THE MAST!" he bellowed, the commanding voice silencing all comment, as his order was swiftly carried out by men too frightened to disobey. The warrior scowled with menace around the ship before his flaming eyes fixed upon the horrified girl. Other members of the crew, hearing the disturbance, began to appear in groups. Tianna was overwhelmed by a sea of faces turning accusing eyes in her direction.

Ezra was swiftly dragged away, protesting and pleading for his life in his native tongue. The warrior's orders were carried out unhesitatingly and the screaming, terrified man, with wrists lashed together, was suspended across the column of the main mast, his shirt having been torn from his back with one ferocious ripping sound

Everything was happening too quickly for Tianna to comprehend. Whatever had Ezra done? It couldn't be this clumsy attempt at a kiss, could it? She could not believe the unfolding nightmare surrounding her and the terror in Ezra's pleading voice chilled her to the bone. She watched in horror as the warrior was handed and unwound a whip of evil magnitude. He took the grip tightly in his fist and cracked it hard across the deck like a thunderclap, stilling everyone in sight.

It was the first time Tianna had seen the warrior since her first terrifying encounter with him. The sense of foreboding then, resurfaced now. The atmosphere on deck was heavy with oppression. He stood erect and all powerful, his strong jaw set in a scowl of cruel harshness. It seemed unlikely that anyone would intervene on Ezra's behalf. The young girl looked around desperately, trying to recognize anyone to whom she could appeal for help. Gideon appeared in the crowd and made his way towards her.

"What is happening?" she whispered urgently.

"They'll be waiting for the Captain," answered Gideon. "He'll decide how many lashes. 'Tis a gruesome thing. They'll carry on until he collapses for certain. I seen it before. The cat can split open a man's back to the bone, it can."

"But you must stop it Gideon, you must. Ezra is your friend."

"I can't be overriding Captain. Here he comes now. I don't like the look of this," he murmured.

Frustration was building in Tianna. Surely the Captain would take control and restore sense to this ridiculous escalation. He was speaking to the warrior. Tianna was well aware the hateful man would tell his own version of events, souring the Captain's opinion. They were clearly speaking about the girl. She saw the Captain look in her direction.

"I don't like the look of this at all," repeated Gideon. The girl swallowed. She was clearly implicated, but still had no notion of why she was feeling accused or what transgression could warrant such retribution. The Captain nodded to Te Manu, and moved aside. Addressing himself so the crowd would hear, but aiming his words at the girl, the Captain looked upon her gravely. She was immobilized by finding all eyes upon her.

"You have been wronged by this mindless buccaneer who chose to disobey an order. The penalty for laying a finger on you is a flogging. Ezra is guilty. His action was seen."

Gone was all the joy of being on deck and the embryonic acceptance she had begun to feel among them. Gone was her belief that although they were pirates, they were also people with histories and expectations. All the effort she had made to try and

105

work her passage was rendered pointless by the barbaric practices of men who were little better than ignorant savages, after all. Tianna was desperately frightened but angered too, and her anger was greatest towards the sinister warrior who brought dread and accusation in his wake. The Captain spoke again. "You have disobeyed my order not to do or say anything to entice my men toward you. For this, Ezra will bear YOUR punishment and take extra lashes." She opened her mouth to protest but Gideon urged her not to speak.

"Keep quiet lass, less they decide to tie you to a mast as well," he whispered. The Captain went on, his manner was cold.

"You have lied to me. You WERE going to meet a contact in Petriah. Unless you confess the names of those who are expecting you, you will remain on my ship as a captive, and Ezra will take the punishment for your silence. Ezra will be flogged until the deck runs red with his blood. Ezra will die this day and for that, you will be responsible."

Tianna needed freedom. She had a mission of urgent importance, but it could not be paid for by the torture and sacrifice of Ezra, and for what? One foolish, stolen kiss? The muscular and gauntleted arm of the warrior ascended slowly to deliver the first fire cracking welt across Ezra's body.

"Tianna, help me!" pleaded Ezra, screaming and twisting himself upon the mast, as the whip rose higher. What happened next was unplanned and totally unexpected. Tianna herself, did not know what took possession of her. Finding herself fuelled by anger, disbelief and desperation, she was not going to cower, no matter what the odds against her. The girl was not going to let anyone lock her up without a fight either.

"Captive indeed!" she thought. The heat rising. As she went to move, the Captain shouted, "Seize her!"

Suddenly with an agility she did not know she possessed, the girl side stepped and leaped onto the rail of the galleon, grabbing the mesh of thick ropes to steady herself. Several men lunged forward but the girl climbed higher and the Captain ordered them to halt. She rounded on them from this lofty perch and grew in determination and resolve, unconcerned for her own fate but intent on reversing Ezra's.

Tianna tapped into reserves that came out of nowhere, too angry to be afraid any longer, knowing she was staring death in the face as she did everything in her power to save a man's life. Her voice, when it came, carried conviction.

"I WILL ANSWER YOU," she shouted, with words clear and resonating. "I will sacrifice my freedom rather than allow you to kill this man. I will throw myself overboard and die in his place if your distrust of me is so great." Her reply was heartfelt and few could doubt the sincerity behind the words. Turning intently upon the Captain, who she now thoroughly despised, she continued for all to hear. "You do not yet know how many innocent lives you will sacrifice by the loss of mine," she shouted down, trembling with rising emotion. "You have read me wrong Captain Jarrus! No man shall die on this ship on my account."

They were all impressed by her daring, but that she was prepared to sacrifice her own life for what was essentially a piece of theatre had never once entered their minds.

"Alright Tianna," announced the Captain. "Come down and talk. If you jump, Ezra will still be flogged. He will not gain by your death."

Fortunately or otherwise, depending on how you view it, Te Manu chose that moment to support the Captain's words by cracking the abhorred whip again upon the deck. It had all the effect of suggesting the brutal assault on Ezra had begun. Enraged by the tyrant standing below her, the girl forgot all thought of jumping. Unbelievably, she returned his glowering look with open defiance, and screamed at the warrior with all the vehemence she could deliver in his direction.

"HATEFUL! REPREHENSIBLE! VILE MAN! YOU SHALL NOT DO THIS!"

There was a horrified intake of breath from below as some men expected a shot to ring out and the girl to slump before their eyes. No-one had ever spoken this way to the warrior before, no one had opposed him and lived. His dark eye brows shielded a sudden flash of fire, the wildness leapt in his beating breast, but he kept himself superbly controlled, as he waited for her to speak again. Standing motionless, his features did not change. Unflinching, he seemed not even to blink, but his eyes continued to burn into hers. He, along with fifty men, was listening.

All noise disappeared. The pirates looked upon the girl as though she might have the power to stop the earth spinning, so great was her determination to arrest this evil man, before he lifted the whip a second time. The flies ceased moving. The clouds halted their progress across the sky. The very wind held its breath. Time itself stopped and hung suspended in the air, awaiting the word of the girl. She had the attention of them all, but her fury was directed to the one man she feared above all others. "If I am the cause of such unrest to descend upon you then it is my duty to dispel it. This cruelty that you call justice, must not take place."

She fixed him with an uncompromising stare. Lifting her chin with regality, the girl addressed the man who she knew hated her very existence as thoroughly as she hated him. "I command you, in the name of the King to reprieve this man." Summoning all the courage her sixteen years could deliver, she swept her grey eyes across the vast galleon. Speaking with what she hoped was a commanding tone, she told them, "I am Her Royal Highness Princess Tianna and in the name of my father, your King, I reprieve this man."

The King's daughter focused upon the Captain and his second in command. Almost directing the very waves upon the sea to obey her, she raised her head and shouted,

"YOU WILL STOP THIS. I FORBID IT!"

Had there been any real intention of a flogging taking place, it would, by now, be of secondary interest to anyone. The profound effect of Tianna's startling admission was that every head was turned in her direction and Ezra freed himself from the inadequate wrist bindings so he did not have to crane his neck any more in order to see what was going on. His part was over. The new drama was centred half way up the mast. To the Captain and Te Manu, both men of reasonable intellect, the girl's admission was most likely to be true, although they were stunned by hearing it. The eloquence of her speech, the dignity behind the presentation and her inspiring self-belief held much more than a ring of truth. They had been acting a part. She had not. Tianna was more than likely exactly who she claimed to be. All activity on the galleon ceased when the girl spoke. There was a long interval of shocked and bewildered reckoning of how they had come to be in the presence of a princess and had managed to upset her to such a degree that she was prepared to jump overboard. They were drinking in the implications of this new reality as she continued to watch from above.

"Bloody hell," said Israel. "Bloody hell." He looked at Gideon, unable to say anything else.

"Who would ever have thought that?" said Gideon, fascinated by the beautiful girl, all over again. Ezra sat down on the edge of a container with a thump.

"I kissed a princess," he murmured, dazed. Gypsy was open mouthed. "I told you to just ask her who she was," he said.

"Aye, you did," agreed Joshua, staring upwards, in disbelief at what he had seen and heard. "What a turn up! We've treated her like she's out to betray us all and she turns out to be the King's own daughter. Think of it."

"I am," said Gideon. "What the hell will Captain do now?" They all turned to look at him. "Bring Her Royal Highness down," the Captain told Gideon, making it plain to everyone that her claim to be a princess was not to be doubted. Gideon moved forward, and bowed before her, snatching off the small cap from his greying hair. Behind him, the others followed suit, all going down on their knees, leaving only the Captain and Te Manu still standing.

Tianna looked upon the kneeling figures before her. She had no quarrel with them, and smiled sadly at the display of respect for her identity.

"Oh, please get up," she told them, suddenly feeling drained and despondent. The girl had given away her secret and would most likely become the most valuable hostage ever taken, as a result. Whatever respect they paid her was of little use. She was still a captive and would be guarded. Her mission to reach Petriah, her plan to escape, her chance of freedom seemed to crumble before her eyes.

"What do you think, Roden?" asked Te Manu, quietly, in a voice deep but without a hint of menace.

"I think she speaks true," he answered.

"As do I," replied the warrior.

"Alright. Everyone take some time," said the Captain, aware that Tianna was surrounded by a gaping crew of pirates who had no idea what to do or say in the presence of a member of the royal family, who was now swinging several feet above them on the rigging. The Princess, quite believing her outburst had prevented the most barbaric assault on Ezra, prepared to climb down. Rivalling the authority of the Captain and his murderous first officer would have dire consequences, but what was done, could not be undone. The last vestige of hiding her true identity had gone. It had been sacrificed for that poor wretched man. Now, they would do what they liked with her, to hold as a hostage or sell in a far land for a high price.

"Oh why did I tell them who I am?" She reproached herself bitterly. "I need not have revealed everything." She cursed her tongue. With something of an anti-climax, Tianna prepared to come down.

Gideon was first to stand close by, offering his large, outstretched hands to the Princess. She gave him a small smile of resignation. It was impossible to maintain further royal dignity to descend a criss cross of ropes whilst wearing boys' britches and with hair flying wildly about her face in the wind, but she was determined to maintain some measure of composure, whatever the Captain decided to do with her.

However, at that moment, Tianna noticed the crashing waves of the sea far below her, beating against the ship. Seeing the water perilously underneath for the first time, the girl was shocked and simultaneously began to panic. The rope she had held, which at first had seemed as rigid as an iron bar, suddenly appeared to be as weak as the string in a tallow candle in her hands. She wobbled, let out a wail of grief, overbalanced and fell, plummeting ungraciously towards the sea. The shock of it was instant. No man waited for orders before moving.

A jumble of shouts could be heard as the men were galvanized into action by this sudden new turn of events. They ran in all directions. Ezra dived from the side of the ship and was first in the water. Israel watched for signs of her to re-surface and then plunged in a few yards further along.

Gideon grabbed the rope ladder and threw it hastily over the side and Josh went down it towards the waves. There was a real chance she might have knocked herself out on the way down or even gone under the vast ship. A great flurry of activity followed.

The other men shouted out sightings of her from the side of the galleon and mercifully she was soon spotted again in the water. Floundering, and going under again and again, the terrified girl was fighting to stay at the surface and growing weaker by the second. Ezra swam strongly and reached her before Israel. Between them, they kept her up, before swimming with the exhausted girl to the side.

Jarrus was beside himself. The expletives rained hard. "I don't believe this is happening," he exploded. "We just find out she's a princess and the next thing we do is drown her." Te Manu merely picked up the vicious cat o' nine tails from the deck and began to recoil it. He had no doubt the girl was safe with so many men leaping into the water, and would be restored to the ship quickly. He appeared to be absorbed in his own occupation, betraying no concern or reaction. In fact he showed no discernible emotion whatsoever, to the dramatic events unfolding on the sea. While chaos surrounded them, Te Manu alone seemed unmoved. Yet something hovered over his well-shaped lips and something was playing behind his riveting, dark eyes that was seldom seen. He remained intent on tying the whip and did not look up. When the rescue was over, Te Manu walked quietly away. He went below deck to the storeroom, ostensibly to replace the rope, but he lingered there, needing to be alone. He had been vociferous about Tianna in the preceding days, although what he really thought about her, he could not work out.

In truth, the girl had got under his skin. He was angry about that. To compensate, he had to convince himself and everyone else that she was an enemy. Te Manu rejected anything approaching sentiment. To him, emotion epitomized weakness in a man and, as such, was reviled. He treated self-doubt as an enemy and therefore would never question his actions or the validity of anything he had done. He was strong in mind as much as in body. He was loyal to the Captain and had values, but there was a core of hardness that was virtually impenetrable. He would not get close to anybody and they must not get close to him. Te Manu kept them all at a distance by making them fear him, and even with those who did not fear him, his insular thoughts and capacity for brooding, meant the ones he called friends, were not allowed to know him.

Today, he had been arrested by the girl's spirit and he now knew she was not an enemy of the pirates or a threat to their way of life. She was, however a threat to his own equilibrium, and that was dangerous. The sooner she left the ship, the better.

Up on deck, the ungainly Princess, coughing, spluttering, and fighting for breath, was dragged from the sea by Ezra and Israel and hauled up the rope ladder by Joshua who locked his arms around her small waist and told her to hang on around his neck for the ascent. Israel climbed up behind in case she fainted and fell before reaching the top. Ezra stayed hanging onto the bottom of the ladder until the others had all gone up. Gideon reached over and unlocking her limp arms from Joshua's neck, took hold of them and hauled her over the side, followed by the soaked rescuers. Tianna fell onto the deck where only moments before she had made a profound impression.

In the long minutes she had been in the water, Tianna had been sure she was going to drown. In the helpless terror of falling, the sea had appeared to rush towards her and hit her with a thwack as it forced the air from her lungs. Winded, she had tried to surface, but water rushed in, determined to pull her down again. Tianna had been hauled from the sea quickly but roughly and her sides ached where Ezra had plucked her from being submerged again and Israel had swum with her to the ship, before Josh had seized her in a tight arm lock as he swung like a monkey, precariously at the bottom of the ladder.

Her senses were deadened by the water making rushing sounds in her ears and the salt stung her eyes. Tianna was exhausted, frightened, tearful and angry but most of all, alarmed that she could not get her breath. She was choking and heaving on the deck, coughing and spluttering as though gasping for the last time. Jarrus squatted behind the girl and locked his arms around her middle, pulling her up. She winced with pain as he seemed to crush her sides.

"Quickly, Gideon. Throw her over your back, head down." Gideon threw her over one shoulder and Jarrus dealt her a thump between the shoulder blades. Whether it helped was anybody's guess, but after two more, she began to cough and groan and seemed to be breathing easier. She lay upside down, limp, gasping, nose running, with arms dangling.

"That'll do it." said Jarrus with obvious relief.

Mr. Baines came hurrying with blankets for the girl and the men who had been in the water. Israel and Ezra stood dripping but began to shake the water out of their ears and hair. They recovered rapidly having not swallowed much of the sea water.

"Is she gonna be alright?" asked Josh. The Captain was confident. "Yes. Put her on the floor Gideon."

Joshua and Gideon lowered her carefully to the deck and placed her on her side. She panted but was recovering. Mr. Baines brought a blanket, which he and the Captain wrapped her in.

"Take her to Rhapsody," ordered the Captain. "He's got brandy down there. He'll know what to do." Gideon threw her again over his shoulder, this time, like a roll of carpet.

"Aye, Sir," he responded, carrying the girl effortlessly towards an area of the galleon she had never seen, down the wide steps towards the lower deck. As Gideon departed, Te Manu reappeared, having disposed of the weapon of correction among a repository of knives and pistols. He walked across the deck, seeing Ezra stripping off his torn, wet shirt.

"Double rations tonight. You played your part well," he said, as he made his way towards the Captain, but the warrior expressed no concern for the girl, nor did he ask where she might be. His face bore not a trace of interest. Josh and Gypsy watched him walk away.

"He's a hard bastard," muttered Josh quietly. "Not one word about what's just happened."

"Has he ever really flogged a man to death, d'you think? I've been here five years and I've never seen it," asked Israel.

"Long time ago he did," said Ezra, still rubbing his long dark hair, the salt water drying rapidly upon his skin in the hot sun.

"It's true," added Gyp. "Ezra's right. We asked Gideon once. He's known him longest." Israel threw the blanket onto the one discarded by Ezra.

"What did Gideon say then?" he wanted to know.

"That Te Manu's trunk was splattered with the blood of his victim, mingling with his own sweat, while he, cool and calm walked about giving orders for the next watch," said Ezra.

"Bloody Hell," commented Israel. "You had a close call then, Ezra. Damn good job you was only acting."

Ezra laughed. They moved away to the duties that called them.

"You know something?" Josh said, turning to his friends,

"What?" they asked.

"She still hasn't said who she was going to see in Petriah!"

Roden Jarrus leaned heavily on arms that rested upon the rail of the ship. His fingers were interlocked in front of him as he gazed across the Sorrello Sea. Te Manu came and stood beside him. The Captain was pre-occupied by everything that had happened. There were many thoughts chasing each other across his mind. Eventually he spoke. "What's the penalty for half drowning a Princess?" he asked.

"About the same as threatening to slit her throat, I should think," replied Te Manu, drily.

"Then you and I will probably swing together," concluded the Captain.

Chapter Nine - Rhapsody

Inside a small cabin, not much bigger than the average larder, Rhapsody was waiting. His crinkled, black hair, oiled and plaited into numerous tight braids were tied with cotton around his head and beaded so they swung, colourfully, whenever he moved in the familiar, rhythmic swagger across the deck, his hands carelessly in his pockets, the gait that everyone recognized. He was fun loving, humorous, and broke every rule that had ever been made.

His dark skin shining, he was the tall and equally virile counterpart of his best friend, Te Manu. They were a pair of opposites, in just about everything. There were very few, if any, men who could speak to Te Manu as Rhapsody did and get away with it. He was the antithesis of Te Manu and a good antidote for his sullen friend. Rhapsody was convinced that hidden beneath that peevish mask, lurked a man who contained passion and had a soul. Where Te Manu suppressed all feeling, Rhapsody wore it openly.

He was not the ship's doctor; the galleon did not have one, but Rhapsody was something of a medicine man. He kept brandy and rum and would use them medicinally if need be. He kept tobacco of sorts and opiates that induced pleasant thoughts, if not an actual cure. Rhapsody had the laid back disposition of all his people. He knew all about tribal rituals as well as ancient medicines. He joined the ship and left the ship at regular intervals to return to his Island of Calypso, where he was reputed, so the pirates believed, to have fathered quite a few children. Naturally funny, always good humoured, his philosophy of life was inherently free, easy going and seductive.

He was somehow immune from the hierarchy on board. It was as if nobody quite knew whose command he should be under, and so he wasn't. He enjoyed a special place alongside the Captain and his first officer, Te Manu. All the men on Zenna Marius liked Rhapsody, and one man loved him like a brother.

Gideon transported the princess like a sack over his broad shoulders. The jostling down the steps, with her head down actually helped dislodge the sea water and force it from her lungs. Gideon placed her upon the narrow bed with greater care than the unceremonious way he had carried her, and attempted to make her comfortable. He sort of bowed before leaving, probably in deference to her royal status, which seemed rather at odds with the heavy handed way in which he had delivered her to Rhapsody's keeping.

Tianna neither noticed nor responded to Gideon. She was in no fit state to do anything. Trembling with shock and cold, despite the heat of the sun outside, the princess was soaking wet. Her eyes were reddened and sore, her throat enflamed from coughing and she was completely disorientated, not knowing where she had been taken. Tianna had never been in this part of the galleon before, and she had only ever glimpsed Rhapsody from afar, his company usually being with Te Manu. She gazed upon him now as he stood in the doorway and blinked as her eyes were stinging, still unable to take in her surroundings. He bent down in front of her.

"Here, drink dis," said Rhapsody, by way of an opening. His voice was deep and velvet. Tianna put out a shivering hand and grasped the tankard, looking suspiciously at the contents which she sniffed, before taking a cautious sip.

"It's brandy," explained Rhapsody, "De very best brandy, make you better reeeal soon."

She took a mouthful and almost choked again.

"Ugh!" she spluttered.

Rhapsody laughed. "Keep tryin' girl and you'll soon get the taste. It will warm you all de way down."

He rotated his hands and pointed down with an extended finger, to demonstrate the journey of the liquid. Much as Tianna disliked the stuff, she persevered enough to swallow some of it and did begin to experience a warm sensation inside. A few minutes passed.

"Why did you jump in de sea?" he asked suddenly, settling himself across the end of the bed and studying her with a good natured air. She moved her toes. Rhapsody was lying on them. He seemed very relaxed.

"I didn't jump in," she said indignantly, "I fell in."

"You said you was gonna jump in. They told me," he persisted.

"That was before," explained Tianna. "I said I would jump in if they were going to flog Ezra, but they stopped." She started coughing again. When the spasm passed Tianna shook out her long, wet hair, twisting it between her fingers. She cleared her throat, beginning to recover. The girl gave an involuntary shiver. Rhapsody remained on the bed, but sat up and leaning forward, drew out a heavy wooden trunk from beneath the bed. He tossed a shirt in her direction from among the contents. "Here, put dis on. You're dripping all over me bed."

"Oh! I am sorry." replied Tianna. "Please turn your back for a few moments."

"Why?" asked Rhapsody.

The question hardly seemed necessary.

"Because I'm going to change my clothes so your bed isn't wet," she explained.

"So?" he countered, as though that wasn't a reason. Tianna stared hard at Rhapsody, unsure what to make of him. "So I don't want you to look at me while I'm doing it," she said and then, looking pained, added,

"Please? If you wouldn't mind." Rhapsody pursed his lips and nodded "Okay." His broad shoulders half turned away from the girl as a concession. It was not very convincing. Rhapsody put his hand playfully over his eyes and as she struggled out of the wet garments, he parted his fingers to reveal his deep brown eyes watching her. He chuckled, mischievously.

"Umm. Nice."

"Oh!" she exclaimed, shocked and cross, pulling the blanket up fast over her knees. Drawing them up, she hugged herself protectively, resting her chin upon them so Rhapsody could see no more of her. The clean shirt would just have to wait. Tianna's wet clothes were on the floor. He had turned back to face her, the appreciation of glimpsing her naked body and young breasts, danced in his amused and sensuous eyes.

"You are one hell of a pretty woman," he crooned. Somehow, Tianna just wasn't afraid of him. She frowned as if to scold a very badly behaved child. This ship was a world of utter madness from which there could be no immediate escape. With the recent memory of what it was really like to be floundering in the sea, Tianna had completely abandoned her earlier plan to jump off the galleon and swim towards Petriah. "Oh, what have I done!" she lamented, thinking back to the sequence of events since she had first seen the beautiful vessel and mistaken its identity.

"What have I done?" she said again, wringing her hands. It was a rhetorical question, and didn't need an answer.

"You jumped in de sea." said Rhapsody, maintaining his position at the bottom of the bed, smiling at her.

"I didn't mean that!" she said, becoming more assertive, despite wearing nothing but a thin blanket. "And I did NOT jump, I fell," she reminded him, but as she spoke, he gave her such a wicked smile of delight, because she'd retaliated to his mischief, that the princess could not keep a straight face. Despite all that had happened to her, she wanted to giggle. It started as a smile that couldn't be contained, and soon developed into insuppressible laughter at the absurdity of what had happened. Rhapsody, who could rarely stay serious for more than a few moments, joined in until the two of them were virtually helpless with mirth. In spite of everything, the princess saw her predicament as funny.

Rhapsody gazed at her with genuine warmth. Their sense of humour was perfectly matched, and in that moment an enduring friendship was born that would remain for a lifetime. Tianna's sides still hurt, she tried to recover herself.

"Oooh that's better," gasped Rhapsody, lying flat on his back across the bed, exhausted. "Laughin' is better than medicine. It warms you up. See? Now you is mended!" He pronounced her cured, and lay across her feet as casual and relaxed as it is possible to be.

"You're not a very good doctor, are you? If all you can do is make your patients laugh," complained Tianna.

"I don't only do that!" retorted Rhapsody, "I can make 'em drunk as well!" The princess's mouth opened like a goldfish. "Oh really! What a terrible thing to say," she admonished him, but as he gave himself up to a fresh bout of laughter, so did she. It was totally infectious and was some time before they both subsided. They smiled affectionately at each other.

"Are you a pirate?" she asked him.

"No," he answered.

"I didn't think you could be," she confided, warming to him even more as a result. "What is your name?" the girl enquired.

"Rhapsody," he told her.

"Oh, I like that very much." Tianna was enthusiastic. "I'm Tianna," she volunteered.

"I know," he replied.

"Do you know lots of things, Rhapsody?" she asked.

"Try me," he challenged, with a grin.

Tianna tried to decide how much she could say to him. She needed to share her misgivings about the pirates and, if Rhapsody was not one of them, maybe his predicament was like hers. She studied the man reclining close by. He didn't seem at all bothered by anything. Rhapsody may have been approaching midlife, but his chirpiness remained irresistible. His smile, she was yet to discover, was generous and freely given and his easy going nature brought out the best in everyone. He held nothing back as would a man with more reserve. Rhapsody's clothes were old. He wore tight fitting trousers, frayed at the knees and tied with a thin rope around his waist. His vest had seen better days. His arms and chest were shining, brown and smooth with well-developed muscles. He was strong with a waist and hips in perfect proportion and had the overall physique plus good health that seemed common to all the men on board. Where Mr. Baines had an undeniable spread around his middle and was still in his early forties, Rhapsody was fitter, although only a year or two younger. His speech and movement bounced with rhythm while his voice was low and the vibrations particularly sensuous. Most entertaining of all was his capacity for humour which was ever present in his face and wide flinging gestures whenever he got excited.

Tianna was fascinated by his hair which was shoulder length in the braids that had been plaited in a perfect crisscross symmetry across his well-shaped head, and were softly oiled. She was bathed in the warmth of his large, liquid eyes that simultaneously wore down her resistance, melting any fear she might have had and making her want to laugh whenever they creased at the corners in good humour.

Rhapsody had everyone spellbound. He possessed a gift of getting up close and personal without ever being rebuffed for his overt familiarity. Tianna had already found herself talking to him in a way she would never have imagined possible. Maybe part of her reserve had been dispelled because she had given away her true identity and in so doing had almost abandoned herself to whatever the consequences of that might be. She had mentally shrugged her shoulders and resigned herself to fate.

Rhapsody continued to lie across the bed, his ankles crossed and resting on the seat of an old chair with a broken back rest that served as a stool. He appeared to have all the time in the world at his disposal. Tianna looked at her new friend earnestly. "Rhapsody, are you a prisoner too?" she whispered. He grinned broadly in response to her question.

"No. I don't t'ink so. Why? Are you?"

She sat up straight, the surprise of his query registered on her face. "Well. Of course I am," she said, "didn't you know?" His smile did not diminish despite the absolute certainty of her answer. Tianna felt obliged to emphasize the seriousness of her plight.

"I stood up to the pirates, and I will be punished severely for it, I know I will," she confessed. "Gideon thought I might even get flogged like Ezra."

Rhapsody's expression was one of amazement at the way her thoughts were turning. Raising himself, he tut-tutted at the mess that certain members of the crew had made in dealing with their stowaway. He shook his head and sat upright too, pulling himself to a sitting position by gripping the base of the bed frame.

"You got this all wrong, girl," he told her. "Now you hear what Rhapsody gonna tell you, 'cos what I tell you is right." She prepared to listen, with no idea at all of what he might say.

"Okay. Number one. De Captain never, never, never hurt no woman, no how." He held up one finger to emphasize the first point and then raised a second. "Number three..."

"We haven't had number two." she interrupted.

"You sure about that?" he teased her.

"Yes. You only got as far as one."

"What was that den?" he pretended to be confused.

"That the Captain would never, never, never hurt a woman," she repeated.

"Oh! You know that already. Good."

For a moment she looked non-plussed, until he winked at her. "You just remember it," he said, smiling. Tianna laughed, realizing what he had done.

"Is that all you were going to tell me?" she asked.

"Yeah. But I can go on if you want," he replied.

"Go on then," the girl urged him.

"Well now. Let's see. Number two. Nobody on dis ship is gonna be floggin' anybody, especially you. They would only have to show you de t'ing for whipping, and you'd be faintin' clean away."

Rhapsody extended his arm to show his hand fluttering like a butterfly, which the princess followed with her eyes. Listening to Rhapsody was proving to be a very visual experience. "Waste of time floggin' you," he declared.

"But they *ARE* pirates!" emphasized the girl.

"Yep. But they was men before they was pirates." His logic was clear. She reflected on this. It would be nice to believe in them. She almost could believe in Mr. Baines and Ezra and maybe even Mr. Gideon; as for the rest! No. "Rhapsody, you don't know what I've done. I shouted at the one called Te Manu. Nobody *EVER* does that and survives." The princess expected her new friend to be horrified by the admission that would surely seal her fate. Instead, he seemed more amused than ever.

"Who you bin listening to?" he asked.

"Look how he hurt Ezra if you don't believe me," she insisted. "They were going to kill Ezra. Didn't you know? Whatever will happen to him now?" She looked anguished.

"He's prob'ly gonna be stone drunk tonight." Rhapsody replied happily.

"Drunk?" she echoed, thoroughly perplexed.

"Sure. He did a fine job with all that hollerin' and shouting so he's got double rations and so has everyone else who went after you when you jumped in de sea. Manu give them all extra for tonight."

Tianna was about to protest again that she had not jumped in the sea, but was too astonished by hearing that the warrior intended to increase their rum rations, instead. "Do you mean Ezra is alright?" she asked, uncomprehendingly.

"Yep. And he's got you to thank for tonight's drinkin'."

The princess had heard the crack of the whip with her own ears. She had heard what the Captain had told her. She wore a frown of concentration, trying to make sense of Rhapsody's carefree reaction to everything she said. It just did not make sense.

"You'll see him later tonight, when he sings," added Rhapsody, breaking into her thoughts. "Or you can go up and find him now."

"Oh no!" exclaimed Tianna, suddenly alarmed by the thought of being found on deck. "Not yet. I would far rather stay with you. I like it here and I really like you."

"Well, ain't that fine!" he smiled. Tianna had not finished with her questions. "If they don't punish me, I suppose I will be kept as a hostage now they know who I am. How will they send for the ransom money?" she asked. This only sent Rhapsody into fresh paroxysms of laughter. "How can you t'ink that? You headed for Petriah, same as us, ain't you?"

"Well yes, but do you really believe they will release me?" she asked, not daring to hope they would let her go.

"Course they will." he nodded.

Tianna would like to have believed him but, turning their conversation over in her own mind, could not marry the events she had witnessed and the ease she saw in Rhapsody. The blood curdling warrior who wielded the whip was the most evil of them all. She shuddered at the expression of hatred she had seen on his face. The Captain had told her Ezra would die for her disobedience. All this she had seen and heard.

"Listen! I's going up to tell them you is okay." announced Rhapsody, getting to his feet. "'Cos it seems to me, they gotta start puttin' t'ings right, real soon."

"Oh dear! Must you?" asked Tianna, anxious all over again.

"Sure, but you stay here. I'll get food sent down."

"I'm not hungry. Oh please do be careful," she warned him. Rhapsody heeded her with a salute. "I'll be careful. Stay put 'til I come back."

For a few minutes after he departed, the girl sat thinking about the extraordinary conversation they had just had. She felt humiliated at falling overboard and having to be hauled up like a fish to splutter on the deck. The experience convinced her there was no way she would try and swim ashore, that plan was a nonstarter.

Tianna absently scrambled into the clean shirt while Rhapsody was away and swept up her soaked clothing that had been lying on the floor for some time. She hung them over the door, before sitting down on the bed once more. Her sixteen year old imagination saw her confined to a cabin, deprived of fresh air and sunlight while her father read the ransom note. Her worst fear was coloured by reality and the Captain's mention of Baron Lussac. The princess shivered at what might befall her if she were sold to him, the very man she had been trying to escape. Tianna had a sick certainty she was finished. In revealing who she was, her plan to give them the slip had vanished. Her admission had cost her dearly.

Rhapsody strode across the sun drenched deck with his rhythmic gait, hands in pockets, and was soon being acknowledged with nods and shouts as he passed the working men with his typical swagger.

"Hey, Jonah! Take Tianna sometin' to eat. She's in my den," he shouted.

Jonah, in usual fashion, jumped up eager to please. He wanted to see her very much and have her tell him if she really was the princess that she claimed to be. He was sure Tianna would be honest with him. They were almost friends.

Rhapsody continued, whistling as he descended the steps to the cabin. He rapped out a powerful knock on the door, depressed the latch and entered before anyone inside had time to reply. Rhapsody swung his legs over the bench and dropped down beside the warrior, brushing against Te Manu's elbows as he sat, facing the Captain.

"Is she alright?" was the first thing Roden Jarrus wanted to know.

"Sure is, except she thinks you're about to flog her too, or Te Manu is gonna finish her off for standin' up to him."

The Captain gave the warrior a long suffering look. "Yes, well, for a time, disposing of her had been a solution for one of us." he said pointedly.

Rhapsody turned round, one leg now either side of the bench. He leaned against the wall, giving Te Manu a hard look. "Hell man! You know you'd never have done that t'ing." he said, fixing his friend with the intensity of his rebuke. Te Manu stared at the table, but chose to remain silent.

The Captain saw they had a real problem on their hands if the girl really was a princess. "Why couldn't she have told me? I gave her enough chances to talk," he said defensively. Rhapsody turned to chastise the Captain. "Oh yeah? Well you don't come outta dis so good. She got de same idea 'bout you bein' just as bad as everyone else. She's reckoning that if you don't kill her, you got some idea to make money by keeping her for ransom. When you did find her hiding on deck, you tellin' me you really t'ink she should 'a said, "Oh, by de way - I'm a princess.""

Rhapsody had decided both the Captain and Te Manu needed to think again. Te Manu brooded, flicking crumbs off the table from their recent meal.

"Why should she think we want her for ransom?" he asked, without raising his eyes. "Nobody said anything about keeping her for money."

"Because you give a pretty damn good impression of doin' your worst, man," retorted Rhapsody, with energy in his voice. "She's terrified of you, man. T'inks you can strike a man dead just by looking at him!"

Te Manu scoffed at this, the way he had with all conversation about the girl ever since she had been discovered.

"She t'ink I'm next for a flogging just because I talk nice to her and then come up here to you. You should've let me have her right from the start," said Rhapsody. "I would've given it to her straight."

"You'd have given it to her alright," said Te Manu scornfully, "knowing your bloody track record with women."

"Alright! Shut up both of you!" interjected the Captain. "Rhapsody, you know damn well you couldn't be trusted with the girl in your cabin. You'd have been all over her."

"He'd have been *into* her!" accused Te Manu. Rhapsody shrugged his shoulders in reply. He wasn't going to deny it.

"Yeah? Well, she wouldn't have been afraid of me, I know dat for sure."

"Do you believe she's really a princess?" Jarrus asked him, to interrupt the tension..

"How do I know?" answered Rhapsody, his voice rising. "De only way you two is ever gonna find out, is if she trusts you enough to talk, and that ain't gonna happen."

"I'll go and talk to her," said Jarrus. "I'll go now."

He stood up to leave.

"Yeah, well don't go wid'out me 'cos that girl is gonna take some persuading' that you is alright," said Rhapsody, as he too, got to his feet, hitching up his trousers with his thumbs.

"Come on then. Hurry up," replied Jarrus, going through the door.

Rhapsody went to follow him, but couldn't resist the last jibe at Te Manu. "Okay, Captain. I is wid you, and we just tell her that as Manu ain't gonna come down, she'll just have to trust my word that she AIN'T his next victim for the cat!"

The Captain raised his eyes to heaven at the two of them and went up the few steps to the hot deck.

"She still could be!" retaliated the warrior defiantly. Rhapsody turned on his heels to have another blast at Te Manu. "Fuck you man! What is wrong with you? D'you hate this kid so much?"

Te Manu snorted. Rhapsody, seeing his perversity, surmised it accurately. "You know what? You gone so far down dis road, you can't find a way back. That's your problem. You was wrong about her an' you damn knows it. Sort your fuckin' head out man!"

Rhapsody went out, banging the door hard behind him. Left alone, Te Manu let out a long breath and almost at once felt better.

Jonah took the remains of his own lunch, along with Tianna's down the wide steps to Rhapsody's own quarters, just in front of the main sleeping quarters for the bulk of the crew on board.

"It's not very big in here, is it?" he announced, trying to negotiate his way around the door with two large plates and tankards. "There isn't even room for a table."

"I rather like it," answered Tianna, trying to perk up and definitely relieved to see him. "I'm glad you've come, but I'm much too nervous to eat anything. Sit on the bed and tell me what is happening."

Jonah wriggled backwards, making himself comfortable against the wall of the cabin. He balanced a plate across his legs and Tianna manoeuvred until she could do the same.

"Are you really a princess then?" asked Jonah, with admiration already in his voice.

She peered at him with her head on one side and a tangle of long, matted hair, all the worse for the seawater, flopped in front of her eyes. She tossed it back. "I fear it is true," she replied sadly, reminding herself again of what this would probably cost her.

"Phew!" went the sound from Jonah's lips. "They was all saying so when I took the food around. How you stood up for Ezra. It must have been something to see. Pity I missed most of it. They wouldn't let me come over. They've been teasing Ezra 'bout the way he's won the heart of a princess. They mean you!"

Jonah laughed until he saw that Tianna wasn't amused, so they talked instead about Tianna falling overboard and how frightening it had been and she tried to ascertain what was being said on deck. Jonah hadn't seen the Captain or Te Manu so couldn't refute the girl's insistent belief that she was in dire trouble with them. He could only say that everyone above them was in fine form and kept talking about it.

"Ezra got double rations as a reward." he told her.

"Reward for what?" she wanted to know.

"Well, carrying out Captain's orders of course; pretending to be scared, you know."

She was on the point of discovering what Jonah meant, when a footfall on the stairs disturbed them. The noise outside heralded the arrival of someone. Jonah jumped up and whispered, "Better go. See you later."

And in a flash was gone, taking the steps two at a time as he passed the Captain.

"Josh has been calling for you, Jonah," he shouted up to the boy's retreating back. "Aye, Sir," he called out happily, as he sprang across the deck. Jarrus briefly wondered what it must feel like to be Jonah and not have a care in the world.

Hearing the dreaded voice convinced Tianna that the Captain had clapped Rhapsody in chains and had now come to get her. She shrank against the wall as he entered. Roden saw how far she recoiled at his appearance. It confirmed all that Rhapsody had said. The girl looked so vulnerable, hunched up in the corner of the small bed that he immediately stepped outside to await Rhapsody's arrival. Tianna was very pale and her mouth had gone dry. As the Captain hesitated in the doorway, he felt a compelling need to say something to reassure her. "Right. Okay. Nobody is going to hurt you. Have you got that? Yes?"

The girl nodded, unconvinced.

"Good! Good!" said Jarrus, with equal lack of conviction, as he looked back towards the steps whilst shouting impatiently, "Where the hell are you, Rhapsody?" He stepped back inside the cabin.

"Alright! I am not going to hurt you. Not me, not Te Manu, not any of my crew. You understand that? Not one of them."

She nodded again, but would not be fooled about at least one infamous member. It was also unnerving when he kept darting in and out of the doorway to stare up the steps.

"Good." he said a second time.

He began to abandon hope that Rhapsody was anywhere near and didn't want to leave the girl alone again in order to find out. He blundered on. "We did not get off to a good beginning, Tianna. You misled me from the start." The girl swallowed. It was evident that her fear ran very deep. She was silent and immobile, crouched in the corner. Rhapsody descended the steps, reappearing in the door frame, which he leaned against comfortably, hands in pockets, ready to listen. The Captain edged inside to sit upon the broken backed chair, remonstrating with Rhapsody as he did so. "About bloody time." he said, crossly.

Tianna looked imploringly at Rhapsody who, she was relieved to see, was not in chains after all. Rhapsody winked at her. His well-developed, folded arms seemed glistening and strong and his demeanour so casual, that the princess knew he was afraid of nobody and was on her side.

The Captain was not so relaxed. He brushed his index finger against his lips in thoughtful reflection on how to progress from here. "Something rings true about your claim to be a princess," he said after an interval. "I'm nobody's fool, Tianna, I will find out, but for now I am going to presume you are who you say you are, and I'm going to make something very clear. I am not the kind of man who has women beaten. I never have and I never would. I do not take prisoners or hostages. I do not run that kind of ship, but you need to believe me and open up."

He fixed her with unblinking eyes of darkest blue, and his close proximity in that confined space, made the tension between them all the more tangible. She looked pleadingly towards Rhapsody for which direction to take.

"He's right, baby," he said, nodding his approval.

"All that crap they give you 'bout floggin' Ezra an' keeping you here is all bullshit, baby. It was just a load of shit to make you talk some."

"Yes. Alright! I think she got the message," interjected the Captain, just to shut him up.

"Yeah? Well I just telling' it how it is man, a load of shit."

"RHAPSODY!" shouted Jarrus.

"Yeah Boss. I got de message."

"Thank you!" said the Captain. "Now sit down."

Behind his head, Rhapsody pulled a funny face, and Tianna immediately softened. The Captain caught the change in her expression and spun round on Rhapsody.

"For Christ's sake, sit down and shut up!" he roared. Rhapsody resumed his former place at the foot of the bed. "So come on, Tianna," said the long suffering Captain. "Talk to me. Tell me about your home and family and why you are on my ship."

Tianna had the full attention of them both. It was such a long and complex story she hardly knew how to condense it. She thought for a few moments before deciding where best to start. The girl would conceal no secrets. They may as well hear it all. "Alright. I will tell you." she said, in a voice barely audible.

Outside, two men hurried noisily up the steps, drowning her words. The Captain got up and shut the door. Tianna began her story again. "I have a sister, five years older than me, called Tasmin."

The Captain and Rhapsody briefly contemplated what a twenty one year old version of Tianna could be like. They dragged themselves back to the present.

"The Baron of Scalos is a man called Lussac. He came to ask for my sister's hand in marriage. He tried repeatedly to convince my father it would be a good match. My father would not countenance it. Tasmin will not accept any suitors. There have been quite a few, but this was different. My father believed the Baron's interest in Tasmin was tied up with his ambition to control the sea passages."

"And you still maintain that your father is the King?" asked Jarrus.

"Yes. Of course," the girl answered.

"Go on," said Rhapsody, entranced by the tale.

The Captain nodded.

"We still had to maintain diplomatic relations with Scalos, because we are a group of four Islands, but during one important formal occasion, where lots of heads of other lands were present, the Baron made a fool of himself and declared publicly that he was to become the consort of the Princess. There was an awful scene. My sister denounced him and stormed out. My father's Ambassadors to the Islands had to refute Baron Lussac's statement. He declared he had been publicly humiliated and demanded an apology and compensation for the sleight. Our own officials believed him to be out of his mind."

"When did all this happen?" enquired the Captain.

"Six months ago," she answered.

"And then what happened?" he asked. The girl went on. "Relations between Auretanea, Petriah and Scalos were severely damaged. The Governor of Petriah brought in negotiators to intervene, but things began to deteriorate. There were accusations in Petriah that Governor Cavendish was exceeding his authority in the matter. He and his ministers had already been criticised by a number of merchant ship owners who believed the looting of their vessels by pirates, on the Sorrello Sea was being ignored or even condoned by him. They wanted to hear Baron Lussac's ideas for change. Governor Cavendish refused to call for any vote to hold such a meeting."

The Captain and Rhapsody were riveted by the girl's story. The matter of their piracy now becoming directly implicated in the telling. "There are threats to Governor Cavendish's leadership, and if he goes, his successors are likely to sweep away the old ways which tolerated many things, like the illicit cargo trade, which he never addressed," she said pointedly, gradually losing her fear of the Captain. "You see Sir, far from being your enemy, my family has been almost impartial to your trade upon the Sorrello Sea, but now, your way of life is threatened just as much as mine."

"Why your life, Tianna?" he asked.

"Because the Baron did not withdraw peacefully," answered the princess. "He had been developing fighting ships and trained an army. An Ambassador came from Scalos, a man named Moreton. He made several visits. He apologized for any discord and brought rubies for Tasmin. The soldiers who accompanied him did not leave the town. He talked of re-establishing cordiality, and wanted more dialogue over the proposed control of the straits. He issued an ultimatum. It was couched in terms to sweeten the poison but it was poison just the same. The Baron would begin to supply ships to protect the straits from pirates and expected to negotiate a favourable marriage in return. He came with an escort of three ships to impress the King, and all the soldiers they could carry. They were sent as gifts.

My father saw it as a pending invasion and Tasmin went into hiding, but was determined to raise the alarm in Petriah before we were cut off. Ambassador Moreton brought an invitation for Tasmin to travel to Scalos. She had gone. He told my father that he must return to the Baron with a favourable response. To that end, he was willing to accept what he deemed "the lesser prize." to take with him to the Baron as a gesture of goodwill between the Islands and who would be lavishly entertained and returned safely. My father did not believe anyone would return safely from Scalos, and would not agree."

"The lesser prize?" queried the Captain. "What did he mean? What is it?"

"Did he get it?" asked Rhapsody.

"No," she answered with a faint smile "but YOU did. I was the lesser prize... He wanted to take me."

Her words hung in the air. Nothing could have had a greater impact upon the men staring at the princess and then at each other in that moment. The Captain's mind was working furiously. He wanted to be sure he had got this right. "Are you saying that if you had stayed in Auretanea, you would have been taken to Scalos against your will?"

"I didn't wait to find out," she replied.

"So you and your sister have both run away."

"Tasmin has gone underground," she explained.

"What?" said Rhapsody. *Underground?*

"That's what she said. She was going to organise volunteers from Petriah to join up with those from Auretanea. They were going to get across in luggars but the Scalos soldiers have started intercepting many boats. Her movements have to be underground."

"And she is doing this alone?" asked the bemused Jarrus.

"With lots of the servants from the Castle. They are being organised by Darius."

He wanted to ask who Darius might be but decided to stay focused on the plight of the two princesses.

"And what was your part in the plan?" he wanted to know. "I have to tell Governor Cavendish urgently. He needs to release more boats and ships at Petriah to help us." She suddenly looked apologetic.

"You were offloading cargo under the cliff. I thought you were a regular carrier. I only meant to hide here for a night and a day."

"And we could have been in Petriah at least two days ago if I had known all this before," replied Jarrus, bitterly regretting the lost time.

"Hey, this is bad, ain't it?" surmised Rhapsody. "We can't take her back to Auretanea and she ain't gonna be safe left in Petriah if boss Cavendish goes under."

"You're right," agreed The Captain. "She's probably safer on this ship than anywhere else. Listen, Tianna, I am also going to see Cavendish when we get to Petriah. While you were stealing aboard, Gypsy was hearing from the Islanders how the straits were jeopardised."

"That was Mikhael and Artemus," she told him. "They are also involved in Tasmin's movement. Darius is Mikhael's grandson."

"Good grief." responded the Captain, "You seem to know a lot about this."

"I can take you to Governor Cavendish, if you don't know him," offered the princess.

"I do know him." Jarrus replied. I count him to be a good man, and one of the few on land I can trust." Tianna flashed him a smile. "I'm glad you like him," she confided, "He's my favourite uncle!"

The girl had supplied the Captain with an overwhelming amount of information. Had he only known this at the start, he could have assimilated it thoroughly with time to consider what to do next. As it was, the galleon was now one day away from Petriah. Roden wanted to speak to Te Manu, urgently. He swiftly dispatched Rhapsody with a message.

"Tell him to meet me in the cabin. You've heard all this, Rhapsody. Fill him in with everything until I get there, to save me repeating it. We have very little time to prepare ourselves for what we may find."

Rhapsody did not need telling twice. He would relish putting Te Manu straight about the runaway princess.

"Aye Captain," he answered happily. "See you later, baby!" He bounced off the bed. Tianna watched her new friend leave. She wondered what she was supposed to do and asked if she might go up into the fresh air. Being here was starting to feel claustrophobic. The Captain had no objection. His thoughts were racing and he was keen to see Te Manu who was also acquainted with Fabian Cavendish. He agreed to the girl's request.

She edged forward, her bare legs and small feet extending beneath the ill-fitting and oversized shirt, which slipped from one delicate shoulder, as she touched first one foot upon the floor, then the other before she could stand. It was a simple manoeuvre made cumbersome by the one garment she clutched around her body, but it revealed to Jarrus the total inadequacy of her provisions. Roden had a girl claiming to be the King's daughter right in front of him, naked but for a borrowed shirt, and shoeless in all the time she had been aboard. It occurred to him that in all that time she had requested nothing for her own comfort.

He looked at the tousled hair, the bruises on her legs where she had bumped herself as she laboured, and her sore hands and dirty feet, where she had attempted the work that he had set her to do with Israel, Gideon and Ezra. Compassion outweighed anything else he might have felt. Roden delayed her exit.

"Stay a moment," he told her. She sat on the edge of the small bed, directly in front of him. "Give me your hands." The girl looked quizzical. He took them firmly but gently in his own, exposing the remaining blisters on her palms. The deep blue eyes were focused on rebuilding trust, after days of suspicion and turbulence.

The princess sensed the former kindness she had seen on that first morning after waking in the cabin. He brushed the backs of her hands with his thumbs, all the time he spoke, comforting and compensating for all that had happened to her.

"Tianna, this situation is too big for you to deal with. There is potential for huge upheaval in the Islands. This requires men to talk to men. I don't want you getting it into your head that you can rush off to Cavendish. We have to be careful when we get there. I know the risks. You do not. There is a safe house I will take you to first." Jarrus had no desire to release her from his protection; not from his command as Captain of the pirate galleon; not from his life now she had infiltrated it. She was a victim of another man's greed, just as he had once been.

The girl emerged from a cocoon of fear that her imagination had spun since she had arrived. She matured in an instant, galvanized by the words of the man before her. Tianna knew he spoke truly and as a result, the last vestige of doubt about the Captain melted away. Her own innate confidence in the task she had set herself, burned bright once more and when she acknowledged him, she spoke as a princess and one who understood their mutual destiny.

"Captain, with your help I will become stronger. With my help, you will receive the credibility you need to be heard by any official in Petriah. Neither of us can achieve as much alone as we can together. I grant that I am just a girl to you, and that you find my face pleasing, but remember who I really am and know that I have power and a voice that I intend to use in Petriah. Men may wish to talk to men of war, but they would do well to heed the King's daughters, for they will find their spirit to be as indomitable as any man's."

The Captain of the Zenna Marius was captivated by her single mindedness. Never before had he encountered such a young girl exuding such intelligence and grace, embodied in ragged clothing, trying to work her passage. He smiled, then he kissed her hand as he gallantly raised her to her feet, before bowing low. "Your Highness, I am at your service," he told her. The Captain and the princess would be friends.

Chapter Ten - The Castle at Auretanea

Miles behind them, on the Island of Auretanea, the King stood alone at the balcony doors. His hands were cupped together loosely behind his back. Only the movement of one hand slapping the other gave an indication that he was agitated. To all other outward appearances, he seemed calm. King Theodore was a benevolent ruler. He found discord particularly uncomfortable and hated upset in his life. It seemed that age had made him less resistant to the changes that were determined to keep him awake at night. He could not understand why some people thrived on making complication. He liked harmony and since his wife had passed away, he actually needed it. Something of him had died with her, all those years ago and he never managed to equal the feisty energy of his beloved daughters, or their zeal.

His craggy features and wiry, receding brown hair, added to his years. He looked for all the world like a tired dish mop, having given years of service, but now flopping, instead of bristling. The Ambassador of Scalos had just vacated the room after an uncomfortable conversation with His Majesty. There were no two ways about it, Tianna had disappeared and despite him sending everyone he could think of to search for her, they had returned without news of her whereabouts, or they hadn't come back at all.

The King professed bewilderment at the disappearance of his younger daughter. He was not going to inform the Ambassador that the young black horse had found its way home and trotted into the stable yard or that the note in Tianna's bedchamber and handed to him by the maid gave the King reason to hope that his enterprising daughters would find a way to bring much needed help to their beleaguered Island. He could only pray for her safety and hope that his years of insistence upon developing both his daughter's skills, as if they had been sons, might at last prove useful. Time for talking was running out. There were soldiers from Scalos all over the place and an uneasy peace was just about holding between the townspeople and their unwanted visitors, and the King's own soldiers who had been instructed to keep the peace but not challenge the interlopers.

His Majesty had remained on cordial terms with Ambassador Moreton, who proved to be far easier to deflect than Baron Lussac, who, thankfully had not come. The problem was the Ambassador's own nerves which were worsening by the day because there were no princesses to be found and the King seemed peculiarly indifferent to their disappearance. Moreton did not like his job, but with a great deal of bluff and flattery, managed to strike a balance of sorts between the Baron and his neighbours, in a situation that was proving to be disagreeable.

He had been under instruction to escort either princess to visit Scalos, or lose his position, but Moreton had already seen what had happened to ministers who lost their positions in Scalos and most of them were keeping company with the rats in the underground cells of the Black Tower. He dare not return to Scalos alone and anger the Baron who would declare him incompetent, but neither could he request the pleasing company of a princess who wasn't even there to ask!

Diplomacy had prevailed, but only just. He had come on an errand of conciliation (He had been instructed to say) and to that end brought lavish gifts to impress and ships to liaise with Auretanea, to enable them to overcome piracy on the Sorrello Sea and protect the straits. As this was neither requested nor desired by the King, his response was muted and the idea that Tianna might favour the Baron in place of her sister was absurd. His Majesty would never permit it. Ambassador Moreton began to apply pressure.

The ill-disciplined Scalos soldiers were becoming bored and restless without direction and so Moreton had given them the job of searching the small ships that sailed between the Islands on the pretext of concern for the missing princesses. Their presence was bitterly resented by the Auretanean people. Moreton began to panic that he was losing control of the situation and so he began to bring his own soldiers closer to the castle.

The King's philosophy was not what one might have expected. He was remarkably slow to react, preferring to be an observer of events than a participant and he encouraged his people to do the same. Consequently, he would not permit his own guards to take any confrontational action but instead, expected everyone to maintain diplomacy and stall for time.

Hard on the heels of the Ambassador leaving the King, after another unproductive audience, His Majesty's eccentric sister, Philomena, breezed into the room. She often arrived as if propelled by a strong wind.

"Well, I certainly don't need to ask how that went!" she exclaimed, having passed the Ambassador on the stairs. "And to add to our problems, Tasmin has not returned so that is two princesses who have disappeared."

"She has not disappeared," cajoled the King, hoping

to placate his older sister. "She is just gathering support for her resistance movement and has probably gone further afield than before."

He tried to sound casual as though this were an everyday activity for any young princess. Lady Philomena raised her eyes to heaven, which she needed to do very frequently when faced with her brother's unconventional ideas on raising daughters.

"This is all your fault, Theodore!" she scolded. "Their poor Mama must be turning in her grave at these events. If you had not brought up the princesses to think like boys, we would not be in this predicament of not knowing where they are."

"I consider it fortuitous that we don't know where they are," responded the King. "It spares me from having to invent a story for the Ambassador."

He tapped his hands more than ever behind his back whilst fixedly watching through the window.

"Unless of course, you think the Baron of Scalos makes a suitable son in law."

"No of course I don't," she replied irritably.

She wrung her hands.

"Look at us!" she implored him.

He turned his head in her direction but had heard most of this before.

"What possessed you to drive such thoughts into the heads of the girls, Theo? They think nothing of marriage, of merging our small Islands with other kingdoms. No favourable liaisons, no promise of children. While other princesses are being courted, yours study politics or ride bare backed over the plains. What good is that to a royal princess?"

The King gazed into the far distance. He was not given to argument and defended his position with a quiet, stubborn dignity.

"They are good daughters and intelligent. They have been a great comfort to me since their mother died. If I leave no heir, at least I leave daughters who will make intelligent choices of suitor one day. They will attract fine and wise partners into our kingdom."

Philomena shook her head despairingly.

"The princesses will not bring husbands into Auretanea," she told him bluntly. "If they ever marry at all, they will leave for other kingdoms. They will go whether you wish it or not. You cannot go on pretending they are a substitute for a son. You do not have a son!"

These sharp words stung the King, but he remained composed and shielded his pain, choosing instead to turn the course of the conversation, as the servants arrived with tea. The interruption served to calm the King's sister, considerably.

"He wants control of the straits more than he wants Tianna, you know. She's just his means to an end," said Theo, stirring the sugar in his cup.

"Can't you negotiate more with the Ambassador?" asked Philomena, who clearly had not been afforded the same political education as her nieces. The King tried to explain again why this was futile.

"The sea is not mine to bargain with," he told her.

"We just happen to be closest to the narrow inlets. They must remain free or there will be a dreadful impact upon the smaller Islands. What about Baruk? Or Marama? Or Urla? How can they survive if they are dependent on the whim of Scalos. They need small ships to supply them." He shook his head.

"We do not know how Baron Lussac has become so strong, or what other territory he has in mind to take."

"Has there been no word from Petriah?" asked Philomena.

"Unless Tasmin reappears to tell us so, I presume not. Maybe she cannot reach him at all under the circumstances." ventured the King.

"Not reach Fabian?" answered Philomena, shocked.

"Oh! But that is abominable!" she declared. "Why, everything we know is shared with Fabian. We cannot be cut off."

"Well, I think you'll find we already are. Scalos is becoming most unfriendly."

The King's sister looked aghast. "Then Scalos must be stopped!" she announced as though it were as simple as swatting a rather persistent fly.

"I think, my dear that is what your nieces may be trying to do," said the King, quietly. "I only wish I knew where they are."

But however far the King's imagination might take him, it would never reach a pirate galleon carrying fifty men and a girl with indefatigable courage who would turn seventeen years, this very day.

Chapter Eleven - The Music of the Night

With the departure of the Captain to meet Te Manu in the cabin, Tianna was left to herself. Rhapsody wasn't coming back. He couldn't wait to impart all he had heard and would savour every moment of telling Te Manu how wrong he'd been, not that Tianna had any idea of the earlier showdown when Rhapsody had rounded on the warrior for his obdurate attitude.

She peered outside of Rhapsody's sanctuary before continuing past the door in the wrong direction, to steal a peep behind the heavy canvas curtain that shrouded the entrance to a mysterious world below deck. She dared not step inside, but through the gap could see a huge and lengthy chamber that still admitted light from where cannons had long ago filled a uniform row of square apertures.

A great number of hammocks were slung across the numerous beams and rafters, like so many bats, suspended and waiting for nightfall. This was the place where men drank, talked and slept and where she would never be allowed to venture. In this very basic underworld, it was not as spartan as she had supposed it to be. She glimpsed evidence of the crew's possessions; clothing, pillow rolls, tankards and jars, bottles, coils of rope and tools of all descriptions jostling together on shelves, while bags slung on hooks, bulging and with contents overflowing, took up what little space remained. There was an overall odour to the place. It seemed a very masculine smell of combined oil, wood, mustiness and heat and the shafts of light that did manage to illuminate the chamber at regular intervals, revealed it not to be an unpleasant place.

A few sweating and soiled individuals crossed her line of vision in the far distance, without realizing they were being observed. Tianna sensed it would be quite wrong to stay. There lingered a murkiness that pervaded every corner and persuaded the girl to retreat. She drew back, realizing for the first time how only a handful of the crew had become acquainted with her, and how many more laboured out of sight under the watchful command of Manmou.

The girl climbed the wide steps, emerging into strong sunlight and a salty spray that whipped up the recent memory of her frightening sojourn to the waves that had threatened to claim her. She took a deep breath of the good, clean air and was at once invigorated by the brightness, and the sounds borne upon the wind.

The deck had lost the sinister atmosphere that had descended when Ezra had been caught. It was as though nothing had happened at all. She wandered to the back of the ship, wanting to be alone with her thoughts for just a little while, to take stock of the changing kaleidoscope that was her life right now.

The girl gazed over the dark, smoothly varnished wood that travelled at chest height, seamlessly stretching away to the bow. She ran her hands along the flat ledges, stroking the warm surfaces, marvelling again at the immense strength of the galleon as she climbed over each projection along the bulwarks and moved between timbers two feet thick. The metal gleamed golden. It gave Tianna great comfort, and she smiled at the memory of her plan to jump overboard and escape to Petriah by swimming there. Thank goodness she wouldn't have to. It had been a wildly optimistic notion, and having fallen in, the princess understood how perilous it would have been.

The girl walked slowly along, sliding one hand along the polished ledges and handrails, following the contours of the galleon, passing groups of activity here and there. Something stirred within her soul in that short interval of time. It was almost as if Tianna's affinity with the gracious ship and the men who breathed life into her, fused together and she suddenly knew, beyond all doubt, that she was glad to be there.

The men on deck stopped to look at her or nodded in her direction. She was hoping to catch sight of Ezra but did not. In truth, she was more self-conscious since shouting above their heads that she was a princess, and they were equally self-conscious, not knowing how to respond to having a princess in their midst.

Eventually, Tianna turned inwards to the area she knew best and went in search of Jonah, although it was Mr. Baines who saw her first. He greeted her with the same unquestioning acceptance whenever she appeared. "Are you recovered from your swim, Lassie?" he asked lightly.

"Yes. Thank you Mr. Baines," she answered with a wry smile.

He nodded and became thoughtful for a moment or two. "I'm sorry you've been wronged on this ship. I hope you'll be forgiving all the times you had to work from the galley. We just didn't know who you were, see?" Tianna smiled. She did not want dear, kindly, agreeable Mr. Baines to carry the blame for the pre-judgment of others. "Please don't apologize Mr. Baines. I have been happy with you and Jonah and I have learned things that I would not even have been able to try doing before."

Mr. Baines face creased into a smile of self-effacing pleasure, like a ball of soft dough. He wore a smile of such magnitude that his small black eyes virtually disappeared into the wrinkles either side of his round face. He brushed back the brown hair that flopped forward. "Well, well, well," he said quietly, with his usual shyness. "All the same, Miss, I hope you'll excuse all them little potatoes you've peeled an' all, not to mention so many pewter plates, as stood there, lining up, awaiting you to wash them. They never knowed they was in the company of a princess, see?"

She laughed. It was natural and without fear. Tianna was sure she would come to no harm on the galleon now. "I hope you'll let me help some more," she said.

Mr. Baines looked surprised.

"Oh! I don't think that would be fitting, not for a princess I mean, not now we know who you are."

Once again, Tianna demonstrated that she expected no favours. She pointed out that if Mr. Baines refused her offer of help, then that in itself was disobeying the wishes of a princess, which left him perplexed for a few minutes, scratching his head, before he conceded that if she insisted on cooking and cleaning things, he couldn't very well stop her.

"Good." she said.

"We'll be eating early tonight on account of the music up on deck later on," he informed her. "Tis allus the last night on board afore we goes ashore and weather looks set to give us one of the clearest, finest skies for singing."

He started to drag one of the heavy sacks towards the tureen, then straightened up to mop his forehead and neck.

"Do pirates sing?" asked Tianna, amazed at the thought.

"Aye, lass. We all sing," he answered, turning aside as Israel came by. "Captain wants to know are we on for early victuals?" he asked the cook, while looking at Tianna with a deadpan face and acknowledging her with a grudging flick of the head.

"Tell him we are. I've just got to get these last root veg into the pot, tis all cooking nicely." answered Mr. Baines. Israel moved away. The girl watched him go. With his fine, straight hair and lithe frame, he was the very opposite of Mr. Baine's more generous build.

Israel's lightness enabled him to ascend the rigging and reach the crow's nest with the speed and agility of a monkey swinging between branches. There was something almost fluid in his movements. He was glimpsed more often aloft than on the deck, or so it seemed to Tianna. She had often seen him climbing the ropes or sliding along the mast rails to raise or lower the enormous sails, when he would be shouting instructions to other crew as the sequence was repeated. Strange names they had, all the parts of the sails; head, throat, luff, tack and foot, leech, cringle and boon. Words she had not heard them shouting to each other, Jonah had supplied. He knew a great deal and made her laugh. Her particular favourites were ratlines and dead eyes, while Jonah favoured something called 'futtock shrouds.'

Apart from shouting across the billowing sails, Israel was not predisposed to conversation and Tianna considered him rather reticent. He passed comment however, on any number of things, without looking people in the eye as he spoke, and his expression rarely changed. He was serious or vaguely disapproving and Tianna was convinced he thoroughly disapproved of her. If she had to describe him in a single word, it would still be "surly", all his comments sounding short and curt. Not that Mr. Baines or Jonah seemed troubled by it.

The cabin boy appeared, bumping another sack up the steps from the stores. The hard vegetables escaped the hessian cloth and began a bid for freedom by rolling across the deck. Tianna leapt up to give chase and before long she and Jonah began the task of chopping them for the pot. "What happens when the pirates sing?" she asked him.

"We all come up on deck. Everyone. It's quite a crowd." he began.

"Out here? Just where we are now?" she wanted to know.

"Yep, and you've never heard anyone like Ezra sing. No-one in the world can match him. If they knowed about Ezra on land, he'd be performing in one of them great houses far across the ocean, so Captain says."

Mr. Baines arrived to join the vegetable peeling. Even with three of them it would still be a lot to get done if they were going to eat the evening fare earlier than usual. "Don't you be forgetting to tell about the guitar playing," said Mr. Baines, settling himself down. Jonah grinned. "You likes the sound of them together, don't you, Mr. Baines?"

"That I do," he answered. "Many's the time I've watched and wished I could make my fingers move across strings like them two, making all those wonderful sounds, but then I s'pose Ezra and Mr. Manmou couldn't make a stew, so it's each to his own really."

Tianna's eyebrows rose considerably while she listened to all this, especially at the association of the two pirate's names. "Do they sing together as well?" she asked.

"Everybody sings," replied Jonah, "The whole ship's company," he went on.

Mr. Baines became quite expansive, forgetting to peel anything at all as he sat with a faraway look.

"It fair lifts your spirits to the sky when you hear it. I've seen men's eyes fill with tears when they sing together as one voice to our beautiful lady."

"He means the galleon," explained Jonah, in an undertone.

"Oh." murmured Tianna beginning to understand.

"But will Ezra be up to singing tonight - after this morning I mean." Jonah and Mr. Baines looked momentarily confused. "Won't he be sore?"

They exchanged a look of bewilderment and then began to laugh. Mr. Baines shook his head and resumed peeling. "He never was hit if that's what you're thinking, lass," he told her.

"But I saw and heard it," she argued.

"You heard it lash the deck. It was never intended to land on him, so don't you be worryin'." And he bustled off to season the food. "I'll have to find someone to give us a hand or we'll be havin' these for breakfast," he shouted back.

The princess and Jonah continued squatting on the deck, working in comfortable silence. The girl's long tangled hair, matted and smelling of the sea, added to the illusion of two urchins, side by side, ragged but happy, beneath a blazing sky. She was far more relaxed and wished now that she had eaten her lunch.

"I am so hungry," she admitted to her friend.

"Where's your plate?" he asked.

"I left it in Rhapsody's cabin," she replied

"You can go down and get it. He won't mind. He's not there anyway, he's talking to Captain."

"Are you sure it's alright?" The thought of trespassing worried her.

"Just be sure not to go any further than the cabin. Beyond the canvas is out of bounds," he warned her.

Tianna retrieved her plate, guiltily aware that she had already been tempted to part the curtain on that alien place. As she emerged with the bread and cheese, the princess saw that Mr. Baines had recruited a few labourers to help, who weren't best pleased with the chore. Mr. Baines reminded them that if it hadn't been for the nonsense of the morning, everything would have been on time. The girl made her way back to Jonah, who looked up.

"Where did you get the shirt?" he asked.

"It's Rhapsody's," she said and held the damp clothes that she had just retrieved, which Jonah recognized as his. "I'll return it to him as soon as my stuff is dry."

She spread the garments in the hot sun.

"After that, I don't expect I'll see Rhapsody again," Tianna sounded wistful.

"Course you will, you'll see him lots of times. He's always up here," beamed the boy as Tianna stood up and tried to roll up the wide shirt sleeves for the umpteenth time. "He's always in and out of Captain's cabin, when he's not working below with Te Manu," he added cheerfully.

"It must be awful for him working down there. Is he afraid of the warrior?"

"No, stupid!" laughed Jonah, whose face revealed an impish grin as he shoved her playfully off balance.

"Course he's not afraid. They're best friends."

"NO!" exclaimed Tianna, correcting her balance to rest on her haunches once again, the dishevelled shirt and loose rope tie around her middle assuming the shapelessness of a sack. She was incredulous that anyone as full of fun as Rhapsody could befriend anyone so dreadful.

"Are you ever afraid of them, Jonah?" she asked quietly. "Of all the pirates, I mean."

"No." replied Jonah, decisively. "No one ever hurt me. It's like we're all on the same side, see?"

The girl took some time to think about this. "Not even the warrior, the one who is so fierce and angry?" Jonah threw the last vegetable into the pot, aiming to make a splash.

"No. 'specially not him!"

"Really?" persisted the princess, intrigued to find out more, "Why not?"

"Cos he's the one who got me on this ship," said Jonah, brightly.

"How?" she asked with growing interest.

"Him and Captain came to drink at the ale house where I was working, but treated no better than a beggar boy. They see me being kicked by the owner, a ruffian, always drunk himself. Mr. Manmou gets up and puts a stop to it. He very near murdered the innkeeper for beating me, then he asks me nice as you like, would I like to leave with them. Captain did a deal of sorts, talking to the innkeeper's wife and paid her, I think, and then they invited me to come aboard. That was when I was eleven or twelve. I've been on Zenna Marius for two years now." Jonah ended proudly. Tianna was fascinated by his story. It was not what she had expected to hear and contradicted her own assessment of the sinister man.

"But he was fierce and dangerous, wasn't he?"

"Oh, yes!" enthused Jonah. "It don't do for anyone to mess with Mr. Manmou. When he took hold of the innkeeper, he got him by the throat and shook him 'til his eyes rolled," went on Jonah with great effect.

The boy grasped his own neck with both hands and sticking out his tongue, he emitted strangulated, gurgling cries and fell sideways, cross eyed, slumped beside the girl he hoped to impress.

"I knew it!" Tianna said with considerable satisfaction, and she laughed at Jonah's antics.

They were both being silly, trying to outdo each other with juvenile grimaces, when Mr. Baines called to them. "Bring that lot over here if you're done."

They carried the heavy pot between them, struggling not to lower it on their bare feet.

"Will I be allowed to stay on deck for the singing?" The girl enquired, hopefully.

"Dunno," replied Jonah. "It all depends if Captain thinks girls are allowed. Mind you, being a princess might swing it. Not that you looks like one with a head full of smelly seaweed!"

He laughed and so did she. Her olive skin was glowing and her complexion, tanned even more by the sun, contrasted with her grey eyes, to make them seem more startling than before. Joshua came towards them. She recognized him as the one who always thanked her when she brought his food. He saw them laughing together. He took the heavy pot from her grasp, to help Jonah. "Well, looks like the galleon has got a second cabin boy now, Jonah," he greeted them, amiably.

Tianna smiled but nervously, her shyness returned. It seemed to the princess that Joshua would like to talk to her if circumstances made it possible. Josh was a man totally comfortable with himself, unlike the wiry framed Israel, although they were often to be found together.

Josh's roles were various but merged depending on what was needed. In some respects he was the ship's mate, in others, the boatswain, but on Jarrus's ship, the roles of his eight closest crew had developed and been fashioned over time. They all complemented each other comfortably as a team. They were mutually dependent on each other for their safety at sea and a bond had developed between them all.

Israel's dual responsibilities seemed to include relaying Captain's orders across the whole deck and this had probably evolved because he was so regularly seen aloft that Jarrus could shout up to him and from his perch, Israel could see everyone with his bird's eye view of the ship.

Late in the afternoon, he shouted that Petriah was visible in the far distance and a palpable wave of excitement and anticipation rippled around Tianna. It was as if everyone relaxed their guard once the shock of discovering her identity had sunk in, and they could behave less suspiciously around her. It was about now that the girl realised the cabin where she had been sleeping was the Captain's own domain and just how much he had given up in order that she should stay there.

Tianna, Jonah and Mr. Baines were kept exceptionally busy but everyone ate at the earlier hour and the Captain ordered that the galleon would remain outside Petriah and sail into harbour the following day.

He seemed energized as he moved among his crew. This was a popular stopping place but with events in Auretanea clouding the horizon, Roden Jarrus wondered just what kind of reception might await them. He would urge caution in everyone.

Evening came. Tianna noticed there were already far more men on deck than usual, talking together in small groups, their discourse amiable, interspersed with occasional eruptions of laughter and jocular spirits as they prepared for their shore leave. Here and there, groups entertained themselves with games whilst others piped a tune for an audience that either cheered or pleaded for them to stop, depending on their taste. A few danced a step or two and all the time, the Captain wove a trail between them, joining in and being welcomed into their circle before moving on. They created a colourful display with scarves and headbands and sashes that meant not one was like his neighbour and their accents, from any number of faraway places united them as migrants all, for not one considered home to be any place but the galleon.

There was still a good bit of tidying up going on in the galley when Israel put his head inside and shouted.

"Captain says everyone's to be present tonight so the young 'uns must be there to give thanks and stay right through to end. That's orders!"

"Yes, got that," called back Mr. Baines, although Israel had already gone. Tianna thought again how offhand he was, never waiting for any reply. She wondered how many of his messages got missed completely as he never bothered to find out if he had been heard. Still, the information he had brought pleased her. She felt a slight thrill. If all the crew were to be on deck it would be quite a gathering. "What does he mean, give thanks. Are we going to pray?" she wanted to know.

"Lor, no!" retorted Jonah "I 'ad enough of that at the orphanage. Didn't do me any good neither. Starving hungry and havin' to be grateful for being given a mouldy crust! This is different, we sing to our ship." Tianna looked confused.

"It might sound daft to you but 'taint when you hear Ezra and we look up to the Zenna like she was a mother."

"I never knew my mother," said the girl.

"Nor me," added Jonah, but his voice was chirpy as he said it.

They washed and cleared the remaining implements, having eaten the last meal on board for maybe seventy two hours. During the stop over there would be more stores to load, but for now the galleon was restful, waiting for entry into the harbour when morning came. The ritual that was important to everyone who had received safe passage, was about to begin. All at once they started to hear the notes of the guitars being tuned and prepared to play. Mr. Baines threw down the towel where he'd been roughly drying his hands and told his two help mates to leave everything and get themselves out on deck. They scrambled into the evening air, the twilight enhanced by lamps suspended at regular intervals along the rails, illuminating the gracious curve of the beautiful ship with amber light. It was the first time Tianna had seen any lamps and Mr. Baines told her they were only permitted when the galleon was very close to land on account of the fire risk.

"That's why you don't see the men smoking their baccy on board," he added. "They chews the stuff instead. Fire is the biggest fear on any ship."

The warm breeze wafting across lightly touched them as they climbed onto the cabin roof, a favourite watching place for Jonah. He and Tianna settled down. She scanned the scene around the deck. A large group of men, wearing bright but ill matched colours, were assembled, talking, drinking, leaning, standing or sitting, all perched somewhere, and in the midst of them, Ezra, tuning his guitar. Her attention was unexpectedly arrested. Beside Ezra, was the unmistakable form of the warrior, also with guitar in hand. They were talking, laughing unselfconsciously together, planning what to play and how to entertain their audience.

The princess observed them both under the cover of a darkening sky. She had never watched the feared one before and had never seen him smile. There had been no opportunity to observe him when he was entirely unaware of her. She sat cross legged and although her eyes wandered over the entire company, picking out those who she recognized and asking Jonah to identify those she could not, the girl found her attention returning again and again to the two musicians, and one in particular. Tomorrow she would be in Petriah. They would entrust her to the care of her uncle Fabian. The ship would sail away and she need never set eyes on any of them again. Her path need never cross that of the brutish one for as long as she lived. She would easily maintain distance from him for the remaining hours. His aversion to her demonstrated that the sooner she left their company, the better. The girl mentally closed a door on them all, in her mind. After tonight, all this would begin to fade in her memory. Strangely, it did not give her the relief that she thought it should.

Suddenly, without introduction, but completely in harmony, Ezra and Te Manu began to play. At the same moment, the Captain, emerging from the crowd, saw Tianna and made his way towards her. Jonah moved aside to make way for him, but the Captain bade him stay. He was not going to join them.

"You are alright where you are, Jonah. Tianna, come across here. I will talk to you about tomorrow."

He strode towards the cabin. The princess had no choice but to follow him. She was disappointed to be missing the start of the music and had wanted to see what happened between Ezra and the warrior to try and resolve things in her mind. The opportunity was denied her because the Captain descended the steps and opened the cabin door, speaking to her before she had even entered the room. "We will arrive in Petriah by daybreak," he informed her. "I will request an audience with Governor Cavendish, but you cannot be seen dressed like that. It will be necessary to obtain garments more fitting. There is a brothel in Petriah, kept by a woman called Romana. She is a good woman who will help us and has links with Cavendish."

Tianna could hear the gypsy music of two guitars tantalisingly reaching her through the open door. She longed to take a look.

"Romana will have access to seamstresses. They will know how best to attire you in the time we have available. It is the best I can do," he continued. "The men take a few days rest in Petriah. They split their time between old acquaintances, the taverns and the brothel house."

Rhapsody appeared at the top of the three small steps to recall the Captain now Ezra was preparing to sing.

"The brothel is just a short walk from the quay," explained Jarrus. It was not a word known to the girl.

"What is a brothel?" she asked, innocently.

"Eh?" exclaimed Rhapsody, coming as he had right at the end of the conversation. He remained on the top step. "What did you say?"

"A brothel... Is it a market place?" she went on, recalling the connection with seamstresses and clothes. The Captain stood behind the girl on the steps as she moved to go up. Above her, Rhapsody laughed out loud. She stared at him, perplexed by his reaction to her question, then peered back over her shoulder into the smiling face of Captain Jarrus, who was trying to conceal his own obvious amusement, not wanting to explain. "It is a market of sorts," he allowed, his blue eyes shining at her ignorance, but would expand no more although clearly, some unspoken joke was passing between the Captain and Rhapsody and the amusement remained in their faces for some time.

"Don't let her out of your sight," the Captain told Rhapsody.

"Right Boss," he replied.

Tianna resumed her place beside Jonah and Rhapsody sat alongside the two youngest on the ship. Of all the people on board Jonah and Rhapsody had been the most fun, making her laugh and being silly. She would miss them. The haunting gypsy music had ended and when she swept her eyes across the wide deck, there was no sign of the warrior, any more.

"Do you know what we is singin' for princess?" Rhapsody asked her in his melodic, deep voice.

"No... Not really," she admitted.

"Well now... Let's see..." he crooned, smiling.

"We gonna t'ank dis beautiful ship for keeping' us safe all the time we bin on de mighty sea. We gonna t'ank her for holdin' on to us and standin' up to de wind and de sun an' givin' us shelter an' bringin' us safe to dis land. You hear every one sing, princess, cos dere lives depend on de protection of de great lady wid de white wings, above you."

The girl gazed upward. "I should thank her too, shouldn't I?" asked Tianna earnestly.

"Sure," agreed Rhapsody. "De words ain't difficult and you're grateful she got you here ain't you?"

"Yes. But I will miss the galleon," she answered almost wistfully. "I will be saying goodbye to her as well as thank you,"

"Well, is that so..." he answered softly. "Do you want to be sayin' goodbye?"

Tianna looked up at the clear night sky, already peppered with a trillion stars. Nearby, Ezra began to play quietly, a mesmeric introduction to the most emotive and wonderful music falling like kisses upon her ears. The men became quiet at the sound. It was as if the whole enchanted ship was waiting for her to reply.

"Sweet and low, endless wonder,
You bear us through your peaceful water,
Sworn to live our lives beside you,
Face the winds and ride you... .."

"Do you want to say goodbye, princess?"

Rhapsody asked again, his voice seductive and delicious, under the darkening sky. He was so close to her that his question was almost silently asked. In fact, she wondered if he had really spoken at all. She felt his words in her mind. Was that possible? She turned her gaze to meet his, and saw the gentlest, knowing smile, as if he could already read her answer. His eyes never left her face.

"No. Rhapsody." She shook her head slowly, surprised to find so much emotion welling up inside. There was a catch in her voice. "I don't want this to be goodbye."

He nodded his head in silent acknowledgement of her confession, strangely satisfied. Although he smiled, he said nothing more.

Tianna's heart and mind were opening to an extraordinary way of life. A world of hard and sometimes dangerous toil undertaken by rapscallions and cutthroats; men whose histories had nothing to link them save for the fact that all had turned their backs on the land and for whom, the galleon was home. She had begun to identify each one of them, her fears lessening, her interest growing.

A hush had descended upon the company. Tianna watched, entranced. Ezra's music was the only sound. He threw his head backwards, throwing the passion of his song to the skies. Ezra sang at first in Italian, with the resonating and sensitive sound that lifted the men's very souls, to the stars. His clear words were held, suspended so they lingered in the air and echoed upon the ears, as he continued.

"The sun and stars that guide us singing,
From heat of day to cool of night,

Under great white wings a beating,
Where our souls rise up in flight."

Tianna gazed at him in wonder, transported to another dimension by the sheer magic of his voice. She felt a surge of emotion, goose bumps radiating across her back and down her arms. She shivered at the immensity of feeling enveloping all of them.

And then, just when she thought that Ezra's song must be ending, he lifted his voice still higher, raising his arms upward to the open night sky above the moonlit galleon to whom they owed everything. Astonished, the princess listened as the sound of fifty men rose up with Ezra, their deep voices rising to a crescendo, as one powerful and overwhelming choir, they sang. It was the most uplifting and emotive sound. They offered their all in that singing. Flushed and impassioned, their faces contorted with the sheer force and magnitude of the delivery, their lungs bursting with power. From the highest to the lowest, from the deckhands to the men who sweated in the bowels of the ship, all came together, united in this song of thanks to the source of their livelihood and sanctuary.

"Let me with your spirit soar,
Oh mighty vessel heaving,
Beauteous lady breathing,
Take my heart and soul and more,
I owe you all I am,
Each poor and simple man.
Hear my voice,
Hear my voice."

The richness and strength of their singing would remain with the princess. It had a profound effect upon her. She watched, transfixed.

Tianna did not need to be told of the loyalty between the men of Zenna Marius and the love of their ship. They were united as one. Mr. Baines had been right, for her eyes grew misty at the sentiment that touched every fibre of her being, as the voices, pure and true, paid homage. The princess vowed to herself that somehow, one day, the royal court and people of her homeland, must hear them sing and in so doing, cleanse themselves of the blind prejudice against this remarkable band of men. Rhapsody watched the princess steadily. Tianna could feel it. The tears in her eyes were threatening to fall. She had the strangest, growing sensation, that between the two of them a journey was beginning, not ending.

Tianna remained on the roof of the cabin with her companions as others came and went. She was in the throes of uncertainty, needing to find the resolve to walk away from them, yet unable to imagine being left behind when the Zenna Marius sailed once more. She heard drifting conversations and overheard talk and laughter. Rhapsody smoked, as the men were allowed to do on deck when close to land. No one ordered her to leave when the men were drinking. As night enveloped the ship like a velvet blanket, Tianna began to tire. Lulled by their voices and strains of guitar or singing, her eyes began to close.

When the Captain came by, she and Jonah were fast asleep on the roof of the cabin. Rhapsody smiled. "You want me to wake them?" he asked with a yawn. "No," replied Jarrus. "Leave them be."

Rhapsody looked around. A lot of the crew would sleep under the stars tonight. He yawned again, and within a few minutes was snoring.

Part Two
Petriah

Chapter Twelve - Romana's House

Cries of "Land Ho." echoed round the ship just before dawn and men went to the side to glimpse the outline of Petriah through the misty haze. There was excitement in the atmosphere on board and the galleon resounded with growing activity.

Petriah was a destination eagerly anticipated since it afforded some of the gayest and liveliest entertainment. Deals would be struck there, old acquaintances renewed, new friendships forged. The ale would flow and girls would flirt outrageously, thrilled by the appearance of the men from the galleon. The ship would have been visible on the horizon for some hours. By the time the gangplank would be fitted, any number of citizens, some known to the crew, and some curious strangers, would be watching eagerly and none more eagerly than Madame Romana, herself.

It did not surprise Captain Jarrus to find several young messengers waiting for him to step on land, bearing cards from their masters. He knew people in high places at Petriah. On this morning, a youth in red and yellow attire handed him an envelope bearing the seal of none other than Governor Cavendish. The missive surprised him, since the friendship between them was potentially dangerous and Cavendish's association with Jarrus was considered unwise. Sending a message to the pirate was risky. Cavendish knew he had enemies in Petriah. Jarrus read the words and scribbled a time on the paper to be returned. He handed the envelope back to the boy.

"Wait a moment. I will send a word to Romana's house. You will deliver this first, then go on to the

Governor's house. Do not await any replies. Inform them I will attend at these times." and so saying he tossed a coin into the boy's hand. "Thank you, Sir." exclaimed the youth as he sped away.

The house of Romana had once been resplendent, standing proudly at the gateway to the town. It still had lawns to the front, but the garden walls had crumbled in places and the outside wore a neglected grandeur that forewarned of the moral dereliction inside. A broad pebbled path curved its way to an attractive porched front entrance that had pillars either side. The front door was seldom locked and a fair variety of callers passed through, and most of those were returning customers.

The house was slow to wake up in the mornings, but began to show signs of life in the early afternoons and kept such late hours that it never fell quiet until the early hours of the following day. The inhabitants of the brothel never saw the sun rise, and seldom woke before mid-morning. Madame Romana herself, was beautifully attired, having made wealth in the trade of bringing together desirable women and men hungry for attention. She was a shrewd business woman, respected for her acumen, and was more than tolerated in the town because of her almost accidental dual role.

In the long past, she had given the otherwise destitute girls food, clothing and shelter and the rudiments of an education to those who aspired to it. Upwardly mobile herself, she had tried to set a standard for the house. She understood male appetites but there existed a strict code of conduct and Romana seldom encountered trouble. Violence rarely erupted at Romana's house. A man in drink would be tolerated but a man intoxicated and aggressive would find himself thrown out by the doormen or even by his peers, who did not want to sour their good relationship with Romana, whose discretion they trusted. She had contacts in high office, among them, Fabian Cavendish. She was well placed to know what was going on, having an ear to the ground via her working girls. Cavendish, in return, ensured that Romana's house received minimum interference.

One of the curious anomalies of her trade was her compassion towards the unfortunates, who, barely beyond childhood, came looking for a life of prostitution. On several occasions, having refused a waif on account of her age, Romana had taken a girl and found suitable work for her outside, in service of some kind. In a paradox of vice and virtue, Romana held that no girl seeking refuge would ever become one of her working girls until they had learned to read and maybe write a little first.

If one of her working girls was careless enough to become pregnant, the fatherless infant would similarly benefit. To ensure that girls took responsibility for themselves, as far as the times allowed, Romana docked their wages if she was supporting a child. At any given time, there might be a number of individuals beneath the canopy of Romana's care, and many others, owing to her insistence upon basic instruction, had found a place in the wider community.

She was tough and did not tolerate any girl given to thieving, drinking or temper, but regardless of her lax morals, she offered more than she took from the society of the time, which made scant provision for the poor. Ahead of her time, her older girls had an opportunity to put money by for when they no longer worked and one or two had even married. The woman had innate good sense and a modicum of class. A lot of people had reason to be grateful to Romana.

She sat now, in the comfort of her large upstairs lounge reading the note that had just been delivered.

"Heavens above!" she exclaimed and a moment later, "I can hardly believe it." then, hastening down the staircase, she bid one of the children to run after the messenger boy who had only just left.

"Go and get him back again Tobias, quick as you can. I want him to take notes to three other dwellings so it will be worth his while to return." Romana gathered her full skirts and puffed her way back up the staircase.

"Angel! Angel! Bring my writing case. Hurry girl."

As several sleepy female heads appeared from various doorways, she told them, "We've a special visitor coming today and you've all got to behave yourselves as never before. Mind your manners and drop a curtsey."

"Who on earth is coming?" yawned Hermione, one of her senior girls, who, at twenty nine, knew Madame Romana best.

"Come in here while I write to the seamstresses," Romana urged her, "and shut the door behind you."

Hermione did as she was told, and then read over Madame's shoulder as she hastily dashed off one letter, and passing it to Hermione, began writing another without even looking up.

"Is this true?" gasped Hermione.

"It's true enough if the Captain writes it so," replied Romana. "Now, don't vex me by asking questions I can't answer. Take these letters to the messenger boy. Oh where is Tobias? And where is that messenger?"

On her way downstairs, Hermione read the notes again.

"What's all the fuss about?" asked Angel who, drawn from her bed by the noise, looked crumpled, her hair a complete mess.

"Well, the ship is in," answered Hermione, and the dashing Captain is bringing a visitor. You'll never believe it but the princess of Auretanea is on her way to meet us."

"You don't mean it," said another girl, coming forward."

"Read it yourself…if you can," taunted the older girl.

"These notes are for the seamstresses to get here as soon as possible."

"Hermione!" shouted the voice of Madame, crossly.

"Don't tell the whole house! For all I know this is meant to be a secret. Oh! Where is the wretched messenger boy? Ah! He comes now! Quick Hermione, give him the letters. Good boy! Good fellow! Make haste."

The lad was paid and dashed off jangling three extra coins in his pocket. This really was a profitable morning for him. Madame Romana returned to her suite and was looking through her wardrobe with a critical eye. "I can't think what he means," she told her maid. "He says the princess will need shoes and clothes fit for presentation. But, presentation for what? And surely princesses come with their own shoes and clothing, don't they? And a good deal more besides, I should think."

"In less than an hour they will be here," interrupted Hermione, "and the girls who already know are very excitable as it is."

"Well, dampen them down for goodness sake," retorted Romana, crossly. "We can't have them frightening the princess. Go and teach them some manners."

Romana called out instructions, bustled about, shouted and cajoled a gaggle of spirited females into a semblance of order and set the maid to straighten out the lounge, before she left to straighten out her own hair and clothing. The house was buzzing with a frenzied anticipation, more usually reserved for the arrival of the men of the galleon. This really was a most unusual morning.

On board the Zenna Marius, Tianna had woken early and got dressed in her shirt and britches which had been washed only yesterday by their brief encounter with the sea. She watched as the cargo began to be unloaded and interest grew around the quay side.

Conversations leading towards eventual transactions had started in places and several of the men from the galleon began to move off down the cobbled streets in groups. Roden Jarrus had been one of the first to set foot on dry land. He waved cheerily to folk and was halted several times by people eager to talk to him or hear what merchandise he carried, but today, he shortened their conversations with a good natured clasp of their shoulders and a promise to catch up with them later at the ale house.

Tianna made her way towards the gang plank which served as a bridge between land and sea and she peered at the busy scene around her. She had only been there for a few minutes when the Captain hailed her from the quay. "Come on Tianna. I've received word that Cavendish wants me to call on him this morning. I will tell him you are safe but will take you first to Romana's house to find clothing. She will know we are coming. I sent word early. The house is not far. Follow me."

The girl noted the Captain's smart turn of dress. He was clothed in well-fitting garments, clean and expertly sewn, with not a button loose or frayed thread to be seen. She briefly regarded her own grubby clothes. He clearly had prepared in advance to pay a call on the Governor of Petriah but had been precipitated by a request from Fabian, himself.

Roden Jarrus waited for her to step on land. As she stepped on to the wide plank, the Captain hailed someone from some distance away, and, to Tianna's consternation, the dubious figure of Te Manu Manmou advanced from some distance, in the Captain's direction. It was obvious by his similar dress that he and the Captain would be paying calls together. Each wore brightly coloured frock coats in shades of emerald and jade.

The girl gave an involuntary step back, going into retreat, which the Captain noted at once. He did not comment but saw the alarm in her face and followed her gaze to the warrior. Roden could do nothing immediately, but made a mental note to address her fear, before they parted company for good. Manmou totally ignored her. In fact it was highly unlikely he had seen her at all as she had drawn so far back on the ship. The two men turned on their heels, and walked briskly ahead, Jarrus in step beside his second in command. What a dashing pair they made! Equal in height and stature, they strode purposefully forward, not once glancing back, their own conversation keeping them fully occupied. They progressed rapidly, in high black boots and with dress swords worn on low slung hip belts, each dressed smartly and striding confidently ahead.

The young princess felt very out of place away from the galleon. On land, these britches were inadequate and her legs and feet were bare. Her beautiful long black hair bounced behind her, swaying to her hips, but in contrast to her past arrivals in Petriah, with escorts and chaperones and carriages to meet her family, she was now quite invisible to passers-by, who hardly glanced in her direction. Some way behind, Gypsy and Israel were following the girl, making sure that she was not approached. They were alert to the possibility that any of them might be intercepted and questioned. The Captain and Te Manu were also watchful. However, nobody bothered them and they were confident that the princess could never be recognized. She walked on, oblivious to the fact that the men from the galleon were not far behind, ensuring her safety.

At first, she was dismayed when handcarts trundled across her path. She endured the rough ground under her feet and the nuisance of being jostled as people hurried past unconcerned if they knocked into her. She found it necessary to side step people who were intent on their own pursuit and she frowned at their lack of courtesy. Despite this irritation, an inner voice reminded the princess that anonymity had its advantages too. No one was keeping her apart from this hustle and bustle and the more she looked around, the more she wanted to see. Tianna had never been free to wander in a bustling market place. She gazed at the street hawkers, shouting their wares to attract custom. She looked upon the goods laid out on display. She passed tables of finely coloured china and baskets with doves and chickens.

Above her head an array of dazzling fabrics danced before her eyes as she passed by. She gazed upon baskets filled with colourful, scented flowers. There were pyramids of fruit and trays of sweetmeats and basket makers demonstrating their skills as she lingered to watch them. Voices called to each other incessantly. Tianna was very interested to see the various craftsmen demonstrating their skills, surrounded by their wares. It was a vibrant, noisy and jostling place, the like of which she had never seen. She briefly halted beside a small gathering of people, attracted by gales of laughter. They watched the antics of three clowning acrobats perform ridiculous stunts and knock each other off balance to delight the crowd.

Jarrus stopped and glanced behind to afford her time to catch up, but although the Captain had thought of it, Tianna noted the warrior's back remained resolutely turned against her. She kept them in sight. How tall they seemed, how broad their shoulders, how straight their backs when viewed from this distance.

At length, the princess followed them through a large lawned garden, and Gypsy and Israel waited until the girl reached the door. There were high white walls but no gates and the pillars were crumbling. Ahead of her, the two finely dressed men entered the house without knocking. The girl hesitated, then glanced behind to see Gypsy and Israel watching her. Gypsy gestured for her to go on. She gazed up at the windows. No one had come forward to greet her. It seemed impolite to just pass through the door, and until now she had not realized that the other two pirates had been monitoring her progress. She felt rather sandwiched between the men ahead and the two behind, with little option but to walk on. She raised a wave of farewell to Gypsy and Israel. Only Gypsy returned the gesture.

"Is that the last we'll see of her then?" he asked, after a few moments, when she had gone.

"I bloody well hope so," answered Israel.

They stood watching the empty doorway for several minutes after she had disappeared from their sight. Neither of them had any need to linger, but they did and it was Israel who was last to turn away.

Only minutes before their arrival, happy chaos reigned inside the brothel house. Girls had fought with themselves and each other, to suppress nervous, excited anticipation as they flapped and fussed, hoping to catch a glimpse of the two most talked about and handsome buccaneers. Only a few knew the identity of the important person travelling with them.

Madame Romana had implored the young, foolish women to use more decorous behaviour, but she was in such a heightened state of nerves that such admonishments were delivered into the general chaos and failed to make any impact. Consequently, the giggling and squealing went on, unabated. Some of the girls would become hot and faint at the sight of the two striking men. One or two would be overawed and put on a pretentious display to cover their awkwardness. They had become wildly excited at the appearance of the galleon coming into Petriah, after months at sea. The two men paused in the doorway and glanced around. They seemed to fill the space with a commanding presence of their own. Knowing that Romana had rooms above the sweeping staircase, the Captain merely glanced at the girls clustered around the doors and took the stairs two at a time, while the silly females sighed and swooned saying such nonsense to each other as "Ooh, he looked at me first," as their hearts fluttered.

Te Manu was close behind Jarrus. He had no patience with the girl's comments which irritated him. He stood on the upstairs balcony, resting his hands on the balustrade, while Jarrus opened the double doors to Romana's private rooms and swept inside, to find her. He had no time to waste this morning and was eager to move on and see Cavendish.

Meanwhile, Tianna, barefooted and quiet, had peered through the imposing front door and stepped onto the large black and white chequered floor inside. She observed a vast open space with a stairway sweeping upwards to her right. The room itself was a strange shape, hexagonal in design, with two doors set between each panel, presumably with rooms behind. There were pillars separating each of the six panels and if one followed these upward, they curved artistically inward at ceiling height, towards a dome of similar geometric design that flooded the area below with light. Between each pillar, tall, broad leafed shrubs in pots, grew up towards the brightness, echoing the pattern of feathered plumes at the top of the plaster pillars. The area was clearly intended for dancing. There were cushioned seats around the perimeters, some deep and wide enough to recline upon, as well as other soft furnishings. The whole was altogether pleasing and unusual. Tianna surveyed the room and wondered what she should do. Unsure of whether to go up or stay down, she stepped on to the foot of the graceful staircase and listened. It was then that the girls in the alcoves by the doors noticed her.

Suddenly there came a rather unkind burst of female laughter. Tianna turned in their direction and was about to say hello, when she realized they were pointing at her clothing and she was the cause of their mirth.

"You won't be comin' in here looking like that," shouted one, mistaking the girl for a destitute seeking work. "Madame's got her standards."

"Just look at her mucky feet!" squealed another.

The princess lowered her head to see how muddied her feet and legs had become walking barefoot through the market place. She felt embarrassed and ridiculed in this strange house, whereas her clothing had been of no importance on the galleon. She had felt free and comfortable in her short britches, when staying clean hadn't mattered too much and her appearance was never criticized. Tianna had no idea whose house she was in or who these mocking women were. For the first time, she felt conspicuously different and out of place as she looked down at herself, ashamed and self-conscious as never before.

"Get back to the gutter. Shoo! Shoo!" one of them laughed.

On hearing their shrill voices, Te Manu Manmou spun around and swiftly grasped the situation, reading it accurately. Suffuced with sudden anger, his reaction was instant. He leaned across the top of the stairs, fixing them with an outraged glower as his temper flared at the three unsophisticated brothel women below. He roared at them, thrusting the accusing finger in their direction, looking angry enough to attack.

"GET OUT OF HERE! OUT! OUT! OUT!" he bellowed. Immediately the simple creatures with no manners looked stupefied and froze in shock.

Te Manu's fury had been impulsive. He was incensed by their behaviour towards the princess. Something inside him burned with a passion. Flashing into his mind came the memory of a starving boy, never dressed as the others, having food thrown to him like a dog, by his tormentors, wearing garments that hung like rags upon his childish frame, and ridiculed because he was illegitimate and looked different. It cut him like a knife to sense that again.

Could those ignorant, painted harlots not see how unspoilt and beautiful the girl was? He condemned them for their blindness and prejudice at only seeing the way she was dressed. The laughter of the three girls ceased abruptly, arrested in an instant by the ferocity of Manmou's voice. When their shock subsided, they scrambled and pushed each other to get back behind the door as fast as possible, which banged shut.

Unfortunately, Tianna had also been traumatized by Te Manu's command to get out, trembling, and not knowing if he intended it for her also, she backed down the steps to get away through the front door and out to the safety of the garden. The Captain came out of the upstairs room in response to the disturbance and saw her leaving, just in time.

"Tianna!" he shouted. "Stop! Where do you think you're going?"

She looked up, her face confused. The Captain's elbows relaxed on the banister rail. His voice softened.

"Te Manu did not mean you," he said. "Come up here so I can introduce you to Romana."

She returned to the stairway. As he waited for her, Jarrus spoke to the warrior quietly.

"You are going to have to make peace with her, Manu, and do something about her fear of you before we turn her over to Cavendish. There is no time now. We are going to run late for our appointment as it is."

The girl hurried past Te Manu at the top of the stairs. He looked away, his back turned against her, but only because he did not want her to register further alarm. His ferocity had been intended to protect her from insult and pain, but it had not been clear to Tianna. He uttered an oath beneath his breath, angry with himself. Why had it mattered so much? Why had he bothered to say anything?

As Jarrus re-entered the room through the double doors, he speedily announced, "Romana, this is Her Royal Highness, the Princess Tianna of Auretanea."

She hardly had time to get inside the room. Romana and her maid were already curtseying low, before lifting their eyes to behold a real princess. As Madame Romana raised herself slowly, she stared. Her hands flew to her cheeks while she viewed the girl up and down. Her face was an extraordinary mix of emotions. "Your Highness!" she started, more in shock than awe, "You're dressed like a cabin boy!"

Outside, on the balcony, beyond the open doors, Te Manu uttered words of derision at Madam Romana's unnecessary comment. The girl knew how she was dressed for fuck's sake! Manu never suffered fools gladly. His irritation intensified as he heard the accusation behind Romana's question to the Captain.

"What *have* you done to her?" she demanded.

Te Manu thumped the balustrade. Really! These brothel women were insufferable. Romana's shocked reaction was received in jest by the Captain, who seizing the opportunity rejoined, "Now you know why we call on your help. Her Royal Highness can hardly walk among society in Petriah dressed thus."

Madame Romana shook her head and tut-tutted.

"No. indeed... no," she replied absently, whilst mentally taking note of the princess's height, probable weight, colouring and shoe size and admiring her youthful proportions, already considering clothes.

Tianna was amused by Romana's reaction, and in contrast to her earlier embarrassment upon the stairs, was now inclined to smile. Captain Jarrus did not intend answering any questions and Romana would not ask any. She was discreet. It was necessary to be so, given her clientele. She would provide what the Captain requested.

"I shall leave the Princess in your safe keeping until nightfall. Provide all that she needs and a purse shall be paid tonight to cover your expenses. The Princess will sleep on Zenna Marius tonight. I do not trust houses. They have too many windows and doors and guarding every entrance is rendered impossible. Before midnight she shall be escorted to the galleon where her safety will be entrusted to the night watch."

He turned to bow to Tianna, "You will be well guarded and quite safe there, princess."

Tianna was not impressed with this plan and her expression clearly told him so.

"Captain. I need to see Governor Cavendish as a matter of urgency. After all, he is my uncle."

Roden Jarrus stood his ground. "But not dressed like this, your Highness. Give Romana time to provide all you need."

The princess saw the dangerous look in the Captain's eye. He was not one to compromise and she had not come all this way to be denied her purpose. "I'm certain he will wish to see me sooner rather than later."

She smiled graciously towards Romana as she spoke, but there was a determined edge to her voice as she levelled her eyes at the Captain, and held him, defiantly in her gaze. He lowered his voice.

"I told you that men must deal with this," he reminded her tersely.

"And I told you that neither of us can achieve as much alone as we can together!" she hit back, whilst matching his tone as quietly as she could. The Captain looked at her as if for the first time, on the cusp of discovering her true tenacity. In deference to her status, and for Madame Romana's benefit, he opted for a chivalrous withdrawal. "Of course, your Highness. Whatever you demand." he said easily, smiling and taking her hand in his own with a flourish as he bent to kiss it in farewell.

"OUCH!" she complained, as his vice like hold on her tightened, gripping her fingers painfully. "I will hasten to your uncle now and tell him of your safe arrival." he smiled menacingly, whist hissing at her under his breath. "Don't you DARE leave the safety of this house until I come for you." Her eyes remained challenging. His were amused. He held on to her fast, feeling her try to wrench her hand free without being seen to struggle.

"Ow!" she mouthed again, silently, but aloud said,

"Please pass my greeting to my uncle, Captain," and added for his hearing only, between clenched teeth,

"Alright. I will not leave. You have my word. But remember I WILL be heard in Petriah!"

His eyes twinkled as he released her, and with a sweeping gesture to the ladies, made to withdraw.

Madame Romana and her maid exchanged a bewildered glance, not comprehending any of what had just transpired between her two guests. Tianna's mouth was set in a determined line. She was furious to see the amusement on his face. *"You will not thwart me, Captain Jarrus,"* she whispered, intent on having the final word on the matter. It was almost certainly a challenge.

He moved to the door. "Romana ... A word..." he muttered. She came forward. His tone became serious, for her ears only. "Do not, under any circumstances enlighten the princess of your profession, nor cause her to witness your women giving or taking pleasure," he warned her. "Her place is up here, away from the revelry below. Find her some innocent companion to engage her time. I will return later in the day to take my own pleasure." Romana understood his meaning. She also quietly assured the Captain that the princess would be protected from all ribaldry. Satisfied his instructions would be carried out, Jarrus closed the double doors behind him, and rejoined Te Manu.

Chapter Thirteen - Cavendish

The two men sprinted down the stairs and out into the glorious morning sunshine. Striding purposefully toward the street, and adjusting the frilled cuffs of his jacket as he hurried along, the Captain remarked they were probably going to be late for their meeting with Governor Cavendish, and would need to move swiftly.

"What delayed you?" asked Te Manu.

"The princess. Dared to argue with me about when she could see her uncle. She's a feisty little thing. I think I've just been challenged," he replied, and laughed at the audacity of Tianna. Even though she was a princess, to him she was no equal. No female ever could be.

"How can she challenge you?" asked Te Manu, interested.

"I'm not sure," replied Roden, "But mark me, she's up to something."

Two girls from the brothel, hanging around the boundary of the house, waved and blew kisses with pouting lips and crude posturing. They giggled. The Captain, always amiable, rotated his hand towards them and gave a broad smile in their direction, but continued walking briskly. Te Manu chose to ignore them and looked unimpressed.

"The harlots should know better than to proposition us in the street," he complained with irritation.

"You'll be welcoming their invitations tonight, and you know it." Roden smiled. Te Manu made a sound like a huff but did not contradict his friend, who laughed out loud. "I wonder why the Governor has requested to see us," the Captain considered as they walked.

"Maybe word has reached him about Auretanea after all," suggested Manu.

"Hmmm. I'll say nothing until we've heard what he has to say." Jarrus decided. They turned the corner and came within sight of an imposing residence ahead of them.

Tianna watched the doors of Romana's private rooms close behind the Captain. She looked at the two women and smiled shyly, whilst appraising them. Romana might have been approaching fifty. She was not very tall but carried an air of dignity, knowing when and when not to be voluble. Her pale, golden hair was swept up most becomingly. Her jewellery was discreet, rather than flamboyant and her gown was expensive and well-tailored.

Romana had a weakness for gowns. Nothing afforded her greater satisfaction than to see the female shape attractively attired. She may not have been able to turn her working girls into ladies but at least they would look like ladies. Her blue, shrewd eyes were small and her nose a little too pointed. She could be severe but despite all that had hardened her as mistress of a brothel, her disposition remained obliging. It would not have been easy to guess what passed through her mind since she tried to maintain a veneer of composure even when her girls were at their silliest. She composed herself now, wondering what demands a princess might make.

"Madame, do you have a personal messenger?" enquired the girl.

Romana was surprised. "Indeed I do your Highness. Shall I fetch him?"

"Yes," the girl answered, withdrawing a small flat envelope from the waistband of her britches.

"Does he know the shortest route to the Governor's house?"

"Most certainly," replied Romana. "I know the Governor very well. My messenger has run there many times taking different routes so that my messages are not interrupted by any who would wrong that fine Gentleman."

Tianna smiled. "I should like him to deliver this letter as quickly as possible," she said.

"Of course." agreed Romana, and rang the bell.

Tianna was pleased with herself. She had used those nights in the Captain's cabin profitably, finding ink and paper in the alcoves to prepare a detailed plan and a request of her uncle. She would not get ahead of the Captain in person, but if the messenger was swift and sure, her words would reach him first.

Te Manu Manmou and Roden Jarrus stood on the threshold of an impressive building, as the doors opened and a man in smart dress appeared to usher them inside. Coinciding with their arrival, a messenger, in bright livery, running along the street, appeared at the front entrance as the door opened, bearing a letter for the Governor. To expedite matters, Roden took the envelope from the gloved hand of the breathless messenger and passed it to the footman.

"If you would like to come this way, Gentlemen, I will inform the Governor of your arrival," the footman said stiffly, and the Captain along with his first officer were shown into a well-appointed library with large leather padded armchairs in a deep hue, the colour of good claret. The footman withdrew, to find the Governor, bearing the letter in his hand.

The library contained deep alcoves filled from floor to ceiling with large volumes and a table, centrally placed, was littered with maps and several heavy ledgers were open nearby. The two visitors had been there for perhaps ten minutes before Fabian Cavendish stepped smartly into the room. He was a tall, distinguished and striking figure with silver grey hair, brushed back, and dark, arresting eyes. His beard was neatly cut and his dress, elegant.

He struck observers as a refined man with excellent manners whose interest in people was sincere. He had obvious strength of character, defined by a quiet air of authority. His height was imposing and it was his habit to wear a purple cape that created a flourish as he walked or turned around, and was fastened with a gold chain. His voice was deep, but smooth and one got the impression that he toned it down, because beneath the surface, he had the power to make the walls tremble, if he chose. He greeted the Captain and Te Manu with enthusiasm. Shaking their hands firmly, he apologized for the slight delay and set about pouring refreshments for his visitors, ensuring they were comfortably seated, with everything at their disposal, before drawing up a chair for himself.

Cavendish noted that his guests had dressed with care. Their tailored coats, one in emerald and one in jade, were as elegant as any gentleman's. He observed they were not poor men, but chose to wear their wealth in gold about their person. These were proud men, not defensive of their choice to live a life at sea, nor afraid to fly in the face of the accepted ethics by dealing in contraband, about which they kept quiet. Only the gold earrings and pendants might have marked them out. Cavendish knew and respected Jarrus. Their association was of long standing, although as Roden looked upon him, Cavendish seemed older and more careworn than he remembered.

"Welcome, Gentlemen. Thank you for responding to my request for this meeting," he began, in his pleasant, cultured voice. "I will come straight to the point, for the situation calls me to forego all usual social discourse and tell you instead, if you do not already know it, of a pending threat to the stability of these Islands and my own future as Governor."

Roden and Te Manu were attentive to his words.

"For years there has been a rumbling discontent over the passage of cargo vessels using the Sorrello Sea. It has remained free and open to all who use it but various merchants have sought in the past to control areas of it or put forward a motion to see it patrolled, with toll charges applied that would cripple the small traders who come to these Islands. I have resisted all call for change that would, in my view, give power to the wrong people. The latest attempt comes from Scalos, and is far more persistent than anything we have seen before. The information reaching me is so far, incomplete. Rumour has it that Scalos soldiers have arrived in Auretanea in large numbers, unnerving the population, but no-one has come forward in any official capacity to confirm this. I have sent several equerries to the King but have yet to hear anything from any of them. Only yesterday, a boat came in, carrying two elderly men in a state of near collapse after a perilous crossing. They say another boat, ahead of their own was attacked in our own harbor. They claim to have come from the castle, which is under siege, and have been seeking men and youths to travel to Auretanea to swell their numbers to resist what they claim is a possible assault on their freedom by Scalos.

There have been thinly veiled threats from Baron Lussac in the past which came to nothing. It seems we should have taken more notice. I am being thwarted by my own ministers who cannot reach agreement as to what should be done, since all is conjecture and rumour. They are satisfied that our own ship will return with reassuring news soon. However, if the boat men speak true, my own niece, Tasmin, is involved with them and was instrumental to their coming here, which frankly is almost too fantastic to believe."

He darted a look at each of the men in the room, suspecting they had something equally fantastic to disclose. "You travel between the Islands, gentlemen. Have you seen or heard anything that could verify what is going on? I would sail myself, but the situation here is far from stable and those loyal to me are rightly concerned that others will look for an opportunity to remove me from office in my absence. If I react to any trouble in Auretanea without waiting for firm evidence of it first, I will have little support here in Petriah."

He sat upright. His eyes betrayed nothing of the letter which had astonished him only minutes before this meeting, which professed to be from Tianna.

"I am in the keeping of one Captain Jarrus who considers he knows better than I. Do not believe him if he tells you it is better for my delicate state as a girl, to be excluded from your discourse, and presents you with a false image of my need for sanctuary. He has shown me kindness but underestimates my determination to play my part in liberating us from the

intimidation of Baron Lussac. There are storm clouds gathering over us. I have much to tell you, of Tasmin and Father, and I have an idea, the execution of which can only be realized with your consent, and time grows short. Tia"

Certainly the tone of the missive conveyed all the indignation that both Tianna and Tasmin were capable of displaying if thwarted, and the letter also testified to Tianna's typical impetuosity. It might well be genuine. If so, how had she come to be acquainted with Jarrus, of all people? Fabian was intrigued to find out. He was a natural diplomat; a man of sound judgment, for he listened well and would not be pushed to any point of view until he heard everyone. He would see what Jarrus divulged first.

The Captain decided he must tell Cavendish everything he knew. "A girl has travelled with us from Auretanea. She refused to identify herself, after being discovered on my ship as a stowaway. I confess we treated her with suspicion at first. She requested safe passage to Petriah, to see someone on a mission of some urgency. She later claimed to be your niece, Sir. I listened to her story, but have delayed bringing her to meet you. She calls herself Tianna and says her father is the King."

Fabian Cavendish steepled his long fingers as he reclined in his armchair. "Do you believe she is the princess?" he asked them. Both men confirmed rather sheepishly, that they did.

"The younger princess IS called Tianna," the Governor informed them. "and she and her sister are lovely to behold. The younger is only just of age to marry, as to further description, I would ask you, has the girl in your keeping hair as black as jet that falls below her waistline and is far longer than usually seen? Does that describe your stowaway?"

"It does, Sir," answered Jarrus, looking at Te Manu pointedly.

"Well, that is the most notable thing about her, and eyes of extraordinary grey, a most unusual colour?" he went on. They confirmed the description.

"Where is she?" he wanted to know.

"At Romana's house being fitted for a gown," came the Captain's reply. "She had neither shoes nor adequate clothing when we found her."

The Governor raised his dark eyebrows at this.

"You've taken her to the brothel house?"

The Captain felt some further explanation for this seemingly irresponsible action was required. Te Manu shifted in his seat, but otherwise remained silent.

"I regret misjudging her and have arranged for her to receive a wardrobe more fitting for being on land. I swear no man has laid a hand upon her. We did not recognize her status and so..... she has worked her passage."

"Doing what?" asked Cavendish, incredulously.

"Preparing meals with our cook. Cleaning dishes, sweeping, that sort of thing... .."

The Captain's voice trailed off. He couldn't believe he was informing the Governor of Petriah that the princess, had been requested to fulfil such tasks on his ship. "She was very conscientious," he added suddenly, and then immediately wished he hadn't. It sounded ridiculous. Te Manu gave Roden a look which clearly said, "Shut up!"

If Jarrus and Manmou were expecting a reprimand from Cavendish, it did not come. Instead the Governor reacted with thinly suppressed mirth. "How long has she been working on your ship?" he enquired.

"Six days," came the reply.

"Six days! but you can sail it in much less than that," exclaimed the Governor, surprised.

"I delayed our arrival because I had not found a way to discover her identity or her purpose," the Captain told him truthfully.

Fabian considered the sanitary arrangements, which he guessed had been basic in the extreme. "Six days without proper clothing and only your facilities for her personal needs?" The Governor was appalled. "Did she object?"

Te Manu cleared his throat. "No… erm… No she did not." he informed him, shifting a little in his seat.

The two visitors were becoming decidedly uncomfortable. Fabian Cavendish pushed back his chair and stood in his purple cape beside the imposing hearth place of the library. "Gentlemen. Let me tell you something about King Theodore and his daughters. I have known Tianna since she was born." He turned towards them briefly.

"I take it the girl in your charge is about sixteen and is about this tall?" He indicated with his hand.

"Yes." They agreed.

"Good." replied Cavendish. "Unlikely to be an imposter then. I am almost certain we speak of the princess." He remained standing, but brought the decanter to the table.

"The King decided to bring up both daughters with all the expectations and advantages normally afforded to a son. Unusual, I know, but His Majesty was widowed at the age of forty eight when Tianna was a small child, about two, I think. I don't believe he ever really recovered. While it would not seem unusual for a male heir to the throne to be educated in state affairs, it is unheard of for a princess. Nonetheless, they have been schooled in history, maths, science and sit beside him at many assemblies. It was the King's way of coping perhaps, after being bereaved. He poured himself into their education. On home and foreign affairs, he invited their juvenile understanding and guided them to see all matters from a rounded perspective. He is a learned man and unconventional, and I believe the princesses take after him."

Fabian replenished their glasses with more excellent wine. Roden Jarrus turned the stem of his, thoughtfully. He remembered her reaction to Ezra's mock lashing on the ship. She had certainly been feisty despite her fear of them. "I felt she saw herself equal to men but could not work out why." he said.

Cavendish smiled. "Both she and her sister would probably match you with the sword too," he said.

Te Manu's eyebrows rose. He was intrigued to hear this. "Really?" he said.

The Governor of Petriah nodded, "Oh yes. The girls are adept swordswomen. They have been trained to fence. They possess determination in sport to win. It is as I have said, all the advantages afforded a son have been bestowed on the Princesses. What I don't understand is why she arrived on your ship in such a manner."

Roden Jarrus outlined the way Tianna had fled from the Ambassador and his plan to escort her to Scalos, which was an insane proposal by anyone's reckoning. Fabian Cavendish frowned. "I was there when the Baron presented a casket of rubies to the princess Tasmin and publicly humiliated himself by announcing a betrothal when there was none. A less arrogant man would have been more circumspect in his approaches. As it was, he did not anticipate being refused. I can quite believe he would expect the younger one to be delivered as consolation, and knowing Tianna as I do, I can imagine she would find the courage to board a ship to ensure it did not happen."

Te Manu's whole demeanour had become more reflective since hearing these things. "She did not know she was among pirates," he said.

"No. She thought she would be in Petriah within two days and did not expect to be discovered," added Jarrus. They both remembered that night only too well. A sudden rap at the door interrupted them and the Governor gave a command to enter. An urgent note was passed to him by a manservant. Cavendish read the contents. "Gentlemen. Excuse me for a few minutes. There is someone I must see. Please help yourselves to more refreshment."

He swiftly left the room. Te Manu got up and walked towards the window. "Did you really need to tell him she'd been working for us?" he asked, disapprovingly The Captain tapped his fingers on the arm of the chair.

"No, but if I hadn't mentioned it, Tianna might have done. There is no knowing what she is going to tell him," he retorted.

Te Manu was no longer listening. A carriage outside the window was bearing away a dapper little man in florid clothes. Cavendish reappeared soon afterwards.

"I apologize Gentlemen. My esteemed advisor, Celeiro, has been dealing with a grave matter which was my reason for summoning you to see me in the first place. Now I know more, we must speak of it. I have already told you of the boats arriving from Auretanea. What you may not know is that early this morning, a boat was found drifting. The occupants were from Auretamea and had been killed. Their throats had been slit."

He paused to allow them time to assimilate this twist in developments, the gravity of which could not be lost on the pirates. "I take it you know nothing of this?" He went on. "It is alright. I am not accusing you, but the crime has coincided with your arrival and has been carried out in such a manner as to implicate pirates. You must be careful. We have acted quickly to suppress the incident and the bodies have been taken under cover to the mortuary, but the silence will break, and when it does, your men will be blamed amid much hysteria. The timing and manner of these murders is no coincidence."

This was alarming news to the two men. Jarrus's crew were already freely abroad in the town and may encounter accusation anywhere. They could not be trusted to react calmly in the face of a charge of murder.

"I will do everything I can to withhold this incident today and maintain calm, for I am convinced enemies of Auretanea are here in Petriah. I will arrange a luncheon in honour of the princess's visit and thus ensure we buy ourselves time before having to confront these murders publicly. Warn your men, Jarrus. Tell them to avoid any affray. Come to me again. Remember there are those who would depose me and very shortly we are going to need your help just as you are going to need ours."

They stood to go their separate ways, a sense of urgency hastening the departure.

"Do I bring the princess or should she stay ignorant of this development?" the Captain needed to know. Fabian realized they had not got the measure of his niece, despite what had been told them.

"I would imagine," he said quietly, "That the princess sees herself as the third part of a powerful liaison already, and that, so far the other two parts are her Captain and his esteemed first officer. If no ill befalls us before then, let the four of us meet as equal minds, Gentlemen. For now, I have much to prepare, and you must find your men and ensure they avoid all provocation until I can find a way to prevent us all falling into a trap."

They bowed low in the hallway, anxious to depart.

"After our next meeting, you need to get away from here and take the princess to a place of safety. If there are Scalos sympathizers in Petriah, the abduction of the princess is possible. It is not safe for her or me but I intend to stay. May the spirit of Yasemin hold you in her keeping, until we next meet." They walked away from the house.

"That's a strange thing to say," commented Jarrus.

"No. I've heard it before," replied Te Manu.

"Oh, where?"

"Rhapsody says it."

"Oh, that figures," agreed the Captain.

Chapter Fourteen - In a Tavern

The next hour was not easy as they tried to assimilate everything they had been told. The situation was almost inescapable. The fact of the murdered Auretaneans discovered with the galleon's arrival would incriminate them if they stayed, but if they left immediately, they might be seen as fleeing. They had to be accepted as having legitimate business in Petriah. If they turned their backs on Cavendish, they would also be abandoning the princess and then there was the matter of the straits, for if Baron Lussac had his way, Jarrus would never sail freely again.

They had a crew to consider and a livelihood to protect. This fracas was not of their making. It was borne of a failure to respond to alarm by a body of inept ministers who had haphazard defences and an inadequate military. Jarrus was rightly contemptuous of their reluctance to act in time. It had taken two girls to risk themselves for the sake of their land and none of this need have happened if the men in power had lifted their heads out of the sand and monitored Scalos more carefully. Te Manu and Roden made their way to a quiet hostelry to take lunch and sup ale. On the way, they looked into every place for a sighting of the men and were successful in giving most of them warning.

The identity of the crew was known to a limited number in the town and this helped preserve their anonymity. A few, like Josiah Baines, had good friends to stay with in Petriah, folk who had known him for long years and welcomed both him and the boy Jonah. There was enough support for the crew of the galleon to help them, but the news Jarrus imparted made them all more alert than usual.

The two settled into a small hostelry. Sitting in the corner of a low ceilinged tavern, where little light permeated the dusty square paned windows, they reflected on their meeting with Cavendish.

"If he's asking us to take the princess to a place of safety, where does he have in mind?" asked Te Manu.

"He never said, and I don't know how far away he means," answered Roden. "But one thing is certain, he expects another meeting with us that will include her and as things stand, she won't even go through a doorway if you are standing near it."

"I know," admitted the warrior. Jarrus continued,

"Find a way forward before tomorrow. Talk to her tonight, when she returns to the galleon. She knows she has to sleep on board but is bristling at my insistence to keep her there. I don't think Cavendish will risk her in his keeping. He looks like a hunted man."

Te Manu listened. He saw the necessity of at least finding a way to say something to Tianna, but how to accomplish it was something else. "Will you agree to take her on to another place?" he asked the Captain. Roden heaved a sigh. "I don't know what to do. My instinct says get out before the murder of those men gets laid on us. We've done what the princess wanted, affording her safe passage to Petriah. There's no obligation on us to stay. We don't want to be mixed up in any of this, do we?"

"Up to a point, we already are," said Te Manu. "What could Cavendish do if we refuse to help anymore?"

"He'd be disappointed in our refusal and make his feelings clear, but he is not vindictive. We could sail away from here tomorrow."

Roden seemed overly sure about Cavendish. It vaguely puzzled Te Manu as to why the Captain was that trusting. They remained quiet for some time.

"Suppose the galleon sails as an escort to one of the smaller Petriahn ships. The girl could travel on one of those to a place of safety and we could shadow them until they reach a mid-way point, then resume our usual route," suggested Te Manu.

"That's not a bad idea," replied the Captain. "It's a fair compromise. Yes. Let's offer to do that."

Jarrus smiled, the responsibility of the princess miraculously lifted from his shoulders, at least for the moment. He buried any earlier thoughts of keeping her in their care, and drained his tankard.

"Come. Let's risk moving through the town and pick up on old acquaintances, then on to Romana's where those women you say you despise are waiting for us."

They paid the landlord and went outside.

Chapter Fifteen - Afternoon at the Brothel

Tianna, meanwhile, was delighted to have feminine company and almost the moment the Captain had left, she smiled broadly at Madame Romana and apologized for her appearance. Madame lost no time at all in offering the princess her bathroom and her maid. The luxury of sinking into the slipper bath, in fragrant, warm water while the maid lathered her hair, was total. Tianna lay back in the deep water and closed her eyes in ecstasy while Madame appeared with various fine cut glass jars which she placed in a row upon the deep window seat.

"Here are the bath crystals and salts," she began,

"These two are oils for your skin and this one is for your hair. I will come back with a choice of brushes and combs, after the hot oil has had time to soften your hair to untangle it. Good gracious! Is that seaweed?" she asked incredulously as the maid held up some fine strands of green algae. Tianna opened her eyes and thanked Madame for all her trouble.

"It is an honour, your Highness," she replied warmly.

"Now, on that table are powder puffs and fine dusting powder for after your bath and the seamstresses are arriving, very excited they are. I have some clean clothes which are about your size and those good ladies will set to work with needles and threads and do their best to alter some gowns for you. There won't be time to create anything new for tomorrow but we will all do all we can not to disappoint you."

Tianna was relishing every moment of the pampering after being at sea with only water at her disposal, and a limited supply at that. There were thick, white towels which the maid slipped around Tianna's shoulders.

They smelled fresh and clean and Tianna wrapped them around her body, hugging herself tight.

When she left the privacy of her bath and re-entered the large lounge, several visitors had arrived. Three seamstresses dropped fine curtseys and a cluster of girls, some only a year or two older than the princess, stood beyond the outer door, hoping to be introduced to her. With Tianna's permission, they would be allowed inside. Madame Romana provided the princess with a silk bathrobe and feeling rejuvenated and clean, she felt comfortable enough to meet them.

Romana opened the door, reminding them not to overwhelm the princess in their excitement. The unsophisticated girls entered coyly enough, curtseyed, and introduced themselves politely while three went very red and timidly apologised for their earlier behaviour.

"You are forgiven," said Tianna. "You didn't know who I was."

The girls were very relieved at the kindness of the princess and simultaneously admiring and envious of her beautiful hair which was being brushed until it shone by Madame Romana's maid. They marvelled at the length and thickness of her tresses and shyly began to ask her questions.

"Has your hair ever been cut your Highness?" enquired one. Tianna replied that she did not think so.

"Have you ever measured it?" asked another. Tianna laughed and said no, and when the girls offered to fetch a tape measure, the princess agreed that it might be fun to guess the answer. They began to warm to her. Any inhibitions about having a princess in their midst were soon forgotten and the girls began to laugh, quarrel good-naturedly and squeal unselfconsciously in perpetual gay high spirits. Far from overwhelming the princess, they amused and entertained her with their ridiculous animation. Tianna had left friends behind in Auretanea. It was fun to make new ones even if their lives were so very different. The younger girls had fun opening the large trunk of clothing that they had dragged with considerable difficulty into the room. There was a great deal of discussion on what colours might suit the princess's complexion and how a garment might best be altered to flatter her.

Tianna stood upon a stool to be measured ineffectually by over enthusiastic girls and then properly by the seamstresses. The older girls and women had become excited by the arrival of the galleon with the promise of all the men arriving from it, who often brought small gifts. The anticipation of being visited by the pirates seemed to send some of the girls into a swoon and caused a frisson in others. To question the princess about them created a near frenzy of excitement, all eager to listen to what she had to say.

They were urgent in their demand for any shred of information about their personal favourites that they would savour and remember long after the galleon sailed away. Tianna was asked many questions, which became more impertinent as the girls started to relax. While colourful garments were measured against Tianna and adjusted with pins for length, the infectious banter of the girls had Tianna laughing too. The oldest listened keenly to the younger girls prattle, intent on learning as much as they could. They envied the princess her week long proximity to the men they considered they knew, and asked the girl to divulge more. "Did any of them try to kiss you, your

Highness?" she was asked when Romana had left the room.

"No!" she answered, shocked, and then dissolved into giggles through embarrassment at the memory of Ezra's clumsy attempt on the day she had revealed her true identity and fallen into the sea.

"Which one would you choose if you had to marry a pirate?" was met with squeals of laughter around the room, as they urged her to name one. "Go on, Princess, if you HAD to who would it be?" They all began to take turns but luckily for Tianna, Madame Romana reappeared in the room. She immediately stifled the conversation.

"Don't be absurd you silly girls!" she said. "You know better than to ask a princess such stupid questions," ensuring their intimate knowledge of some of the men was not up for discussion. That was a golden rule of the house. She did permit some divulgences however, being intrigued as to how Tianna had coped on the galleon, and the princess was able to reveal little things she had discovered about Ezra, Gypsy, Israel and Joshua which were lapped up eagerly by her new friends. She spoke with a fondness for them, strengthened by the memory of that incredible last night of singing on the Zenna Marius.

However innocent her memories, during the afternoon at Romana's, the princess's passion stirred in what had been a hitherto sleeping libido. Tianna became interested by the romantic sexualizing of the pirates, viewed through the eyes of the brothel girls. At first she was shocked by their forwardness. There was a sadness to their frivolity, for they would never know the crew in any other capacity than one and would only dream of what it might be like to share any part of other men's lives. "Have you ever been in love? What is it like to dance with a prince?" were questions fired in rapid succession, along with "Have you ever been kissed, Princess?" Tianna had to confess she had no answers to satisfy them. She had never considered such things before but suddenly, she wanted to be able to say "yes," and enthral them.

"Close your eyes and imagine a prince standing in front of you," they giggled, all wanting her to pretend. A career of prostitution had not yet robbed Romana's girls of the desires and aspirations to find love. Tianna remained on the footstool but her dream of a faceless lover ready to hold her in his arms was short lived when, with eyes shut, she lost her balance and toppled sideways, laughing. Seeing the princess stumbling over the footstool served to make Romana remind them all that futile dreams of pirates or princes would end in similar loss of balance. She steered them back to reality. "It's no good any of you dreaming of being wedded, least of all to a pirate," she admonished them. "Why, those men are wedded to the sea. They forget your names just as soon as that anchor is pulled up, so don't you lose your heads or hearts over them."

Until now, such an idea would not have even entered the princess's mind and she was able to laugh at the girl's wistful notions. There had been nothing in the least romantic about actually being on board among men who spat and cursed and sweated and smelled as they toiled and rarely washed. She suddenly felt quite immune to these silly females who had little else to think about and was restored by Madame's redress.

It did little to diminish this gaggle of pretty females, however, who thrilled and imagined themselves the cherished subject of the pirate's conversations. The older women were coarser and more hardened to their life, but still laughed at the optimism within them all.

Tianna gained an unexpected insight to the generosity of Captain Jarrus, and the likely reason for the girls believing they had found special favour with him. Of course, she knew nothing of the payment in return for sexual pleasures, which was the lucrative trade of the brothel, but several girls chose to bring their trinket boxes and showed the princess their treasured keep sakes. It was quite usual for the Captain and the other pirates to bestow small gifts upon the women they had chosen to spend time with. Madame Romana was willing to concede there was a side to their nature's not usually seen in her experience, and certainly unheard of among men from the sea, who were usually a rough necked lot. She had decided long ago that Captain Jarrus was a gentleman.

"He can hold a conversation with any man of breeding so it's natural he would choose a crew with some care. In the years I've known him, I've never been wronged by any one of them and that's a fact. Seems funny when you think about it, why such a man should take to piracy and run such risks. Of course they spend a lot of money in this town and you'll find many folk in Petriah with good cause to like them. When I think of all the sailing vessels you might have sailed on, your Highness, I would say you chose one of the best, much as it surprises me to think that a pirate would ever be allowed to escort you."

"Oh, but I didn't choose them, Madame. I thought it was a cargo ship. I made a terrible mistake and boarded the wrong vessel." Tianna corrected her. But just as she said it, she was struck by the seed of an idea. Supposing she *had* chosen to board the pirate ship? What would people say then? An idea began to grow in her imagination.

She stopped herself just in time from revealing the drama involved in becoming a stowaway. They must not find out the princess had been that subversive. To tell them the truth about Auretanea would precipitate an avalanche of questions that Tianna did not want to answer. As luck would have it, these simple girls seemed more intent on showing her their pieces of jewellery and small vials of perfume and hair decorations. Nobody professed to be afraid of any man from the galleon and the older girls seemed to boast of it, if they had been chosen for what Madame Romana referred to as "companionship." by the Captain or Te Manu.

"The Captain gave me this," called Angel, holding a pretty compact case containing a mirror that was a delicate piece with small coloured stones set around the edge, and was much admired. Not to be outdone, a rival stepped forward.

"Manu gave me this," said the sultry voice, belonging to a languid beauty who revealed a comb studded with glittering stones that she pulled from her dark hair. Tianna felt intimidated by these older women, who might have been ten years her senior and had a superior, cat like way of looking that suggested they enjoyed a certain exclusivity with the ship's crew.

"Te Manu asks for me, whenever he's here," purred the sultry, superior one. The princess decided the woman couldn't really know him at all. Why, the warrior was a monster! Tianna did not comprehend the petty hierarchy in this den of females. There was strong competition for the Captain's favours and the senior men of his crew, whenever they returned.

Something feline with spitefulness combined to make them fight for supremacy. Jealousy, sultry expressions, withering looks and scorn were poured onto each other at times. Their behaviour could be brazen and it was not unknown for them to erupt in temper with hair pulling and scratching each other being the women's favourite method of getting even.

"Yes, well never mind the jewellery," said Romana, frowning at Angel and Marni, who were now intent on trying to outdo each other in displaying their treasures.

"They won't be presenting you two with marriage rings, just remember that! Let's put everything away and have some lunch."

Tianna was rather relieved. These older girls were rather frightening, in a forward, posturing way, and they seemed to look at the princess with some resentment for her knowledge of the crew. It was a jealousy Tianna would not have understood. Madame clapped her hands and issued instructions so that the garments and fabrics lying across every chair and sofa, could be moved safely beyond the spillage of food.

Trays were brought up from the kitchen and luncheon began with potted meats. Madame would reserve a genteel tea for her royal guest and the seamstresses later, when the girls had departed to dress and pretty themselves for the afternoon and evening visitors. For the time being, the room buzzed with chattering and laughter, and Tianna was delighted to be among them. She was on the point of being invited to see some of the attic bedrooms where the younger girls slept, when the call came that a visitor had arrived to see the princess, and thus prevented her tour going any further.

Chapter Sixteen - Uncle Fabian

Madame Romana was enamoured of Governor Cavendish. That much was obvious as she stood beside him in the lounge. The princess entered, delighted to see him. He beheld his niece with a look of great affection. "Where might we speak privately, Romana?" he enquired.

She opened the door of a smaller but well-appointed interior room, which served her for all manner of confidential purposes and would now be made available to Fabian. He thanked her and gestured for the princess to enter ahead of him. Romana discreetly closed the door and left.

"Oh, Uncle Fabian, At last I have reached you!" she said with feeling, overcome with relief at being reunited with one of her close family. Tianna ran to his arms and he stroked her head against his chest. He was an exceptionally tall and imposing figure, made all the more so in his cloak, in which the young princess buried herself. "You have read my news?" she asked after a few minutes, still clinging to him tightly.

"I have your letter and your suggestions for Petriah. I support your ambition unreservedly and you'll be pleased to hear, I have put your instructions in hand, already, my dear child."

She hugged him. "I knew you would," she told him gratefully.

"Time for preparation is short, Tia, so I will not stay beyond an hour. Tell me quickly, who knows you are here."

She looked up at him, sensing his concern. "Only the pirates and Madame Romana's girls," she replied.

"Nobody from Auretanea knew you were coming?" he wanted to know.

"Only Tasmin," she answered.

"Good." Fabian Cavendish sounded relieved. "Then nobody else in Petriah must know you are here tonight. It will be much safer that way."

He went on to explain about the murders and how incriminating it could be for the crew from the galleon and him. "Someone means to have them arrested and overthrow my position for befriending Jarrus. I can only keep these murders quiet for so long, before there will be an outcry. You must be hidden tonight against any attempt to abduct you."

"Do you really believe that might happen?" she asked. "I thought I'd be safer here."

"We do not know who to trust, Tianna," he replied, gravely.

She dropped heavily into a chair. "The Captain said I was probably safer on his ship," she admitted, ruefully.

"And he was probably right," confirmed Cavendish.

"For tonight at least. I want you to be there."

The princess protested and her mood became petulant. "But I don't WANT to remain among them another night, Uncle. I want to sleep in a real bed in your lovely comfortable home like I always have before, and be with you." Tianna implored him to change his mind. "Besides, I cannot go back, one of them wants to kill me!" she claimed, dramatically.

"Who wants to kill you?" asked Fabian, who was used to his niece when she could not win with persuasion.

"The warrior. He can be terrifying. He scares me," she confessed.

"What has he done to you?" enquired the Governor, studying her closely.

"He hasn't done anything," she replied with large, round eyes.

"What has he said to you, then?" he asked, reasonably.

"Well. He hasn't actually said anything to me since the first day I went on board." Tianna searched her mind for a convincing offence. "He doesn't acknowledge my existence at all. He despises me. He will kill me with his look alone, if not his action. I know it!"

Fabian sat down in the opposite chair. His silver grey hair, illuminated by the reflection in a mirror, made him look older and wearier than his fifty seven years, but he did not succumb to the tiredness he felt. His ram-rod back lent him automatic authority as he addressed his young relative.

"You are not making a great deal of sense, child," he told her. "Believe me, if I thought this intimidation had substance, I would act upon it, but you tell me he has ignored you and therefore wishes you harm."

The princess chose not to divulge how threatened she had been on that first night and how, as a result, she had wet herself. That was just impossible to admit. Fabian Cavendish watched her intently, wondering what was in her mind. "Is there more you wish to say about it?" he probed gently.

"No," she replied.

"It is a grave charge to say he wishes you dead, when we may be surrounded by those who also seek our demise, whilst professing to be our friends. Had you thought of that?" he warned her.

"N-no," she whispered, hesitatingly.

"The greater danger may come from the one who pretends to like you and invites your trust, rather than the one who dislikes you and will not pretend otherwise, for he is honest."

The princess backed down. Her uncle was a wise man. "Tia, I know this has been a difficult journey for you, without comforts and in the strangest company, but I have more reason to trust the pirates than half of my own ministers right now. Bear with the situation for one night more and we will spring the surprise of your arrival, tomorrow."

Tianna considered it. Having grown up alongside any number of dignitaries, her point of view had always been respected. Unlike the hierarchy on the Zenna Marius, where the Captain expected her to obey him without question, the princess had never been told what she may and may not do by her own family. Instead, her dear father and her uncle had calmly explained the pros and cons of even complex situations and, without being judgmental, presumed she would learn how to make her own evaluation. She usually could. Tianna understood that her own personal welfare was balanced against the freedom of her beloved country. When it came to it, both she and Fabian understood that sacrifices may have to be made. Petriah was rumbling like a volcano that could erupt at any moment. It could so easily take Fabian with it. Tomorrow's assembly was pivotal. She had to remain undiscovered tonight. Tianna agreed to stay on the ship.

"There is more you must be told," said Cavendish. "For some weeks I have been championing your sister's resistance to Scalos, but cannot do so officially."

Tianna's eyebrows rose and her lovely eyes widened.
"How so?" she asked him quietly.

"There are fishing boats taking volunteers across
from Petriah to Auretanea. They leave your Island
with just one or two men and return with eight or ten,
dropping them off at remote points under the cliff,
before returning with the same men as started the
journey. Older fishermen and those who could pass as
fishermen have come over to us that way, bringing us
news. This end of the operation has halted since
yesterday's murders. We have sent out a vessel to turn
back anyone else coming across while we decide what
to do. So far, Tasmin has at least eighty men and
youths from here to join her. Most of them have
relatives living in Auretanea. My authority here is
becoming increasingly challenged and may collapse
taking me with it. Celeiro says he has hidden two
elderly fishermen in a tavern. They were sent by
Tasmin and have links with the castle. We will have to
get to them before whoever is behind these murders
reaches them and with their own methods expose her
plan."

"Did Celeiro get the fishermen's names?" asked the
girl.

"No." answered Cavendish.

Tianna was enthralled by the conspiracies going on.
Intrigued by her uncle's involvement and her sister's
enterprise, the girl realized that far more had been
happening than she'd known.

"I must go and organize for tomorrow," declared
Fabian, standing up. "Trust the Captain, Tianna. He
got you here." He stroked her cheek. "I would give
anything to welcome you under better circumstances,"
he admitted, kissing her forehead.

"That day will come," she replied with more boldness than she felt. They were separating far sooner than Tianna would have liked, but there was no time for sentimentality. Romana and Fabian parted with discreet affection. As he kissed the back of Madame's hand, he looked back at his niece.

"I shall go and prepare for a huge reception tomorrow. Word will be sent out at once. We must galvanize the people of Petriah. You will be safe here tonight. No-one would ever think of looking for you among the girls in a brothel. Romana will protect you. She knows everything."

Chapter Seventeen - The Evening Begins

When Tianna re-entered Romana's lounge, she was just in time to witness the last minute preening of some of the girls, sitting before the dressing table mirror, reddening their cheeks with alcanet root powder and ground cochineal. The air was rather too heavy with scent. In fact everything seemed rather heavy in its application. They wore dresses that accentuated their bulging breasts, rushing past Tianna excitedly as they tumbled over each other on to the sweeping staircase, adjusting bodices and hair adornments as they descended to tease, torment, flirt and ultimately give their all to the visiting men.

With their disappearance, the room became altogether quieter. Madame drew out the leaves of an oval table onto which would be placed fine pastries and sweetmeats. The delicacy of the tableware was in sharp contrast to the heavy plates and tankards used on the galleon. Alone with Romana and the older seamstresses, the atmosphere became more refined and they made faster progress with sorting a number of garments for the princess. Occasionally, Romana seemed distracted and kept going to the window to glimpse who was coming into the garden below. She would also disappear below for varying periods of time, before returning to see what progress was being made with the princess's gowns.

Tianna was more content to stay since talking to her uncle. It would be quite a few hours before she would be expected to retire for one final night upon the galleon. A young girl, much on Tianna's years, arrived with a silver tray of delicacies and was introduced to the princess. She bobbed an awkward curtsey. Her name was Christa, and she was as fair as the princess was dark. They smiled at each other, instant companions.

"Why haven't you any clothes?" asked Christa, bluntly. Tianna, realizing she could be cornered by the question that everybody pondered, decided on the spot to make up the reason.

"Alas! My trunk fell in the sea and all my gowns were lost."

Madame Romana considered this catastrophe almost as terrible as the princess going down with them.

"Oh!" she lamented. "To think of all those fine royal garments among the fishes. It is too much to bear." She looked anguished by the thought of it and how her own heart would break if it happened to her. The other ladies expressed great sympathy at how terribly difficult it must have been.

"Your Highness, can you recollect how many you lost?" asked Romana. Like so many people having to digest an almost intolerable piece of bad news, she still wanted to hear all the details.

"Well," began Tianna, thinking on her feet, and went on to invent a preposterous list, adding, "and of course my slippers went too."

At which, Christa brought forth a favourite pair of her own. They were dainty flat sandals that were worked with such fine gold threads and tied behind the ankles, that Tianna felt guilty in accepting them.

At six o'clock the noise downstairs was audible and Romana dismissed the seamstresses, who would work with the assistance of their families at home, having been sworn to secrecy. It would be a busy night for them but they would be paid well. The Captain had promised that. The princess thanked them. Each woman curtseyed as she withdrew, thrilled to have taken tea with a princess and honour bound to keep her secret until disclosure was deemed safe.

It was yet another reason for Tianna to be spirited away to the galleon before midnight, lest anyone should put two and two together. Only Romana knew where the princess would really sleep.

Madame herself would also withdraw, but was less certain of how to do it. There was a fair amount of distracting noise and activity below her room, which would draw the princess's interest if the door opened too often, letting in the sounds coasting up the sweeping stairs.

"I really must go down and attend to the guests," she told the two girls. "It is a pity I cannot stay and your uncle was most insistent, as was the Captain, that the gathering down there is not suitable for your tender years. That is on account of the...er...drinking, smoking. And er... Well everyone has to be older to be admitted. Yes! That is it."

The princess thought it rather an odd speech but gratitude for the kindness she had received, prevented her from objecting. "Thank you, Madame," she replied happily. "I shall be perfectly comfortable with Christa's company. My uncle told me, that as an unexpected guest, I should not venture down to the working part of the house. He no doubt meant I must make no demands upon your servants."

She smiled. Romana was greatly relieved at Fabian's ingenuity. The "working part" of the house was decidedly off limits tonight! What a lucky association the princess had made with the servants. It spared telling her anything at all. Romana made her exit from the room and switched mode instantly to listen to the baser requirements of her guests.

Only Christa and Tianna remained in the upstairs lounge. The princess was comfortable, her skin and hair cleaner than in many days. The evening was hot but the two girls entertained each other, choosing light garments to try on, brushing and braiding each other's hair and decorating themselves with dress jewellery and ornaments.

Tianna, aided and abetted by Christa, chose a revealing, low cut gown of vermillion, with golden accents in a dress spangled with flame and orange highlights that sparkled as she moved. She had never worn such a garment and, peering into the mirror, gasped at the effect. Christa plaited Tianna's heavy hair behind her, setting a matching band across her head. The princess observed her reflection in the mirror and for the first time in her life pulled down her bodice to accentuate her own breasts, as she had seen the other girls do.

"You are very pretty, Tianna," admired Christa, pleased with her handiwork. "It is a shame no-one will see us up here in our finery. I should like us to be admired."

Chapter Eighteen - Entertainment

The noise from downstairs became louder. There were far more voices than before and the regular opening and closing of doors. The women of Romana's house received their visitors warmly. The large central hall, overlooked by the balcony, was alive with activity. The tall foliage reflecting against long mirrors maximized the light and created an even greater depth of space and there was plenty of sumptuous seating around the perimeters. Musicians would later set up in the centre of this area to sing and play when the hour grew late. The women saw to it that the men were made comfortable. They had been trained to be discreet and must cause no irritation by their presence. The girls stood back if men seemed occupied by conversation. Romana knew that her house was a valuable meeting place and if the men were unhurried, the longer they stayed, and the more likely they were to return.

The women were patient. They decorated the sofas or stood around the walls like resting butterflies, sunning themselves on a warm day, occasionally fluttering their wings. At a given signal, a subtle hand gesture or a casual glance, one would pick herself from the wall and slowly passing a man, would see if she caught his attention by gliding by. She might allow her gossamer scarf to trail across his reclining body as she moved provocatively, encouraging him to grasp the lightly perfumed garment. She might pause to entwine her long painted fingernails through a man's hair or snake her arms softly around his neck, and if the man was receptive to any of these ploys of seduction, she would linger. If the man glanced at her but continued his discourse, she simply fluttered on to the next.

Overseeing this elaborate game was Madame Romana herself, presiding over, and occasionally indicating, across the crowded room, where a receptive man might be sitting. Not all nights were busy, but when ships came in, it was always worthwhile for Romana to engage singers and musicians and turn it into a night long event.

The women used many ploys to attract a man. Some men would ignore the advances they received until a particular girl attracted them. Some men might just wave them away like flies on a hot afternoon, but always, interest was aroused and men would respond to the women. After all, that was the game, and it was what they had come for. One by one, they would reach for a girl and begin to fondle or grab and kiss her, and the girl, having been successful, would lead the man away from the large, hexagonal hall with the chequered floor and through one of the doors to the privacy of the rooms beyond.

Te Manu Manmou and Roden Jarrus paid only scant attention to the overt approaches of the women. Their preference was to select a woman from across the room, then move purposefully across the floor and take one. There was much jealousy and disappointment for females who, having been favoured before, were not remembered again. They would resent it, squabbling and even fighting among themselves, believing their possessive right to the two principal men of the galleon had somehow been usurped by the girl led away to take her place. Nonetheless, any woman who was chosen would consider it a rite of passage among her peers. Passing through those doors with either the Captain or the warrior, she would be forever elevated above the other girls.

Inside these chambers men exorcised their lust for women after weeks at sea and they were rewarded handsomely for the more extreme favours. The earthiness and crudeness of the men was taken for granted. Some appetites were insatiable. There was a hunger and lewdness making them predatory as they submerged themselves in the debauchery with women who encouraged them with their wanton and provocative behaviour. Just as the men knew their favourites, so did the women, and among the men were those who sought to give pleasure as well as take it, and acted more like lovers. Consequently there were always one or two girls who deluded themselves it was love, especially if their assailants were young and virile.

Roden would charm women into cavorting with him and they loved it. Te Manu would excite them with erotic techniques of arousal. They each controlled women and had them submit in very different ways. Both were dominant forces. They used and abused the brothel women, engaging them for elicit pleasure but were only really sated if their women lay exhausted beneath them, having been taken to a shattering climax. Hot and spent, in the aftermath of such powerful sexual tremors, those women pleaded for time to recover. Te Manu and Roden were demanding men who ensured they left their women sated. Such was the prowess of the Captain and the warrior. They had a reputation to maintain. No wonder the poor harlots were prepared to fight each other over them!

Not all men went to the brothel. Among Jarrus's crew were those with family links to the Island. Men came by asking for occasional voyages when money and work were in short supply and returned to their homes when the journey was over. Some of the crew had old friends or neighbours and even remnants of a family from years gone by. As some of Jarrus's trade was legitimate, not all the crew considered being in Petriah a serious risk to their freedom, especially if they had been citizens of the place. Some of Jarrus's older crewmen passed the time with ancient seafarers who would exchange stories, exaggerated and embellished by the years of telling. They were content to sup and smoke and talk.

Jarrus, Manmou, Gideon, Rhapsody and others had enjoyed being in the town. Although they were wary at first, it soon became apparent that no news of the recent murders had been leaked and they went about safely. They had renewed past friendships, made fresh acquaintances, drank freely and eaten well. New deals had been struck in the ale houses, monies and goods were satisfactorily exchanged. Now they were making their way to the brothel and the promise of a night of revelry.

At Madame Romana's, the evening was progressing well. The place was crowded. Upstairs, the two girls, Christa and Tianna, heard the sound of musicians tuning their instruments, preparing to play. The princess adored music and although her education had not included the usual accomplishments of playing a fine instrument, she could still dance and sing, enjoying it just as much as her companions even though her steps had to be invented as Tianna lacked any of the skills to be found in girls who had received lessons in graceful movement. "I know I'm not supposed to leave here until I go back to the galleon," confided Tianna, "but no harm can be done if I just open the doors and watch from the balcony, can it ?"

Christa smiled encouragingly at her new friend.

"You can see a lot from upstairs without ever being noticed. I learn a lot just by watching how the older girls do it," she announced.

Tianna was quizzical. "How the older girls do what?" she wanted to know.

"Come on. I'll show you," offered Christa, who bounced off Madame Romana's large sofa and bounded towards the double doors of the upstairs room.

The balcony afforded a good view of the chequered floor below and being wide, enabled any onlooker to draw back to the wall and not be visible to those on the ground beneath. No clients were permitted access to the upper floors and Christa had perfected an art of watching everything and pulling back if Madame ever came into sight below. Pillars supported the balcony with attractive plaster scrolls decorating the architrave above the upstairs doors, but it was not the architecture that captivated Tianna. Her eyes swept over a scene so unexpected, so incomprehensibly wild, and abandoned, that for the first few minutes she could make no sense of what she saw.

Chapter Nineteen - Awakening

Men and women, drunk with liquor and merriment, reclined on the furniture below. Doors opened and closed. People passed through, entering or leaving together. They walked or they staggered. Men swept women off their feet, gathering them into their arms and carried them, laughing together, into the rooms. Sometimes men kicked open the doors, becoming quite unbalanced by the voluptuous women, unable to see past the ruffles and layers of their petticoats.

Dishevelled and in various states of undress, the women behaved provocatively and were teasing. They tossed their hair, beckoned to their admirers, loosened their bodices exposing their breasts and invited attention. They raised their skirts to dazzle with glimpses of well-shaped thigh. The princess, transfixed by the scene below, watched as a man crawled on all fours beneath the volumous skirts of an ample woman. She saw a second man bury his face in the buxom cleavage of another. It was some moments before Tianna began to identify some of the men from the Zenna Marius and recognize the women with them as those who had asked her questions earlier in the day.

That any of them could abandon themselves to such activity, shocked and bewildered the girl. Yet, fascinated, she could not withdraw. Expecting to be reviled and shrink from the scene, instead the minutes went by with Tianna still watching, transfixed. For as long as they were unaware of her, she remained. The princess glanced across at Christa whose elbows were on the rails of the balcony, a wide grin on her face. She was enjoying the lascivious behaviour hugely, expecting Tianna to do the same. The princess saw no displeasure on any face, but was relieved to merely be an onlooker, and a secret one at that, for nobody thought to look up to the balcony. Those participants were lost souls engrossed in the debauchery below.

In one of the side rooms, Te Manu stood by the side of the bed, and prepared to take his leave of the one they called Marni. She lay naked and panting, her dusky skin hot and glistening as she recovered from his recent assault on her body. He looked at her. She rolled over to raise herself languidly upon one elbow, sultry and spent, watching him begin to re-dress as he moved away from her.

"Do I please you, Manu?" she purred, hoping he might yet stay. He turned his head to look at her again. He did not smile. His voice, when it came, sounded flat and slightly bored. "You please me. You always please me," he replied, lacing the front of his tight trousers more comfortably now that the throbbing desire to have the girl had been satisfied.

"Then why are you leaving?" she asked, rolling on her back, spreading her long painted talons and clawing playfully at the bed sheets.

"I must," he answered simply.

"Don't leave me for another. Stay with me." she simpered, whilst stroking herself and patting the silken sheet. He watched Marni attempt to seduce him all over again. Her full red lips parted, the flashing dark eyes narrowed like a cat's. She massaged her swollen breasts, inviting his assault upon her heated body for a second time. Te Manu enjoyed the performance as her fingers stole provocatively down her body to the silky mound and she parted her long, shapely legs to stroke herself and compel him to stay. He watched her appreciatively, as she pleasured herself before his eyes, but he continued to dress, broodingly. Why he was in this mood he couldn't tell. He couldn't shake it off. Today he was not himself. He looked at Marni, arching her back and moaning for him, teasing him to return as her restless body writhed upon the bed. It was all an act; of course it was. But, suddenly, the shallowness of the performance irritated him.

It was as though he'd never really seen through her until now. What was this undulating, snake -woman really like? There was no resistance to him. She would do anything he requested, be anyone he wanted, anyone that is except her true self. He could teach her nothing. She had probably indulged in every bestial practice known to man, used every past experience to perfect a pantomime of sexual gratification from the neck down, but what the hell was in her head? He was suddenly dissatisfied, knowing that her mind would make dull company. Irritated with Marni for being what she was, he was more out of temper with himself. This just wasn't enough anymore.

In truth, he had been preoccupied since the meeting with Cavendish, although it had not obstructed his pleasure whilst penetrating this salacious beauty who writhed beneath him. After he had thrust into her again, his thoughts had returned, remarkably quickly, to the words of the Governor and, more particularly, to the princess. Of her, he tried not to think, but could not help himself. When he had re-entered the hall earlier that evening, Manu had recalled her vulnerability at the taunts of those ill-mannered trollops. It was an image that involuntarily resurfaced in his mind.

"Find another man to conquer, Marni," he told the curvaceous woman who breathed heavily upon the bed. "I am done with all this tonight and cannot be good company any longer."

She sat up, switching off the provocative performance in an instant. "You have had enough?" she asked.

"I have had enough. There is just too much on my mind," he added as an afterthought, but he chose not to look back, or wait for her reaction, and departed abruptly.

In another room, Roden reclined beside Hermione. Sexually gratified, he lay staring at the ceiling, his thoughts also in another place, while she threaded her fingers through the mat of dark hair that covered his chest.

"What are you thinking about?" she asked, lazily.

"The ship," he told her, which was partly true.

"I guessed your mind was elsewhere." she said, pouting, affecting disappointment that wasn't convincing. She moved her shapely leg across his thigh as if hoping to recapture his attention.

"You can stop that. I have to leave soon," he told her. He stroked her smooth skin and then playfully slapped her rounded bottom hard, as he eased himself away. She jerked at the smack, raising herself on all fours, and knelt with her head down, rocking on her parted knees and rotating her curvaceous hips for him to do it again. He laughed at her brazen display, unable to resist the invitation.

"You're a temptress Hermione," he said, kneeling up.

"Oh well, what difference will another half hour make?" and aroused once more, he pulled her roughly down the bed and dragged her hips against his, to take her from behind. He got no further. Outside, the strains of musical instruments tuning up, signalled that time had flown and the hour was later than he realised.

"Shit!" cursed Roden, remembering Tianna. "I have to go. Romana will be waiting."

"Waiting for what?" asked the dishevelled girl.

"Never mind." he answered.

"It's the princess who'll be waiting, isn't it?" guessed Hermione.

"Sort of," he answered, struggling to put himself back into his clothes. She sat abandoned on the bed, her long red hair untidily spread across her white shoulders, as she waited for him to say more, but he merely blew her a hasty kiss for her services, then winked and smiled that self-assured smile and disappeared from her perplexed gaze.

The atmosphere in the grand hall became calmer. Those emerging from the side rooms were noticeably languid. The entertainment beginning at this late hour was of a different kind. It no longer demanded participation. A more subtle mood was prevailing. Outside the door, Te Manu stood momentarily and was soon spotted by Rhapsody, sprawled on a deep sofa, flanked by an attractive girl on either side. Rhapsody hailed his friend. Te Manu approached him.

"Hey, friend." Rhapsody greeted him, raising his hand. He was even more laid back than usual.

"I bin sucked dry man! I bin t'ru hell wid dese beautiful women. I can't feel my legs, man!" he complained cheerfully.

"You're drunk, Rhapsody. Just how much have you had?" Te Manu asked him.

"Hell, I don't know," Rhapsody answered, then grinning at the two girls resting in his arms, he said happily, "Okay. Go away now and let me friend siddown." The two girls peeled themselves from Rhapsody's body, and sloped away, pouting at Te Manu as they moved.

"Two at a time, Rhapsody?" asked Manu. "You had both of them?"

"Sure did!" his friend closed his eyes with satisfaction.

Te Manu leaned back into the sofa. They watched four gypsy dancers who had just moved into the centre of the room, and began stamping their black heeled shoes upon the marble floor while the guitars set the rhythm. It was a vibrant and spirited sound, the dancers were fuelled and defiant in their posturing, driving their feet hard into the ground, their expressions fiery. "They match my mood," admitted Te Manu. "The music, the dancing, I feel something like this within me tonight. I am stirred up and restless like them."

Rhapsody opened one eye to see Te Manu staring ahead at the whirring movement, which had started slowly and was rapidly gathering a frantic pace with strong, rhythmic hand claps and shouts from the performers as they strutted proudly, then began to move in a rush of energy and colour around the musicians. "Something is gnawing at me. I have an appetite that I thought Marni would assuage, but the brothel does not stem it. These women do not satisfy me tonight," he complained.

"Well, you sure has been bad tempered this week," agreed Rhapsody. "Per'aps you is ill man."

Te Manu drew on his cigarette, but said nothing. Rhapsody sat up.

"Course it could be that somet'in is getting under your skin," he suggested. "or someone."

"Like?" asked Te Manu.

"Like the princess. You gonna have to make peace wid her."

Te Manu scoffed.

"She won't let me talk to her. Not now. The chance has gone," he declared with finality.

"Den don't talk to her, man, Kiss de girl."

"Kiss her?" Te Manu rounded on him. "You don't know what you're saying. You are drunk, Rhapsody!" And he folded his arms, a set expression of contempt in his eyes once more. Rhapsody was well used to his friend's moods and was undeterred.

"Sure t'ing," he continued happily. "Somehow you gotta get t'rough to her before tomorrow. You said so yourself. Now here's what I would do man, if I don't have de words to say - I kiss de girl."

Te Manu flicked ash on the tiled floor.

"I had enough of that with Marni," he declared, defensively. Rhapsody turned on his friend.

"What the hell you god damned talkin' bout, man? Marni is sex! I ain't talkin' bout sex man. I is talkin' bout bein tender wid de princess. I guess you just don't know what that is!"

Te Manu's mouth hardened. He was being bawled out by Rhapsody again over the blasted girl and did not want a showdown with him here in the brothel house. He fixed his gaze upon the performers. The tempo of the music had increased. The guitars played in perfect synchronization with the dancers who dominated the floor. The strong chords vibrated with the thudding heels that drummed so rapidly, sparks almost flew from their feet. The music was vigorous, compelling the dancers to swirl ever faster across the marbled floor.

Te Manu was transported back in time. In his mind's eye he was a child again, watching the glare of the crackling bonfire burning in the night. Always on the perimeter of the gypsy encampment where he was obliged to toil until he could hardly stand, and scavenging for extra food because he never received enough. They had denied him the right to belong to the clan, even though the gypsy music was so much a part of his soul. He shook himself back to the present and shifted in his seat, oblivious of Rhapsody still talking, and watched the strong rhythmic hand clapping of the men drumming their heels arrogantly, like peacocks dominating the floor. It set his pulse racing to hear it.

He drifted again, seeing with the eyes of a child, the gypsy women dancing, their earrings catching the light from the dancing flames of the fires at night. Concealed beneath the wheels of a trailer, he would watch entranced, absorbing the sound and movement but always from a distance because his mother had broken the cardinal rule and had conceived him outside the clan. Illegitimate, and looking very different, he was subjected to neglect or brutality, yet they never quite succeeded in extinguishing his spirit. Visions that had been so long buried in his past resurfaced tonight. For the first time in his adult life, Te Manu struggled to fight them down. He thought again of the princess, barefoot on the stairs and the stupid, mocking girls of the brothel house. He knew what ridicule felt like. Feelings long suppressed, about the mindless, ignorant pigs who had tried to destroy him, but failed, bubbled dangerously near the surface of his turbulent mind. Is this why he had been so angry this morning. Damn the princess! She was the reason all this had been resuscitated in his head.

There was a smouldering eroticism in the dancer's rhythm that stirred the warrior's stormy passion as he watched them. Dark and intense, the powerful dancer threw his partner away from his body, then pulled her in close with aggressive determination. She was as provocative as him, sliding down his torso as his head inclined towards her neck, to control and caress her. There was almost a fight going on between them, their bodies hot and sensual as they moved. The woman's swirling black hair brought Tianna to his mind again. Beside him, Te Manu could hear Rhapsody, still protesting that he needed to do something about the princess and soon. He was sick of hearing it. She was the reason everything was in turmoil. She had brought trouble to them all. Damn the girl! Damn and blast the little witch!

Since she had come on board, he had found himself at odds with just about everybody and even now, it was still fucking well going on! Rather than start a fight and bash Rhapsody to shut him up, or knock him out, Te Manu decided to switch off completely, and sank deeper into the sofa, closing his ears to the tirade, determined not to listen. That man who seldom smiled and rarely sighed, slowly moved brown, resentful eyes around the room, surveying everything, missing nothing, imagining that everyone save himself, was a happy, carefree fool, untroubled and having a great time.

Above him, on the balcony, Tianna had been watching the dancing couples tap out the strong gypsy rhythm, banging their heels and tossing their heads proudly. She had never seen anything like this and was captivated by the way the women held their vibrant skirts and thrashed their colourful layered petticoats from side to side. There was tremendous energy and power behind each sharply defined movement accompanied by enthusiastic clapping from the audience. The dancers bowed low at the end and withdrew with wide, breathless smiles to great applause. Then, the mood became quieter, softer, and the guitars began to play a gentle, sensual rhythm. People quietened.

Tianna, hearing the dreamy music, gradually became entranced by it. Everything else in the room seemed to fade far, far away. She leaned forward. Her soft eyes widened. She was drawn helplessly into the magic; spellbound by the haunting voice of the lone minstrel who moved forward to the centre of the room and sang of love.

Te Manu felt the quietness descending all around them like a blanket as the atmosphere began to mellow. His eyes gradually revisited those faces he had seen before. They were attentive now and still. Those eyes slowly moved to the lone musician and rested there for a moment, before slowly surveying the rest of the room. Some of the brothel girls had emerged quietly. Their sweated labour finished, they were equally curious to see the minstrel.

People were everywhere. They congregated around the main door, occupied the porch, and leant over the fine carved handrail at the base of the wide stairwell, trying to see and hear the minstrel play, captivated by his song. Te Manu's gaze travelled over a crowd of many faces, observing them closely, a soothing balm washing over them all, in stark contrast to what had gone before. His own slow eyes began to ascend, his gaze sweeping steadily upwards, past those sitting on the stairs, towards the balcony, where a slight ripple of movement caught his passive, wandering eye, and he stilled... unable to believe the sudden impact of what he saw.

Rhapsody, two thirds inebriated and deaf to the caressing sounds being played, was still holding forth.

"Are you gonna louse this up with her just like you have every day?" he asked, provocatively.

Not gaining one word in reply, let alone the thump which he was half expecting, Rhapsody sat up to see what had arrested Manu's attention. He followed the direction of his friend's entranced gaze, his own eyes coming to rest at the top of the stairs. Rhapsody's mouth opened: "Wow man! there ain't no woman more lovely than that," he exclaimed, and he emitted a long, low whistle.

It was impossible for Te Manu to drag his gaze from the vision of perfection at the top of the stairs. He was held as if invisible forces were at work, drawn to a girl whose beauty was oblivious to his presence, as she listened, totally absorbed by the music. Serenity and gentleness shone in her face. He was drawn towards her as if by a powerful magnetism. Something happened to him in that moment. Perhaps it was triggered by the lighting of the chandelier illuminating her hair and smooth shoulders, or the flickering candles causing the vermillion gown to shimmer, or the softness of her expression that made her seem a dreamlike creature.

There was suddenly no capacity to see or hear anything else in the room. Te Manu stared at this incredible girl. The source of all his bad feeling, arguments, turmoil and inner conflict was standing upstairs, completely unaware of him or anybody but the musicians and the haunting song that held her, enraptured.

Every fibre of the warrior's being was tuned to this girl. He had not the vaguest notion how to follow the Captain's orders to make peace with the princess. Until this moment, he hadn't even wanted to, considering that after tomorrow, their paths need never cross again. But now, something powerful fuelled him with an overwhelming desire to reach her and make her listen, and no matter what else may happen, he could focus on nothing else until he had been afforded that chance. Roden entered the hallway. It was later than he'd hoped and he needed to get Tianna on to the galleon quickly and double the night watch. Seeing Te Manu looking towards the balcony, he automatically glanced up, expecting to see Romana. Instead he saw Tianna, dressed as he had never seen her. She was without doubt, an apparition.

"Phew," he breathed out, appreciatively.

In a room full of females, extravagantly dressed and over painted, the simplicity of the princess stood out in innocent contrast. The Captain's reaction, like Rhapsody's, was to stare. Te Manu, however, could not stand still. Like a man in a trance, he got to his feet without taking his eyes off her. The warrior made his way to the foot of the great staircase, determined to engage her, edging closer to the girl who bewitched him, without even knowing he was there.

Tianna smiled softly to herself and sighed deeply as the last notes of the music came to a gentle end and drifted away on the air. She came out of her reverie long enough to clap her hands and smile at Christa, having totally forgotten that she shouldn't even be there. "Oh, that was the most beautiful sound I ever heard," she told her new friend. "Will there be more? I wish he would start all over again."

She swept the expansive room with her smiling gaze, wanting to see, if like her, the people would call for the musicians to play again. As she peered down, Tianna had the curious sensation that she too, was being watched. It was an odd feeling. She decided to investigate, blowing caution to the wind, and stretching her arms along the balcony rail, dared to lean over.

Suddenly her eyes widened in startled surprise and her mouth opened enough to allow a sharp intake of breath as she flattened herself against the wall. The Captain and Rhapsody were down below and they had definitely seen her. The princess instantly felt a surge of guilt for being there and wondered if it was wiser to retreat into Romana's room or go down the stairs to explain herself. With a racing heart, she tried not to panic.

Deciding it was better to face the music rather than delay the inevitable retribution, the girl opted to walk down and brazen it out. She had the excuse of enquiring of the Captain when she was meant to leave this house. It was fearfully late, and he had said he would come for her. She would say she had been looking for him. She took a deep breath. Tianna moved onto the top step to go down and instantly froze.

"Oh My. It can't be !" she exclaimed, almost unable to believe her bad luck, for there, on the lowest treads of the wide stairway was the all-powerful figure of Te Manu and with eyes fixed determinedly on her, like a hunter, he was creeping up the steps, noiselessly making his way towards her. It was his gradual advance that affected her most. She suffered an immediate chaos of the mind. A thrill of panic seized the girl. It was fear but inexplicable excitement too as she sensed the eroticism in his large, dark eyes, and his total fixation upon her told her that she was his prey. He could devour her with such a look, and in this feverish moment, she would let him. Her reaction was instinctive. A tingle spread from her stomach radiating throughout her body, reaching the inside of her thighs.

Thrill and terror fought for supremacy. She could not control either. Such panic and surprise became interlocked with a primitive excitement in thoughts that overcame the princess which she could not shake.

How long any of them had been watching her, Tianna could only guess. She only knew for certain that all the vehemence of the warrior would be released upon her for this disobedience. A fresh wave of panic sent her sprawling back through the double doors of Romana's lounge, which she tremblingly locked behind her. Calm reasoning had deserted the princess. Despite the doors being locked, she looked desperately around the room for a hiding place. She was frightened of Manmou's slow ascent, and even more frightened of the way her body had responded to the anticipation of him reaching her. The little girl resurfaced as she scrambled behind Romana's curtains and shut her eyes against the world.

Seeing the princess retreat with almost violent haste, arrested Te Manu's progress when he had only reached the third step. He halted there abruptly with the slamming of the doors above, and was joined by Rhapsody, who had seen the whole thing.

"Are you gonna let this go on?" Rhapsody asked him. Te Manu continued to watch the doors at the top for several more seconds.

"No," he answered. "I will find a way to set things right." Running through his mind was the dilemma of what to do and how to succeed. Rhapsody, as usual could not be quiet. "You gotta show de girl that you is okay. How you gonna do that if she runs when she sees you comin' eh? This is one big problem, man."

They were approached by the Captain.

"What was that all about?" he asked, wondering how Tianna had disappeared so fast.

"She caught a look from him!" replied Rhapsody.

Te Manu began to wish he'd belted Rhapsody when he'd had the chance. Roden got the picture.

"I've just asked Romana to bring Tianna down the back stairs so she can be escorted to the ship. Four men are going on watch now. If you go with them..." He did not need to finish the sentence.

"I'll go," replied Te Manu, understanding the implied direction from the Captain, which had nothing to do with the duties of the night watch. Roden nodded, and hastened away to meet the princess outside.

"Don't ask her nothing'," said Rhapsody helpfully. "Cos that girl ain't gonna speak one word to you, she's shit scared. Go real slow. I can see what's bin wrong wid you. She's got under your skin from de start an' you've bin fightin' it and fightin' it."

"Will you SHUT UP Rhapsody," responded Te Manu. Rhapsody chuckled, hiccoughed and swayed unsteadily on his feet. "Just don't want you messin' up. You gotta make her like you, man," then he whispered, *"Kiss de girl!"*

Christa knocked repeatedly on the heavy doors on the upstairs landing and rattled the lock to no avail, trying to be heard above the musicians.

"Princess. Let me in," she called, rapping more insistently. "Tianna, it's me, Christa. Let me in."

Eventually, a key turned on the inside and a rather embarrassed face appeared through the crack in the door. "Has he gone?" Tianna whispered urgently.

"Has who gone?" asked Christa.

"The one called Te Manu. The one who looks like a tribal warrior."

"I don't know their names," answered Christa, "but there's nobody here." She looked puzzled and pushed her way into the room. "What's the matter? I didn't think you'd ever let me in."

"He saw me on the balcony listening to the music and looked so angry and was slowly coming up here. I just ran inside and locked the door," Tianna explained.

"But you're a princess. You can do anything you like, can't you?" enquired Christa, surprised at Tianna's fear. The princess thought about this. Now they were on dry land, she supposed she could.

"I didn't think about it," the girl confessed.

"Well, if I were a princess, I wouldn't be scared of anyone," boasted Christa, "and if you're frightened of the one I think you mean, the one with the shaven head, well, I know a lot of the girls are crazy about him."

Tianna began to question herself about this. Everything she heard about him contradicted her own perception. It was very confusing. The sight of the warrior had stirred her, arousing an excitement within the princess that was not purely fear. She had wanted to study him on the ship when he played the guitar with Ezra, and try to fathom him out, but had not been given the chance. Walking behind him and the Captain in Petriah, she had studied his height, his gait, his straight posture and broad back suited so well to the beautiful frock coat he had been wearing, cut so becomingly on his waist and hips. He and the Captain had received many approving glances as they proudly strode ahead, but he had never once turned around to consider her welfare on that walk, the arrogant, pompous man! Tianna chided herself for thinking such things. She still held that he was an animal; that his dislike of her was intense, the result of her intrusion into their lives, she could almost pardon him for that, but his behaviour since then had been abominable. He was the scariest, most ill-mannered, graceless, bad tempered savage she had ever encountered. It was best that they studiously avoided each other. Their mutual disregard was the result of a deep loathing. Tianna was sure of that.

But, what might have happened had she not panicked outside Romana's door? Christa was right. She was a princess in Petriah, not a stowaway on a ship.

Romana's voice on the stairs broke into Tianna's thoughts as she came puffing up the steps. "I must say the musicians really are excellent," she enthused as she entered the room. "Ah. There you are your Highness," she said, breathlessly, as if surprised to find the princess where she had left her. "A trunk with some clothing and a supply of toiletries has been placed downstairs, though I cannot imagine how you managed before. Men make do with such crude facilities. The bearers will carry the trunk to the galleon just for tonight and the Captain is waiting for you outside. We will leave by the back stairs. The way is well lit."

Tianna paused to say goodbye to Christa and to thank Madame Romana for all she had done.

Outside the building, Roden Jarrus waited with Te Manu. The night air had hit Rhapsody who had slid down the door frame and was now on the ground in a happy, drunken haze.

"If you like, I can say something to her first to put her at ease." offered the Captain. "In fact, it might be better if I do it."

"No," responded Te Manu decisively. He was adamant. It was a matter of pride. "What passes must be between me and the girl," he declared, concealing the fact that he hadn't the faintest idea how to go about it. Roden frowned, unconvinced. "Just don't end up frightening her even more. A lot rests on this. We've got to see Cavendish in the morning and it's turned midnight already."

Te Manu wore a long suffering look. He did not need reminding. As Romana led the way down, she apologised to the princess for the necessity of using the back door. "The Captain expressly forbade you to see even a hint of their manly pleasures," she laughed, "but I hope you were entertained enough with Christa and did not find the time tedious."

Tianna exchanged a smile and a guilty secret with Christa, who had followed them down. "It has been very interesting," admitted the princess, thinking back to the antics of the fevered men and women she had seen. "I look forward to returning tomorrow. I hope the seamstresses will not tire themselves too much on my account. Thank you Madame."

Romana beamed. "Such pretty, pretty manners," she cried, dabbing at her eyes. "If only some of that could rub off on my girls, what a happy woman I would be."

Captain Jarrus was there to greet them outside. The night air was still and fragrant with the sweet smell of orange blossom, the perfect white flowers hanging in abundance on the trees near the house. Lamps had been lit, throwing pools of light like glass pebbles onto the path all the way to the harbour. Two bearers stood ready with the trunk and several of the ship's crew waited to escort Tianna to the ship and relieve the first watch from their shift.

She flushed slightly, aware that she had seen them embracing the women and briefly wondered what they would think of her had they known how much she had been affected by their exhibition. The Captain, seeing her dressed so prettily for the first time, complimented her with sincerity. She smiled and dropped her eyes shyly. The girl had no idea how to respond to the complement. Her absence of vanity was very appealing, but said much about the lack of a mother in her life to guide her through such situations and a father who thought all such feminine things too frivolous to encourage. Tonight she was poised between girlhood and womanhood once again and dressed to reveal the beauty of that blossoming, in a shimmering gown.

It is not easy to be on a precipice. One is apt to fall.

"You have achieved well to find so many garments in a short time, Romana," the Captain said.

Romana was pleased. "By morning the best gown will be ready. At what time shall I expect her Highness?" she enquired.

"By mid-morning," he told her. "Then we go to see Cavendish, by mid-day."

"Heavens! That does not give us long, Captain. Dressing a lady in style needs time you know. Can we have longer?"

He laughed. "Alright. Earlier then. Although I can't see anyone in your house fit for waking at such an hour. I am in need of rest to nerve me for the day but shan't get it either."

Madame curtsied. She and Christa withdrew.

Just then the princess saw Rhapsody lying on the ground. Forgetting any royal protocol, if indeed any existed for such situations, she bent down to raise his head upon her lap, her face full of concern.

"Oh, Rhapsody, what happened?" she asked, anxious to hear him speak. The Captain had not bargained for this further delay to her departure.

"Tianna! The man is drunk, and I need to get you out of here quickly. Leave him be."

She hesitated. "But he may be ill," she retorted, defending her action, trying to cradle him against her breast.

"Tianna. I will attend to Rhapsody. It is not safe to linger. Somebody may be watching. Go to the ship at once. That is an Order!"

She got to her feet, the anxiety of leaving her friend registering on her lovely face. One minute a princess, the next a member of the crew and answerable to the Captain. "Aye aye, Sir." she responded as he had taught her to do, trying to effect a salute in her panic.

The incongruity of the situation was not lost on any of them as she saluted in her dazzling vermillion gown that seemed to float as she moved. She could not have looked more beguiling than in that outfit. Tianna hastened away with the bearers and several of Jarrus's men. Roden shook his head with amusement at the retreating figure of the princess. The girl was dazzling.

"Once they reach the galleon she'll be safe enough. It's over to you now, Manu. Make peace."

Out of the shadows stepped Te Manu, who without a word, began to follow the girl towards the ship.

The Captain watched him go, unconvinced, before turning to another of his crewmen. "Give a hand here," he said, indicating Rhapsody who had turned on his side and was now slumbering like a baby.

Chapter Twenty - Enchanted Midnight

Tianna skipped alone in the still night air, with Joshua and Gypsy to escort her just behind and the two bearers ahead, looking out for danger as they went.

Not a leaf stirred on the branches as she passed beneath the trees. Her heart was surprisingly light. Her thoughts were dominated by visions of the thrashing skirts of the dancers and the sounds of the guitars. It awakened romance in her soul. The bearers were well ahead of her with the trunk. The princess held her skirts as the shimmering fabric swept the ground. She danced along, the music from the house still drifting towards them as they went.

"So you are happy tonight and dressed like a real princess," said Joshua, smiling as she twirled around.

"Oh, yes," she sighed. "Tonight I feel as though I could fly." The small golden sandals that she had borrowed were delicate but after a week on the galleon, Tianna wanted to feel the ground beneath her feet. She slipped them off, savouring the freedom of cool grass under her toes. The music now became distant. She stepped as though she might be one of the dancers, her bare feet touching the ground with fairy lightness. The girl attempted to swish her petticoats whilst swinging the sandals around. She tripped and lost her balance but did not fall. Gypsy and Joshua were amused. The princess might imagine she was able to fly, but she had clearly never been taught to dance! They laughed, and so did she. She did not care.

The night was idyllic and the girl relished a freedom so newly acquired which she had started to value very much. She had encountered people and situations today that would never occur in her life at the castle.

Tianna breathed deeply and happily, exhilarated by the night, but above all by the adventure of it all. She was prepared for tomorrow. She did not have any plan for what might happen afterwards and might have to think on her feet, but that was the future. Tianna wanted this night to go on and on.

There were lanterns all along the quayside and lamps had been lit on the galleon, giving it a welcoming glow. The Zenna Marius creaked slightly as she rested upon the water. Tianna understood how the pirates believed the ship possessed life and an ethereal spirit for she was never completely silent or motionless. The princess felt enveloped in the galleon's protection as she came aboard.

Behind her, the revelries of the night continued, but Tianna was content at leaving at this hour. She could not drive the shock of the cavorting men and women from her mind, but this was offset by the kindness she had received and the music that had held her entranced so that overall, the memory of the day would become one satisfying whole.

The bearers deposited the box on the quayside and it was taken on board by Josh and Gypsy, who did not allow them access to the ship. The princess thanked the bearers and they left. She chose to take the smaller of several boxes with her, although her head was still in the clouds as she made her way to the cabin, and singing softly, she day dreamed.

They all exchanged greeting as the first watch was relieved of their duties and eagerly set off for Romana's. The night watch were laughing about something when Gypsy caught sight of Te Manu arriving unexpectedly behind them to go on board. They looked surprised to see him.

"Shit! She won't be dancing about for long if he's coming," said Joshua perceptively.

"What does he want? There are ten of us for the next four hours already," asked Gypsy. They hung around, waiting to find out.

"I think the party just ended for all of us," murmured Josh.

Meanwhile, Tianna felt comfortably alone, fancying that the old ship could speak to her with its comforting noises. She had recovered from the fear that had gripped her on the balcony. Christa said no one had a problem with the warrior and Jonah had said the same. The princess had also been struck by Christa's affirmation that if she had been a princess, she wouldn't be afraid of anyone. However, Tianna had no intention of having her own plans railroaded. Tomorrow everything would change in her life. There was only tonight to get through and then she would never have to set eyes on the warrior again.

In the privacy of the Captain's cabin, the princess unfastened the alluring dress. It had been a refreshing change to wear for a few hours but she had almost forgotten how restrictive a long gown could be. It forced her to take smaller steps. She could neither run nor climb. It limited all movement. The old Tianna would have accepted these restrictions. The new Tianna would not. She searched for her britches and then remembered they had probably been left in the trunk, up on deck. Small matter. She would collect them all in a few minutes. The night was sultry and hot. She searched the boxes she had carried and pulled out a floating, white garment that was sheer and light with a daringly low bodice, but as there would be no one about to see her until morning, it hardly mattered. She loosened her plaited hair, removing the pretty band and went up the steps to retrieve her britches for the start of tomorrow. Tianna was confident she could steal across without being spotted. She knew where Gypsy and Joshua had left the trunk and they would be guarding the ship by the quayside. She paused to gaze dreamily up at the full moon as it cast a silver light upon the water.

Te Manu was preoccupied. In less than twelve hours, a meeting would take place in Governor Cavendish's house, and as things stood, the princess would not participate if he appeared. He left the quayside, protected by the shadows and gave instructions to the night watch who had boarded just ahead of him.

"Patrol once." he ordered. "Then keep your position here. I will be on board for the next hour or so and do not wish to be disturbed. After that time, resume your patrol as normal, understood?"

"Aye aye, Sir," they responded.

Te Manu perfected a severity to maintain discipline of more than forty men. He was not hated. He was respected. Te Manu demanded that and always got it. A man who respects himself will find others respect him also, he said. This self-belief was pivotal to who he was and went back to the days when ignorance and prejudice towards him, on the margins of the gypsy clan, had made his beginnings unendurably difficult. His back still bore the faded, silver scars of childhood beatings. Determined to show no weakness, the youth had worked hard and developed a powerful physique, honing skills that became indispensable to the gypsies. As he grew to adulthood on their perimeters, they began to fear his increasing strength but still needed him, until one night he had seized an opportunity to escape and left them behind forever.

All men were generally wary of Manu, the common feeling being that it was wiser not to upset him. His temper was explosive. His whole adolescence had been spent in the pursuit of power and domination. He had to survive. He must win. He must keep his pride among men. Women, on the other hand, adored him; only the princess could not know that. He was smoulderingly good looking with a way of fixing someone in his gaze that could terrify, but had a primeval magnetism for women. Commanding with a fierce look and few words, his attributes seemed few. A man with scant patience and low tolerance, he abhorred stupidity, ignorance and prejudice but respected intelligence, fearlessness and spirit.

At his core seemed few redeeming features but those that existed were the essence of the man, and had been forged by the deprivations of his childhood. He would rail against injustice and would defend youth. For some reason, they alone saw the raw honesty of the warrior and never had cause to be afraid of him, as Jonah could testify.

He crossed the deck silently and descended to Rhapsody's empty quarters where he removed his footwear, jacket and shirt. Te Manu sat on the edge of the narrow bed to think. The night was oppressively hot, especially down here, but it was some relief to feel air against his bare skin even though he needed to get outside again as soon as possible. The cabin was stifling. The man needed inspiration but found none. He had seen the princess's flight from him less than an hour ago. To move upon her in the cabin would alarm her, to creep upon her stealthily in the gathering darkness was just as bad. He decided the whole situation was bloody stupid and he would stride out there noisily, and command the wretched girl to listen to sense. He would say he wasn't going to hurt her and draw a line under their differences. It was the only way to go. Right? Well, maybe, except that he did not move. Heaving a frustrated sigh, he put his head in his hands and moved his foot. Something engaged with the back of his heel beneath Rhapsody's bed. Instantly remembering what he had left there on their last night on board, he reached down and carefully withdrew what he hoped might become the answer to his dilemma.

Tianna left the moonlight glittering on the peaceful water and crept in the shadows to retrieve the contents of the trunk on deck. She avoided the amber glow that fell in regular streams across the deck, not daring to be seen in her flimsy attire. Her intention was to take the things she needed for the early morning to the cabin and then sleep. However, sleep was only appealing if it allowed her to dream of romance which had begun to stir the girl's embryonic passions. Her fantasies of love, of kisses, all suggested by the girls of the brothel, were very much in Tianna's mind. What must it feel like to be touched by a handsome man? To be kissed? To be held tight in someone's arms? The air was still heavy after a scorching day as she made her way back to the cabin, having not found the trunk. She was puzzled and lingered a while wondering where else to look when she fancied she could hear faint sounds of the gypsy guitars.

The princess stopped. There it was again. The most beautiful sound. She stood absolutely still to listen. It was! It was the spellbinding tune that had captivated her on Madame Romana's balcony, and it was having the same effect on her again. It was such a romantic sound, but was it coming from the distant house or was it in her head? Tianna had the whole deck to herself and could not resist dancing in the darkness, sending the delicate fabric fluttering around her. She opened her arms wide in the darkness and spun around sending the floating garment into a whirl of cloud before it came to rest as light as vapour around her again. Abandoned and carried away by the memory of Romana's house, she was at first only vaguely aware that the music she could hear was almost certainly in the very air surrounding her. The girl stopped quite still to listen. It must be Ezra, she imagined, and forgetting all about the trunk of clothing, she began to follow the sound as if mesmerized.

So quietly into the night sky were those notes played that the princess could not quite trust that they weren't formed from her own imagination. Protected by the cloak of night, she ventured further away from the cabin, bolder than she really wanted to be, curiosity heightened. Standing some distance away with his back towards her, was the silhouette of the player. His knee was bent to support the guitar with his foot upon a trunk. Her trunk of clothing! He faced the moon over the sea. His head was bent slightly forward, towards the instrument that he played. He seemed absorbed and comfortable, his broad shoulders turned away from the softly approaching girl.

Fascinated by the intricacy of the music, Tianna crept forward, barefoot and a little scared, silently approaching the musician. She came closer than might have been wise. The flickering amber lights caught the man's ear ring and glinted upon the gold band tight around his strong upper arm. The girl's pulse quickened. This was not Ezra. She stood stock still, knowing she had come too close. Tianna could feel her heart thumping in her chest, and tried to control it. The man lifted his head, only very slightly, but enough for the girl to give a sharp intake of breath, recognizing in an instant, that the tall, well-built figure in front of her was no other but the warrior !

Rendered motionless with shock, the princess wondered what to do. She was certain he was not aware of her. Perhaps she could take silent steps backwards, retreating into the black night. If she was really careful and controlled each movement with stealth, he need never know she had been there. She recognized the hauntingly beautiful chords as those played by the musician at Romana's house, the same sensuous rhythm that had captivated her then, was her undoing. How could such a savage play with this emotion? She almost derided him more for possessing the skill.

Tianna underwent the same thrill of fear, the danger inherent in igniting this strong, masculine being. She was now, at this moment, closer to him than she had ever been. Panic was uncontrollably seizing the girl, threatening the rhythm of her breathing. The rising palpitations were enough to make her whole body tremble violently. She feared they would give her away, but it was pointless to expend the effort to control herself. Te Manu already knew she was there. His acute hearing missed nothing; He sensed her, and almost imbibed her fear. Guessing her proximity, he knew she would hear him if he spoke. One mistake on his part would send her running from him. Whatever he did next had to cause her to stay. He did not want to spring after her by giving chase and then force her to listen, although he would do it if there seemed no choice. Manu was caught in the moment, just like Tianna. He toyed with the idea of asking her if she remembered hearing the song, but remembered Rhapsody's drunken warning not to ask her any questions. Even when not sober Rhapsody seemed to know what was needed. He had to think, and then, in his mind's eye, Te Manu knew the answer. He saw the girl in a new light:

She reminded him of a fawn, a curious graceful animal which had stepped too close to retreat and would now stare quietly so long as no sudden sound or movement disturbed her. The image ran counter to his baser instinct, where in his imagination, he had already sprung, tightening his hands around her slender wrists, dragging her resistant body hard against his, holding her firmly, needing to subjugate the frightened girl in order to make her listen.

But that is not what you do with a beautiful fawn. You reach out very slowly and with luck, it may even allow you to stroke it. Te Manu would reach her too, and stroke her with words. There was for him, an illicit, sweet satisfaction in knowing he had made an impact on this girl, even though it was fear she displayed. His had become a deliberate game of detachment, when in truth, his fascination with her had been growing steadily over the days. She existed totally beyond his experience in age, in status, in innocence. He had encountered no one like her. She was beyond his reach, yet he wanted to overcome the obstacles that separated them.

Still resisting the urge to turn around, Te Manu continued to play the guitar, but more slowly as though the music was drawing to an end. Closing his eyes to help himself find the perfect timing, he opened his mouth and began to speak with the deep exotic voice that aroused the heat in every woman who heard him. He knew full well that she would hear every word in the near silence of the deserted ship.

"I spoke to Fabian Cavendish today. He told us a lot of things about you, Tianna."

He had spoken her name. The guitar played with tantalizing softness. He could sense her breathing behind him. "He is a wise man, your uncle, dealing with many things. I think we will help each other."

She was startled. It was a shock to find he knew she was there and to hear him say her name made her heart skip a beat. She did not move. It had been clever of him to speak of Fabian. His name was almost guaranteed to hold her attention.

"I misjudged you," he said. His voice was steady. The words were delivered as a statement of fact, not an apology. Tianna was so shocked she could not move. As he spoke, he very slowly turned towards her and gazed upon her exquisite expression. In the moments that followed, when they beheld each other closely for the first time, something profound and inexplicable was exchanged. It was a connection neither could have anticipated or explained.

In those precious seconds, each drank in the physical reality of the other. The warrior's nostrils dilated as he drew a deep breath, his chest expanding as their eyes locked for the first time. It was a defining moment. He saw the perfect symmetry of her face. Her head was tilted ever so slightly, with an expression frozen by fear yet questioning. He searched the flawless softness of her cheek, the lips parted in surprise and above them, round, startled eyes of smoky grey, fringed by long, dark lashes that stared intently into his own. The chemistry between the two of them was instant. His smouldering brown eyes held hers with a language that needed no words. She blinked. The attraction was mutual and could not be disguised. It took him by surprise. Te Manu had never expected to be so powerfully affected. Just as before, when he beheld her on the balcony, he was fighting with himself, resisting the desire to possess her. He knew he must keep talking. While she heard him, she would stay. If he moved suddenly, she would flee. He knew she was intrigued. His penetrative gaze became a shade softer and the beginnings of a smile, almost of satisfaction, lifted the corners of his mouth. She saw it. His eyes began to move very slowly across her body as he spoke quietly, bathing her with his deep, sensuous voice.

She really was a beautiful fawn. Unblinking, doe eyed, soft, timid, curious; giving away nothing in her expression, but looking at him expectantly. She was wary, but just about daring to trust. His voice continued to keep her captive. She was under a spell.

"Rhapsody told me you would not speak," he said, laying aside the guitar with slow deliberation.

Tianna watched the movement with a flicker of tension. She tensed again, ready to dart. Te Manu saw it, but continued to talk quietly, holding the girl with words. "Rhapsody was right, but then, I guess he knows you." He moved one foot towards her. She

262

blinked again, shocked and took a step back. It was now or never. "I would not have hurt you," he said quickly, watching for a reaction. "Nor Ezra. The whip hit the deck, not Ezra."

A slight questioning furrow crossed her brow.

"We had to frighten you enough to get to the truth. Pirates do not make many friends. We had to know if you were an enemy." There was a long pause. The girl swept large eyes across his ruggedly handsome face. She was still embittered for all he had put her through.

"And... do you think me an enemy now?" she asked, nervously, her voice barely more than a hesitant whisper. Immediately his smile widened. Te Manu's little fawn was beginning to paw the ground. She had spoken. No. It was more than that. She had asked him a question. She was going to stand her ground and not run away. The creases at the corners of his molten eyes deepened. "What do I think?" he repeated. "No. I do not think you are an enemy. I think you are bold, determined, and proud. I think a fire burns within you because an injustice has been done to your Island and you desire to right that wrong. I think you believe I have been unjust to you and you are angry with me but still afraid, deeply afraid of me, at the same time."

Tianna's rigid self-defence dropped at the accuracy of his words. It was as if he had fired them from a bow. "Perhaps you are right," she admitted quietly. Her shoulders relaxed a little. She lowered her eyes from his in order to compose herself. Te Manu took the advantage to move closer. She instantly bridled.

He was fully six feet tall, close and intimidating. It was too much. Panic returned, flooding her at his intrusion. The sudden resurgence of alarm could not be contained. Attack being her only defence, the words burst from her lips. "You held a knife to my throat!" she accused him, the mixture of fear and recrimination evident in her voice as she retreated a step, trying to distance herself from this determined being. Te Manu was taken aback. Then, he raised his eyes to the sky. "Oh that!" he breathed out heavily. "It is what I do. It is what I am. I am a pirate, not a shepherd!"

There was a long pause. This exchange was getting him nowhere. He seemed to be searching his mind for a way forward. When he spoke again, he was less intense but his words were delivered with a hint of customary exasperation. "Look, we are pirates. Wanted men. Always suspicious. Never trusting. We take risks. The life hardens a man, but if he's hard, he survives. I have killed, but I never killed just to see a man fall, and I swear no woman or child was ever harmed by me." His face was serious. "You do not need to look so afraid," he said sternly. It sounded like an order.

The princess was in some turmoil, struggling to reconcile herself with all she had heard and how she felt. She was shaking. He had just admitted killing for goodness sake!

"Let me show you," he said, trying to approach her again. She would have none of it and jumped back, leaving him standing. Tianna was drawn to him like a magnet but would not trust him just because he demanded it. "Stay back! You will not touch me. I KNOW that you despise me for daring to board this ship and I told my uncle you will probably try and do away with me." she told him bluntly. Te Manu was surprised. Events had moved on since then. Surely she knew that. This was ridiculous.

Tianna almost believed he could search her mind and read her thoughts and make her do whatever he wanted. His hypnotic hold weakened her defences and frightened her. She had to be angry with him. It was her only weapon. Suddenly he understood what was happening. She had to do this. They needed to argue to find a way forward. Te Manu began to enjoy her.

"Oh. Come on!" he retorted. "Do you really believe the Governor of Petriah would let you sleep here if he thought I would kill you?" She had no answer to that, but frowned, annoyed.

"Haa!" he exclaimed as if he'd gained a victory. Scoring the first point opened the way to win another. "Do you think Jarrus would keep me on board if any harm befell you now? Well. Do you?"

The girl visibly jumped backwards. He was so vehement. She pouted, turned her back on him and folded her arms in defiance of his power, still scared, but also irritated and demonstrating this conversation was going nowhere, she stood her ground, but her mind was racing.

"How can I say anything if whenever I move, you jump like a frightened rabbit?" he complained, mimicking her by turning his back and folding his arms too.

Stalemate.

For a few moments they both stood like that, their backs turned on each other, but knowing the conversation was far from over. He broke the silence. The sensual voice returned and became irresistibly provocative. "I stayed with you all night when you came aboard," he said quietly.

He had delivered the master stroke. She immediately stepped around him, forgetting all her fears, and looked up at his face in total amazement. Her gaze was exquisite. There was something so appealing in her expression that Te Manu was affected deep inside.

"I woke up wearing a shirt," she replied, her eyes darting across his, with the unasked question.

"Mine," he answered, "and yes, I undressed you, but I never did anything to make you ashamed."

Tianna was desperately trying to think back. "Why don't I remember this?" she asked more of herself than him. She struggled to recall anything from her first night in the cabin, upset with her lack of memory.

All thought of running away from the warrior evaporated with this revelation. Tianna needed an explanation. On that terrible night, she had wet herself. It was the last thing she remembered. The humiliation was as real now as it had been then, when she had fallen down. The princess grimaced at what must have followed. She had never considered it before this moment. He had seen what had happened, and Oh for the shame of it! He had removed her soiled garment and dressed her in his own shirt! Is that what he was telling her? Is that really what happened?

"You hit your head on the corner of a packing case. Gideon carried you to the cabin. Roden told me to stay with you." Te Manu explained.

His voice was steady and completely self-assured. Tianna tried desperately hard to recollect any of this. She was discomforted by the lack of memory, unable to guess how much of what he told her was true.

"But you undressed me," she protested in some anguish at this unfair advantage he held over her.

"Twice. If you include now," he commented, drinking in her body, his eyes provocative and seductive, as she stood in shimmering gossamer of white, the lightness of which caught the softest breeze, like a wispy cloud.

"Oh," wailed the princess, realizing the garment was virtually transparent. She was furious with herself, and wrapped the fluttering layers around in a hopeless attempt to conceal herself. She looked ready to cry in frustration.

"It's too late to hide, I've seen you." he said quietly, as if it was of little consequence to him, although the vision of her standing in the lamplight was magical, and was affecting him deeply.

"No it's not," she insisted, distress making her bolder. "I need to take my trunk of clothes to the cabin, and you're standing in front of it."

The dialogue between them was becoming easier. He had her at a disadvantage and was not done with surprises. She was weakening. He was growing stronger. "I kissed your lips in the cabin that night," he told her, provocatively.

"You did not!" she countered, crossly.

He was amused by her protest. "I had to," he replied, provocatively. Te Manu was enjoying this. Every word he spoke was true.

"What do you mean, you had to?" she demanded, forgetting to be afraid any longer.

"You'd had nothing to eat or drink all day for all we knew. You had been unconscious. I tried to rouse you to take water. It was the Captain's orders. It was not easy to keep you awake, or get you to open your mouth and so..." He stopped talking, and watched her.

"And? And so what?" Tianna had to find out.

Her eyes widened with an expression almost irresistible to him. It was taking all his self-control not to touch her. He looked at her intently, captivated by her questioning gaze. "I moistened your lips with drops of water and kissed them until you responded to me." There was a sharp intake of breath. Her face was a picture of bewildered shock as she tried to assimilate the information. He waited.

"And... did I?" she enquired almost too timid to hear the answer.

"You did," he answered "I roused you several times and got you to drink by kissing you, before you turned back to sleep." The effect upon the girl was profound. Te Manu watched as she struggled with the information, his smouldering eyes concentrated on her face. He was so close to her now, but she hardly noticed. Her mind was whirring.

"I'll show you if you like," he said quietly, lowering his face towards hers. A small noise escaped her mouth. It was nerves, fear and anticipation all at once. He pulled back to look at her. His face was severe, his eyebrows questioning, but his voice was not. It bathed and caressed her with a sensuality she could not resist.

"It was only a kiss," he chided her. "You do not need to fear it. Close your eyes. Do this for me,"

There was an insistence to the man. His strong, dark voice resonated not only in her ears, but somewhere deep inside her being. Waves rippled throughout Tianna's body that took her breath away. Her eyelids closed, the lashes sweeping her cheeks. Her heart was pounding. He was hypnotic. She felt the lightest, kiss upon her forehead and another fell softly upon her closed eyes. The girl melted at the whisper of his warm lips as they brushed her face, with tiny kisses.

She could not believe his tenderness. It was in total contrast to his severe manner. She succumbed to this first touch. The tension in her body began to subside. She was floating away. She wanted him.

Te Manu drew his fingers under the girl's ear, along her jaw line until he reached her chin. She felt the pressure of his thumb as he tilted her face up to meet his. There was a growing insistence to his movements.

"Keep still," he said very quietly. "Don't move."

She held her breath. His finger stroked the outline of her mouth and suddenly Tianna felt a soft but firm pressure against her lips. He kissed her lightly once, twice... and then, combing his fingers through her long hair, tilted her head slightly to one side. Her eyes opened to see his own focus intently upon her mouth.

Te Manu's heart was pumping faster, fuelling his strength to even greater purpose. The girl sensed his whole being was becoming more powerful, more focused, if that were possible. She felt his energy, a force that told her there was no going back, and he would ignore all resistance. He was in control of her and she felt her own defences slipping away as powerful feelings washed over her, and she became completely absorbed in his sensuous touch.

Massaging the back of her head, his lips descended upon hers with new determination. She felt his tongue forcing her lips apart and her breathing quickened, as she started to panic, frightened, not only by him, but by the heated sensations flooding her mind and body. Feeling the tension in her, Te Manu stopped and drew back just enough to look at her again, trying to appraise what was happening. She felt she would drown in those dark eyes. Unlike his slow, controlled breaths, hers were fluttering with nerves. Her heart pounded. The girl could not cope and she drew back from him in sudden panic.

Te Manu knew he could lose her in that moment. she could run away and they would become enemies once again. He had to do something and fast, but what? *"Kiss de girl."* Rhapsody had said. Well, he was trying his best. Manu grasped her hands firmly, and decided that was exactly the way he had to go.

"You're hurting me. Let me go." she protested.

Instead, he raised her hands aloft so that her arms encircled his neck, drawing her closer to his body than ever, stifling her protests.

The princess felt Te Manu's arms slide beneath hers, and cross the small of her back, drawing her body up hard against his, enveloping her in his tight hold, as he lowered his mouth upon her lips once more. This time, she could not move at all.

"It is only a kiss." he murmured, urging her forward, his hot breath falling onto her cheek. Oh but it was heady stuff. His probing tongue resolutely parted her lips further. Secure in his arms, Tianna stopped struggling as the first waves of desire washed over her and she finally gave herself up to the man she had condemned less than an hour ago. While his tongue searched her mouth, awakening sensations that she could not control, Manu rotated his hips against the girl. She experienced his heat and his passion until, completely lost in his embrace, every part of her body yearned to be in contact with his. She could not help herself. She instinctively moved with him.

Tianna felt a throbbing sensation as the blood rushed to her sex, his kisses weakening and loosening all her resistance to him. The dominance of his lips on hers, whilst exploring her mouth, was felt in the depths of her body as if his tongue caressed her inside. Her arms dropped from his neck, as her legs buckled and she moaned, her fingers opening and closing, clawing his forearms, as she scratched the coarse hair that grew on his skin. She was intoxicated by the man. She absorbed his taste, his body heat, his breathing, as she responded to his control. Te Manu did not want to release the stunning girl. Astounded that she was responding so sensually to him, he held her all the more tightly against his groin. Conscious of becoming swollen and heavy, losing all sense of responsibility and reason, Te Manu rotated his hips, pressing his pelvis forward, forcing the girl to feel the full extent of his arousal, throbbing through his clothing against her own sexuality. Unbelievably, her body swayed with his. They were oblivious to anything else. Unlocked by the most passionate kiss, the chemistry between them rose like smoke from two fires, curling together, inseparable and drifting skyward.

It was past one o'clock. The second watch had waited the hour and were starting to patrol the ship. Te Manu suddenly heard them talking in the distance, and came to his senses. Instantly alert, he pulled Tianna even deeper into the shadows. Her own dreamy eyes opened. "Sshh!" he told her, pressing a finger against her lips. "It's the night watch."

She blinked at him and turned her head. The warrior exhaled deeply, needing some minutes to come down from his plateau, not fully knowing what he had done. He continued to hold the girl closely. Both needed time to recover. "Hush now." he warned her. The princess nodded, but she was shaking. "We're alright here for a short time," he said. Her head rested on his perspiring chest. Against her ear was the steady drum of his strong heartbeat. They were hot. She nuzzled against him, breathing in his unique masculine smell, feeling his chest hair against her cheek, supported and comfortable in his arms. She wanted to stay there forever. Te Manu's mind was working fast. "Listen to me, Tianna. I have to speak to the men, then I must go to the tavern to meet the Captain before I rest. You must go to the cabin. Get some sleep."

She nodded. He searched her face as if they might never be so close again, and he needed to memorize every detail of the girl before they parted.

"It is just as well they came. I only meant to kiss you. I took you too far." he confessed. "Come with me quickly now." He took her hand and hastened to the cabin steps. Just outside, he withdrew something from his belt. It was a gold band. "Give me your ankle," he said. She didn't understand.

"Quickly, your ankle." he repeated impatiently, bending down.

"Oh!" She comprehended at last, as he grabbed her leg. The warrior unclasped the gold piece and placed it upon her, locking it into place. He stood up and looked steadfastly into her eyes, placing the small key into the locket he wore around his neck. "When you waken, you will know tonight was no dream. You wear pirate gold now. Like all of us. One day, I will explain what this means. For now, all you need know is that you are one of us, and that I will protect you, just as we protect each other." He stepped away from the girl, his demeanor changing, already distancing himself from her, he drew himself up tall. "Now GO," he commanded her, severely, with all the usual authority returning to his voice. The princess obeyed instantly, narrowly missing the approaching night watch as she slipped silently into the cabin. Te Manu went towards his men. The usual glower had returned to his eyes.

Chapter Twenty One - Roden's Idea

Te Manu walked towards the crewmen. He felt rejuvenated, energized but also mystified by something going on within himself that he would not find words to describe. Two other members of Jarrus's crew had brought Rhapsody with them, who they had half walked, half dragged back to the galleon.

"Where shall we put him, Sir?" they wanted to know. "Throw him into one of the cots," answered the warrior. "There won't be many returning tonight. He can sleep it off there."

Te Manu left instructions for one of them to guard the cabin where the princess would be sleeping, then he sprinted through the town to meet the Captain.

It was already half past one when he arrived to find Roden sitting alone in this comfortable hostelry, reclining in an ample chair, planning for the days ahead. His crowded thoughts and ideas needed voicing and he wasted no time in coming to the point.

"By eleven o'clock I have to tell Cavendish whether we are sticking with them in their troubles or sailing away. Either way, I don't believe Petriah has enough resistance to outflank Scalos. They are too slow in reacting and have no idea of Lussac's strength."

Te Manu sat down in the opposite chair, turning Jarrus's paperwork towards him.

"I may be wrong. They may be evenly matched. I don't know where Cavendish might obtain ships, but the outcome is far from certain. If we pull away, we leave them to face it alone," he continued.

Te Manu fixed Roden with a comprehending look.

"And you don't want us to pull out and leave the princess heading in another direction," he concluded.

"Right." admitted the Captain.

"So where does Cavendish have in mind for her?" asked Te Manu.

"I don't know," answered Jarrus, "But I think she's safer kept on board with us for the time being."

Te Manu thought back to his recent amorous encounter with Tianna and briefly wondered if Jarrus ought to redefine the word "safe." His face, however, betrayed nothing of what he had done. Roden had the ghost of an idea forming in his mind. It was vague, but he was working on it. His mind was not on Tianna.

"What would you look for if you were trying to identify a ship far out to sea?" he asked Manu.

"What?"

"Come on. What would you look for?" He repeated the question. Manu was finding it hard to think of anything but Tianna. "How far out?" he said at last.

"Just beyond clear visibility. Still in your line of vision, but only just." Te Manu considered.

"The number of masts. Two or three would give me her size," he said. "The figurehead if she was in profile. The colour of her flags, and if I could see them, the cannon portals. Why?"

Roden Jarrus leaned forward. "And first. What would you notice first?"

"The colour of the flags she was flying, I guess," reasoned the warrior. He could not for the life of him see why Roden had become so intense.

"Exactly!" said Jarrus. The colour. Now, suppose you recognised the flags, would you carry on trying to identify it?"

"Probably not, or at least, I'd assume that if everything else seemed okay, I wouldn't make too close a study of her. If the ships were where I expected them to be, I'd read the flags."

"That's it exactly!" agreed Jarrus, thumping the table. "If you expected them to be there, you'd accept you'd read them right."

"What is this all about?" asked Te Manu, who was tired. The Captain did a quick calculation of whether his first officer might be receptive to hearing a wild idea. He decided to go for it. "We persuade Lussac that we support his attack on Auretanea, and then we double cross him."

"What?" responded Te Manu, not believing what he had heard.

"We find out just how many ships and men he's got," Jarrus replied.

"You mean we actually go to Scalos and call on him?" asked Te Manu,

"And offer him our support," added the Captain.

"Really?" commented Manu, dryly. "You think he's going to want our support?"

"I can persuade him to it," suggested Roden.

Te Manu did not want to play devil's advocate, but had to point out they had nothing to bargain with, except their ship, which had all but two cannons left, having been stripped out years before Jarrus had even acquired it. Roden was forced to admit the idea was crazy. He got up to leave the tavern, still wrestling with some half-baked notion to outsmart the Baron, while Te Manu told him once more that the idea was insane. They decided to walk back to the galleon. Neither man wanted to leave Tianna on board all night without being there.

"Did you talk to her?" asked Roden, as they neared the ship.

"I did." Manu confirmed.

In their manly arrogance, they assumed that presenting the girl to her uncle wearing a clean gown and in a decent state of health would be about the extent of their obligation. The fact that neither of them considered any contribution from Tianna at tomorrow's meeting, merely confirmed their lack of foresight. It only mattered to the Captain that she didn't appear terrified of them and thus cause her uncle to think she had been mistreated.

"So, is the princess alright with you now?" Roden persisted after an interval. Te Manu gave his friend a keen look. "I am okay with her. She is okay with me," he replied and would not give away one word more. Roden frowned slightly, not believing it had been quite that simple. The two men approached the ship.

Chapter Twenty Two - Turnaround

Tianna had entered the cabin as if on a cloud. Once inside, she had flung open her arms in a gesture of abandonment at the memory of her entire evening at Romana's and what had just happened on board. She twirled around, euphoric. Passionately stirred up and thrilling with excitement, Tianna found it almost impossible to rest. She rolled on the bed, staring into darkness, exhilarated. Once or twice she grinned or began to giggle, alone with her thoughts. Tianna could hardly believe what had taken place and relived every word spoken. She recalled the warrior's richly sensuous voice, his smell, his touch, all the sensations flooded her mind until she was intoxicated all over again. It was madness, but she couldn't rest.

When the princess eventually calmed down, she reached for the gold band that Te Manu had placed around her ankle. It was reassuringly solid. It was neither a dream nor her imagination. The warrior had been alone with her and he had kissed her. "Pirate gold," he had told the girl. "Now you are one of us." She sighed, liking the sound of it.

Suddenly, she sat bolt upright and began to think. She had no plan for what happened after tomorrow. Tianna had only asked for passage to Petriah. No one would be expecting her to be on board after tonight. She would have to watch the galleon leave without her. "It isn't what I want!" she declared, with rising emotion. Since Te Manu had aroused her passion, she did not want to be left behind. The more she tried to find reasons for travelling with them, the more logical the ideas became. She must find a way of being indispensable to the Captain and what better opportunity than tomorrow. With schemes and ideas running helter skelter through her mind, Tianna eventually fell asleep.

On the far side of the Zenna Marius, in the airless night, Te Manu, Jarrus and Rhapsody would all sleep on deck in temporary hammocks or cots hooked to the rails, which they sometimes did on balmy evenings. They were tired, sexually gratified and in Rhapsody's case, slowly emerging from a deep restorative sleep. He massaged his temples with his fingertips, not quite sure how he'd got there.

Te Manu lay in a hammock, arms behind his head, staring up at the density of stars though focusing on nothing in particular. The hammock was slung low enough for him to have one foot upon the floor, with which he was slowly rocking. Across his generous lips, a wry smile played. There was no mistaking the newfound contentment on Te Manu's face. His eyes had a faraway look. For him, the day couldn't have ended better.

Roden Jarrus relaxed nearby. He had got nothing out of his friend save for the affirmation that he and the princess had made their peace. Rhapsody, despite suffering from a hangover, was determined to find out more. "You kiss de girl like I told you, man?" he enquired lazily. Te Manu turned his head in Rhapsody's direction.

"Uh Huh!" he answered.

"You *kissed* her?" interrupted Roden, sitting up.

"Uh Huh!" Te Manu responded.

Rhapsody let out a long howl of approval, which ended in a groan as he clasped his aching head.

"Was it good, man?" he continued, although pain shot through his temples.

"Uh Huh!" came the reply.

"You *kissed* the princess?" interrupted the Captain again, incredulous at the nerve of the warrior. Rhapsody chuckled, then groaned. "De princess like you better now, man?" he probed, enjoying every minute, despite suffering.

"Uh Huh!" re-joined Te Manu.

Roden was astounded. He hadn't seen Te Manu this laid back in months, but how far had this gone?

"I don't believe I'm hearing this," said Jarrus, running his hands across his head. "You kissed her?"

"Uh Huh!" Te Manu said again.

The Captain got up. "Don't bullshit me, Manu. If you set this up to have your way with the girl, you'll tell me now."

"Look. I kissed her. Alright?" admitted the warrior. His manner became terse. Rhapsody tried to sit up. His head hurt and he shut his eyes, lowering himself back down, as if dazed. "Hey man. Cool it," he said, clasping his head.

Roden wasn't for stopping. "Did you move in on her?" he demanded. He was wondering whether confronting Manu was enough, or he should go the extra distance and break his neck.

"I kissed the girl. That was it," Manu repeated, determined not to become angry.

"I believe him. There weren't no time to do more with her." said Rhapsody, opening one eye. He spoke from experience.

"You'd know more ways than most of us. He'd have had time. What I want to know is, how far did he get?" retorted the Captain.

It was true, Rhapsody was an opportunist when it came to seduction. Te Manu was getting fed up with the inquisition. "I kissed her for fuck's sake. The next watch started patrolling the deck. I told her to go to bed. Then I came to the tavern to see you. End. Ask her if you're so bloody sure there's more," said Te Manu, with finality.

Jarrus relaxed. "Okay," he said, "but this whole episode could backfire and end very badly for us. Just remember that."

Te Manu acknowledged that Roden was right. The immediate danger of a run in with the Captain had just passed. He would not admit how close he came to taking the princess further. Rhapsody lay back, happy.

"It's alright man. It's all...right," he soothed with a slurred voice. "You want me to shut up now?" he asked with a huge grin.

"Uh Huh!" answered Manu closing his eyes.

"You got it man," said Rhapsody, happily.

The Captain shook his head. It was past two in the morning. In five hours they would have to be up. Roden wondered what the princess would be like later.

"I never expected things to go this far," thought the Captain, wondering if this would cause more problems than it solved. He was still angry when sleep finally overcame him.

Several hours later, Tianna was disturbed from a deep sleep by the arrival of the Captain. He hastened to the cabin, not hesitating to enter, banging the door behind him. He immediately began looking for things. The girl raised her head but would like to have slept longer. She groaned.

"You'd better wake up," he said. "A lot will happen today. Here, read this." and he threw a message on to the bed whilst raising a foot on the long bench to fasten the buckle of his boot.

Tianna sat up bleary eyed and combed her long hair back through her fingers. The note was to advise them that a meeting of some kind had been arranged with luncheon at one o'clock for as many attendees as could be assembled in so short a time. It was signed, Cavendish.

"The note is rather cryptic," commented the Captain, "but then I suppose he didn't want to risk saying too much in case it got intercepted before we meet him at eleven."

"Who is meeting him at eleven?" she asked.

"You, me and Te Manu." he answered.

The Captain slung his wide belt around his waist and began to fasten it.

"Do you hear all this, Tianna? We need to be prepared for today."

She watched him rushing about. "I know," she answered, sleepily.

"Well, should you not rouse yourself? You will see your uncle today." She smiled to herself. The Captain did not know of her earlier meeting with Cavendish at Romana's house.

"Have you prepared for what you will say to him?" he asked her, concerned for her reply.

"I have," she replied, simply.

Rolling on to one side, the princess produced two scrolls and sat up, careful to keep the blanket high over her scant clothing. "I worked on these most nights while I've been in your cabin."

"Have you, indeed!" replied Jarrus, alarmed.

He unrolled one but gave it only the most cursory attention. It carried no reference to himself or Manu, Just lines and lines about Baron Lussac and the threat to Auretanea. If that was all she had to say to Cavendish, it was a relief after the revelations of last night. "You wrote all this?" he commented, suitably surprised, before carelessly tossing the scroll back to her. "We've got to get the Zenna Marius out of these waters soon, because I'm not hanging around once word is out that you are here, and it isn't safe for my crew either. Your uncle wants us to find you a safer place than Petriah for the time being. So, whatever your reservations are about my first officer, I need him here, now."

The princess seemed to come alive at his words, suddenly remembering last night. The memory of Te Manu was instantly restored to her mind. She reached for the gold anklet and felt its reassuring presence. It wasn't a dream! It was there, solid and as real as she was, placed by the man who had caused her such a restless night. She threw herself back into the pillows with an enormous, ecstatic sigh, and a dreamy smile remembering everything, not least the sensations he had aroused in her.

Roden Jarrus watched her reaction obliquely, but guessed it had everything to do with Te Manu's method of making peace with females. He left the cabin abruptly to find the warrior and show him Cavendish's note. "Oh Hell!" he despaired inwardly, looking at the languid girl. "TIANNA! GET UP! We leave on the hour." he yelled.

"What have you done to her?" demanded the Captain, accusingly, as soon as Te Manu had read the message.

"What do you mean?" he replied, still holding the unread note in his hand.

"The princess. Soon as I mentioned your name, it's like she's lost her senses, sighing, throwing herself back on the bed, no idea about how late wer'e gonna be if we don't move soon." complained Jarrus.

"That was what you wanted, wasn't it?" asked Te Manu.

"I told you to talk to the princess, not start making love to her!" argued the Captain.

"Well, it just kind of... you know." answered Te Manu, defensively. "You got your result."

"Why is it always extremes with you!" protested Jarrus, but he didn't wait for an answer.

"Come on!" he said, striding towards the cabin, irritably. "I just hope she's really okay with you and we're not back to square one."

Refreshment for the three of them had already arrived by the time Jarrus opened the door and Tianna was sitting on the long bench, waiting. It was the first time she had ever seen the warrior by day in such close proximity and she had never been in the cabin with them both before. Jarrus sat down opposite the girl and immediately tore open a roll of bread for himself. He caught sight of the princess looking round eyed at her conqueror.

Te Manu, still standing, massaged the gold locket he always wore around his neck in which he had placed the key to the ankle band she now wore. He gave her a long look as he fondled it. The gesture was not lost on the girl. Their eyes held each other and needed no translation. They read each other intuitively, remembering last night. The Captain sensed this unspoken transmission going on and was compelled to break it. "Oh for pity's sake," he exclaimed, thrusting the plate of rolls with excessive force at Tianna to break the spell. The plate caught her in the chest. As bread went all over the table, she caught some along with the Captain's reproof, and gave him a small, apologetic smile.

"Hmmm," he muttered, watching her. She knew the real rebuke would be for Te Manu and not her. The warrior was unperturbed. He brought three tankards to the table in his fists and poured liquid into each, placing one before Tianna, before serving the Captain and himself. It was a simple gesture, but a significant one, aligning the three of them for the first time.

The men talked as they ate. Beneath the table, Te Manu accidentally encountered the girl's small bare foot as he stretched his legs. He pressed his naked foot upon hers. Their eyes met. She bit her lower lip and looked down. She did not move as the men continued talking. Had Jarrus been aware of it, he would have exploded with anger and belted him, and Manu would have found himself on a charge, or embroiled in a fight, or both, but the incident passed without him being betrayed.

The girl listened to their conversation, knowing the answers to things they did not. She wisely kept her counsel. They were too dominant a force on the galleon. She would wait. The princess heard their opinions of the Baron, of the possible might of Scalos, of the options open to Cavendish, but not once did they think to include her or invite her opinion. To them, she was a pretty little thing who needed protection. Tianna brought to mind her beloved father's wisdom. It served her well as she sat quietly in the pirate's company. "Diplomacy is a skill. Learn what to say, how to say it and to whom you say it with utmost care, but most of all, learn when to speak and when to listen, for timing is everything." The princess smiled inwardly, and remained quiet.

Jarrus decided to send Tianna to Romana's house with an escort while he honed ideas to present to Governor Cavendish. To that end he continued to bounce suggestions off Te Manu. The bread rolls and tankards served to hold down maps as they contemplated the aggressive threat to the sea straits posed by Scalos and the impact such action would have on their freedom. They still had not decided if they were simply going to sail away, and considered that during the conversation with the Governor at eleven o'clock, Jarrus would decide how soon they departed, with or without the princess. There was the matter of corpses in the mortuary. If and when that news broke, it would be better if the pirates were elsewhere. Cavendish was obliged to address the matter, it was unavoidable. All in all, matters weighed heavier on the Captain's mind the longer he stayed.

Tianna walked beside Rhapsody, with pirate escorts ahead and behind, covering the short distance to Romana's house. Jarrus was taking no chances about a possible kidnap and considered that keeping her identity secret was, like the murders, impossible to conceal for much longer. He chose not to alarm her with that thought. Rhapsody was in high spirits and did not appear to be suffering any hangover.

"Well, a sure lot of things is happening with you," he said as they left the ship.

The girl beamed at him, considering Rhapsody to be her friend and ally. "Rhapsody, I am not afraid of pirates anymore," she declared, confidently.

"Well, that's no good thing. Some pirates are real bad. Don't you go joining no other pirate ship, cos it sure as hell won't be like this one!" he advised.

Tianna laughed. "I won't be looking for another one," she promised. "I just wanted you to know I'm not afraid of anyone on this galleon."

Well, that's okay with me." he joked. "I told you that you got them all wrong 'bout flogging and shooting an' them things. Now you know Rhapsody told you right, girl."

"Oh, Rhapsody! You were right," she sighed.

"Somet'ing happen las' night?" he asked, knowing full well it had, and at his own suggestion. She danced along the path to Romana's house. He grinned and joined the beat, doing steps of his own. "You gonna tell what happened?" he suggested.

"Oh, I want to, but I can't. I just can't," she replied, dreamily.

He shook his head, sending the long beaded plaits bouncing around his ears, and laughed at her. Funny how Te Manu and the princess had managed to tell him everything without saying anything at all. Rhapsody took delight in all kinds of mischief and approved wholeheartedly of the skip in her step this morning. "He sure as hell kissed that girl," he said to himself as they went inside the house.

Chapter Twenty Three - Celeiro

"Is Captain Jarrus here?" enquired the small, slightly stout man with grey frizzed hair standing at the quayside. "It really is most important that I find him."
Several of the crew were on deck, but did not seem inclined to be helpful, and eyed the newcomer suspiciously. They stared at the overdressed little man, who glanced at their naked torsos with apprehension and distaste. The pirates made him all too aware of the knives they carried and which one of them had now drawn, casually fingering the hilt and turning it over.
"Who wants him?" demanded Israel, with an unfriendly tone, pointing the dagger at the stranger, which caused the poor fellow to jump and stumble over his reply.
"My...My name is Ce...Celeiro... Sir," he offered,
"and I come on an errand of some urgency." He swallowed.
Gypsy had also approached and frightened the man further by walking slowly around him in a circle, observing his dress and curious at Celeiro's almost effeminate appearance and manner. He grinned at Israel as if they might have some fun with the unfortunate dandy placed between them.
Roden and Te Manu came up the steps from the cabin, unaware there was a visitor. Celeiro was just about to make enquiries of them, when he was arrested by the powerful presence of the warrior, and took a step back. Roden appeared alongside him.
"Captain Jarrus?" enquired the poor fellow, in some desperation. "I really must see him. I come from Governor Cavendish."

Te Manu and the others continued to stare at the stranger in a most suspicious fashion, which was thoroughly disconcerting for him, but their Captain introduced himself. "We were just preparing to go and see Cavendish," he said.

"And I come to tell you. DON'T. Not now. Not yet," added Celeiro, keeping a nervous eye on the warrior and the other two semi naked pirates.

"You'd better explain," commented Jarrus, and indicated a couple of stacking crates where they might sit. Celeiro took one gratefully. "There has been another murder," said he. "Found floating in the water with his throat cut, just like the others. The body was discovered at first light this morning."

"I see." said Jarrus slowly, as he looked at Te Manu for his reaction, "and the implication being?"
He already guessed the answer.

"The Governor is with a man called Salgari who is calling for immediate action. Salgari is whipping up antagonism against your presence in Petriah, Captain. He wants the Governor to have you arrested on suspicion of murder at once,"

"I see." said Jarrus "and have you come to arrest me?"

At this question, the crew took a step nearer as though they were closing in. They would easily cause the visitor to exit in a hurry. Celeiro looked astonished by the Captain's question. "No. I come to warn you," he explained. "The Governor has told Salgari he has called a luncheon with all the dignitaries he could summon and that it is to discuss the situation in Auretanea. Therefore, he refuses to do anything until the luncheon has taken place. Salgari has issued an ultimatum, that because Governor Cavendish's association with pirates implicates him, he must either arrest you this day or step down from office. He has a stay of execution only because of the luncheon, but after that, Salgari and Rastille and others will call for a vote of no confidence in Cavendish. There is deep division here in Petriah, Captain, and the citizens are uneasy about the rumoured developments in Auretanea. Men who have so far not fallen in with Salgari will not ignore murder, especially when it is discovered we suppressed what occurred yesterday. They will vote against Cavendish for certain. Salgari and Rastille will almost certainly use the meeting to deliver this at the end."

Roden Jarrus considered the situation.

"Does Salgari know the princess is here?"

"No," Celeiro confirmed. "The Governor told no one in case she was kidnapped."

"Good," said Jarrus, "and I take it that nobody can take action against me or any of my crew until after the meeting?"

"Yes. In theory, but there is an uneasy peace, Captain, and I strongly advise that your men return quickly and you prepare to leave at once."

The Captain's eyebrows rose.

"I cannot do that," he replied.

"Why on earth not?" asked Celeiro, greatly concerned.

"Because of the princess. We cannot leave her here. If the Governor is toppled, what happens to her?"

Celeiro had no reassuring answer.

"You see," went on the Captain, "whether it is dangerous or not, we have an appointment with Cavendish that we intend to keep."

Celeiro looked at him with considerable respect, but tinged with growing anxiety at what may happen.

"Oh dear, Oh dear," he replied "I will go and tell him so, right away. I don't know what he'll say."

Te Manu watched the retreating figure.

"I take it then, we are now staying?" he asked.

"You bet we are," answered Jarrus. "As protectors of Her Royal Highness, the princess, and that means we are in this up to our necks!"

Chapter Twenty Four - Assembly

Within the hour, Tianna had received every pampering that could be bestowed upon her. Everyone had worked hard with the hours left to them to ensure the princess looked and felt the part she needed to portray. She was pleased that her uncle had supported her wish for an open assembly, where ordinary citizens as well as those in office would attend. He had promised to send messengers further afield to bring in a greater number from across the land. No doubt the ordinary citizens were a safer audience than many who purported to be Fabian's own supporters.

She knew there were several treacherous men in office, who would be surprised by her unexpected appearance today. What reaction those dignitaries would give to her arrival could only be guessed, but at eleven o'clock, her arrival in Petriah would be announced using criers and heralds and the ensuing excitement should guarantee a packed assembly. Although, very soon, the whole of Petriah might be talking about her imminent arrival, the princess was sure nobody would guess where she was being dressed and still less, who her travelling companions had been. She bathed again.

Her hair was swept up as she sat before the mirror. The gown was of such fine craftwork that Tianna was astonished by the seamstresses work. A cloak had been fashioned to slip around her shoulders. The result was an amazing transformation and everyone in the room stared appreciatively at what had been achieved. Romana had more surprises. "Whilst you are away today, these good ladies will fashion one or two things to make you more comfortable. The cobbler has also been asked for his assistance and if you are pleased by his efforts, wonders if he might hang a notice to say he made footwear for a princess?"

Tianna laughed and agreed.

"But who asked the cobbler?" she wanted to know.

"Why, the Captain, your Highness, and it was him who made the suggestion for the other garments."

"What other garments?" the girl asked.

"Items for use on the ship," Madame replied.

Tianna was taken aback. Did this mean the Captain was expecting to take her on to a place of safety as he had mentioned this morning? Her uncle had said nothing about this in their hurried conversation yesterday, but in fairness, there had been so much for them both to impart during their short meeting, that time had passed in a flash.

"So we will alter a few shirts and britches to match your size and the cobbler will bring boots." Romana swept on, leaving the princess to digest the implications of all she was saying. Boots? Britches? These were not the items of a lady being escorted elsewhere. Tianna began to smile.

Leaving the galleon, Te Manu and Roden had very little idea of what lay ahead. There had been no word from Cavendish on how the princess was supposed to arrive at his house only that he expected to see them all at eleven o'clock. They anticipated the princess attending a luncheon of some sort, without knowing where they should dwell as it commenced, because as pirates, they could not expect to be invited. Since Celeiro's unexpected visit, they were understandably apprehensive about Cavendish's survival and what that might mean for Tianna.

"Is she expected to say something at this meeting," asked the warrior, as they trudged along, looking furtively around them as they progressed.

"I doubt it," answered Roden, "but according to Celeiro, Cavendish wanted to use the luncheon to discuss Auretanea, so maybe she will be asked questions about the welfare of her people while they are eating."

"Then what do we do after?" Manu wanted to know.

"Then we get away as quickly as possible, because much as I like the Governor, I can't see any way he's going to stay in office. I will ask Cavendish beforehand, to get the princess out to us before the meeting is over." The crew of Zenna Marius had been recalled after Caleiro's disturbing news and would be ready to depart as soon as the Captain returned. As they regrouped, the two men were nearing Romana's house.

In the upstairs room of the brothel, much progress had been made.

"Now, I will show you another thing." Madame Romana was in full flight and quite unstoppable. She produced two handsome capes. "One is for the Captain and one is for his first officer. I mean them no disrespect when I say this, for they are good men, but there is a difference, if you know what I mean, between them and the Governor, in the matter of dress, shall we say. I know how stubborn the Captain can be and nothing on this earth can make the man do what he doesn't want, as Fabian, I mean, your uncle, will bear me out, but these are rich, masculine and becoming garments, if they could be so persuaded," she ended, breathlessly. The princess laughed gaily.

"Why, these are in keeping with my own, Madame, and very subtle to suggest that the wearers and I are linked in some way. It is very clever. I hope they see the advantage and accept the dress for the occasion."

Madame Romana beamed. "It was the left over fabric, your Highness, and I did wonder if you would object on those grounds, but I see you are entertained by my idea and it would give those two the appearance of being gentlemen, if they are to escort you by carriage."

The seamstresses and Madame were deeply gratified by the enthusiasm of the princess. It was approaching eleven o'clock when Romana opened the double doors on to the balcony and saw Captain Jarrus and Te Manu entering the hall below. In great excitement, she hastened down the stairs to greet them, before running immediately back up the stairs in a flurry of anticipation. "Your Highness! They are here!" she called, flinging open the doors, ready for the dignified and composed princess to pass through. Tianna seized control of the moment. Until now, she had been under the command of the Captain. She was about to turn the tables. She wondered how they would react.

At the foot of the staircase, the two men watched Romana's comical ascent and deduced from her flustering they would be late for their appointment with Cavendish once again. They waited without much in the way of expectation and were therefore unprepared for the impact when it came.

Suddenly they stared at the top of the stairs and their faces changed so totally that Madame almost wept with joy. Above them, the princess stood, a radiant beauty with an aura of supreme self-assurance. She was like a thing of fantasy. An aura surrounded her which was ethereal. Te Manu and Roden were entranced. She descended slowly, with lightness and grace in her steps, the train of her turquoise gown slipping like a waterfall behind her on the stairs. Tianna's movements were fluid as she came closer to her protectors. Her slender arms were caressed by long silk gloves of matching colour, her bodice was tight across the swell of her breasts and tapered to the fitted waist where gold embroidery edged the flowing skirt falling to the floor like a pool around her feet. She was illuminated by the sunlight shining upon her from the glass dome above which caught the sparkling tiara in her hair. Her smile was demure, her face, tranquil. She paused at the third step where the stairway widened, and met the overwhelmed gaze of the two men who had called for her.

Only at this moment could either Roden or Te Manu begin to assimilate the true significance of having a princess standing before them. Romana's excitement had brought forth the entire occupants of the house. The ground floor swelled with the domestic staff while the young brothel girls, who had run down the back stairs, out of one door and in through the front, jostled to see Tianna. Others peered over the balcony while still more waited to see her in the garden.

Romana held the capes for the men, who, adopting the same dignity as the princess, accepted them without a murmur. Tianna smiled warmly at this, and took the last remaining steps to stand before them. Madam Romana curtseyed low, and like ripples on a pond, the rest of the household followed. The Captain and Te Manu watched the spontaneous gesture, awed by the deference shown to the beautiful young girl. It seemed the most natural reaction to bow, and they did, before turning to escort her through the door. Outside, a carriage, sent by Cavendish, awaited the princess.

The three of them took their leave of the house and its occupants, as if they were taking part in a pageant. The princess waved a gloved hand to the people around and behind her. She had been transformed from the barefoot and dirty urchin who had been jostled in the market square and who had lowered her head in shame when the three ignorant girls from the brothel had sniggered at her clothes.

Te Manu could not take his eyes from her. There was something in her demeanour that neither he nor Jarrus had seen before. It simultaneously fascinated and troubled them, a portent of what was to come.

The Captain took her hand as the carriage driver opened the door and the princess stepped inside. He gathered her train and bundled it in beside Tianna, while Te Manu entered via the far side and moved her flowing skirt. Sitting down was not easy without their assistance. The princess sat centrally on the velvet buttoned cushions, flanked on either side by the two men who kept watch through the windows of the compartment.

Not one word was spoken on that journey as the horses made their way, but the silence was not uncomfortable. They were so occupied by thought, that to voice anything at all would have been inadequate. When they did look at the princess, she allowed herself a small smile that secretly delighted in the extraordinary circumstances that united them.

As the carriage drew close to the Governor's house, there seemed to be a growing crowd of people waiting.

There was no sign of trouble, just excitement in the air.

"Word must have got out that you are here. We must be very careful," said the Captain, watching from the window. Tianna remained calm. She already knew more than they did. "My Uncle will have announced my arrival, in time for the luncheon," she told him.

Jarrus looked concerned about the wisdom of this but he also wondered how Tianna was in a position to know anything Fabian Cavendish had done. He was prevented from enquiring by the footmen opening the carriage door. Fabian was there to receive her, amid cheers from well-wishers. He looked resplendent in his own robes of high office which he wore in defiance of Salgari's earlier ultimatum, and kissed the princess's forehead before taking her hand to escort her into his comfortable home.

"Sit down Gentlemen," Cavendish requested of Roden and Te Manu. He began to pour them a drink from a crystal decanter. "I am delighted you both decided to come. Celeiro was most impressed by your attitude. I see you are not a man to be easily intimidated, Captain. No more am I. Come! I drink to your continued good health." He smiled.

The Captain was impressed by the Governor's calmness but questioned the reason for so many people thronging outside. The princess smiled and continued to sit demurely in a wide armchair with her finery reminding her to maintain dignity. She listened as Cavendish talked.

"There is safety in numbers, Captain. I have more support among the citizens than I do among ministers. There will be an open meeting following our luncheon which will infuriate my opponents but make it far more difficult for them to obstruct the event. However, by coming here, you have placed yourselves in equal danger alongside Tianna and myself, and so I propose that we remain together for the official meal, which at least I may conduct without interference. Is there anyone who could identify the two of you by sight?"

"I came because we are concerned for what should happen to the princess if you are displaced, Sir," replied the Captain. "We do not expect to be entertained at your luncheon, and will draw our swords to get her away at the first sign of trouble."

"See this as a responsibility to the princess then, Roden. She understands the risk we are taking but must take the chance to appear. If you stay with her as escorts, no one will impede you, but it would be helpful if your true identity is not immediately revealed, especially to men like Salgari."

Te Manu picked up on Cavendish's use of Roden's first name. It was suggestive of a stronger association than he had first believed they shared. The Captain hesitated. Tianna and the Governor watched him.

"Very well. We will do as you wish. Some of the townsfolk would readily recognize us. I do not think we are known to any ministers by sight, but our reputation as pirates and our ship readily condemn us. When this luncheon is over, I intend to get us away from here and hope that you will trust my judgement in escaping with the princess."

The Governor of Petriah agreed.

"Our enemies will be at that assembly, gentlemen, whoever they are. On the surface there would appear to be no connection between our internal unrest and the fate of Auretanea, but these murders suggest otherwise. If I am correct, they will not usurp my authority while I am with the princess, but none of us can be certain. I entreat you to save her and yourselves if matters escalate."

Tianna withdrew with her uncle to finalise the departure for luncheon. They would all soon be leaving. Te Manu had been silent throughout, but was full of condemnation for the Governor.

"Am I losing the plot?" he demanded of Jarrus when they were alone. "The girl wanted to find her uncle to ask for his help, but he arranges a lunch party to shield himself to prevent his enemies removing him. Is that it? Is that what the gentry do?"

Roden was baffled by the situation just as much as Manu and neither of them had anticipated being expected to attend the meal. He hastily scribbled a note for a messenger to take to the quayside. "If we are going to be at this bloody assembly, I want some of my best men present to give us our best chance of escaping from here alive," he told Te Manu. "There is no sense to this at all. It's like some game, and the girl needs taking out of this fast. There's no hope of Auretanea getting help from anyone here."

Much as they liked Cavendish, the pirates considered he had no concept of what was needed and what was to follow would be a sham. The matter was hastily dropped when a message came that guests were arriving at the assembly hall and it was time to go.

Two carriages now waited at the door. The first would take Cavendish ahead with the princess. There was already a crowd outside the assembly rooms. All wanted a glimpse of the princess but most ordinary townsfolk were already aware of the rumoured invasion of Auretanea. Many had relatives living in that kingdom and some had sons and brothers who had volunteered to go there. Already frustrated by the slowness of any official response from the Governor, they were unaware that he had been thwarted by his own ministers who had argued that there was insufficient evidence of any threat, and had refused action.

The princess alighted from the carriage to cheers from the crowd who had hurriedly left their daily chores in response to the town criers and tolling bells that had successfully spread the word of this extraordinary meeting. Fabian's own guards escorted them inside. The Captain and Te Manu looked out of the second carriage on hearing the noise, and for the first time, began to get an idea of just how big this reception could become. They were completely taken aback.

"How is she going to cope with all this?" asked the Captain as they tried to estimate the number of bodies lining the streets. It was an overwhelming scene.

"Look. Here are some of our men," he added. They climbed out of the second carriage as Joshua approached. "We received your message Captain. The men you requested are here and armed. The others have prepared the Zenna for sailing and have moved her out. Our longboats are in harbour and ten men are ready to cut all the other boats adrift if the signal is given."

"Well done." said Jarrus. "That will slow down any attempt to stop us leaving.

"What's going on here?" asked Josh, bemused at the throng of people. "

I don't understand this any more than you." answered Jarrus. It seems the Governor is taking an insane risk exposing the princess like this. Spread out around the building but make sure you are all close to an exit. Watch the main table for any sign of disturbance. At the first sign, fire into the air to cause confusion while we get the princess out."

"Aye Aye, Captain," replied Josh.

"Is everyone accounted for? Mr. Baines and Jonah?" demanded Te Manu.

"Aye Sir. Mr. Baines is here and Jonah knows to give the signal back at the harbour."

"Then we are as prepared as we can be," Te Manu confirmed. "Go to your places now. We have to stay at the table."

"Sir?" asked Joshua, uncomprehendingly.

"We have to dine with them," explained the Captain. Josh raised his eyebrows at the incongruity of the situation, but said nothing. Celeiro approached them. He was far more comfortable with these proceedings than he had ever been on board the galleon. The pirates were all clothed, which was a relief, and not as embarrassingly conspicuous as they might have been. He addressed the Captain. "I will walk ahead of you to the top table. Few, if any, will know your real identity. I have arranged seating for you beside, and directly opposite, Her Royal Highness. The Governor's personal guards will protect us if necessary, should you attract unwarranted attention. Are you ready to enter gentlemen?"

Roden and Te Manu had no confidence in Fabian's own guard and kept quiet about the measures they had already put in place. Mystified, they prepared to follow the small and dandyish figure of Celeiro. Inside the vast assembly rooms, the pirates were surprised by the magnitude of the occasion. Noblemen bowed and clapped as the princess entered to a fanfare. She did not appear to be surprised by her reception and graciously acknowledged those dignitaries being introduced to her, taking special note of the ones she knew to be a thorn in the Governor's side. She was astute enough to evaluate those who were genuinely pleased to see her and those who fawned over her arrival in a show that was insincere.

Everyone found a place at the luncheon table that filled the length of the assembly hall, while the general public were being admitted to stand at the sides, and jostle for places along the public balcony. There were pretty speeches of welcome, which the princess courteously acknowledged before people ate. Minstrels played for them. Food and liquid refreshment flowed. Celeiro heard rumblings of discontent from those seated about the presence of the masses. He was delighted that so many had come and still more would arrive before the end of the meal. Like the Governor, Celeiro had more faith in the tradesman than the politician and firmly believed that including them had been justified. The occasion had a slightly theatrical feel to it with an ominous undercurrent.

Captain Jarrus was more adept in society than Te Manu who could not see the merit of feasting and entertainment as a prelude to the purpose of the meeting, if indeed there was a purpose. He remained sceptical and scowled at the food placed before him without gratitude. The array of fine cutlery perplexed and irritated him further. Manu had no experience of social dining, and skewered the meat on his plate with the knife he drew from his belt, to the astonishment of those guests seated further along the table. He was far more comfortable in these strange surroundings with a weapon in his hand. They were vigilant, watching, more than listening, to surrounding conversation, keeping a sustained guard over the proceedings as the rest of the crew positioned themselves among the growing crowd, around the inside of the hall.

Fabian Cavendish maintained accord with everyone who approached. He and the princess were subjected to the opinions of others. Throughout the meal it was the fashion to move about and mix conversations, bringing points of view to the host and his guests. Tianna heard several dignitaries hint at appeasement as the solution to ease Auretanea's plight.

"The majority of these present will be sympathetic, your Highness." declared one, dejectedly. "But many will need to be swayed. Nothing will be achieved quickly."

"The members are pacifists," announced another, as if he spoke for all. "and we believe conflict is best averted by negotiation." Some points of view sounded so feeble that Te Manu snorted and scowled with menace at the bearers of such comment. They tended to retreat rather hastily, wondering who on earth he could be. The princess however, remained serene throughout and, like Fabian, was dignified, composed and unhurried.

The Governor was polite to everyone and uniformly respectful, whatever he was thinking. He studied his niece's demeanour, admiring her resistance to giving anything away, save the courteous attention she afforded each person who approached. She listened graciously to the absurd, the condescending, the pompous and the cowardly with the same unfailing charm. No one could have guessed if the princess was possessed of any strength of feeling. She espoused nothing.

Tianna's mind began to concentrate less on the mindless prattle. It did not deter her from her own thoughts. Her uncle watched her with attentive affection. Something like a mild amusement illuminated his smile when their eyes met. He recognized she would not be influenced by anything she heard. He could hazard a guess what was going through her mind. The princess might have been disillusioned by the surrounding company but if anything, it galvanized her thinking. Were these men or puppets masquerading as ministers? Could they not confront the fact that decision, courage and action must replace rhetoric before it was too late?

She was scathing of their superficial understanding of the crisis and of how complacent their privileged lives had made them. The simpering good manners, expressing polite but insincere concern for Auretanea, affected the princess and fuelled her. She turned to her uncle and said softly,

"I should like to address the assembly now."

Fabian alone looked confident. It was as if he already knew the card he was waiting to play was an ace.

The Captain and Te Manu however, were totally unprepared for this and exchanged long looks, revealing their anxiety at hearing Tianna's request to speak. The exposure of this girl already compromised her safety without her standing up. There was also the possibility that she might default with nerves, by fainting clean away just as she had on that first night on the galleon, or be rendered mute, anything in fact that might turn the next few minutes into a fiasco. She had to be stopped.

To Te Manu's horror, Fabian called the assembly to order. The Captain fervently hoped she would make a pretty speech of thanks and be done in a trice without incident. They had no idea of what to expect from Tianna. This was beyond their control. They were merely spectators. Tianna declined to look at either of them. When Fabian called the meeting to order, she quietly rose from her chair, opposite the Captain. The room became silent. All eyes were turned towards her. Occupying various positions in the room, Gideon, Gypsy, Ezra and the others were conscious of the changing atmosphere. The Captain could hardly believe that this young girl had asked to speak before several hundred people.

The pirates, standing around the perimeter, looked from one to the other, mystified. Te Manu focused hard on the pepper pot on the table in front of him, beneath troubled brows, and just about managed to dart a concerned look at Roden, whose own jaw was so taut with nerves that one could clearly see the pulse in his neck throbbing, the rest of his body rigidly immobile, as he stared at the princess. There was an awful tension in them both. Anything might happen. Seated so close to the girl, they could feel the weight of attention, several hundred pairs of eyes, turned in her direction.

The princess raised her beautiful face very gradually to gaze at the full assembly of people stretching way down the long table. She swept her gaze across people standing against the walls. She saw faces she knew from the galleon and then saw Romana, who had been offered a chair at the far end of the long table, and now sat waiting for the princess to address them all. Making sure of their full attention, the princess spoke.

"Good people of Petriah," she began, "I thank you from the bottom of my heart for your generous welcome and the comments passed so freely during luncheon." Speaking clearly and with effective dignity, as though she had done it all her life, Tianna dumbfounded the assembly by informing them next,

"The great galleon, Zenna Marius has been my safe passage out of troubled Auretanea. She was commissioned by my father, the King, to give me protection and to deliver a message of the utmost urgency to the citizens of Petriah."

Fabian had to conceal a twitch of the lips at this falsehood and the Captain and Te Manu were totally unable to believe their ears. Across the room, Israel folded his arms and smirked at the girl's audacity. He had to admit the girl had pluck. "That's right," he said, proudly to his friend, Gypsy. "Asked for by the King himself, we were."

"Did I hear that right?" asked Gideon, turning to Mr. Baines. "Aye 'appen you did. The lass has just told a whopper but it's in our favour, so it is. Wonder what she'll think of next."

They almost held their breath as she spoke. Assured of the full attention of her audience after the revelation about the Zenna Marius, the princess talked to them of the instability of Scalos, of the threat it posed to its neighbours and the disenchantment of its people who were rumoured to be paying the price for accepting a dangerous philosophy. She described the doctrine of the powerful Baron spreading like a canker throughout the Islands. She talked to them of their own freedom now threatened, just as certainly as her own enslavement would surely follow any invasion of her land. There was awestruck attention to her words, and a steadily growing momentum to her speech.

The pirates looked at one another across the table. They gazed at Tianna in disbelief. The mass of people were riveted by her command of language. Their sons and brothers had gone willingly to help Auretanea but until now, no one had told them officially what was going on there. The princess knew what she was talking about. Geographically accurate, the girl made them consider the fate of outlying Islands and she told them in no uncertain terms the grievous result of inaction. The princess conferred upon her rapt audience, a sense of responsibility and a duty towards their neighbours who were part of the same kingdom.

Her timing was superb, her delivery swift as arrows. She began to build to the climax of her mission. Tianna told the people of Petriah of her loyalty to her father, the King, who had raised daughters with his own spirit, firing her with the courage that brought her here. If she, the youngest princess could risk her life, could pledge to return to the sea and fight for her beloved land, then who could refuse to follow? Tianna ended on a stirring call to arms, addressing every man of office sitting at the tables.

"STAND UP AND BE COUNTED IF YOU ARE FOR YOUR KING!"

At this, Fabian Cavendish immediately rose, as did the Captain, followed by Te Manu and like a rolling wave, the rest followed, shooting out of their seats to pledge allegiance to the King and the courageous princess. The applause was thunderous and continued unabated for many minutes. Governor Cavendish took advantage of the opportunity to immediately put the call to arms to the vote and the room was full of assent. Celeiro obtained signatures in full view of the townspeople who were witnesses to the occasion. Petriah would provide the help that the princess requested. The excitement in the room was palpable.

Those ministers who had hoped to reduce Cavendish's power were dealt a bitter blow, for who could threaten the Governor without betraying himself amid the frenzy of support surrounding him?

Tianna stood to a crescendo of goodwill and a public demonstration of loyalty that could not be stilled. The speech had been inspiring. Unrehearsed and heartfelt, it had struck the target. The Captain and Te Manu were astonished by the whole affair, the triumph of which registered on the faces of the citizens present. More volunteers were already approaching the ministers to offer their services to defend the King. Romana dabbed her eyes and said, "Wonderful! She was wonderful," as one of Fabian's personal attendants took her arm and escorted her to a waiting carriage. The princess left the assembly rooms with some difficulty, escorted by Fabian and retired to his private rooms, accompanied by the Captain.

Closing the doors behind them, they sank into armchairs, exhausted and overwhelmed by the reaction of the crowds. Fabian pressed his palms together and with steepled fingers, prodded his lips, thoughtfully.

"You have surpassed anything I could have hoped for," he told her.

She gave him a grin that immediately replaced the façade of serenity she had worn earlier to great effect. Jarrus regarded the princess anew. She was, he concluded, highly intelligent, well-educated and possessed of an innate confidence he had not seen before. Her radiant and impish smile suggested a character trait that would challenge him, given the chance. He recognised that this playful princess had reserves of mischief and daring and was going to use them. Right now, she was riding the crest of a wave. The Captain could not quite believe what had been achieved that afternoon.

Te Manu walked across the hall to Gideon and several of the others at the close of her address. They were all amazed by the performance she had given and the resounding support she had received.

"Well I never. Well I never," said Mr. Baines, as he watched her withdraw from the room, surrounded by jostling, noisy well-wishers. Gideon was similarly affected. "She's such a little thing an' all," he muttered. Gypsy approached the warrior.

"What do we do now, sir?" he enquired. The threat to overthrow the Governor and arrest the pirates had been averted by the princess. Te Manu had to think where to go from here.

"This victory will rile the Governor's enemies. I need to get instructions from the Captain. Stay between the ship and the brothel until I send word. Arrange for the ship to be close enough for boarding and be prepared for anything. Maybe no one will displace Cavendish, but we cannot be certain. The Captain is with him now."

"Will we be able to say goodbye to the princess?" asked Ezra.

"Aye, Will we be able to do that?" enquired Josh as well. The others waited eagerly for a reply.

"No one will say anything to the princess," answered Te Manu, firmly, "until we have received orders." They would not challenge him, but certainly looked disappointed. The warrior revealed nothing in his indifferent expression. He stared into the middle distance, choosing his moment, before adding. "But I cannot see us leaving her in Petriah." At once there was a marked change in all of them. They were recharged.

"Now hasten to the ship!" he ordered. With renewed enthusiasm, they hurried away. The warrior watched them go and slowly smiled. He had underestimated Tianna. They all had. Not one of them wanted to leave her behind, not now.

Chapter Twenty Five - Roden's Plan

Inside Fabian's rooms, the atmosphere buzzed for some considerable time and everyone was on a high. It was only later that the conversation veered towards where sanctuary might be found for the princess. The Governor suggested Calypso Island, unspoilt, primitive and off the beaten track. Tianna had no interest in being found a place of safety and she wandered towards the window. "Where are the men from Auretanea who need safe passage?" she asked her uncle, changing the subject.

"You mean the fishermen who helped recruit Tasmin's volunteers?" he answered.

"Yes. I think you said they claimed to be from the castle. If that is so, I may know them. May I go to them?"

Captain Jarrus believed her request would be denied. Moving about in Petriah when kidnap was a distinct possibility seemed irresponsible but, unfortunately he could not overrule the indulgent Governor who would grant his niece anything right now. "They are in a tavern. If you go to them you must be properly guarded, Tianna. I do not know who we can trust, especially now you are known to be here."

Tianna was undaunted. She turned a smiling face upon the Captain and Fabian. "Well, don't trust Salgari for one. Did you see how deferential he was towards me this afternoon? He will not press for anyone's arrest while I am here, but he probably curses me for coming. He would have me disappear, I'm sure of it." She laughed dismissively, which unnerved Jarrus. After all the man was a real threat.

"We did well together uncle, but I still wish to find the men who have been helping Tasmin."

Cavendish agreed. "You see, Roden, the princess and I are possessed of similar determination when faced with opposition. Very well, child. Under cover of darkness and with some disguise, a way will be found for you to take word to them tonight. Meanwhile, we must begin to work on a strategy for harnessing the Petriahn ships and training men in sufficient numbers to fight. The trouble is, we cannot guess how many ships Lussac has."

Roden could not believe the Governor would sanction the princess's desire to go out at night, but was mindful to remain neutral. "I should like to do more than take the princess to a safe Island, Sir." Jarrus responded. "My future is also threatened if Lussac succeeds. I propose escorting Her Highness to Calypso Island for the duration of the struggle to free Auretanea. From there I could sail to Scalos with my regular cargo, and find out more information on what is happening."

"That will take too long, Captain. No. I fear we will have to go into this guessing his strength." The Governor looked upon Jarrus with an almost fatherly eye. "Do not think I am ungrateful for your offer, but we need to know quickly whether we are facing just the three ships already outside Auretanea, or more.

"Six." piped up the princess, returning from the window. Fabian gave a small smile. He turned around in his large leather chair.

"Six Tianna? Sit down, child and explain what you know."

"Ambassador Moreton told my father that Baron Lussac boasted six ships. Three sailed, two were almost fitted and one was under construction, at the time of the first sailing."

"Did Theodore believe him?" enquired Fabian, referring to the King. The princess considered this.

"I think so," she replied. "Moreton was trying to impress Father, so had there been above that number, I think he would have said."

The Captain pondered this. "And three of them are already sitting within sight of Auretanea expecting Moreton to escort the princess to Scalos, or they invade. Time is indeed running out," said Jarrus, impatient for some decisive plan.

"If he has six we cannot outnumber them. Not without help from further afield." The Governor remarked. Captain Jarrus seized the opportunity to revive his outrageous plan.

"We could sabotage them," he suggested. Tianna put her elbows on the table and cupped her chin in her hands. This sounded interesting.

"Sabotage them! How? Please explain yourself," demanded Cavendish.

"I will need paper, pens, half a dozen ink blotters and three small tot glasses," began Jarrus.

"Shall I go and look for them?" The girl asked her uncle. He waved her away. Tianna went to find what she could, being familiar with the layout of the house.

"I can only find four wooden handled ink blotters," she told him. Fabian discovered two more on the library shelf. Tianna was prepared to be fascinated, Fabian, less so. "Do you need a decanter for the glasses, Captain?" she asked.

"No. I do not propose drinking. They represent the Scalos ships," he responded, spreading the roll of paper across the table and holding it down with paperweights. Tianna knelt on a chair and rested on her elbows, prepared to become absorbed.

Te Manu arrived at the house alone, and was admitted. His arrival was announced but the focus of attention was more on the peculiar assortment of items spread out upon the table, and he slipped into the room without much of an acknowledgement.

Tianna gave him a devastating smile. It stirred for him, the memory of last night. It seemed an age away. He tried not to respond, choosing instead to blend in and concentrate on what they were doing. They all pored over the table. The Captain was ready to begin. He stood and leaned across the cluttered table.

"These paperweights are the ships from Petriah, concealed behind the east coast of Auretanea. They will not sail into Auretanea until a flare is given by the cigar box." He hesitated to enable the Governor time to assimilate all this.

"It represents the Zenna Marius, Sir. She is coming from the south towards the bay. These tot glasses are the three Scalos vessels we know are there already."

He drew a rough outline of the coast on the sheet of paper. Everyone stared at the tot glasses. Te Manu began to recognise the outline of the plan that had so obsessed Roden yesterday. Surely he wasn't going to propose it to the Governor of Petriah as a viable idea?

"This is the remainder of Baron Lussac's fleet. The Zenna has brought them across from Scalos and has joined Lussac's men to fight you."

He manoeuvred the ink blotters behind the cigar box.

The Governor regarded Jarrus critically, wondering if the Captain had taken leave of his senses. Te Manu was acutely aware of his misgivings, which he shared.

Roden ploughed on, undaunted. Tianna watched intently, and appeared to follow what was going on.

"Have you switched sides?" she asked, accusingly.

"Watch!" replied the Captain, tearing small strips of paper and marking them either red or green. "Three Scalos ships with red ensigns already in Auretanea and more following the galleon with no ensigns at all. Now, the Petriahn ships come into view."

"That's wrong!" protested the princess. "You've given them red Scalos flags instead of green Petriahn ones."

"Exactly." responded Roden. "So what will the crew of the tot glasses be thinking?" Fabian Cavendish threw his hands up in despair at ever understanding this nonsense. Te Manu tried to stop Roden with a reproving look. He failed. Tianna alone was enthralled. "Wait," she said. "I need more time. You asked what can the crew see inland. Why, red flags of course. More ships from Scalos. Oh! They will think the remaining ships from Scalos have come in from the other direction. Is that it?" she suggested excitedly.

"Yes," said the Captain, greatly encouraged by his young ally, who found the whole exercise to her liking. "Now, what do the crew of the tot glasses think of the ink blotters coming behind the galleon?"

"Oh. I don't know," said Tianna, disappointedly.

Te Manu shifted uncomfortably in his seat. "Roden. I really think this should wait," he intervened, shaking his head. Jarrus, undeterred, placed a green piece of paper on the cigar box galleon.

"Oh! Oh! I've got it," cried the girl,

"Well?" encouraged the Captain.

"They will think the ink blotters are the Petriahn enemy following the galleon, because you show OUR flag." She drew herself up proudly and beamed at him. The Governor was a patient man, but found all of this impossible to follow. The princess on the other hand had played the game, and was of one mind with the Captain. "Six ships with red flags and three with no flags. The right number of ships but the wrong way round," she proclaimed. "Then what happens?"

"The galleon pulls away into the bay and fires into the sea separating the tot glasses and the ink blotters. Result? Chaos. And with luck, the tot glasses open fire on the incoming ink blotters, or in other words the Scalos fleet wages a battle with itself, and doesn't recognise the mistake until it is too late."

"It's brilliant!" announced Tianna, "But won't you be fired on by the original three ships?"

"Not before they fire on the vessels behind us because the original three are now sandwiched in the middle, and if the timing is right, will believe the enemy is coming in behind them." The Captain sat back, pleased with himself.

Tianna gave the Captain every encouragement, not that he needed it. The Governor injected a dose of reality, more akin to Te Manu's reasoning.

"This is outrageous, and you know it," he protested. "Tot glasses and cigar boxes! Whatever next? You know nothing of the strategy involved in battle and are not a man of war, no matter how much you think you can be. Let us face facts. You spend much of your life raiding cargo vessels and for the most part, you actually raid them with the complicity of their crews, who are only too eager to give you the goods!"

The Captain toyed with the cigar box. It was all true. Cavendish continued. "The scheme you are proposing is ridiculous. It is unrealistic. Lussac is not a fool. He is not going to entrust you with anything, let alone ships. There's a price on your head. Don't forget that when you propose a meeting with him, and he wants an end to piracy. He'll be after your blood. No. The truth is this will have to be a conventional battle, conventionally fought, with losses on all sides and a very uncertain outcome."

Governor Cavendish sat pensively after this outburst. It was as if in describing what they were up against, there was no room left for optimism. They all became preoccupied with thought. The Governor was first among them to raise his eyes. He considered it might smack of ingratitude to the Captain to reject the plan totally when he had already chosen to stand by them in this hour of need. He seemed to be mulling it over.

"You'd have nothing to barter with Lussac; nothing to make him listen to you." He voiced it as if racking his brains for inspiration. The princess got up and walked around the table. She perched on the arm of her uncle's chair. "Do the vaults hold anything other than gold?" she asked. The Governor gave her a smile and patted her hand. He clearly cherished her.

"Are you considering bribing the Baron or buying his ships?" he asked lightly.

"Neither," she replied, "I just wondered."

"Well. There is your dear mother's jewellery, some of which passes to Tasmin. The state crowns and tiaras, then there are rings and the rest is made up of gifts that have been bestowed on the family across the years." he told her.

"What happened to the rubies that the Baron brought to Tasmin when he sought betrothal?" Tianna wanted to know.

"Ah, well. Those have proved difficult. Tasmin did not accept them of course, but Lussac stormed out after what he perceived to be a public humiliation, and left them with his emissary. Then it was inferred they should come to you. Now we know why of course. He expected your father to send you to him. The rubies are still in our possession. There has been no easy way for your father to return them without causing even greater offence. Our diplomats have failed to find a way forward. Why do you ask, Tianna?"

"May be the Captain could return them for us," she said, brightly.

"What's this?" questioned her uncle, cautiously.

"He might return them and sort of suggest he purloined them from the Castle when he kidnapped me."

The Governor of Petriah turned to stare at the girl by his side. "Are you suggesting yourself as a hostage, taken by pirates, to induce Lussac to accept the Captain's plan?" he asked. (Of course it was. Tianna thought her uncle was being remarkably slow.) "Because if you are, it's the most audacious thing I ever heard. What is wrong with both of you? You see, Roden, where your outlandish ideas take you? Into a world of complete fantasy." Jarrus was too busy turning things over in his mind to be offended. It was gratifying to win the princess's support for what he considered a daring plan.

Te Manu would like to have silenced them both. He managed to suppress himself only in deference to the Governor's authority and for no other reason. The escalation continued apace. The girl who had been a timid fawn in his arms not twenty four hours ago, was lively, impudent and in suppressible. He was angry at her insubordination with her uncle, yet fascinated by her unbridled vivacity. She was far from finished.

"If neither Auretanea nor Petriah are safe places for me, if your ships cannot outflank the Scalos vessels, if Petriah is poised to suffer heavy losses in a conventional battle, then why not give the Captain a chance to succeed?" she protested vehemently.

"Because you are just a child. A royal child and a royal daughter must be protected at all costs." he reminded her forcefully.

Te Manu gave her the most reproving look which failed to have any impact. She did not even notice. Tianna was in full flight.

"Would you say that if I had been born a prince?" she challenged him. "To be sent to some faraway place to hide while my father's life is at stake and his people, threatened?"

"No. I would not," admitted Cavendish squarely. "You are right. I would say take your army. Face your enemy. Trust in yourself and your beliefs. But you are not a prince. You are a princess, a girl. It is not the same."

Te Manu's expression was one of suppressed anger. He was finding it difficult to remain silent. It sounded to him as though the princess had picked up on Roden's ideas and was fighting his corner for him. Even Jarrus believed the argument had gone too far

"The Governor is right, princess. We should stop. My ideas have no substance in reality," he said.

Tianna disagreed. Loudly. "They do!" she insisted. "They do. They do!" The escalation in her voice was becoming embarrassing.

"Tianna. You are as foolhardy as the Captain," declared Cavendish. "You cannot become the bait to trap Lussac."

Te Manu managed to catch her eye at last.

"What are you saying, princess?" he asked her, in sombre tone. His head was inclined. The smouldering eyes became censorious, burning into hers, arresting her attention with his levelled voice. Te Manu would have cheerfully shaken her but settled instead for the glower he usually reserved for his men on the galleon. She stilled and looked back at him with large, innocent eyes. The warrior was not for playing games. Tianna recognised it. She may try to argue to get her own way, but his own determination was greater. Controlling the impetuous nature of a princess was going to be difficult. Te Manu glared at her and she stared back. Intelligent, beautiful and spirited with infuriating will power and unstoppable self-belief. She stood her ground, but curbed her tongue. The Captain waited for the Governor to direct her, but when he did speak, it sounded more like capitulation.

"Content yourself with what you have achieved for now," he told her, wearily. Go instead to find your fishermen in the tavern, if indeed that is who they are, and put your energies into obtaining them safe passage for they must live in fear of being murdered like the other poor devils."

Tianna was on her feet in a second and bounded towards the door. The Captain raised questioning eyebrows at the Governor, who looked very tired.

"Your men can see to it, Roden, but I want you to stay here awhile, at least until Celeiro returns." he said.

Jarrus and Te Manu exchanged a look of mutual disquiet. They realised the girl would use her status to persuade everyone to her ideas in Petriah. She had single handedly won them a reprieve by telling several hundred people, among them local grandees, that the King had commissioned their ship, and as a result of her speech had won the support of the entire town, and was now bursting to get out there again. Te Manu had no doubt she would give whole hearted support to Roden's ill-conceived plan for Scalos too.

Governor Cavendish left the room to summon the carriage to take Tianna to Romana's house to find more suitable clothing. Te Manu was astonished that she was permitted to go out into the night, but neither he nor Roden felt able to oppose the plan.

"Doesn't anyone ever stop her?" he complained.

Jarrus told Cavendish's personal guard to take a message to his men at the brothel to provide her with an escort to the tavern.

"What is this all about?" asked Manu, when they were alone.

"She may know the identity of the two men hiding in the tavern," replied the Captain. "The Governor wants us to take them back with us rather than risk them being murdered too."

"She doesn't need to go. One of us could have visited them," reasoned the warrior.

"I know that," retorted the Captain. "Are you going to try telling him...? Or her?"

Te Manu gave it up. Roden carried on writing.

"I'll send Gideon and Israel with her," he decided and passed the note to the waiting footman.

Fabian Cavendish returned to the room having organised the carriage. The princess scooped up the fabric of her train that she had detached on arrival at the house and had left on the window seat. Her piled up hair was starting to tumble around her shoulders and the perfectly placed tiara slipped a fraction. She showed no concern for any of it.

"Celeiro is arriving, gentlemen. I should like you to stay and hear what he has to tell us," announced the Governor, thus effectively preventing either of them from making the short journey to Romana's house with the princess, much to their constination.

Celeiro arrived, flushed with excitement and more at ease in front of the pirates than he'd so far been. "Congratulations on a most stirring speech, your Highness," he began. "There has been a huge response and we have taken advantage of the mood of the people to gain ground. Salgari and other antagonists will not risk displacing your uncle under these circumstances. It is my belief that until the opposition has had time to assimilate the impact of what has happened today, we may presume the authority of our Governor will not be questioned again, at least not immediately. You will not need to hasten away either, Captain. People are already at the quayside hoping to glimpse the princess again, if and when she boards the Zenna Marius. Your ship has never been more popular. The people of Petriah are for us."

This was satisfying news for the Governor. His spirits lifted at once. "Excellent!" he said. "With accusations against you being shelved, we can retire in comfort and look more closely at your ideas Captain, and perhaps devolve a strategy less alarming than your first suggestion. Perhaps we should take some extra ink blotters and paper weights to the next room," he continued, moving purposefully towards the front door with the girl.

Celeiro looked mystified, but the princess gave the Captain an impish grin. Her uncle would reconsider the plan, after all. She passed through the hall and out into the early evening. The Governor decided to see her off. Roden followed him outside. Fabian took hold of Tianna's elbow to steady her as she climbed into the waiting carriage. As she seated herself he tightened his grip on her arm, causing her to pause and look round at him. "Promise me your stay at the inn will be brief, and dress differently for the journey. Cover yourself well. If approached by anyone at all the journey must be abandoned and you are to return to this house or the ship, whichever is nearer without delay. Remember our enemies will be smarting and angered by today's turn of events."

Cavendish was still apprehensive of Tianna's inclination to do her own thing. "Do you understand me?" he asked her. "You are not to take unnecessary risks."

"Yes. I do understand, and I will be careful," she answered, in haste to get on with it. The Captain shook his head, unable to accept that this was wise or that enough had been said. "With respect, Governor," he intervened. "I need the princess to understand more than this."

The Governor graciously side-stepped, indicating that Jarrus had his permission to speak. Roden placed both his arms against the door frame of the carriage, and the tread of his boot on the foot rest, completely filling the aperture of the carriage door, while Tianna perched on the cushions inside. "Israel and Gideon will go with you tonight. You will do exactly as Gideon and Israel command, every step of the way," he told her, firmly. "In my absence, they will decide what is safe and what is dangerous, and if you object, just once, they will drag you out or carry you over their shoulders if necessary and in my note I have already given them the authority to do just that. It will be my orders, not yours that will prevail, princess."

Fabian's dark eyebrows rose at such a suggestion, but, to his credit, he did not object. The Captain had her safety at heart and he sounded determined, brooking no argument. The pirates would never have sanctioned this mission and did not approve the indulgence of her independent spirit. The princess grinned, but did not argue. She was asserting a freedom on land that she never could at sea, but was wise enough to stay quiet.

Chapter Twenty Six - The Servants

The short carriage ride was uneventful. The girl was escorted by Fabian's personal guard who bore the message from the Captain and ensured it was delivered to his men. Tianna was received at Romana's house and the coachmen departed. Gideon and Israel waited for her by the door.

"This is bloody stupid if you ask me," complained Israel, who was grieved at being interrupted having just decided to spend the night with a girl called Arabesque, or at least something that sounded similar.

"Now then, now then!" growled Gideon, who disliked any criticism of the Captain.

"Well, it is," persisted Israel, who was irritated at being at the beck and call of the princess.

"Captain can't cross the Governor of the place now, can he?" said Gideon, patiently. "And if that there Cavendish has told princess she can go to a tavern, so she goes. Ain't nothing our Captain can do about that is there?"

"Alright," conceded Israel, grudgingly, "But the Captain can't be taking orders from a girl, can he? I mean, who are we s'pose to listen to once she's back on board?"

"Aye. That's gonna be an interestin' one and no mistake. Sparks are sure to fly," agreed Gideon.

Upstairs, the princess turned sideways to check her profile in a long mirror. A cape and tricorn hat completed her cover. She stuffed her long hair, which had been so neat only hours before, under the rim of the black velvet hat, where it refused to stay. Hair flopped over her nose. Romana and Tianna laughed at the effect.

"It has been a pleasure this last two days, your Highness" said Romana. She looked a little wistful and rather sad at the approaching departure, but the moment passed. She had much to impart. "There's britches and shirts to fit you properly and by the time the galleon sails, maybe the boots we spoke of as well. For now the sandals are all we have managed. Oh, we are going to miss you!" she said, becoming emotional all over again.

The excited girl arrived with Romana at the door and was passed into the care of Gideon, who stared at the disguise but was unable to find anything suitable to say, and Israel who scoffed at the stupidity of it and thrust his hands into his pockets. As they moved away rather quickly, the hat began to descend over Tianna's dark eyebrows and sat stubbornly on the bridge of her nose. Walking between the two of them with their long strides was rather difficult, but the princess kept up. Still animated by the achievements of the day, Tianna found it impossible to be quiet. "I've never been in a tavern before," she confided brightly. "How shall I behave? What shall I say?" Israel smirked unkindly.

"We'll do the talking, not you, ma'am," he answered curtly. He sounded as unfriendly on land as he had on the galleon and was clearly not going to behave any differently towards the princess. She frowned beneath the hat at his perversity.

"Why?" she asked. Israel narrowed his eyes and his thin lips set in a resentful frown. "Your ways of speaking would draw attention in a second," he answered, whilst looking straight ahead and striding forward, his thin, lithe frame making easy work of the distance.

She had to hold on to the hat and try to keep up.

"How?" she demanded, not giving up. He cursed under his breath but was careful not to let her hear.

"Your voice is too high," he informed her, dismissively, hoping to shut her up. He did not intend to talk to the princess more than necessary, and refused her the satisfaction of eye contact.

"Oh. I thought I could pass for a youth, like Jonah perhaps," she said. This went unanswered by Israel, unless one considers a snort of derision a suitable response. Gideon was more amenable. "Tis not the pitch alone as betrays you, ma'am, but the way you sound. You speaks like a princess," he explained pleasantly, taking huge strides, matching Israel.

"I will have to work on that." she replied, breathlessly. "Can we slow down please? I'm losing my sandals."

They progressed through the cobbled streets quickly, soon arriving at the tavern. Gideon pushed open the heavy, dark door, passing only a few men imbibing in the dingy atmosphere. Tianna looked around with interest. It opened a whole new world to her unaccustomed eyes, of stale smells in airless recesses, of grimy windows and men with yellowed teeth or none at all, who sat hunched, protectively, over their ale, who looked for all the world as though they hadn't moved away from those stained, old tables in years. Any attention the three of them received was cursory, the dimness within the low ceilinged room helped deflect interest away from the new arrivals. This old tavern was not a place frequented by the young, or the better off. Gideon made enquiries of the landlord, who indicated a door at the top of a flight of uneven, well-worn stairs. He watched them go up but was not interested enough to question their purpose. Gideon's gruff voice and heavy presence ensured they were not impeded. The landlord considered them an odd trio, especially the little one with a cape so long it touched the ground as he moved upward. A call for more ale distracted his attention. He returned to his customers.

Gideon glanced over the rickety bannisters. Nobody looked up and the slow hum of conversation continued in the gloom below. He hovered on the landing, deciding if they had reached the right moment to make a surprise entry. Satisfied, he nodded to Israel who brought his fist to the door with a resounding thwack and entered immediately, drawing his pistol upon whoever might be lurking inside. The two occupants, taken completely unawares, shot to their feet, either side of a small table.

"Well, really!" began the emboldened princess, thinking this was a most impolite way to come visiting.

Gideon clapped a massive hand upon her shoulders and halted her on the spot. "Beggin' pardon ma'am, you jest wait wi' me 'til we knows it's safe in there."

One mighty hand was enough to hold her in place. Nature had bestowed twice the normal materials when she shaped Gideon. Taller and broader than most men, he had considerable power in his arms and hands. His size fascinated Tianna, yet of all the pirate crew, he had a gentle fondness for the princess. He smiled at the impulsive girl, knowing exactly how to talk to her and not upset her. They waited for Israel to motion her inside.

Seeing there were only two men in the room and they bore no weapons, Israel allowed the princess to pass, but he held the pistol and glared menacingly.

"You men from Auretanea?" he demanded.

The two figures inside were unnerved by this.

"We m...m...might be." stammered one, frightened to confess it.

"Oh good!" proclaimed the black cloak and hat.

"I come from Auretanea too." The occupants stared from the one brandishing a pistol to the enormous outline of the one at the back of the trio, who blocked the doorway, then to the smallest of the three who had spoken. With uncertain recognition, Tianna made a guess. "Mikhael?" she said, "and is that you, Artemus?" They were surprised to be identified by the curious stranger, and stood with their hands raised owing to the pistol, unsure what to say next.

"Look. It's me!" announced the one who had spoken last, and like a conjuring trick, she whisked away the hat to reveal the girl beneath.

"Well. I'll be blessed!" exclaimed Artemus, with overwhelming relief. "It's our princess."

"And isn't that Mr. Gideon too?" ventured Mikhael. Israel replaced his pistol. They shook hands with great vigour, made all the better by the information that Israel was also from the Zenna Marius and one of Jarrus's men, who they may have seen once or twice before. Drawing the rickety chairs around the table and perched on the ends of the two narrow beds, the five caught up on events since they had last seen each other. The only possessions belonging to Artemus and Mikhael were rolled in bundles and hung from two large hooks on the back of the door. Tianna confessed to leaving without even that much!

"How did you get here?" asked Gideon. "We only pulled out of the bay some eight days gone."

"It were my grandson, Darius." replied Mikhael. "He and the princess Tasmin have got a proper movement going back home, that we could not speak of before we saw you sail."

Tianna knew Darius well. She had grown up spending time with the castle servants, who had known her since she was an infant.

"Them Scalos blackguards, beggin' your pardon, princess," Artemus excused himself for language, before continuing, "They stopped boats leaving and began searching what came ashore. Darius says they'll have to find a more secluded landing place and the only boats left alone were the fishing vessels. Trouble was, young Darius don't look nothin' like a fisherman do ee, Mikhael?"

Old Mikhael chuckled. "Not a bit, but we are grizzled enough to pass for fishermen, so we got out on the fishing boat to pick up the boys coming across, and had made a few good trips afore these dreadful murders stopped us."

"What did you do?" asked the young princess.

"We heard about it from the Governor's gentleman. A dandyish sort, not meaning him no offence, but a good man. He had us take shelter here and wait 'til things died down a bit," explained Artemus.

They were amazed to hear Tianna's adventure, given the fact that at the time they had been on the beach, telling Gypsy what was happening, the princess must have been clamouring down the cliff towards the cove. They also knew nothing of her public address. Israel wanted to know more about the underground movement in Auretanea.

"The princess Tasmin started it, six months ago, after that nincompoop Baron upset her. I mean no disrespect, princess, but nincompoop he was in my opinion. She started with Darius, in the servant's hall and they soon had a group of volunteers collecting weaponry." Artemus explained.

"We didn't give it much thought at the time, but they got the secret passages behind the kitchens opened. There's a hideout some distance away," went on Mikhael. "Numbers are growing on account of the people being so afeared of what Scalos intends to do. They don't want to sit around doing nothing until it's too late." The two elderly servants were justly proud of what seemed to have taken root in the domestic quarters of the castle and which had spread to include the volunteers of Petriah.

"Our lads are with the princess." Artemus declared proudly, "and what we lack in skill is more than made up for in guts and determination to protect the castle and the King."

"Oh, well said!" chirped Tianna. "That is just what I told them at the assembly this afternoon."

"Darius was first to start coming over here, long afore we got involved and took lads back with him, but when all but the fishing boats were stopped, being on the old side, we took over. We passes easy for fishermen." ended Mikhael.

Israel was impressed. There was something very likeable about the two old friends. Working side by side for years and living cheek by jowl had given them an almost comedic delivery, where they could often finish each other's sentences. They were two halves of one whole and chivvied each other, praised each other and conspired with each other like mischievous children. Tianna had known them for ever. She sat with them now, as comfortable as she ever was, and looked upon them protectively.

Artemus was the taller of the two. Thin, with a gaunt look, owing to prominent bony cheeks, that gave him almost a raw-boned look, he had greying brown hair that grew thinly to his collar and a grey brown beard to match. Above the ruddy cheeks were two brown eyes that generally approved of what life dealt him, until that is, Scalos had begun to make things less comfortable. It took a lot to ruffle old Artemus, but this had, although he so disliked thinking badly of anyone, that when his words found expression, he felt duty bound to apologise for every comment. The princess was amused.

Mikhael was the shorter and plumper of the two. Despite a receding hairline, he had a mass of silver white curls and enormous blue eyes set in an almost cherubic round face. Even his white whiskers didn't seem to age him. Good natured and prone to mischief, Tianna had grown up accustomed to his misdemeanours. He tormented his long suffering wife in the castle kitchens, by never being around long enough to fulfil any errand and would dodge out of the way if he heard her calling, chuckling as he went. The fact that these two old friends had even tried to cross the sea and masquerade as real fishermen to bring sympathisers back, was something of a miracle. It just went to show how much they wanted to protect the castle and the life they had there.

"How many volunteers have you got?" asked Israel. Mikhael surprised him with the answer.

"Tis on the way to a hundred already. They moved in among the townspeople in Auretanea and are meeting secretly when they can. The princess Tasmin has got it all organized, and has lots of support. She's found men to train them."

"Don't look like we'll be much use to them now though," said Artemus, "not holed up in Petriah."

"We will be taking you along with us tomorrow." Gideon told them. "Captain says as The Governor wants you to get out safe." This was welcome news.

"We ought to start back," said Israel, suddenly reminded of the Captain.

"You come to the ship early morning, before dawn." Gideon instructed them. "We'll be ready for you. Gyp is on that watch and you knows him. He'll look out for you. We'll see you alright."

They were relieved and grateful to be going home. The princess pulled the cloak around her shoulders and replaced the hat. The mass of thick, black hair resisted being concealed. At the doorway Gideon paused.

"Ask Gyp to fetch me when you arrives tomorrow. I'm sort of quarter-master on board the Zenna." he informed them. "Now lock the door behind us and take these, just in case." He handed them two pistols, which the old pair looked upon with considerable apprehension.

The trio emerged on to the street, the two pirates watching and listening, interpreting every sight and sound as a potential threat while the princess, totally unconcerned for her safety, chatted on. "Are you really a quarter-master, Mr. Gideon?" she asked as they hurried along. "I never heard of a quarter-master. What does it mean?"

Israel, irritated by her stream of questions, perkiness and total oblivion when it came to the lurking dangers, muttered with characteristic surliness, "She'll be ruddy well running the ship next!" Tianna stood stock still, then rounded on him with explosive indignation. She retorted, loudly.

"OH NO I RUDDY WELL WON'T!"

Israel halted on the spot. He stared at her in total amazement at what she had dared to say. His face was suddenly frozen and dangerous, the anger seeming to build from within, fuelling his rage. Then he looked her in the eye for the first time, and, met her defiant, girlish resistance. Slowly, unable to maintain his prejudice any longer, his mouth began to turn upwards into a smile which broadened in the next instant to laughter. Israel had been determined to dislike the girl from the start for disrupting their lives, but he just couldn't keep it up.

Gideon had never seen Israel get a retort to his own acerbic tongue before. They were equally stunned by Tianna's feisty outburst, and were rooted to the spot. After a moment of disbelief, they roared with laughter at what she had said, which coming from a princess, struck them both as particularly funny. The girl had not expected them to laugh.

Realising the danger in rounding on Israel, her hand had flown to her mouth. She could scarcely believe what she had said, and had shocked herself, but as they began to laugh, her dancing eyes lit with similar, irrepressible humour. The men retraced their steps from the tavern barely able to suppress their amusement at the girl who was becoming a match for them all.

Chapter Twenty Seven - Day's End

The hour was late. The day, almost done and Fabian's greatest need was for information about Scalos.

"Our enemy is time, or rather, the lack of it," he reflected.

Cavendish had no volunteers for approaching Lussac in his lair. There wouldn't be any more ministers in Petriah volunteering to go to Scalos with a message declaring the battle lines had been drawn. Nonetheless, Fabian needed to know what the odds against them were likely to be. He could plan no strategy with confidence, without knowing Lussac's power and would need to talk to his naval support in the morning. Fluxton and Chimera were intelligent men and would listen. Fabian had no choice but to revisit the madcap idea he had earlier, summarily dismissed. With the certain knowledge that the galleon would depart in the morning, he could not let the one chance that Captain Jarrus offered, sail away. "If we are ill prepared, our losses will be high. If we are prepared but outnumbered, our defeat will be certain," he reflected.

The Governor of Petriah revisited Roden's ludicrous idea again. He did not like it, but it was all they had. Celeiro contemplated the matter. He sat before the strategically placed cigar box and blotters. The plan was ridiculous, but what if it worked? It was improbable because of its daring, but how improbable was the concept of two pirates and a princess, hurrying through the streets of Petriah, to a tavern? Whichever way you looked at it that was happening outside, right now. The thought that the Scalos ships could be duped into firing upon each other was growing in appeal to both Fabian and Celeiro. With little else on the horizon, they began to convince themselves that the idea was not impossible, just heavily weighted towards failure.

Roden felt he could do no more. At least they had listened and Te Manu was no longer pouring scorn on it. Once they began to consider the plan viable, they set about how to sell the idea to the ministers. This would not be achieved if too fantastic. A little poetic licence in the wording, a suggestion that they were possessed of more information than they actually had, and the stage would be set. Between them, an idea began to emerge that could be approved. The four worked effectively. Captain Jarrus was most enthusiastic, Governor Cavendish, becoming more so, Celeiro, representing the response of the ministers and Te Manu injecting a low key realism into the mix. They put together a time scale for preparation and action. When Jarrus and Manmou were ready to leave, a bold plan, despite the odds against it, had been drafted and was ready to be approved. The Zenna Marius would take the princess to safety on Calypso Island and then sail on to Scalos.

"Why are we going to the ship?" asked Tianna, as Gideon and Israel turned their direction away from the town.

"Captain's orders, ma'am," responded Gideon.

"But I want to stay at the Governor's house tonight," she objected. " He will be expecting my return."

Israel exchanged a look with Gideon that clearly said

"Here we go." The princess had stopped walking, and did not intend taking another step unless it was in the opposite direction. Roden and Te Manu took their leave of Cavendish. It had not been difficult to persuade the Governor to entrust the Princess to the care of the substantial crew of the galleon. For one thing, the population of Petriah were under the illusion that it was the King's request, and for another, Celeiro had suggested that the Governor himself would be wise to vacate his premises overnight, lest he should fall prey to a backlash from his enemies. There was no telling if the princess's speech had done enough to thwart his strongest critics, although it seemed likely to have succeeded. For Salgari and others to denounce Cavendish was one thing, to oppose his Majesty, quite another.

When the Captain and his first officer neared the harbour, Gideon and Israel had been remonstrating with the princess for some minutes. The lady wasn't for budging, and neither wanted to manhandle her.

"What's going on?" asked Jarrus as he drew near.

Tianna launched in with her demands to return to her uncle's house immediately. He patiently explained why she should not go and added that Cavendish would be leaving also, in the next hour. Somehow, that hour afforded an opportunity to head back and make him change his mind, as far as the girl could see. She was not going to be done out of a cosy bed in a beautiful house for a second night. Tianna held her ground, arguing that everyone was being over cautious.

"Come on Tianna. We are going to the ship," dictated the Captain. There was no wisdom in hanging about, drawing unnecessary attention. The risk of danger still lurked in the shadows.

"You go to the ship!" she directed. "I wish to see my uncle. I'm hungry too. I've had no supper and I'm tired. I will stay with him tonight. He needs me."

She turned on her heels. They hesitated no more than a moment. Te Manu, had seen enough of her high handedness and swiftly followed the girl who took no more than a half dozen steps, before he caught her arm, swung her round and halted her progress. The hat, precariously balanced, fell to the ground as her black hair tumbled free, rebellious as the girl herself.

"Let me pass," she demanded, although as their eyes met, she gasped, a mixture of emotions crossing her pretty features. Te Manu saw the momentary flash of fear in her eyes, which she tried to conceal, but the chemistry between them was unexpected and powerful, drawing them together despite her resistance to him. He said nothing, but pulled her determinedly towards the galleon. "Let me go!" she shouted.

This had become very physical. Furious at being given no choice, she wrestled to free her arm from his grip, but stumbled back as a result. The warrior dragged the girl to her feet before sweeping her up into his arms to carry her, arms flailing. His hand silenced her protests by covering the girl's mouth as he set her down in front of them all. She tried to kick him. Her vocal protests were restricted to a mumble. "Mmmm," was all she managed, from behind Manu's firm hand.

"Don't fight my orders, Tianna," the Captain warned her. "You'll lose. Carry her to the ship, Gideon. Get her something to eat," he commanded.

Gideon shrugged massive shoulders. Orders were orders, but he wasn't sure it was right. He picked up the angry girl who gave him little option but to bundle her over his shoulder. This was becoming rather frequent. "Sorry, ma'am," he grunted, as her feet left the ground for a second time. The Captain moved fast along with the others, not entirely sure what the Governor might have thought of their tactics. Still, it got her to the galleon.

Once on board, Gideon carried the girl to find food for himself and the princess. She was humiliated and incensed, but no longer fought. Tears of frustration threatened to undo the girl. Gideon found that difficult.

"We'll see Mikhael and Artemus in a few hours ma'am," he said, setting her down in a corner. "Them will feel better fer finding you here when they gets aboard. It will make 'em more easy like."

He rummaged around finding hard biscuits. There wasn't much else to be had at this late hour. She pouted at him, but her anger subsided. It wasn't Gideon's fault, and he was trying to give her a good reason for being brought here. Tianna had been so full of bounce and chatter in the streets. It pained him to see her so quiet. Somehow, the girl being feisty and angry was alright, and so was her attempt to kick them, but to see her cry, well that didn't sit comfortably with Gideon. She sat, for a time, with her face downcast, a tumult of emotions washing over her. Tiredness did not help the girl to think.

She had felt the surge of great power delivered into her hands while she commanded the assembly. She had risen to a great height and still high from that rush of supremacy had given total support to the Captain's plans, arguing for him against all opposition.

Yet he had reduced and dismissed her in a moment when she refused to return to the ship on his orders, and diminished her status in front of his crew.

He infuriated her, but his authority frightened her too. She knew it was potentially dangerous to antagonise pirates. Unlike her Uncle and dear Papa, these men were not predictable. She had been in their company less than two full weeks. It just seemed much longer.

"I'll see you to the cabin when you've taken summat to eat," Gideon told her.

"I wanted to talk to my uncle," she answered quietly.

"I know ma'am." The big man acknowledged her so kindly she wondered if she might dare to say more.

Joshua had just returned from the town. He saw them and came over. "You made a big impression on everyone today," he said, squatting down beside them.

"Aye, you did that," agreed Gideon. "I don't reckon I'll ever see anything like it again.

"People are talking about you everywhere, princess." went on Joshua. He looked a bit confused that she seemed so down. She looked at both of them steadily, but did not smile. "I held Petriah in my hand today and meant everything I said. I have the respect of everyone between these two Islands, except your Captain tonight." Joshua looked puzzled but Gideon shifted in her direction. "You cannot be questioning Captain's orders, ma'am. That's the first rule for all of us," he said.

"Are you going to be leaving or staying, princess?" asked Joshua, "Manu said you were sailing with us."

"There is a lot to do," she told them. "I can't do any more if I stay in Petriah, and your Captain may not heed my wishes even though I have proved I really am the princess and you all know that now. I don't know what to do. I wish I weren't a girl. I'd be treated so differently."

341

"With respect, Ma'am, we are rather glad you are a girl." replied Joshua with his provocative wink.

Tianna smiled.

"Don't be thinking of leaving the galleon just yet," said Gideon. "Our Captain's got good reason for being the way he is. We are all for the King, ma'am, and all for you, too. Remember that."

She softened at their loyalty. Tianna finally smiled and Joshua rolled his eyes at her in the way that always embarrassed the girl since they had first met. Tianna laughed at his efforts to humour her. She had such fondness for them both. The princess retired in better spirits but with many conflicting thoughts in her mind.

Jarrus and Te Manu were less concerned with the girl and more occupied with all that had been discussed. Inside the cabin, the two of them kicked off their boots and spent some time reflecting on details and looking at maps in the poor light afforded by the lamp, suspended over the table. The Captain was convinced that if he could only grab forty winks, he'd be refreshed enough to work into the night. But when the princess returned to the cabin, she discovered the Captain sound asleep on one side of the mattress, his face to the wall and Te Manu, the opposite side, like a pair of bookends, each blissfully unaware of her, snoring or grunting as they slept.

Tianna sat at the table and chewed her last biscuit, thinking one of them at least might wake up, but as time passed, and it didn't happen, she asked herself, "Now what am I supposed to do?" She was cross to think that after all she had achieved today, it was they who slept, and indignant that they, having denied her the chance to stay with her uncle, had reclaimed the cabin as though she didn't exist.

Tianna had no idea what to do or where to go. Her journey with them should have ended. The future was far from certain. She was weary and it was too dark to venture out. She was also nervous of disturbing them. The princess removed her sandals and fingered the gold band around her ankle. It was only then that she had the time to look at it closely in the amber light.

Raising her foot upon the bench, she saw how beautiful a piece it was. The gold had a delicate pattern of laced leaves and tiny flowers woven all the way round. She was fascinated all over again that the warrior, of all men, should be in possession of something so lovely, and that she had been the recipient. Any vestige of anger at their behaviour towards her was diminished further by this reminder of his gift.

Watching the broad backs of the two men, the girl felt altogether unsure of securing a bit of space for herself, but decided there was little option unless she lay upon the bare floor, or went outside again. Moving gingerly, Tianna placed one knee upon the centre of the high mattress. She stilled for a moment, in case they moved, and when neither man stirred, she crawled tentatively towards the pillow.

It was scary and thrilling to be this near to them, wondering if they might waken at any moment as she began to nestle down. They were powerful and dominating and frightened her. She was still deeply unsure of them. Tianna's head touched the pillow. She kept as still and quiet as possible. Closing her eyes, the princess relived the events of this extraordinary day.

She listened to the occasional voices beyond the

cabin as more of the crew returned from the town. Tianna recognised them. First Joshua, then Gypsy, exchanged greetings with the ones on night watch, who patrolled the ship while it rested, in the harbour. Fearless men, all of them, protecting each other from danger, all gradually becoming familiar to her now. It was strangely reassuring to hear them outside. The girl knew she would be prevented if she tried to leave. There were always at least two on duty beside the gangplank, which was likely to have been drawn in by now anyway. Somehow it didn't upset her like it had earlier.

As the noises outside drifted away, she heard the distant strains of Ezra with his guitar and listened in the quietness to the regular rise and fall of the men breathing either side of her. She peered at them, in the darkness, lying on their sides, silhouetted, their bodies turned away from her, yet affording her protection. Never had the girl felt such close proximity to the leaders of the galleon. The princess's grey eyes travelled across the dim outline of the warrior's broad shoulders and down the wall of his back, to his hips. Tianna remembered their embrace. This was the man who had caused her to shudder when she glimpsed him for the first time. He had made her tremble in a vastly different way since them. She reflected on how he had intercepted her tonight and disregarded her protests by overriding them. He had been rough with her. He had the power to frighten her. And yet... she wanted, more than anything, to feel him again.

The girl nervously extended her hand towards his back in the dark, and tentatively turning on her side, brought her palm to rest against the warmth of his skin. He was like some large slumbering tiger who might roar into life, unpredictable and savage. She held her breath. He did not waken. The danger passed.

Tianna closed her eyes and exhaled deeply, having dared to touch him while he slept. The slow, delicious sensation of bodily contact washed over her, intensified by the fact that this slumbering wild animal knew nothing about it. He moved only slightly, but did not waken. With her hand resting against him, the girl relaxed at last and fell rapidly into a deep sleep. Tomorrow the beautiful galleon would turn once more towards the waves on the next part of her journey, but for now, beneath the moon, Ezra's song drifted unheard into the silent air.

'There's a whisper in the trees,
and it's speaking through the breeze,
that is telling me the dawn
brings something more.
It will change our lives forever,
It's the wind for something better,
Things can never be
the way they were before.
No. They'll never be
the way they were before.'

He lay the guitar down beside him and yawned. The mighty galleon fell silent. Exhaustion had finally overtaken them all.

The story continues in Book Two

Rhapsody's Secret

When the events at Petriah result in Captain Jarrus deciding to go to Scalos, neither he nor Te Manu want to take their leave of the princess. It seems that fate intends she should be their travelling companion once again, although their ideas and hers do not always coincide... Sparks will fly!